THE NARROW HOUSE OF CLAY

Forbidden Love

~ Book One of the Langdon Family Saga ~

JUNE ENGLISH

First published in Far North Queensland, 2024 by Bowerbird Publishing

ISBN 978-1-7635643-5-0 (print)
ISBN 978-1-7635643-6-7 (digital)

The Narrow House of Clay, Forbidden Love
June English

First edition: 2024

Edited by: Crystal Leonardi, Bowerbird Publishing
Interior Design by: Crystal Leonardi, Bowerbird Publishing
Cover Design by: Crystal Leonardi, Bowerbird Publishing

Cover Artwork: 'Summer Courtship' by Adrien Moreau. This artwork was produced in 1880 in France. Any work produced before 1924 is now in the public domain and can be freely used.

Distributed by Bowerbird Publishing
Available in National Library of Australia

Bowerbird Publishing
Julatten, Queensland, Australia
www.crystalleonardi.com

For my father, Don. The setting of Cornwall is for you.
And to my cousin, David. For being such an incredible inspiration.

About the Author

June English was born in Devon, England, and emigrated with her parents to Australia as a young teenager. Later in life, June discovered the joy of writing. Encouraged by her writing cousin, she began creating stories in her retirement to keep her mind active.

Email: juneenglishauthor@gmail.com

Author Website: www.juneenglish.com

Facebook: June English Author

A NOTE FROM THE *E*DITOR

Dear Reader,

As you delve into the pages of this unique literary work, you may notice the presence of spelling errors and unconventional language within the dialogue and letters written by the characters. I wish to assure you that these are not oversights but deliberate choices made to enhance the authenticity and depth of the narrative.

The author has chosen to depict the slang and vernacular of the characters as a reflection of a particular time in England's history when education was not universally accessible. This stylistic decision helps to convey the realities and nuances of the characters' lives, their social backgrounds, and their regional dialects.

The author drew inspiration from her own father's language and accent, which significantly influenced the writing style of this book. This personal connection adds a layer of authenticity to the storytelling, enriching the reader's experience.

Together with the author, I hope you appreciate the effort to maintain historical and cultural accuracy through these intentional choices. Thank you for embracing the spirit of the story and understanding the deliberate artistic decisions made in its creation.

Warm regards,

Crystal Leoanrdi

Editor

STOKEBRIDGE VILLAGE
To Bradford
To Penstowe
Trevelen Manor
Freds Farm
Snowdrop Cottage
Lilac Cottage
Daffodil Cottage
Crocus Cottage
Rose Cottage
Bluebell Cottage
To Roweshorne
N

CONTENTS

Disclaimer: This is a work of fiction. Names, characters, business, events, and incidents are the products of the author's imagination. Any resemblance to actual persons, living or dead, or actual events is purely coincidental. This book contains scenes depicting graphic violence and sexual content. Reader discretion is advised. The material in this publication is of the nature of general comment only, and does not represent professional advice. It is not intended to provide specific guidance for particular circumstances and it should not be relied on as the basis of any decision to take action or not take action on any matter which it covers. Readers should obtain professional advice where appropriate, before making any such decision. To the maximum extent permitted by law, the author and publisher disclaim all responsibility and liability to any person, arising directly or indirectly from any person taking or not taking action based on the information in this publication.

$\mathcal{P}$ROLOGUE

As Elizabeth walked up the gravel path with Samson, she felt as if the fifteenth-century grey stone church was watching her. The high, square tower, with its stained-glass window in the belfry, gazed down at her like a disapproving eye.

She was reminded of centuries-old hymns as the solemn tolling of bells reverberated through the crisp morning air, creating an ethereal melody that resonated with the timeworn stones. The scent of ancient wood lingered in the air as she felt the heavy weight of judgement radiating from this gothic structure. Or was it the memory of the sin she had committed haunting her?

Samson gently squeezed her hand as they entered the church through the heavy, weather-beaten wooden door. She gave him a nervous smile and hoped he would help her atone for that sin. Was that possible?

Standing in front of the Vicar in Stokebridge Church, Elizabeth looked at Samson with despair.

Matthew, I love you, why aren't you standing here beside me? But she dared not say the words out loud.

Reverend Ellacott's solemn eyes swept over the gathered congregation as he spoke, "Is there anyone here who objects to the marriage of these two people?"

She stopped herself from looking around. How she wished Matthew was there to say something, but the only people in the church were her immediate family and Samson's. Matthew was nowhere in sight.

Elizabeth wanted to scream. She was marrying the wrong man and the sorrow was making her dizzy. She didn't want to marry Samson any more than Matthew wanted her to, but she had no choice.

Amidst the anguish, her mind wandered back to the days when Matthew was more than just a friend. He was a shy teenager from a wealthy family, struggling with a stutter that became the target of cruel mockery. Elizabeth, recognizing his pain, had reached out to him, becoming his steadfast friend during that difficult time.

As the marriage ceremony proceeded, Elizabeth's heart ached, not just for the man she loved, but for the dear friend she was leaving behind. Matthew's absence spoke louder than any other objection could have.

So, with no objections from the congregation, Reverend Ellacott continued, "Do you, Elizabeth, take Samson as your lawful wedded husband?"

She glanced at Samson once more. She loved him, but he didn't ignite the same passion she had felt with Matthew, and her mind raced over the events that led her to be standing before the young Vicar, marrying her friend instead of her lover.

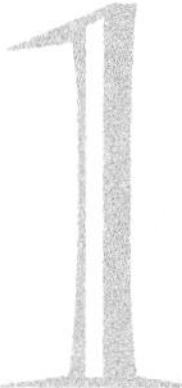

Elizabeth finished her breakfast, stood up and stepped around her younger sister Jane as she stirred a pot over the fireplace in the back corner of the cottage. She reached for her shawl hanging on a peg, feeling the warmth from the fire in the wool as she put it around her shoulders. Through the window in the back wall, above the stairs, she could see fog.

Her father and four brothers sat at the large table in the middle of the room, eating their porridge. Cold air seeped from the sitting room; she walked over to close the door, passing her father and giving him a kiss on the cheek. "Goodbye, Da."

She was about to open the side door near the large cupboard, when her mother walked in, carrying a basket of eggs.

"Goodbye, Ma." Giving her a quick peck on the cheek.

When Elizabeth stepped out of Bluebell Cottage, the fog hit her face like a light mist of rain. She could barely see in front of her, but it didn't matter, she was certain she could find her way even if her eyes were closed. The routine had been the same since she began working at Trevelen Manor as a domestic servant three years ago. She enjoyed the walk in summer, but in winter, the icy wind would whip around her face, causing her lips to chafe and freeze the tips of her ears. Pulling her shawl tighter around her shoulders, she began walking through the village.

The church wall could be seen on her right, and within a moment, near the gate, she saw the headstone of her grandmother's grave. Elizabeth glanced at it briefly, and although she couldn't read, she knew the engraved words by heart.

Elizabeth Pooley

Died 2nd October 1832

Aged 58 years

Was it really three years since her beloved grandmother had died? It only seemed like yesterday her grandfather had told them she had gone to sleep and never woken up. Elizabeth still missed her.

She thought of her grandmother as she walked, the church suddenly appearing like a big grey mountain through the shifting fog. On her left, she could see the whitewashed stone of Daffodil Cottage. She wondered if Mr. Parsons and his son Luke, would ever get over the shock of his eldest son being sent to Australia as a convict.

Elizabeth knew her good friend Samson would be waiting for her at the front gate of his parents' home, Lilac Cottage. As usual, he was smoking his pipe. Cupping his hand around the bowl, he put the stem between his teeth occasionally to inhale the smoke.

Samson greeted her with his usual farmers' drawl. "Mornin' Elizabeth. Another fog hangin' 'round today." He opened the gate to join her.

Smiling, she spoke, "And when is Cornish weather any different at this time of year?"

They had walked about a hundred yards when Samson began, "Elizabeth, wo-yo-wou-"

He put his pipe into his jacket pocket, removed his cap, scratched his head, and ran his fingers through his fair hair.

"Yes, Samson?" To hide her smile from him, she turned to watch a bird as it flew to a nearby tree.

Out of the corner of her eye, she could see Samson twist his cap in his hands, his face red and blotchy, and his mouth opening and closing. She felt so sorry for him, but at the same time, she didn't want him to ask.

Finally, he replaced his cap, took a deep breath, and let it out. "Um… how are they treating you at manor?"

"I'm treated well most of the time." She giggled. "Yesterday, I accidentally knocked an ornament, and it fell off the sideboard."

"Good heavens."

4

"Thankfully, it didn't break. I managed to catch it before it hit the floor," she gave a big sigh. "I think I'd have been dismissed if it did."

Samson feigned horror. "Just as well it didn't break. Who'd I walk with in mornin' if you'd lost your position there?"

His cheeky grin brought a glint of mischief to his pale blue eyes. Elizabeth pushed him playfully, causing him to take a side-step. They laughed and continued up the road.

When they reached his Uncle Fred's farm just before the crossroads, Samson said goodbye, and Elizabeth turned right to continue up the gentle slope to the manor house.

The familiar banter with Samson momentarily distracted her from the weight of her thoughts about Matthew. As she continued to walk, her mind oscillated between the gentle morning routine and the unresolved tension with Matthew. The fog seemed to mirror the haze in her mind.

~

Samson slumped his shoulders as he watched her walk away. When he lost sight of Elizabeth, he bowed his head and walked into the farmyard. He saw his uncle herding the milking cow out of the yard.

"Well, did you ask her today?" He asked.

Samson kicked a dry cow pat, sending dust and small dung pieces flying into the air.

"No, and I'm ruddy annoyed with myself for losing the courage, yet again."

Fred gave him a friendly pat on the shoulder, "You can always try again tomorrow."

"Maybe, if I find the nerve," Samson said.

"You'll find it." His uncle gave a hearty laugh. "How long have you been trying to ask her to wed you?"

"Over a year." Samson sheepishly replied.

"One day, Sam, you'll ask her, and she'll say yes. Now, come on, these fields won't plough themselves."

~

Elizabeth giggled to herself the rest of the way to the manor. She had lost count of the times Samson had tried to propose to her, but he had never got the words out. He always changed the subject.

She liked Samson and looked forward to his company every morning. She was certain her parents assumed she would marry him, though she could only think of him as a friend, nothing more. She loved Matthew.

~

Further up the road, the fog slowly disappeared, and Trevelen Manor appeared. It was an imposing three-storey building with grey stonework, the early morning rays reflecting on the windows like sunlight on a stream. Plumes of smoke rose from the six chimneys in the gabled slate roof.

Elizabeth caught up with two other servants heading for the back entrance. The only servants who lived at the manor were the housekeeper, cook, assistant cook, butler, valet, and lady's maid. All the other staff came from the local villages.

She was hanging her shawl on a peg when the housekeeper, Mrs. Bailey, approached. "Will you help cook today? Betty's not feeling well."

Elizabeth knew that the narrowed eyes and taut lips of the housekeeper meant she could only give one answer. "Yes, Mrs. Bailey."

Thinking to herself, it would make a change from her usual task of cleaning fire grates, sweeping floors and dusting furniture.

~

At the end of the day's work in the kitchen, Elizabeth set off home. In the afternoon, she preferred to walk through the walled garden of Trevelen Manor and the woods behind them, even though it added an extra quarter of a mile to her journey.

The gardeners occasionally talked to her whenever she stopped to admire the flowers. It was mid-October, and the air was brisk. Most of the flower beds had been turned over ready for the next spring, and only a few hardy blooms remained.

She gasped when she heard the head gardener say. "Afternoon, Elizabeth."

Hand on her chest, she turned. "Sorry, Tom, I was daydreaming."

"I didn't mean to scare ye." Handing her a small bundle of sacking. "I thought ye might like these."

Elizabeth peered inside to find three flower bulbs. "Are they the white daffodils with the dark yellow centre?"

"Aye, I remember how much ye liked them when they were in bloom during the summer. I saved some for ye when we dug up the garden."

She thought his smile made him look twenty years younger. Elizabeth put the bulbs in the pocket of her apron. "Thank you, Tom, I'm sure Ma will love them in her garden."

~

Saying goodbye to the gardener, she walked through the back gate into the woods. The autumn leaves stirred in the gentle breeze. She listened to the birds tweeting as she strolled along the path, stopping occasionally to watch a red squirrel scamper along the thick branches. The soft breeze lifted loose strands of hair off her face. Leaves floated down onto the path. Dappled sunlight caused her to squint occasionally as it peeked through the oak, beech, and chestnut trees.

Lost in the beauty of her surroundings, Elizabeth did not see the hand reaching out from behind the oak tree. For a moment, her heart nearly stopped in fright as the hand grabbed her arm, pulling her off the path and causing her to stumble.

"Oh. It's you, Matthew." She held a hand to her bosom. "You scared me, I wasn't sure if I'd see you today."

He gave a brief laugh. "I crept out while Father was in his office." He blew out his cheeks. "I couldn't bear the thought of not seeing you after what happened today."

He took her hand, and willingly, she followed him to their secluded spot. He wrapped his arms around her, kissing her tenderly, as they lowered themselves onto the fallen leaves and bracken.

Gently pulling away from their embrace, she asked, "What happened?"

He frowned. "Father had a visit today from Lord Falmouth and his silly daughter, Susannah."

Elizabeth laughed. "And your father wants you to marry her?"

"That's what he wants, but I don't want to." He brushed his light brown hair back from his face. "I don't want to think about him right now, I only want to think about you." He kissed her again.

Elizabeth's body quivered as he gently fondled her breasts while nuzzling her slender neck. He lifted her dress as she wrapped her arms around his chest and surrendered to his advances. She shuddered as he ran his fingers up her naked thigh, giggling slightly when he tickled her waist. He kissed her again with more passion than she had ever experienced before, she could not help herself, she opened her legs and let him enter her.

She felt weak as rapturous delight filled her body and sent a tingling feeling to her fingers and toes, leaving her almost incapable of any movement. She wondered if Matthew could hear her heart beating as she struggled to breathe. She had never experienced this bliss with him before.

Matthew gasped and finished, then rolled off. They lay on their backs, smiling at each other, holding hands while trying to catch their breath. Elizabeth didn't want the feeling to end, and she could hardly wait for it to happen again.

He pulled her shawl over them both when she began to shiver in the chilly air. He gazed into her hazel eyes as he twirled stray strands of her light brown hair between his fingers.

"Elizabeth, these past three months with you have been wonderful," Matthew said tenderly, gazing into her eyes.

"It's been the best time of my life too." Elizabeth agreed.

Matthew continued. "When I was growing up, I was always nervous around girls and would stammer terribly. If a girl came near me, I looked for the quickest way to get away from her."

"What changed? Why aren't you nervous around me?" Elizabeth asked, intrigued.

"I think it was the first time I saw you after I returned from London. You looked at me and smiled that sweet smile of yours, my heart skipped a beat, and the nervousness disappeared." Reminisced Matthew.

She looked into his pale blue eyes and whispered, "I'm glad."

"I didn't think I would ever feel this way about a woman." He caressed her cheek.

She said softly, "We've learnt about love together."

"Yes, we have." He slowly ran his fingers over her lips. "Will you marry me?"

Elizabeth's heart stopped for a moment as she reached for his hand and kissed the tips of his fingers, her eyes wide with delight.

"Of course, I'll marry you." Then she hesitated. "But will your father approve of you marrying one of the servants?"

"I'll come of age in just over a year, so I can marry whoever I like. I love you Elizabeth. I want to marry you!" Matthew embraced her as he spoke.

"Oh, Matthew." She kissed him again, and once more felt that frenzied ecstasy she had enjoyed so much. Finally, it was time for them to tidy their clothes before parting with a passionate embrace; Elizabeth continued her journey to Bluebell Cottage.

~

The love she felt for Matthew, the next lord of Trevelen Manor, consumed her. When she was at home with her family, he was the only person she could think of, and she often daydreamed about him, remembering stolen moments together in the woods or the attic.

Peeling potatoes for the evening meal, she was startled by Jane, clapping her hands sharply. "Elizabeth, can you help me with supper? You're off with the pixies again."

Elizabeth shook her head and looked down at the knife and potato in her hands.

"I wasn't off with the pixies," she sighed. "I was thinking how nice it would be if I were the next lady of the manor."

Jane laughed. "You've as much chance of that as I have of becoming the next Duchess of Cornwall," she turned back to stir the pot over the fire.

Elizabeth slammed the knife on the table and demanded angrily, "And what makes you think I can't be the next Lady Trevelen?"

With one hand on her hip, the other waving the ladle, Jane turned and said firmly. "Because the land of gentry don't mix with poor folk like us." Calmly she added as she turned back to the pot. "Now, will you finish cutting those taters, or we'll be eating this stew for breakfast instead of supper."

"You just wait, Jane Saunders; I will be the lady of the manor one day, and don't think because you're my younger sister, I'll give you any special attention when you become one of the servants."

The sides of Jane's mouth drew up into a smirk, and her shoulders quivered with laughter while she stirred the stew.

Under her breath, Elizabeth said, "Just you wait."

Samson was waiting for Elizabeth as usual. He had been worried about her since the beginning of February, she was not her usual self. She had snapped at him more than once, and that, too, was worrying. He hoped she would confide in him one day about whatever was troubling her. He was just about to put his pipe in his mouth when he heard her footsteps on the gravel. He opened the gate to join her.

"Mornin' Elizabeth." He cheerfully greeted her.

"Mornin' Samson," giving him a brief glance, she continued to walk.

"What is it, Elizabeth? I haven't seen you smile for a while. Is it anything I can help with?" He wanted so badly to fix whatever was wrong.

She smiled briefly. "That's very kind of you to offer, but I'm sure it'll be sorted soon. We'd better hurry, or we'll both be late for work."

"I don't think Uncle Fred would mind if I'm late."

Elizabeth grimaced. "But Mrs. Bailey would."

Samson nodded. "Well, we don't want you to get on the wrong side of housekeeper, do we?" He quickened his pace to keep up with her.

~

Elizabeth arrived at Trevelen Manor; a grand estate nestled in the picturesque landscapes of Cornwall. The manor house itself stood proudly with its imposing structure, a symbol of the Trevelen family's wealth and status. The exterior was surrounded by well-manicured gardens, and ivy clung to the walls, giving the estate a timeless charm.

Entering the servants' quarters located at the back of the manor, Elizabeth tuned in to the familiar sounds of domestic life. The space had a sense of routine and camaraderie yet reflected a more subdued ambience compared to the manor. She hung her shawl on the convenient hooks along the walls. Picking up the dustpan and brush, she walked to the library.

She was cleaning the fire grate when Matthew walked in, followed by his four-year-old brother, Robert. Matthew turned his head slightly so his younger brother could not see the smile he gave her. He turned back to the bookcase when Robert asked.

"Will you read to me, Matthew?"

"Maybe," Matthew replied.

Elizabeth stood up and bobbed to a curtsy. "Mornin', Master Engels."

"Morning, Elizabeth."

Elizabeth finished cleaning the fire grate, picked up the dustpan and left the room. She needed to talk to Matthew, but she couldn't do that while Robert was with him.

Elizabeth ignored the oil paintings portraying ancestors of the Trevelen family as she entered the grand hallway. Her body went rigid, and her hand tightened around the dustpan as the breath caught in her throat. A flush of warmth crept up her neck, betraying her inner turmoil. She avoided meeting Matthew's gaze as she exited the library, her eyes welled with unshed tears, mirroring the vulnerability she felt within.

Elizabeth uttered a long sigh when she entered the drawing room and saw Matthew's stepmother seated in a chair with a book in her hands. If Matthew had followed her, she could have spoken with him, but Lady Trevelen's presence made that impossible.

She curtsied to Lady Trevelen before moving to the fireplace to begin sweeping the ashes. Elizabeth turned her head slightly at the sound of the door opening. Matthew slid her a guarded look as he lowered himself into an armchair. He crossed his legs, trying to look relaxed as he sat with his elbows on the arms of the chair, fingers interlocked and twiddled his thumbs.

She wondered why his stepmother didn't acknowledge him. A moment later, without looking up from her book, she asked, "Are you going riding today, Matthew?"

"I'm not sure," he replied.

Once Elizabeth finished her task, she stood up, giving Matthew a quick glance before walking towards the door.

Just as she put her hand on the handle, he pushed himself from the chair and said. "Maybe I will go for a ride after all."

She stood like a statue in the hallway, the dustpan still in her hand. She knew her face was red and her eyes tearful.

Matthew put a finger to his lips as he went to the library door and peeked inside, gesturing for her to follow.

He said as they entered, "We're alone. I gave Robert the atlas and told him to take it to Nanny."

She nodded and put the dustpan on the hearth, took two steps into his arms and began crying on his chest. The feel of his heart beating against her cheek was reassuring. "Oh Matthew, I'm so happy to see you."

He stroked her back tenderly. "I can see there's something bothering you; what is it?"

After a moment, she pulled back, wiped her eyes with the back of her hand, and looked at the floor. "I'm…," She swallowed. "I'm with child."

Looking up again as Matthew's eyes widened and his jaw hung open. "With child? Are you sure?" He finally managed to say.

She sniffed. "Yes. About a month ago, I thought it might be possible, but now I'm certain."

The image of Matthew standing in front of her blurred as more tears pooled in her eyes and dripped down her face, leaving wet streaks on her bodice.

He pulled a handkerchief from his waistcoat pocket and gave it to her. Wiping her face, she mumbled. "Well, aren't you going to say something?"

Matthew pulled her towards him and hugged her once more. "It's all a bit of a shock, that's all. I do love you, Elizabeth." He looked into her eyes and smiled. "If you remember, I did ask you to marry me."

Elizabeth wrung the handkerchief in her hands. "Yes, you did, but you don't come of age until just before Christmas. Given my condition, will your father give permission for us to marry now?"

"I think so, I've always intended to marry you." He picked up her hand. "Come, we'll go and see Father right now. He's probably working on his ledgers."

She nearly fell when he opened the door and pulled her towards his father's office. After a couple of steps, Elizabeth tugged on his hand to hold him back. "Matthew, please slow down."

He stopped and faced her. "What is it?"

She wrapped her arms around herself, looked at the floor and softly replied, "I'm worried about what your father will say." She couldn't bring herself to believe it might end happily.

"I'm going to tell him we want to get married straight away and that I had every intention of marrying you when I came of age." Reaching for her hand once more, he continued down the grand hallway.

"But what will he say when we tell him about my condition?" Elizabeth questioned.

"I'll tell him that I love you, and I want to do the right thing and marry you." He knocked on the door. "He's not an ogre, I'm sure he'll give his permission."

Elizabeth nodded, but she wasn't so sure.

"Enter." Came a voice from the room.

Lord Trevelen was sitting at his desk when they walked in. He looked up from his ledger, rolled his eyes and frowned.

"What do you want, Matthew? I don't need interruptions when I'm trying to balance the books."

The Lord of the Manor was an influential man who was admired by his peers; his large size only added to his authority.

"And who is this servant you've dragged in here? And more to the point, why?"

Elizabeth saw Matthew swallow hard, and it didn't surprise her when his stuttering returned.

"Father, I... I have something to s... say.'

Lord Trevelen's eyes narrowed. He banged his hands on the desk and snapped. "What is it?"

Matthew pulled her closer, their hearts seemed to beat as one. "Elizabeth and I want to get married."

Lord Trevelen looked up and down at her. "Who is she? A servant? Don't be so ridiculous. Why would you want to marry a servant?"

"Because I love her." Matthew pleaded.

Lord Trevelen stood up, his face like thunder. "Nonsense, you cannot marry a mere servant girl. You will marry someone from your own class."

"But I love Elizabeth, and this morning she told me she's with child. I want to marry her so our child will be born in wedlock."

Lord Trevelen threw his hands in the air. "I really despair of you sometimes, Matthew. How do you know the child is yours? She could be just saying that."

Elizabeth gasped and pulled away from Matthew.

"The child is mine, and I know because Elizabeth loves me as much as I love her."

Lord Trevelen walked towards the window, turned around and glared at Matthew. "Complete and utter gibberish."

Elizabeth's body shook as she burst into tears. Matthew pulled her close to him again. "Father, how could you be so cruel? We want to get married."

"Well, I won't give my permission, simple as that." He walked behind his desk, sat down, and continued. "Your poor mother is probably turning in her grave right now. How could you be so stupid as to take up with a servant? There are a good number of young ladies in the district who would be much more suitable for you to marry."

Matthew took a deep breath. "Elizabeth is the only girl who doesn't laugh at me, unlike those silly daughters of your friends who giggle whenever they see me. Elizabeth loves me as I am."

"What do you know about love? You're only a child?"

"In case you have forgotten, I'll come of age at the end of the year, and I'm hardly a child. I know my mind, and I want to marry Elizabeth."

Slamming his hands on the desk, Lord Trevelen raised his voice. "And I've told you, I will not give my permission."

Elizabeth stood open-mouthed as Matthew walked up to the desk and set his palms down heavily on its leather surface. "Don't you care about the fate of our child! Your grandchild?"

She jumped when Lord Trevelen stood up quickly, and his chair fell backwards, the thump echoing around the room. He braced his hands on the desk, leaning towards his son, his chest heaving. Even from where Elizabeth was standing, she could smell his whiskey breath when he shouted. "I don't believe it is my grandchild!"

He turned to Elizabeth, pointing. "And you, girl, are dismissed. Come back in the morning, and I'll have your wages ready for you. Now get out, both of you!"

Elizabeth turned, rushing out of the room, lifting her skirts as she ran down the grand hallway to the servants' entrance. She ignored the housekeeper when she shouted. "Where are you going?"

She could feel the eyes of the gardeners as she hurried towards the woods, only slowing as she reached their secret place. Falling to her hands and knees, she lowered her head and cried. Tears fell on the leaves under her hands.

~

Matthew followed Elizabeth to the door and closed it before turning back to Lord Trevelen, he began to sway.

"Fa-father pl-please. I want to marry Elizabeth. I was planning to marry her when I came of age anyway."

Lord Trevelen's shoulders slumped as his fiery temper subsided; he turned to him and sighed. "Matthew, you are my son, the next Lord Trevelen. One day, the manor and the estate with all the cottages from the surrounding villages will be yours."

Lord Trevelen picked up his chair and sat heavily, leaned back, and continued. "You cannot marry a servant, it's simply unheard of. You would be the laughing-stock of all the gentry in the district, and you would lose the respect of the tenants."

Matthew sat on the chair in front of the desk and buried his face in his hands. "But I love her."

Lord Trevelen let out another deep sigh. "I know you think that at this moment, but believe me when I say what you are feeling for this girl is simple lust, nothing more. You can have your fun with the servants if they're willing, but when it comes to marriage, you must marry a girl from your own class."

"But what about Elizabeth? Our child?"

"That's her problem. Now, will you please leave me to finish my work?" Picking up his pen, he dipped it in the inkwell and continued with his ledger.

Matthew hesitated, and his father looked up once more.

"I've given you my answer Matthew. I'm not going to change my mind." He gave his son a hard look with his deep-set grey eyes. "In time you'll thank me for saving you from yourself."

Matthew knew his father was a man of considerable influence and authority. His reaction to Matthew's request reflected a man moulded by tradition and duty. From his father's perspective, the prospect of Matthew marrying a servant was not just a breach of social expectations but a stain on the Trevelen name.

Matthew slammed the door behind him as he left the office. He felt as he had at five years old after his father had given him a beating when his dog had chewed his father's best shoes. There was no chance to argue or set things right. His father's words were law in the house and in his life.

He stood outside his father's office and thought, *If I had a different father, I could marry Elizabeth, and we could raise our child together.*

One of the servants came out of the dining room and gave him a strange look as she bobbed a curtsy before returning to the servants' hall.

Matthew didn't care what the servants thought about him at that moment; he needed to find Elizabeth. It suddenly occurred to him where she would be, and rushed from the house, running through the garden, only slowing down as he reached the edge of the woods and followed the path.

~

Elizabeth was still crying as she sat amongst the bracken fern when Matthew sat beside her and pulled her close.

She put her head on his shoulder. "Oh Matthew, what am I going to do?"

"I honestly don't know. I wanted to do the right thing and marry you, but Father doesn't believe our love is real." He kissed her softly on the top of her head.

"It's such a mess, I'm with child, and the man I love is unable to marry me. And now I've lost my position as a servant."

"I do want to marry you, and I'm sure if my mother were alive, she would have been able to persuade father to allow it. Susan doesn't care, she only cares about Robert."

Elizabeth faced him. "You do believe me when I say it's your child, don't you?"

He tilted her chin and kissed her. "I never doubted it for a moment, and I know you wouldn't lie to me."

"Oh Matthew, what am I going to do?" she said again as she put her head back on his shoulder and her sobs became louder.

"Let's stay here for the rest of the day. We may be able to think of something. I don't want our child growing up not knowing who I am."

After a few minutes, Elizabeth sat up. "Could we move to another village where we can get married and live?"

"I don't know. I'm too well known around the district. Father would find me and bring me back here and we'd both be disgraced."

They spoke very little as the shadows of the trees moved along the ground. Eventually, Matthew asked, "Are you hungry?"

She nodded.

He stood up. "Stay here, I'm going to see Cook and get us something to eat."

She nodded, wiping her face with the handkerchief.

While he was gone, Elizabeth had time to think. She assumed when she told Matthew about the baby, he would marry her. After all, he had asked her over six months ago, but now Lord Trevelen had called her a liar and refused to give his consent. It was clear he wouldn't budge, no matter what Matthew thought. She had no option but to make other plans.

Matthew returned a while later with a wooden tray holding a china plate with a matching cover, a pot of tea and two cups and saucers.

He sat down carefully and placed the tray on the ground in front of them. "Voilà." Smiling as he lifted the cover off the china plate to expose the neatly cut, cold, chicken sandwiches underneath. "I think the cook has a soft spot for me."

Elizabeth picked up a sandwich and gave a small smile in return.

"Thank you."

Matthew picked up a sandwich and made himself comfortable so he could see her face. "It's nice to see you smile again."

"Sandwiches and tea aren't going to change your father's mind, are they?"

Matthew's smile disappeared as he lowered his head. "No, they aren't."

He demolished another two sandwiches before asking. "Have you thought about what you're going to do?"

Elizabeth took a deep breath and let it out slowly. "I'm going to move to another village or even Callington. I can't stay here; this would bring shame to my family." Overcome with humiliation, she looked at the half-eaten sandwich in her hand. "I'll be cast out as a fallen woman and I couldn't do that to them, especially Jane. I might be able to work for a middle-class family in exchange for my keep."

"What about the baby when it's born?"

Elizabeth shrugged. "Maybe the local Vicar will help me find a family who'll raise it as their own."

Matthew stood up and shouted. "You can't do that!"

She stared at him with wide eyes, her voice angry. "But—."

"I don't want our child raised by strangers."

He began pacing around and running his fingers through his hair. When he was calm, he sat beside her again. "I'm sorry, but there has to be an alternative."

"I don't want our child raised by strangers either, but I can't think of another way. I have a few shillings saved, but that won't last for long."

Elizabeth stared at the tea leaves in her cup. Was that a child's face she could see? Or an empty cooking pot with holes in it?

"All my money is held in trust, I can't touch it without Father's permission, but I'll go into his office tonight while he's having his brandy and cigar in the drawing room, see if I can find some money to give you."

A flash of resentment rushed through Elizabeth that he wouldn't even try to ask his father. She covered her displeasure by putting her hand on his arm. "Thank you."

"I'm sorry for shouting at you before Elizabeth, I just wish there was another way." He gently stroked her cheek. "After you collect your wages tomorrow, will you wait for me here, and I'll give you what money I can find."

She leaned over to kiss him. Money would help, but her problem was much bigger than that. She needed a solution.

They sat together till late afternoon when Elizabeth stood up, straightening her dress. "I'd best be going home."

Matthew stood beside her. "I'll meet you here tomorrow."

She nodded and kissed him before turning towards the road, and Bluebell Cottage.

~

As Elizabeth's figure disappeared along the road, Matthew's gaze lingered on the path she had taken. His mind buzzed with echoes of his father's disapproval. The rustling leaves overhead seemed to carry whispers of doubt, making him question the nature of his feelings. The memories of their secret rendezvous in the woods and the shared moments in their attic hideaway played like a haunting melody in his mind. Was it truly love, or merely the thrill of forbidden moments. A heavy sigh escaped his lips as he turned away from the vanishing trail, each step towards the manor feeling like a step deeper into uncertainty.

~

Elizabeth lost count of how many times she burst into tears as she walked home. She kept thinking about leaving her family for good, and how much she would miss them. The need to leave was urgent before the baby showed, and the villagers began talking.

She would have to sneak out of her room the following night without her parents or siblings noticing. She wished she could confide in Jane, but this was something she had to deal with on her own.

Elizabeth's feet crunched on the gravel as she approached Lilac Cottage. Samson opened the gate to join her. "Mornin' Elizabeth."

She gave him a quick glance, kept her head down and didn't bother to acknowledge him.

She stopped when he stood in front of her and asked, "What's the matter? I see you've been crying."

Elizabeth was trying to catch her breath. "I'm sorry, I've got a lot on my mind."

"Something's upsetting you, what is it?" He guided her behind a nearby tree, away from prying eyes.

"Oh Samson, I've been such a fool." She wiped her eyes with the handkerchief Matthew had given her the day before. "And I think you're the only person I can talk to."

"What's happened, and how have you been a fool?" He bent down so he could look into her face.

Elizabeth managed to stop crying before saying. "I'm with child, and I thought the boy would marry me when I told him, but he can't, and now I'm not sure what to do."

"Why can't he marry you? He's not married himself, is he?"

Elizabeth shook her head. "He's not, but his father won't allow it."

Samson growled. "What right does his father have to refuse his son doing right thing by you?"

Elizabeth hesitated. He had recently asked if he could help her in any way; maybe he would. But she still wasn't sure whether to trust him with the father's name. Would he keep her secret? She certainly couldn't talk to her parents about her predicament. Finally, after some thought, she decided to tell him the truth.

"Because his father is Lord Trevelen."

Samson's eyes opened wide. "Does Lord Trevelen know about your condition?"

"Yes." She repeated what had transpired in the office the day before. "Even though Matthew told his father how much he loved me and wanted to marry me, His Lordship still wouldn't allow it. That's when he dismissed me." Tears rolled down her cheeks again.

"What are you going to do now?"

"I don't know," she said, wiping her eyes again. In a strange way, she felt relieved by telling Samson. "I'm on my way to the manor to collect my last wages. I'm thinking about moving to another village, maybe even Callington. If I stay here, I'll be branded a fallen woman, and it would bring terrible shame to my family."

"Seventeen is too young to be on your own in Callington. Please don't move away, Elizabeth." He pleaded. "If it means you'll stay in Stokebridge, I'll marry you as I've just come of age. Then at least, the child will have a father."

Elizabeth took a deep breath and thought of his proposal. Marrying Samson would solve her problem, but could she do it? She had no doubt he loved her, but the simple fact was she did not love him.

Eventually, she asked, "Are you sure you want to marry me?"

He smiled at her, "Yes, I'm very sure. I've loved you for a long time." Samson held her hands as he continued. "Once you've collected your wages, come see me at Uncle Fred's farm. I'll explain we're going to see Vicar about getting wed, he won't mind me leaving for a while."

The grin on his face gave her no doubt of his feelings. Maybe it was right to trust him after all. They walked along the road together, and she waved at him when they parted at the gate.

~

Thoughts swirled in Samson's mind like leaves caught in a tempest as he watched her walking toward the manor, her dress fluttering behind her. Marrying Elizabeth – his childhood dream – felt like it was within reach, yet an uneasy tightness clenched at his chest. He found himself questioning the sincerity of his actions. Was he offering a lifeline out of love, or was it a desperate attempt to salvage his fantasy? He had never imagined himself as the second choice, the fallback plan.

Samson took a deep breath, pushing his doubts aside. The offer was genuine, his love unwavering, but the journey ahead seemed fraught with uncertainties.

Samson cursed the next Lord Trevelen for what he had done to Elizabeth. He picked up a rock and threw it at a nearby tree with as much force as he could muster, watching as it ricocheted off the trunk and rolled into the ditch beside the road.

"That bastard! He should never have taken advantage of her like that."* A rock the size of an orange near his foot was also booted into the ditch before he stomped into the gate of his uncle's farm, kicking it shut behind him, looking around to check no one had heard his outburst.

~

Close to the manor, the uneasy feeling in Elizabeth's stomach increased. At times she had to stop and take a few moments to calm her nausea. The thought of facing the other servants, all wondering why she had been dismissed but not brave enough to ask her. They would find out later when her condition became noticeable. She tried to calm herself and stop crying; she didn't want to walk in with red eyes. *Think about what Samson is prepared to do for you instead.*

Elizabeth took a deep breath, held her head up high and walked into the servants' entrance with renewed confidence. She was immediately confronted by Mrs. Bailey.

The housekeeper had her head tilted back, looking down her nose at Elizabeth. "I have your wages here. His Lordship said I was to give them to you and tell you that you are never to set foot in the manor again."

Elizabeth stood up straight and flicked her hair behind her shoulders. Holding her hand out for the coins, she quickly put them into her apron pocket. "Thank you, Mrs. Bailey." Turning on her heels, she marched to the door.

"Elizabeth," Mrs. Bailey called out. "What did you do for His Lordship to dismiss you like that?"

Elizabeth stopped for a moment and smiled to herself. She had no intention of giving the housekeeper a reason.

Without turning around, she replied, "Nothing, I told him I was getting married, that's all."

She stormed out as the housekeeper shouted. "There must be more to it than that."

Elizabeth had only been waiting in the woods a few minutes when the sound of leaves being crunched under boots reached her. She peeked out from behind the tree and was relieved to see Matthew coming towards her. She raced over and hugged him. They quickly sat down behind the fern. Avoiding her eyes, Matthew pulled some coins from his pocket and put them in her hand. "I know it's not much, but it was all I could find."

Elizabeth counted the money. "Four shillings and seven pence."

It's not enough, she thought as she closed her fingers over the coins. "Matthew, I have something to tell you."

"What is it?" He lifted his head to look at her.

"I have a solution to our problem," placing the coins in her pocket.

"Really?" His eyebrows rose in question. "What kind of solution?"

"Samson Keslake asked me to marry him."

Doing his best to keep the smile off his face. "Your friend who walks with you every morning? The man you say keeps asking you to marry him but can never find the words?"

Elizabeth giggled and nodded. "I was very upset when he saw me this morning, and I told him about my condition. He offered to marry me so our child would have a father. He said he's loved me for a long time."

Matthew reached over and held her hand. "I don't want you to marry Samson, I want to marry you. I want to make you the lady of the manor, it's what you deserve, now you'll only be another farmer's wife." He reached up to stroke her cheek. "I'm sorry."

Elizabeth wiped her face with the back of her hand. "I don't want to marry him either, but at least this way, you'll be able to see our child if I live in Stokebridge."

He hung his head. "Watching another man bring up my son or daughter and not being able to claim him or her as my own, it's going to be so hard."

"It's the only answer I have, other than moving to Callington." She tried to hide her groan of disappointment from Matthew. He was offering no help except a few paltry shillings, which wouldn't last for long.

She wanted to scream at him; he had no idea of what it was going to be like for her. She was the one who had to sacrifice her life by marrying another man just so their child would not be born a bastard. But she knew Matthew was bound by his father's demands.

She heard Matthew sigh. "Do you know when you're getting married?"

"Samson and I are going to see Vicar today." Her voice choked as the tears began to fall again. "I won't be able to see you anymore."

They both lay on the ground; Elizabeth rested her head on Matthew's shoulder until her tears stopped. She opened her eyes and looked at the sun filtering through the foliage, his hand rested on her waist.

She was stroking his hand but stopped when he said. "I want you to remember this time with me, so when you're lying with Samson, you can close your eyes and think about this moment, being together in the bracken fern."

"And when you're with your wife, whoever she may be, you can think of me also." She lifted his hand and kissed the back of it. "I'll never forget you, Matthew. I love Samson as a friend, but you'll always be my true love."

"You'll always have a special place in my heart too." He raised himself onto his elbow and looked at her.

She laughed nervously. "Why are you staring at me like that?"

"I'm trying to remember you at this moment." Matthew then ran his finger down her cheek. "And wonder if I'll feel anything as soft as your skin again."

Reluctantly, they both stood up and kissed one last time before saying goodbye and going their separate ways. Tears flowed as Elizabeth thought of how she had left her lover for the last time.

With a heavy heart, she walked to Samson's uncle's farm. Part of her wanted to run away, but the little money she had would not last long. She knew she had to marry Samson, or she would not be able to keep Matthew's baby.

She saw Fred and Samson on their way to the barn from the house, and called out to them.

Samson beamed at her as she walked towards him. "I were beginning to think you changed your mind about getting wed. We've just finished dinner." He turned to his uncle and said, "Uncle Fred, do you mind if we go and see Vicar about getting married?"

"No, I don't mind." He gave a hearty laugh and turned to Elizabeth. "I couldn't believe it this morning when he said he'd found the nerve to ask you to wed him." He turned back to Samson. "But you'd better change out of those clothes, you smell like a cow pat. I don't think the Vicar will appreciate the church smelling like a herd of cows."

Samson glanced down at his muddied trousers and grinned. "I'll stop at home and have a quick wash and change."

Fred waved the couple off and continued to tend to his cattle.

~

They were near the gate and out of earshot when Elizabeth spoke, "Are you sure about marrying me, Samson?"

He reached over and held her hand while they walked. "I've never been more certain. I've been trying for a long time to ask you to marry me, but you were in love with His Lordship's son."

She stopped, and Samson turned to her. "What is it?"

Elizabeth raised her head to look at him and said firmly, "Matthew, his name is Matthew."

She was beginning to think marrying Samson was a mistake; could she love him as she had loved Matthew? She reached over and picked up his other hand, and looked down at them. Was this a sign that he would always resent the father of her child? Should she go to Callington after all? If she did that, she would have to give up her baby. No, she wanted to keep it as a reminder of Matthew.

"Samson, I'll try hard to be a good wife to you." Elizabeth raised her head again. "But you must remember he'll always be my first love. If you can't accept that, you need to tell me now before we go to the church."

Elizabeth could see him thinking about what she had said, and she wondered if he was having second thoughts. She was surprised when he put a finger under her chin and looked into her eyes before saying, "I know you don't love me same way you love him, but if we get married, you'll be able to keep his child. It's what you want, isn't it?"

She nodded; she could hardly speak as tears welled up again. Wiping her face, her voice croaky as she asked, "What are you going to tell your parents?"

"I'm going to tell them I found the courage to ask you to marry me, and you've accepted."

Elizabeth swallowed. "What if they guess about the baby?"

"Then I'll tell them it's mine. Only you, me and Matthew will know I'm not the child's real father, and I'll never give your secret away."

She nodded, knowing he was her only hope; she had to trust him. "Thank you, but we need to talk to my parents too."

"We'll see them before we go to the rectory," Samson replied as they continued to Lilac Cottage.

She hoped her red face had vanished when they walked in the front door. Only Samson's little brother Billy was at the table, playing with some blocks of wood.

He walked past Billy to the back door and called out, "Ma, Elizabeth and I have something to tell you."

A few moments later, Louisa Keslake came through the back door with pieces of firewood held up in her apron.

"Hello, my dear. What a lovely surprise to see you." She dropped the wood on the hearth and straightened her apron. The grey of her dress showing through holes caused by fire sparks.

Samson was still holding her hand when he said, "Ma, I've come home for a quick wash and change. We're on our way to see Vicar." Smiling, he looked down at her and said excitedly, "Elizabeth has agreed to be my wife."

"At last." She turned to her son again. "All this time, you were so worried; I knew she would say yes. Sit down, Elizabeth, while I get some water boiling for fresh pot of tea."

Louisa gave Billy a nudge. "Go tell your Da Sam's here with Elizabeth."

The boy raced out the door as she went to tend the fire and straighten the dropped pieces of wood. While Samson was upstairs, Louisa and Elizabeth sat at the table, enjoying a cup of tea. Louisa sat with her elbows on the table as she held the cup in her hands.

"Samson talks about you all the time, but I didn't think it would take him this long to ask you to wed him." She admitted.

"He's a kind and gentle man." Elizabeth smiled, "And I know he'll be a good husband." Her smile quickly vanished when she tried to visualise what it would be like to lie with Samson, as she had with Matthew in the woods.

George Keslake walked in the back door just as Samson returned downstairs in his best clothes. "Billy said Sam were here with Elizabeth. What's happened?"

Louisa smiled as she replied, "They're getting married. They're on their way to see Vicar."

George gave a hearty laugh and shook hands with Samson before kissing Elizabeth on the cheek. "Well, that is grand."

"Thanks, Da." He leaned over to give his mother a quick peck on the cheek. Reaching for Elizabeth's hand, they turned to the door. "We'll go now, Ma."

As they walked out the door, Louisa called out. "Go and see your Grandda and tell him the news."

~

Samson and Elizabeth walked past the church to her parent's home at the other end of the village and found her mother in the kitchen kneading dough. She immediately stopped and raised her eyebrows. "Why aren't you at manor?"

Elizabeth forced a smile and turned to Samson before saying, "Because this morning Samson asked me to marry him."

Emma Saunders smiled as she wiped her floured hands on her apron and quickly walked over to hug her daughter and future son-in-law. "That's wonderful."

Turning to tap five-year-old Ted on the shoulder. "Get your father from fields."

Elizabeth watched as her brother rushed out the side door. Emma was pouring water into the teapot when her father, Henry, rushed in the door, followed by Jane.

"What's the matter, Em?" he asked, slightly out of breath. He stopped, his eyes popping open in surprise when he saw Samson standing with his eldest daughter.

"Lizzie's getting married." She replied with a grin.

Jane rushed to give her sister a hug. "How lovely."

Henry walked over and shook Samson's hand, saying, "Welcome to the family Sam." The grin on his face mirrored his wife's.

"We're on our way to see Reverend Ellacott. Will you please give your consent?"

Henry gave Elizabeth a warm hug. "Of course. We couldn't ask for a better man to marry our daughter."

Elizabeth's smile wavered as she thought of the other man who was prepared to marry her but refused to disobey his father.

~

As they closed the door of Bluebell Cottage, Elizabeth glanced across the road to Rose Cottage. As if reading her mind, Samson said, "We'll come back and see Grandda after we've seen Vicar." He held her hand as they walked diagonally across the road to the church.

Still holding hands, they walked through the gate of the church and followed the path to the rectory located behind. Elizabeth glanced at the colourful dahlias standing up tall in the small garden under the window to the right of the door.

Elizabeth stopped just before the door and turned to Samson, whispering, "Before we go in, are you sure about giving your name to another man's child?"

He smiled as he nodded and said, "I'll raise it as my own."

Samson knocked on the door. A moment later, Reverend Ellacott looked from one to the other.

"What can I do for you, Mr. Keslake, Miss Saunders?" Extending his hand, the Vicar invited them inside.

Elizabeth had no doubt the Vicar knew why they had come to see him. She could hear the joy in Samson's voice as he spoke, "We'd like to get married."

"That's wonderful to hear," the Vicar delighted, shook Samson's hand. "Of course, the banns announcing your marriage must be called three times, and you cannot be married until after then."

Samson nodded and asked respectfully, "Will the first calling be this Sunday?"

"If you wish." He then looked to Elizabeth.

She nodded and smiled, "Yes, please."

Reverend Ellacott moved to his desk beside the door. "Very well, I'll call the banns for the next three Sundays, and you can get married…" looking up at the calendar depicting a painting of Jesus on the cross, he began counting three Sundays of March with his chubby finger, before lifting the page to April. He turned back to the young couple, "Easter Saturday, April second?"

Samson smiled at her, and without looking at the Vicar, he replied, "Easter Saturday would be perfect."

After leaving the rectory, Samson and Elizabeth walked to Rose Cottage. Samson called out, "Grandda, where are you?"

Walking around the cottage, they found Bill Rowe standing in the vegetable garden beyond the back door. He stood with his hands on the handle of the hoe in front of him, waiting for them. "What are you doing here, Sam? Shouldn't you be working with Fred?"

As Samson walked towards him, holding Elizabeth's hand, he said, "We thought we should tell you we're going to be married."

"Well, that's grand." The smile nearly reached his eyes as he dropped the hoe and walked lopsidedly to shake Samson's hand and gave Elizabeth a kiss on the cheek. "I only wish your grandmother were still here for ceremony. She loved weddings."

Bill Rowe walked in between them, spread his arms, and gently steered them towards the cottage. "Well, never mind standing here, let's go inside. We might even open a bottle of cider to celebrate news like this."

Elizabeth was trying to be caught up in the joy of Samson's parents and grandfather, but all the time, she hoped everyone would assume Samson was the father of her baby when her condition became obvious.

She wasn't really paying attention to what Samson and his grandfather were talking about, she was more concerned about what the future would hold for her and the baby. Would Samson keep his promise to raise it like his own and not reveal the child's real father? Glancing at her hands, she realised they were shaking and quickly put them on her lap, returning her attention once more to Samson.

~

Elizabeth and Samson sat side by side in church, an acceptable distance between them. While waiting for Reverend Ellacott to step up to his pulpit, he resisted the urge to hold Elizabeth's hand. Instead, he glanced at the magnificent stained-glass windows, and the beautiful stone arches inside the church, with the pews built around them. Nearly half the pews were filled with the residents of Stokebridge and those from the neighbouring villages of Penstowe and Roweshorne.

Reverend Ellacott began his sermon, but Samson wasn't really paying attention to what he was saying, he was wondering what Elizabeth would do when their banns were called. Would she look over to Matthew sitting in the front pew with his father, stepmother, and brother, or would she focus her attention on him?

Samson reached for Elizabeth's hand when Reverend Ellacott said, "I am authorised to publish the banns of marriage between Samson Keslake of Stokebridge and Elizabeth Saunders, also of Stokebridge. This is the first time of asking. If any of you know cause or just impediment why these two persons should not be joined together in Holy Matrimony, ye are to declare it."

Samson watched Elizabeth, wondering what she would do next, but she kept her head still and looked blankly ahead. He glanced at Matthew, who also sat still. He wondered how the man could possibly remain silent. The woman he was supposed to love was about to be married to someone else; surely, he would have stood up straight away and said he had cause. But Matthew had a domineering father; what else could he do?

Samson gave Elizabeth's hand a gentle squeeze and thought, *at least I'm not too scared to stand up for Elizabeth when it matters most.*

~

In Bluebell Cottage, Elizabeth was seated at the end of the table, working on the skirt of her wedding dress. While at the opposite end, her sister was kneading dough, taking no notice of the occasional bits of flour that fell on the flagstone floor.

Elizabeth sighed loudly and threw the half-completed garment on the table; it slipped over the side and landed on the bench seat. Elizabeth dropped her head and arms on the tabletop, her voice muffled when she sobbed, "I can't get the seam to sit right! I'll never get this dress finished in time for my wedding."

Jane wiped her hands on her apron, picked up the deep, sky-blue fabric and looked at the seam. "You're pulling the material a bit tight when you're sewing, that's all."

Elizabeth looked up, "Why can't I sew as good as you?"

Jane laughed, "But you make much better bread than I do."

She reached over and put her hand on Elizabeth's arm. "Would you like me to help you with your dress?"

She nodded and moved to the other end of the table. "I'll finish kneading the dough, shall I?"

Jane sat on the bench and began unpicking the stitches of the skirt. "I'm going to miss sharing a bed with you once you're married."

"I'll still be in Stokebridge, I'm not moving to Callington." Her heart skipped a beat when she thought of moving there when Lord Trevelen wouldn't let Matthew marry her.

"Yes, but at the other end of the village, living with Sam's family."

"I'll still visit, and you'll always see me at church."

Jane put the fabric on the table and stood up. Taking a few steps, she put her arms around her sister. "Even though we argue and make fun of each other, you know I love you." Jane pulled back to look Elizabeth in the face. "Don't you?"

Elizabeth put a floured hand on her shoulder, leaving white dust on her dress. "Of course I know."

They heard a knock on the door; Jane opened it, and was surprised to see Samson and his grandfather standing there.

"Come in Sam, Mr. Rowe. What can we do for you today?"

Bill Rowe quickly took off his cap as he followed Samson inside.

Before addressing their guests, Elizabeth placed the dough on a plate to rise, then returned to the table. "How nice to see you Samson, Grandda." She looked over to her sister as she put the fabric on the cupboard. "Will you put kettle on, Jane? I'm sure we'd all enjoy a cup of tea."

Samson looked at Elizabeth. "Grandda came to see me this morning."

Bill's eyes shifted from Elizabeth to Samson and back again. "I've had a long talk with Louisa, and it's about time I gave up my farm. I've already spoken to Lord Trevelen, and he's happy for Sam to move in."

Elizabeth's mouth opened wide. "But it's your home, surely you don't want to leave?"

Bill shook his head, "I'm nearly seventy years old, and since my dear wife died last year, I'm struggling to manage. Besides, it's a big cottage, too big for only me."

Elizabeth looked from Bill to Samson and back to Bill. "What about if we move in with you to help? That way, you won't have to give up your home."

Bill leaned back and gave a loud throaty laugh. "You'll need your privacy once you're wed. I don't want to interrupt anything." He turned to Samson and winked, "If you get my meaning."

Elizabeth had never seen a man blush before and turned her attention to Bill again. "That's very generous of you, but where will you live?"

"I'll move in with Louisa and George, she'll only have Johnny and Billy at home once you're married, so there'll be room for me."

Samson replied, "I thought you'd be happy to have a cottage of our own. Anyway, it's all been arranged, I'll move into Rose Cottage a week before wedding, and Grandda will move out day before."

Elizabeth opened her mouth, about to speak, when Jane spoke from beside the fireplace. "I like that idea, if I want to visit you, I only need to walk across the road."

~

Samson entered Rose Cottage with his cloth bag of belongings. His grandfather was sitting at the table, enjoying a cup of tea.

"Mornin', Grandda."

"Mornin' Sam, take your stuff to the main bedroom; I moved into the front room yesterday."

Samson raced up the stairs, calling out as he went, "Any tea in that pot?"

"Aye, there is."

Returning downstairs, Samson sat opposite his grandfather, reached for the cup, and took a big mouthful.

"Now Sam, tell me, are you nervous about getting wed?"

"A little. I hope we'll be as happy as you and Gran."

Bill sat up straighter and thoughtfully tapped his fingers on the table. "Well, it wasn't always happy. We had rough times too. But there's one thing you must do if you want a happy marriage."

Samson laughed, "What's that? I could use all the help I can get right now."

"Well, main thing to remember is to treat every woman like a lady, regardless of who they are."

Samson smiled, "I remember you telling me that when I were young, you clipped me round the ear because you said I were being disrespectful to Ma."

"And you deserved it. Never forget that women are fickle creatures." He leaned forward. "If you treat Elizabeth with kindness, then you should have a happy life together."

Samson drained his cup and studied the tea leaves at the bottom, wishing he could see what his future would be. He looked up to his grandfather again, "I'll try to remember that."

~

Elizabeth stood in her corset and petticoat as she looked at her new dress spread across the bed. She scanned the neatly pleated skirt sewn into the waistband, the bodice gathered at the waist, with five wooden buttons up the centre front to the neck, and the long sleeves gathered at the wrists with a small cuff.

Reaching for the garment, she put her arms into the sleeves, then pulled it over her head. "Jane, you've sewn this dress beautifully. I don't know if I'd have finished it on time."

"I'm sure you'd have managed." Jane replied, walking behind Elizabeth to ensure the dress fitted properly.

"Maybe, but it wouldn't have looked as good as this." She straightened up after doing up the last button. Grabbing the side of the skirt, she tried to imagine feeling silk instead of the rough, homespun fabric.

Jane looked at her, tilting her head slightly. "Elizabeth, forgive me for asking, but are you with child?"

Elizabeth sat on the bed heavily, causing the bedframe to creak, and blushed at the question, hoping Jane would not ask whose child it was. "Does it show?"

"I've noticed your waist has thickened slightly."

"Does Ma know?"

"She's the one who asked me. She had a feeling it might be possible, especially with the wedding happening so quickly."

Elizabeth's heart sank as she realised her mother knew about the baby. She thought she had hidden from her that her courses had stopped. She was hoping she could wait until they had been married for a month before announcing her pregnancy. It worried her that her mother may even suspect Samson was not the baby's father. She would have to do everything possible to hide the truth from her parents.

"As soon as I told Samson, he said he would marry me," Elizabeth explained.

Jane nodded. "He's a good man."

"Yes, he is," Elizabeth replied as she thought about what Samson expected from her that evening. She glanced at her thickening waistline and thought of the growing baby. Was she doing the right thing? If she wanted to keep Matthew's baby, she had to accept what her life would be like with Samson and hoped she would be a good wife to him.

"Well, get your boots on." Jane nagged, "Or we'll be late."

~

Reverend Ellacott's voice echoed through the church. "Do you, Elizabeth, take Samson as your lawful wedded husband?"

She looked up at Samson again, there was no fluttering of her heart when she looked at him. He stood beside her, but all she could think about was Matthew, wishing it was him standing beside her. But Lord Trevelen had made sure that would never happen.

Elizabeth could feel her legs begin to shake, and she wondered if they might refuse to hold her upright. She bit her bottom lip and shook her head, trying to rid herself of the guilt, and focused her attention on what the Vicar had said.

She swallowed hard to prevent the nausea, reminding her again of why she was standing here with Samson. She took a deep breath and let it out before saying. "I will."

Resisting the urge to look for Matthew in the crowd, Elizabeth wished she could have taken those words back, but they were like a freed bird. Once released, they were gone forever.

"I now pronounce you man and wife."

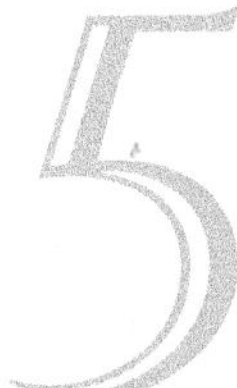

Elizabeth looked around Rose Cottage after Samson carried her over the threshold. It was only the second time she had seen the inside but was seeing it again through the eyes of a new bride. Graced with large windows, natural light illuminated the room. The big kitchen was dominated by the fireplace to the right of the front door, with two hooks over the fire. One holding a large kettle, the other holding a big cooking pot. In the back of the fireplace, she could see the bread oven.

Straight ahead she saw the table about eight feet long with bench seats on either side, beyond that was the back door.

Against the wall to the left of the table was the staircase she assumed led to the bedrooms upstairs. Looking through the window to the left of the door, Elizabeth could see the stone tool shed with the corner of the sheep field behind.

Looking around her new home, Samson smiled at her as he opened the door leading to a room on the other side of the ground floor.

"This is sitting room, but Grandda never used it after Gran died. I don't know if you'll want to use it or not." Samson explained.

Elizabeth took a couple of steps to look inside, it was the same size as the kitchen. A chair stood in front of the spinning wheel in the centre of the room, and a loom was in the far corner. On the opposite wall, a dust-covered rocking chair was by the fireplace which hadn't been lit for a while. The only other item in the room was a chair with a broken leg. She stood back and let Samson close the door.

"I'm sure we'll use it sometime," Elizabeth smiled at her husband as she walked towards the table.

Samson joined her and they stood shyly facing each other.

He reached down and gently picked up her hands, looking down at them. "Would you like to go upstairs?" he asked her.

The rough callouses on his hands rubbed against hers, and it brought back memories of Matthew's smooth hands, and she found herself comparing the two men again. She chastised herself and shook her head, forcing her attention onto the man standing in front of her, she looked into his eyes, "I'll make some supper first."

He let go of her hands, "I'll check sheep and feed pigs and chickens."

Elizabeth watched Samson as he walked out the door. Now they were married, she knew what was expected of her in the bedroom later. It was her husband's right, and she knew she had no choice but to obey. She slowly lowered herself to the bench by the table and cried once more for her lost lover.

~

Samson fetched some grain and threw it to the chickens before climbing the gate and throwing some old corn cobs to the pigs. He reached over and began scratching the back of the boar, telling him, "Elizabeth and I got married today."

Moving to scratch the black and white pig, he continued, "I'm a little nervous about taking her to my bed. You see, I've never been with a woman before."

Another sow walked over to the bucket in his hand and gave it a nudge, Samson responding, "Sorry, Gutsy, it's empty." The pig walked away in disgust.

Samson climbed the gate and leaned on it to watch the pigs, "You'll meet Elizabeth soon enough. When I feed you tomorrow, I'll tell you all about it."

He reached down to scratch the boar's ear, "At least you don't tell anyone things I tell you."

Smiling to himself, he walked back to the cottage.

~

Elizabeth was stirring the pot over the fire when Samson returned and sat at the table. She kept her back turned to him as a rush of heat reached her cheeks when she thought of his expectations.

Joining him at the table while the food cooked, she looked down as she began pleating the material of the dress. After a while, she looked at Samson and asked, "Do you want me to help you in fields?"

"I can manage fields. If you can look after vegetable garden and chickens, that would help. Besides, I don't want you to hurt yourself or the baby," Samson replied.

Elizabeth released the grip on her dress, put her hands on the table and took a deep breath, finally having the courage to tell Samson, "Ma and Jane know about the baby."

Samson's hand stopped halfway as he was about to put his pipe in his mouth. "Did you tell 'em?" he said, now placing the pipe between his teeth.

She shook her head, "Ma guessed, and Jane asked me."

She stood up and walked to the pot over the fire, scooping stew onto plates and returning to the table.

Samson removed his pipe and asked, "Do they think I'm the father?"

"Jane didn't ask, I only said when I told you about the baby, you said you would marry me."

Reassuring Elizabeth, Samson thoughtfully replied, "We'll keep it that way; no one need know truth."

~

It was nearly dark by the time the meal was consumed, and Elizabeth knew she could no longer delay going upstairs. Samson reached for her hand, she stood up and allowed herself to be led up the stairs. When they reached the top, Elizabeth wondered which door he would open. Would it be the one straight ahead or would it be the other on the right? Instead, Samson released her hand, turned left and walked to the end of the landing, opening the remaining door. He stood aside and waited for Elizabeth to walk in.

In the wall opposite the door was the fireplace, a continuation of the one from the kitchen. There was a window to the left and another to the right, with the bed up against the same wall as the door. Samson lit a candle and placed it on the mantelpiece and turned back to join her as she stood by the bed. Elizabeth looked into his eyes and saw the gentleness of her friend. She took his hands in hers, quickly looking down, "Samson, forgive me if I don't please you tonight, it will take a while for me to fall in love with you."

"I'll be patient and hope you fall in love with me soon," Samson replied respectfully.

She nodded and walked to the other side of the bed and began undoing the buttons of her new dress. Samson pulled his braces over his shoulders and began pulling out the shirt from his trousers.

He stopped and grabbed his nightshirt off the end of the bed, saying, "I'll go out to landing while you change into your nightgown."

Elizabeth looked to the door as it closed behind him, she sighed as tears began welling up. *Oh, Matthew, I wish it was you who was waiting for me to undress.*

In the corner of the room, Elizabeth found the cloth bag of clothes her father had given to Samson the day before; she rummaged through it and found her nightgown. Once she had changed, she opened the door for Samson to re-enter the room. She stood in front of the fire shivering, but not from the cold. Her arms were crossed as she held her elbows with her hands.

He gently put his hands on her upper arms, moving slowly to her shoulders, leaning down, he kissed her. Another contrast to Matthew. She wanted to run from the room to Trevelen Manor, but she knew that would achieve nothing. As Samson's wife, it was her duty to serve her husband.

Leading her to the bed, they both lay down. Very soon Samson was lifting her nightgown and climbing on top of her, pushing her legs apart with his knees. All her instincts were telling her to push him away as he thrust rhythmically into her. She closed her eyes and tried to imagine she was lying in the bracken fern with Matthew.

After it was over, she lay looking at the ceiling by the light of the fire while Samson snored beside her. Although he was a gentle lover, he didn't spark that blissful delight she felt when she was in Matthew's arms. Tears rolled down her cheek when she realised she would never experience that again. She rolled onto her side facing away from Samson and cried herself to sleep.

~

Elizabeth dressed and went downstairs to make breakfast. Samson was pulling his braces over his shoulder as he reached the bottom step. Elizabeth put bowls of porridge on the table for them both. They ate in silence before Samson left to feed the animals.

Tears cascaded down her cheeks again as she cleaned the kitchen and began making a batch of bread. This was what her life was going to be like from now on. This was the sacrifice she had made so she could keep Matthew's child.

After putting the dough on a plate to rise, she put her hands on her lower abdomen and spoke to the baby, "I hope you grow up to be a wonderful man like your father." In her mind, the baby was a boy.

Going upstairs to change into her Sunday best after the first church bells had rung, there was no sign of her husband when she returned to the kitchen. She opened the back door and yelled, "Samson, first church bells have rung, hurry up or we'll be late."

She turned as he rushed in the door, "I were checking pigs, looks like a couple have been fighting. A sow had blood all over her face."

Waving her hand towards the stairs, "Never mind about the pig. Will you get ready for church?"

Samson raced up the stairs two at a time and returned just as the second bells began to ring. He crooked his elbow for Elizabeth's hand, asking, "Shall we go to church Mrs. Keslake?"

Elizabeth saw the smile on the face of the man who was prepared to do anything for her and the child she was carrying. He was her friend and she hoped she could turn that friendship into love. Only time will tell.

She smiled back and put her hand on the offered elbow, responding, "Yes, Mr. Keslake."

~

Elizabeth scooped stew from the cauldron onto plates on their return from church. Samson stood up after their dinner was eaten and turned to Elizabeth.

"I'm going to plant some corn in bottom field. Would you like to come with me, I'll show you around the rest of farm?"

"Yes, that would be nice." Pulling her shawl off the hook, she wrapped it around her shoulders.

Balls of cotton floated in the sky as they walked outside. He gently guided her to the right and shortly they reached the large vegetable garden. The water well with its circular stone wall about three feet high, was to the right of the garden, a bucket with a rope tied to the handle lying on the ground beside it. Looking at the garden again with several raised beds in rows, she let go of Samson's hand and walked along the paths in between, touching the leaves of different plants growing before facing Samson and smiling.

"Grandda planted a lot of taters about a month ago, as well as carrots, cabbages, onions, turnips, peas and beans."

Elizabeth nodded, "We should be able to keep some for winter." Returning to stand beside her husband, "I'll enjoy looking after garden."

Samson pointed to the right. "Over in front of hedgerow is the orchard; there are some apple trees, a couple of plum trees as well as a cherry and a pear tree."

She looked over to the mature trees and saw lots of flowers, "Has all the fruit been picked?"

"Grandda picked it a couple of months ago, it's stored in shed." Pointing to the left of the cottage, Samson continued, "Over there."

Elizabeth turned and saw the two stone buildings, one she knew was the tool shed where all the farming tools was kept, with the wood store attached. The larger one, beside the tool shed, covered in ivy, she assumed was the food store.

Samson reached down and held her hand again, "Come, I'll show you sheep, then we'll look at pigs and chickens."

Elizabeth allowed herself to be led to the lush green field behind the sheds, in the corner was a shelter made from wood with woven willow reeds on the sides and top. Three black-faced sheep had their heads down eating grass while four lambs frolicked around in the warm sunshine, and another was having a drink from its mother.

"How delightful, how old are they?" Elizabeth enquired.

"These lambs are about two months old; I'll kill one for meat soon. When t'others are about eight months, I'll take them to Bradford markets."

She lifted her shoulders in a half-shrug, "Sad to see such lovely creatures being killed, but I understand it's necessary." Looking again at the sheep grazing, she asked, "These are all ewes?"

"Aye, I'll borrow Da's tup towards end of summer, we'll have another crop of lambs in spring again."

Samson took her hand, and they walked back to an area behind the vegetable garden, separated by another hedge row. In the corner of the pen, lying underneath a similar shelter to the sheep, was a black and white pig. Another three white pigs were nosing in the mud. Samson leaned on the gate, and all the pigs rushed to see if he had any food. He pointed to a sow with a tear in her ear and dried blood on her face, "That's Pinky, she's the one who's been in fight. I don't know which one she were fightin' with; none of t'others have wounds."

Elizabeth stood beside Samson and pointed to another pig, "Is that one due to farrow soon?"

Samson laughed and reached down to scratch her back, "Grandda called her Gertie, but I call her Gutsy because she loves her food." Watching as the pig twisted her head in pleasure, he said, "She's not due to farrow for another month or more."

Elizabeth asked, "What's the name of the boar and other sow?"

He pointed to the male, "That's Monty, he's a Large White, and that's Blackie, she's a British Saddleback. Grandda only got 'er just before Christmas."

Samson reached for her hand, they walked towards the tool shed and the chicken run in between the shed and cottage. Elizabeth spied the big barn behind the food store and asked, "Is that for animals in winter?"

"Aye, it's too cold for them outside."

Also made from woven willow reeds, the chicken enclosure had a three-sided shelter with wooden boxes in the corner. Samson opened the wooden gate hung off an upright post. Elizabeth followed. He picked up an egg lying in one of the boxes and handed it to her before putting his hand under another hen and pulling out two more. Elizabeth pulled the corners of her apron to hold the eggs while Samson looked for more. When they walked out of the run, six eggs rested in her apron.

Samson shut the gate and looked at Elizabeth, "Would you like to take a walk to stream?"

"Yes, I would, but I'll take eggs inside first."

Walking briskly to the cottage, returning a moment later, she held Samson's arm, "Let's go for a walk, Mr. Keslake."

Walking down the gentle slope beside the hedgerows, they would pause occasionally to gaze over the gate into a field. He would tell her what crops were growing or were going to be planted. Stepping carefully towards the edge of the stream, Elizabeth wrapped her arms around a small weeping willow. The slow-moving water bubbled over rocks. Under an overhanging tree, a flash of silver caught Elizabeth's eye, and she pointed, "Is that a trout?"

Samson walked closer to the edge, followed her finger, and spied the fish, slowly moving its tail against the current, "Yes, it is," Samson replied as he slowly stepped into the knee-deep water after removing his boots and woollen stockings, and rolling up his trousers.

Elizabeth watched in fascination as he carefully walked towards it, extending his fingers under the fish, and quickly flicked it out of the water onto the bank, not far from where she was standing. She laughed and hurriedly put her foot on the fish, "Looks like we have our supper."

Samson picked up a small branch after climbing out of the water, giving the fish a hefty clout on the head. He smiled and sat on the ground to put on his boots and roll his trousers down, "Grandda taught me how to tickle trout when I were a lad."

Elizabeth looked to the woods on the opposite bank, asking, "Is the stream the boundary of the farm?"

Samson nodded and stood up again before pointing towards the sheep field, "The hedgerow that goes beside the church, and behind it, also behind Abe Bosley's forge, and down towards the stream, that's the boundary on that side."

He turned around and pointed behind the fruit trees, "That hedgerow in front of wood is the boundary on t'other side. Grandda used to collect extra firewood from there if he needed it." He turned to face Elizabeth and continued, "You'll notice the farm is wider near stream than it is at the cottage."

She nodded as she viewed the farm. "It's a lot bigger than Da's."

"Yes, I'm luckier than most; I have about twenty acres. We should be able to feed ourselves and livestock."

Elizabeth held Samson's elbow again and leaned on his upper arm. "I'm sure we will."

"I may have to do other work every now and then to earn money to help pay our rent to Lord Trevelen." Looking up towards the church tower standing behind the barn, "And our tithe to church."

Elizabeth followed his gaze. "Yes, of course. Would you be working for local farmers, or will you have to go to other villages?"

He shrugged, "All depends on where I can find work."

He picked up the dead fish and gently led her towards the cottage.

As Elizabeth and Samson continued their daily routines on the farm, a subtle shift occurred in the air between them. Samson, while tending to the animals or working the fields, stole glances at Elizabeth, his eyes betraying a mixture of admiration and understanding. He noticed the way she meticulously cared for the vegetable garden, her hands gently cradling the fragile plants as if they were delicate treasures.

Elizabeth, in turn, found solace in the quiet moments shared in the kitchen or walks by the stream. As they navigated the intricacies of married life, unspoken gestures became their language. A comforting touch on the small of her back as they walked, a shared smile across the dinner table. These small exchanges held a weight, an unspoken promise of companionship.

As days turned into weeks, their relationship deepened. Each moment of vulnerability, carefully exposed and delicately handled, wove a tapestry of emotional intimacy that bound them together in a way neither had anticipated.

~

While working in the garden one day, Elizabeth felt a sensation in her lower abdomen, likening it to the gentle flutter of a butterfly's wings. She stood up, placed her hands on her belly and realised it was the baby moving. She looked over to Samson in the pigsty, his back towards her, bent over. He was probably checking the pregnant sow. Should she tell him about it now, or wait until they were eating supper? A single tear rolled down her cheek. Oh, how she wished she could tell Matthew about the movements of his baby. She took a deep breath and returned to planting potatoes.

~

After a day filled with the toil of tending to the vegetable garden, Elizabeth wearily climbed into bed, her muscles protesting each movement. The cool linen sheets brushed against her fatigued skin as she settled in, hoping for the embrace of sleep. As Samson curled up beside her, his rough fingertips traced a pattern on her forearm. A fleeting annoyance flickered within her, but dissipated as quickly as it came. In the dimness of the room, she found herself relishing these intimate moments with him. Closing her eyes, she surrendered to the warmth enveloping her. In the throes of passion, the rustling leaves and the scent of the forest invaded her thoughts, and in a husky voice, she whispered, "Matthew."

Samson halted; the cessation of his touch palpable. Her eyes flew open, a gasp escaped her lips. "I'm sorry!" she exclaimed.

"Forget about him; *I'm* your husband now." Samson responded, rolling off and turning towards the wall, his silhouette a stark outline against the moonlit room.

Elizabeth lay in the darkness, listening to him snoring. The sound was different from his usual snore, and she realised he was only pretending to be asleep. The anger in Samson's words was unmistakable. How could she hurt him like that? She looked to where he lay, realising she *was* falling in love with him. Calling out Matthew's name was the biggest mistake she could make.

Since her marriage to Samson two months ago, she had only seen Matthew in church on Sundays and it was usually a brief glance as he walked past her on his way to the carriage with his family.

Her body fatigued from the day, sleep still eluded her. She didn't know how she was going to face Samson in the morning; would they argue over it? She rolled onto her side away from him and shortly she heard his usual snore. She closed her eyes and eventually, she too was asleep.

~

When Elizabeth woke in the morning, she realised she had been dreaming of Matthew and the guilt hit her again like a blow to the stomach. Dressing quickly, she went to the hen house, opened the gate, and began throwing grain at the chickens. They squawked as they fought over the scattered wheat. Reaching under a hen, she found two eggs, not disturbing the next hen sitting on fertile eggs. With six eggs in her apron pocket, she opened the door of the smokehouse attached to the food store shed. Cutting bacon from the hanging carcass, she returned inside.

~

Samson was woken by the smell of frying bacon, and it made his mouth water as he dressed. The fog lifted from his brain enough to realise why Elizabeth was cooking his favourite breakfast. Well, bacon and eggs were not enough for him to forgive her. Not yet.

Elizabeth turned at the sound of his footsteps and smiled at him, "Good morning."

Samson grunted as he walked out the back door, "Mornin'."

After throwing some food to the pigs, he leaned on the gate to watch them, but the antics of the pigs were his least concern. He was thinking about his wife's behaviour the previous night. He knew when he married Elizabeth, she still had feelings for the next Lord Trevelen, and he hoped she had gotten over him by now, but he didn't think she would utter his name in their bed. He could confront her about it, but that would only lead to an argument. Right now, that was the last thing he wanted. Taking a deep breath and slowly letting it out, he picked up the bucket and returned to the cottage.

~

Elizabeth placed the plate in front of Samson as soon as he sat at the table. Picking up his knife and fork, he began cutting the meat. He asked, "Did you find many eggs this morning?"

She sat on the other side of the table and answered, "Six, but one hen is sitting on a clutch of nine, we should have some chicks soon."

"If there're any roosters amongst them, I'll kill one for supper."

"That'll be nice; make a change from smoked pork."

Samson stood up after he had finished his bacon and eggs, "I'll be working in field behind pigsty; I'm going to plant some barley. I'll see you at dinnertime. Bye, love."

As Samson closed the door behind him, Elizabeth put her head in her hands and sighed. She was waiting for him to say something about what happened last night. Since their marriage, she didn't feel the urge to push him off like she did on their wedding night. She had become accustomed to Samson's lovemaking, although it was different to Matthew's. She shook her head. For her own and Samson's sake, she must put Matthew from her mind. She stood up and looked out the window at Samson's retreating figure as he walked to the tool shed, silently thanking him for not mentioning her mistake. Chastising herself once more for the hurt she had caused him.

The faint light shining through the window reached Elizabeth's eyes, forcing her unconscious mind awake. Samson snored beside her, and she wondered how he could have slept during the warm night. Tossing and turning trying to find a cool spot on the sheet, it was nearly impossible to sleep. She only fell asleep in the early hours of the morning. It had been a very hot day for July, and it didn't cool down as the night closed in.

Lying in bed with only the sheet covering her, she had a brief thought of Matthew, thinking if she was the lady of the manor, she wouldn't have to cook breakfast, a servant would be doing it for her. She scolded herself again for thinking of him when Samson was lying beside her.

She softly said, "No time for dreaming."

Throwing back the sheet, Elizabeth was about to swing her feet onto the floor, when the pain in her stomach took her breath away, and she felt fluid trickling between her legs. She looked down at the sheet and saw a dark patch. She screamed.

Rubbing the sleep from his eyes, Samson sat up quickly. His hair sticking out at awkward angles, he managed, "What, what's the matter?" His eyes widened at the blood-covered sheet. He dressed quickly, "I'll fetch Mrs. Bosley."

It should have been funny when Samson nearly fell over while pulling on his boots, but this was no time for laughter.

As Samson closed the door behind him, Elizabeth lay back on the pillow, putting her hands protectively over the small bump in her belly, hoping the gesture would protect Matthew's child. The returning pain kept telling her the effort was futile. She remembered her mother telling her of the pain of childbirth and knew she was probably experiencing those same pains. She rolled onto her side and cried, knowing it was too soon.

~

Samson hit the wall as he pulled his braces over his shoulders, he was certain he would have a bruise there in the morning. He cursed the door sneck when it wouldn't open, but after trying a second time, it opened. The early morning sun blinded him for a moment as he ran in front of the stone church wall to Snowdrop cottage.

~

With Mrs. Bosley in tow, Samson raced back to Rose Cottage where Elizabeth waited for the midwife.

On her arrival at Rose Cottage, Mrs. Bosley, a stout woman with silver-streaked hair tied neatly in a bun, stepped into the humble abode. The scent of herbs and lavender, a hallmark of her calming presence, trailed in her wake.

In the close-knit village of Stokebridge, Mrs. Bosley was not just a midwife; she was a matriarchal figure, a soothing force that seemed to emanate from her very core. The worn wooden steps groaned slightly beneath her weight as she made her way up to the bedroom of Rose Cottage.

Sitting up when Mrs. Bosley entered the room, Elizabeth pleaded through her quivering voice, "What's happening to my baby?"

Mrs. Bosley turned to Samson, "You can leave us now, dear; I'll look after Elizabeth."

Before he moved, he turned to the midwife, "Please take care of Elizabeth, Mrs. Bosley, and the baby." Leaving the two women alone as he closed the door behind him.

With eyes opened wide, Elizabeth pleaded again, "What's happening to my baby Mrs. Bosley?"

Concerned, she replied, "I wish I knew, but this shouldn't be happening, it's too soon. How long have you been feeling the baby move?"

Tears streamed down her cheeks as she replied. "Only a few weeks."

Mrs. Bosley sat down on the edge of the bed and held Elizabeth's hand. She looked into Elizabeth's eyes that were dulled by grief. She met her with a compassionate gaze and said, "I'm going to do everything I can to help you and your baby, dear."

~

It was nearly midday when Samson saw the midwife walk into the honeysuckle-covered, stone privy attached to the back of the cottage. He dropped the digging fork and raced towards it. Mrs. Bosley walked out with the empty chamber pot in her hand, her eyes narrowed against the bright sunshine after the gloom of the privy.

"How's Elizabeth?"

The midwife threw her hands in the air and the chamber pot flew in an arc before it landed on the ground behind her. Leaning on the door of the privy, she put her hand to her chest and patted her ample bosom, "Ooh, Sam, you nearly made my heart stop."

Samson picked up the pot and handed it back to her. "How's Elizabeth?" he asked again.

Mrs. Bosley shook her head, "I wish I knew why she's gone into early labour, but even if she survives, the baby may not."

Samson ran his fingers through his hair, spun on his heels, facing the midwife again, looking down at her. Usually, she always had a smile on her face, and the fact it had disappeared, worried him.

"Please don't let her die, Mrs. Bosley, please don't let her die."

She looked into his wide pleading eyes, "I'll do everything I can to help her, I hope it doesn't happen."

Samson's shoulders slumped as he looked at the ground. He felt a reassuring hand on his shoulder before she returned inside, he was grateful she did not say anything. No words of comfort would make any difference right now.

~

Mrs. Bosley woke suddenly when Elizabeth gripped her hand. Glancing at the candle on the mantelpiece, she noticed it had burnt down a substantial amount.

"I think I've wet myself," Elizabeth said.

The midwife quickly stood up and threw back the covers. "You haven't wet yourself; your waters have broken."

Elizabeth's fingers desperately clawed at the flesh of her forearm. Her eyes wide open. "What does that mean?"

The midwife gently took Elizabeth's hands off her arm and sat on the edge of the bed, glancing at their reflections in the window. She replied softly, "Your baby will be born sometime tomorrow."

Lowering her head, she swallowed and whispered, "And it will probably die, won't it?"

Mrs. Bosley reached over for a rag to wipe the beads of sweat off her forehead before nodding her own head. Elizabeth flopped back on the pillow, turned away from her and wailed.

A moment later, Samson opened the bedroom door. He stood in the doorway with one hand on the handle, the other on the door frame. Mrs. Bosley gently guided him onto the landing, closing the door behind them.

"What's happened to Elizabeth?"

"I'm sorry Sam, your baby will be born tomorrow, and there's nothing I can do to stop it."

She watched as he slowly walked along the landing and down the stairs, raking his fingers through his hair, before returning to the bedroom.

~

Mrs. Bosley looked out the window at the sound of birds twittering. Little patches of pale light appeared above Crocus Cottage, and somewhere in the distance, a rooster crowed. Mrs. Bosley looked back at Elizabeth when she felt the bones in her hand being squeezed as another contraction gripped her. Although she released it once it had passed, another one quickly followed. The midwife thought Elizabeth might crush her hand with the strength of her grip.

"I don't think it'll be long now, Elizabeth." Pulling the covers back and lifting her knees.

Elizabeth gave another groan and the midwife said, "I can see the head."

Her cries became louder, and the tears rolled down her cheek as she gave another push. Mrs. Bosley prepared herself to receive the baby and very soon she was holding the little boy. The midwife looked at him, he was hardly bigger than her hand, and the cry he gave was no louder than a mouse squeak. Mrs. Bosley wrapped a blanket around him before cutting the cord. Standing up, she gently placed the tiny boy in Elizabeth's arms.

~

Elizabeth looked at the perfectly formed baby with his dark pink skin and reached out to hold the tiny hand which was hardly bigger than the top of her thumb. His blue eyes seemed too big for his face as he looked at her, Elizabeth couldn't help it, her lips trembled as tears cascaded down her cheeks. Her dream of having Matthew's child as a reminder of their love was about to be shattered.

~

Samson was at the table, asleep with his head on his arms. The smell of tobacco hung heavy in the air, a small plume of smoke rose from his pipe on the table in front of him. Mrs. Bosley gently touched his shoulder.

He sat up quickly and his eyes opened wide, "What, what?" He shook his head. "What's happened?"

"Elizabeth has just given birth to a baby boy, but he's arrived too early. I'm sorry Sam dear, your son is going to die."

"How's Elizabeth, can I see her?"

She nodded. "She'll recover from the birth, but she's understandably overcome with grief."

He was on his feet and halfway up the stairs before she'd finished talking.

~

Samson slowed down as he walked into the bedroom, sitting on the chair by the window. He looked at Elizabeth, the trail of tears reminded him of snail trails on the soil. The tiny baby in her arms.

"Mrs. Bosley said he's not going to live."

"I know, but I want to hold him for as long as I can." Elizabeth's voice trembled as she spoke, her eyes never leaving her precious baby's petite face.

Samson tried to control his own tears which were threatening. He lost the battle as he looked at the tiny baby he was going to claim as his own. He was shocked when Elizabeth slapped his hand as he reached to touch the baby's cheek. She lowered her eyebrows and glared at him, "Don't you touch my son."

With tears running down his cheek, he whispered, "I was going to call him my son too."

Elizabeth let out a breath, "I'm sorry." More tears flowed down her face.

"What do you want to call him?"

"I want to name him Henry, after my father."

"Do you want me to fetch Reverend Ellacott to baptise him?"

Elizabeth nodded.

Samson stood up. "I'll go to church right now."

Samson saw Mrs. Bosley sitting at the table with her head on her arms. She looked up when she heard him walking down the stairs. "Has he died?"

Samson shook his head, wiped the back of his hand over his eyes and swallowed a couple of times. "I'm going to fetch Vicar."

The midwife stood up and gently touched him on the arm, "You stay with Elizabeth, I'll go."

He nodded and slowly walked up the stairs.

Samson glanced up when Mrs. Bosley returned with Reverend Ellacott. He knew his face was red, but he didn't care. He looked at the baby in Elizabeth's arms and could barely see his little chest moving. He wondered how long before he died.

The midwife stood by the door as Reverend Ellacott walked up to Elizabeth. "Mrs. Bosley has told me about your son." Pulling a bottle of holy water from his bag, the Reverend asked, "What name have you chosen for the little boy?"

As Elizabeth looked up to Reverend Ellacott, Samson could see only sadness in her red and puffy face. "Henry," She whispered.

Reverend Ellacott nodded, pulled the stopper from the bottle, and put his thumb over the opening before tipping it upside down. Samson stood up and pulled the chair out of the Vicar's way.

While making the sign of the cross on his forehead with his thumb, he said, "I baptise you 'Henry' in the name of the Father, the Son, and the Holy Ghost."

Samson glanced at Elizabeth and could see fresh tears running down her cheek. He wiped his own face before shaking the Vicar's hand, "Thank you for coming so quickly, Reverend." He looked towards his wife lying on the bed holding the baby. "I'll come and see you later at vicarage."

There was no need to say when. Reverend Ellacott nodded and left. He felt Mrs. Bosley touch him gently on the shoulder as he stood looking at his wife and she whispered, "I'll be downstairs."

His eyes were on Elizabeth as he nodded. She discreetly left the room.

Samson moved the chair closer to the bed and sat down, reaching for Elizabeth's hand, tenderly rubbing his thumb over the back of her fingers.

She turned to face him. "Samson, I'm sorry for what I said earlier." Looking at the baby again, "I was upset about Henry. He's my only link to Matthew and soon he'll be gone too."

"I know," gently wiping a tear from his eye, "I was prepared to look after you and call him my son. I'm sad too that he's not going to live."

Samson stood up quickly when he noticed Henry's chest barely moving, saying as he raced from the room, "I'll fetch Mrs. Bosley."

Samson found the midwife pouring hot water into the tin teapot.

"I was about to bring you both a cup of tea. Has he gone?"

Samson shook his head, "Not yet, but I think you should be with Elizabeth when he dies."

"I understand," she agreed.

Samson watched as she waddled up the stairs as fast as she could. He sat at the table, put his head in his hands and thought about how just over twenty-four hours ago he was looking forward to becoming a father in a couple of months, even if the child wasn't his. But this morning, the unthinkable happened and Elizabeth's baby was born too early.

His mouth was dry, probably from all the crying, he saw the teapot on the cupboard and poured himself a cup. He sat down and waited for the inevitable.

He looked over to the corner near the front window and saw the cradle, he only needed to put on the curved rocker feet. He wondered if it would ever hold a sleeping baby.

He had just finished the tea when he heard a wail through the ceiling and knew immediately that Henry had died. Mrs. Bosley was standing in the doorway with the baby in her arms when he reached the landing. She stood still and whispered, "I'll take him downstairs and put him in the cradle."

Samson nodded and stepped around her. He sat on the edge of the bed and saw Elizabeth lying facing away from him. He touched her lightly on the arm and she turned to him and sat up. They put their arms around each other, their bodies wracked with sobs.

~

As Mrs. Bosley was leaving the bedroom, she glanced again at the young couple consoling each other. This was not the first time a baby she delivered had died, she was no stranger to seeing new parents grieve. She didn't like it as it always made her question whether there was anything else she could have done to prevent it. She turned towards the stairs.

~

When Samson answered the door the next morning, he found Mrs. Bosley standing on the threshold with her basket over her arm. He ran a hand through his unruly hair and returned to the table.

"Mornin' dear, I've come to check on Elizabeth, is she upstairs?"

"Aye, spent most of night crying."

"I'm not surprised," she said, walking to the fire, "I'll make a pot of tea and take a cup to Elizabeth." She gave him a sad smile. "Would you like one too?"

Samson gave a slight nod, pushing the empty porridge bowl away. He glanced at the cradle in the corner of the room.

"I were looking forward to being a father." He put his head on his arms and cried. "I still can't believe he's dead."

Mrs. Bosley stopped pouring water into the pot, rushed over, and sat next to him and began rubbing his shoulder, "You will become a father one day, Sam, and I'm sure you'll be a wonderful Da to your next child."

He sat up, wiped his eyes, and turned to the midwife. "Elizabeth and I really wanted this one."

"I know you did, and I wish I could tell you why Henry died, but I'm afraid I don't know." She stood up to tend to the teapot.

She placed a cup in front of Samson, before pouring two more cups and taking them upstairs.

~

Lying on her side, Elizabeth watched the setting sun. The shadow of her mother-in-law crossed in front of her, temporarily blocking her view through the window. Louisa stood by the end of the bed, a plate of salted pork and bread in her hands. "Are you feeling better?"

Sitting up, she accepted the plate of food and slowly began eating. "I keep thinking I did something wrong, and that's why Henry died."

Louisa sat on the end of the bed, "I don't think you would have done anything that would've hurt him. It was God's plan. We must accept it."

Elizabeth picked up the bread and took a bite. "I don't know if I want to accept it. I wish I'd have died with Henry."

Dropping the bread on the plate before placing it on the chair, Elizabeth looked up when Louisa said, "I felt that way when my Richard died, I didn't want to live either."

Elizabeth reached for her hand. "You lost a child too?"

She nodded. "About a year before Sam were born."

The lump in her throat was hard to swallow as she asked, "What happened?"

"He were about ten months old, for some reason he kept getting sick, and after two days, he died."

Elizabeth wiped her face with the back of her hand. "So, you know what it's like to lose a child."

Louisa's tears fell onto the bed. "I lost a son, and even though it were many years ago, I still think about him," She took a deep breath and let it out, "Now I've lost a grandson."

Elizabeth flinched and gently pulled her hand away, pretending to wipe away more tears. She couldn't let Louisa see her face in case she guessed the truth about Henry's father.

~

In the afternoon, Samson stood with Elizabeth in the church grounds and watched as Henry's little coffin was lowered into the ground. Elizabeth cried openly as she leaned on him.

56

Staring into the hole as the gravediggers began filling it, Samson tried to understand why the little boy died. Unfortunately, infant deaths were a fact of life, but that didn't make their loss any easier to endure.

Entering Rose Cottage after the burial, Samson saw Elizabeth glance at the cradle near the window. Her body shook with sobs as she raced up the stairs. "Will you take that away; I can't bear to look at it."

Samson's own tears flowed as he carried it to his tool shed.

Returning inside, he made a fresh pot of tea, poured two cups and took them into the bedroom. Elizabeth was lying on the bed, he put the cup on the chair next to her.

"I've brought you some tea, love," Sitting on the bed with his own.

She turned to him. "Will this pain ever go away?"

"I hope so." He took a mouthful and looked at her thoughtfully.

Elizabeth sat up, leaning on the bedhead. "I keep praying it's all a bad dream, and I'll wake up to find he's asleep in the cradle."

"I'm sure the pain will ease, maybe when we have another baby. Then hopefully you'll remember Henry with love and not sadness."

Elizabeth rubbed her forehead. "I can't even think about another baby now." Picking up the cup and taking a sip. Tears streamed down her cheeks as she continued, "I can't even tell Matthew his son is dead; I'm not allowed at the manor anymore."

Putting his cup on the chair after drinking the final dregs, "If you'd like me to, I'll have a quiet word with him after church on Sunday."

"Will you?" Elizabeth closed her eyes, let out a breath and slumped her shoulders. "I'd be most grateful if you could," Putting a hand on his.

He nodded, picking up both cups, and he stood up. "You rest now love, Ma's coming later to prepare dinner for us."

~

Seeking solace, Samson found himself drawn to the familiar embrace of the church pews before others arrived for Reverend Ellacott's service. The hallowed silence wrapped around him, offering a brief respite from the thick atmosphere of sorrow he left behind at Rose Cottage.

Soon, Lord Trevelen walked by with his wife and two sons. Matthew looked at him questionably sitting by himself. Still, he continued to walk behind his father and sat in their pew beside his brother Robert.

Samson listened to the sermon but wasn't paying attention. His mind kept wandering to Elizabeth at home. He was also thinking of how to tell Matthew about his son's death, which Reverend Ellacott mentioned at the end of his sermon. "I think you'll all join me in giving our heartfelt sympathies to Mr. and Mrs. Samson Keslake after the passing of their infant son, Henry, who died five days ago."

Reverend Ellacott seamlessly wove messages of hope into his teachings, addressing the universal themes of loss and healing. His words that day were not just of spiritual guidance but practical wisdom for navigating the intricate journey through life and loss.

Samson glanced over and saw Matthew turn around to look at him. He knew exactly what he wanted to know, but he would have to wait until the service was over before he could tell him. The air thickened with the unspoken words between them, the tension building with each exchanging glance.

Instead of walking towards the road, Samson turned and walked to the small mound of fresh earth that covered Henry's grave and waited. Within a minute the next Lord Trevelen was standing beside him.

"My condolences to you Mr. Keslake, and to your wife. I only returned from London yesterday, I had not heard of the death of," He swallowed, "Your son."

"Thank you for your kind words, Master Engels, I'll tell Elizabeth when I get home, she's resting now."

Samson watched Matthew as he glanced around, aware of people nearby. He whispered, "I'd like to visit her if I may."

Samson stood up straight and stared at him long and hard. "I think that would only upset her; besides, you and your father have done more than enough."

He turned on his heels and walked away quickly without a backward glance, leaving Matthew standing in the church grounds alone.

Samson was washing his hands in a bucket on the cupboard after walking inside, when he heard a plate being put on the table. He turned around, his mother stood there, her forehead puckered.

He moved a step closer. "What's the matter, Ma?"

"Is Elizabeth outside?"

Samson shook his head, "No, she hasn't been outside since before Henry were born. She not in bed?"

"No, I've checked all the rooms, there's no sign of 'er. Where on earth could she be?"

Samson wiped his hands on his trousers, his mother following him as he raced out the door. He added. "You look in privy, I'll check to see if she's gone to feed hens."

When he returned to the cottage, Samson saw his mother standing by the privy, shaking her head, "She's not with chickens either."

The sound of urgent knocking at the front door reached them as they walked inside. Samson was surprised to see Reverend Ellacott standing on the doorstep with Elizabeth, her hands and nightgown covered in dirt. It was her face that worried him. She was staring ahead. It was obvious she was not focusing on what was in front of her.

"Where was she?" Samson whispered, looking from her head to her bare feet and back again.

Reverend Ellacott's shoulders slumped, "She was in the church ground at Henry's grave, digging with her hands. When I asked her what she was doing, she kept crying; *I want to hold my baby.* I eventually convinced her to get up and brought her back here. I didn't know what else to do."

"Thank you, Vicar." Samson replied.

Louisa put her arm around Elizabeth's shoulders, "Come Elizabeth, let's get you cleaned up." As if in a dream, she allowed herself to be guided inside.

Reverend Ellacott stood at the doorstep, "Is there anything I can do?"

Samson could see he was relieved to pass the responsibility of her care to someone else.

Louisa turned to the Reverend, "Yes, would you fetch Mrs. Bosley, please?"

Samson closed the door after the Reverend left. Helplessness washed over him as his mother led Elizabeth to the table and encouraged her to sit. She fetched the bucket of water he had been using earlier and a cloth. He watched his mother as she tenderly began washing Elizabeth's hands, being careful not to hurt her ripped fingernails.

Gently brushing the hair from her eyes, Samson knelt beside his wife. "Oh my love, what have you done to yourself?" Silence was her only response.

A moment later, the door opened and Mrs. Bosley walked in carrying her basket. "My goodness, Reverend told me briefly what happened, has she been like this since he brought her back?"

Louisa and Samson both stood up. "Yes," Louisa replied, "She's off with pixies, she won't talk to us."

Mrs. Bosley took the cloth from Louisa and began washing Elizabeth's face and neck. "Sam, you go and tend to your fields, your Ma and I'll take care of her now."

Samson ran his hands through his hair, "This shouldn't be happening; Henry's been dead a month."

"I've noticed she hasn't been to church since then. How's she managing?" enquired Mrs. Bosley.

He looked at Elizabeth as the midwife washed her, she was paying no attention to them discussing her.

"If it weren't for Ma and Elizabeth's Ma bringing pots of food, we'd starve. Not that she eats much."

"Oh dear, she should be better by now."

Louisa added, "She walks around in a dream, she hasn't fed chickens or tended vegetable garden since before Henry were born."

Samson's shoulders slumped. "I don't know what to do."

Samson looked at Elizabeth sitting at the table and noticed her empty gaze.

Mrs. Bosley put a reassuring hand on his arm. "We'll take her upstairs and I'll give her something to help her sleep. Hopefully, she'll feel better tomorrow."

"Whatever you think is best," Samson said sadly before leaving the cottage.

~

Mrs. Bosley dropped the cloth in the bucket, gently putting her hand under Elizabeth's upper arm. "Come, my dear, let's get you changed into a clean nightgown and back into bed."

Leading Elizabeth up the stairs, Mrs. Bosley turned to Louisa, "Can you fetch some fresh warm water and bring it upstairs, please.'

Mrs. Bosley gently removed Elizabeth's dirty nightgown, leaving her standing in her cotton drawers. A short while later, Louisa walked into the bedroom with the bucket, placing it on the chair beside the bed.

"Sit on the bed Elizabeth and I'll give you a good wash."

Louisa stood with her hand on the door handle, "If you don't need my help, Mrs. Bosley, I'll go downstairs."

The midwife nodded and gazed again at Elizabeth, and wondered if she was seeing what was outside the window. She hoped she would be able to help this poor woman overcome the tragedy of losing her firstborn.

~

Mrs. Bosley walked into Rose Cottage the following morning and found Samson's mother washing plates.

"Mornin' Louisa, is Elizabeth still upstairs?"

"Aye, but she's very quiet."

Mrs. Bosley shook her head. "I've never heard of a woman doing that sort of thing before."

"Do you think she'll get better?" Louisa asked.

"I hope so, for hers and Sam's sake. The loss of a baby affects women in many ways."

Louisa gestured to the fire, "I've just boiled kettle if you need hot water."

"I might take up a cup of tea for Elizabeth, see how she is today."

The midwife picked up the cup, walking carefully up the stairs. The sun streaming through the window shone in Elizabeth's face, as she lay on her side with her eyes open. She seemed to be oblivious to its glare. Mrs. Bosley put the cup on the chair beside her and sat on the bed.

"How are you feeling this morning'?"

Elizabeth didn't move when she replied, "I want to be with Henry." Her voice soft.

Mrs. Bosley barely heard what she said, but replied, "You can't mean that, you can still have another baby."

"I don't want another baby, I want Henry."

Mrs. Bosley pushed a strand of hair back from her face. "Do you remember what happened yesterday?"

Elizabeth remained motionless as she replied, "I remember walking to the church to visit Henry's grave. After that, I don't remember anything till I woke up this morning."

"Reverend Ellacott found you digging at his grave, you kept repeating, *I want to hold my baby*, don't you remember that?"

Elizabeth turned her head slightly to look at Mrs. Bosley and whispered, "No, I don't."

More tears ran down Elizabeth's cheek as Mrs. Bosley asked, "Have you had any porridge this morning?"

"Ma brought some up, but I didn't want it."

"You must eat to keep up your strength," Mrs. Bosley insisted.

Elizabeth sat up so quickly that she took the midwife by surprise when she shouted, "What do I need strength for, my baby's dead. I have nothing to live for," she sobbed as she fell on the pillow.

"What about Sam, he loves you and needs your help on the farm."

Wiping her face on the pillow, "I'm sure he can get someone else to help him, I just want to be with Henry."

Feeling defeated, Mrs. Bosley stood up, "Drink your tea Elizabeth; I'll get something to help you sleep."

Mrs. Bosley walked downstairs and found Louisa sitting at the table, shelling peas.

"How be she?"

"Elizabeth seems to have lost the will to live," confided Mrs. Bosley.

"She don't eat much, and 'er clothes just falling off 'er."

"I noticed," Mrs. Bosley replied as she rummaged in her basket, pulling out a bottle of amber-coloured liquid. She poured enough of the mixture to cover the bottom of the cup and then topped it up with water.

"This will help her sleep, but she can't have too much. I'll take this up to her now and give her some more this evening."

"Thank you, Mrs. Bosley, we can only pray she gets better soon."

~

Emma Saunders called out as she walked into Rose Cottage with two tin bowls of porridge.

"Sam, I've brought you and Elizabeth some breakfast."

Hearing no reply, she put the bowls on the table. Walking outside, she found Samson working in the vegetable garden. Emma walked over to him. "How's Elizabeth this morning?"

Samson stood up, shaking his head, "Still the same, won't get out of bed and spends all day and night crying."

"She should be up by now; she can't spend all day in bed. What did Mrs. Bosley say?"

He shrugged and began walking to the cottage, "She said she should be up too, but each woman suffers differently when they lose a child. I don't know what to do."

"Do you want me to talk to her?" Emma asked as they walked in the back door.

Samson shrugged again as he sat down, "If you want." Picking up his spoon, he began eating the porridge. "See if you can get 'er out of bed," bits of porridge fell from his mouth as he talked.

Picking up the other bowl, Emma walked upstairs. Opening the door, she was not surprised to see her daughter lying in the bed, tracks of tears on her face. Not even moving when the door opened.

"Lizzie, I've brought you some breakfast."

Rolling over towards the other window, she replied, "I'm not hungry."

Emma rolled her eyes and placed the bowl on the mantelpiece. Stamping her foot loudly on the floor, she shouted, "When are you going to get over Henry? The poor little boy died. You're upset and that's understandable, but Sam needs you to take care of him. I can't keep doing it, neither can Louisa, we've both got our own families to look after."

Elizabeth turned back to her mother and whispered, "I wish I were with Henry."

"My Ma always used to say, *if wishes were horses, all beggars would ride.*" Walking to the side of the bed and folding her arms, she continued, "If the Good Lord had wanted you in heaven, you'd have died with your baby, but that wasn't what He wanted. There's a good reason you didn't die when Henry were born."

Elizabeth sat up quickly, her eyebrows lowered and pulled together when she shouted, "And what is that reason?"

Emma was startled by the angry tone of her voice but sat on the edge of the bed and said softly, "I don't know what the reason is, and neither does anyone else know what God has planned for us." Standing up again, she continued, "We must have faith He knows what He's doing."

Elizabeth sat silent as she looked at the bedclothes. Emma put her hands on her hips and squared her shoulders. "Well, are you going to get out of that bed and start behaving like a wife? Me, Louisa, and Sam aren't going to do your work forever."

Elizabeth sighed, threw the bedclothes back and sat on the edge of the bed. "If I'm not meant to die, I suppose I'd better get up."

Fetching the bowl of porridge, Emma pushed it in Elizabeth's face. "Good. You can start by eating this."

Elizabeth shoved her hair away from her face and took the bowl offered to her. She glanced up at her mother once more before she took the first mouthful.

"I'll see you downstairs dreckly." Emma closed the door behind her.

~

Samson stared open-mouthed at his mother-in-law when she returned to the kitchen, his eyes followed her as she went to the fire, poured fresh water in the teapot, and poured three cups before sitting at the table.

"Is she coming downstairs?"

"I hope so. I told her we were all fed up with doing her work and that she'd better get out of bed. And I walked out."

Picking up his cup, Samson asked, "I heard a bang, what were that?"

"I stamped my foot on the floor to get her attention. It seemed to work."

The sound of footsteps reached them, and soon, a dressed Elizabeth placed her empty bowl on the cupboard, before sitting opposite her mother.

Samson stood up to greet his wife, "Hello love, Ma's poured you a cup of tea."

"Thank you."

Samson drained the last of his tea, "I'll go and harvest more wheat down by stream." He bent to kiss Elizabeth on the cheek, "I'll see you at dinner time." Picking up his cap, he briskly walked outside.

Emma finished her tea and asked, "Will you cook something for Sam's dinner?"

Elizabeth picked up her cup and looked over the top at her mother, responding, "I suppose I have to."

"Good, there's plenty of eggs in basket, and you can get some bacon from smokehouse. I know Sam would enjoy that."

She stood up to leave. "We don't expect you to do everything right away, but each day try to do a bit more. That's all Sam, Louisa, and I want."

Elizabeth closed her eyes and nodded. "I'll try."

"Goodbye, Lizzie."

~

The smell of bacon cooking was unmistakable when Samson returned to the cottage.

"That smells good. Are you feeling better, love?"

"Not really, but Ma said I have to look after you."

A great weight seemed to settle on Samson's heart as he sat down. "I didn't want Henry to die either, I were looking forward to the baby arriving, even though I weren't his father."

Putting the teapot and a plate on the table, Elizabeth stood beside him as he swallowed a mouthful of bacon. He stopped mid-chew. "Aren't you having anything to eat?"

"I'm not hungry." Turning to walk up the stairs.

Quickly eating his food, Samson followed her. It didn't surprise him to find her lying on the bed with her back towards him. Walking to her side of the bed, his shadow fell across her face, he said firmly, "When are you going to stop feeling sorry for yourself? I need you to help me on farm."

Elizabeth turned her head slightly, "What sort of help, it doesn't take much effort to feed chickens and collect eggs."

He remembered what her mother had said that morning. Samson stamped his foot on the floor too, causing Elizabeth to look back at him. He drew his eyebrows together and narrowed his eyes before shouting, "It's not just chickens, the sheep have been shorn, and their fleece is in sitting room waiting to be spun. And I need you to tend vegetable garden. Like your Ma said, she's got her own family to look after, and my Ma needs to look after Da, Grandda and my brothers."

Elizabeth glared at him. "When I'm feeling better, I'll help you."

He stomped towards the door. "Good, I'll tell Ma you'll be cooking supper tonight." With his hand on the handle, he shouted, "And I hope you're going to eat some of it. You can't go without eating, it's not good for you."

Samson picked up his teacup and quickly drained it before walking outside. He desperately wanted to slap her around the face and tell her to forget about the baby. Even though Henry was not his child, he was grieving too. But what he was going through was nothing compared to what she must be feeling. He would have to wait for her to get over his death.

He grabbed the bucket of pig food and walked to the sty, climbed the gate, and poured the contents into the trough. Reaching down to scratch Gutsy's back.

"What am I going to do about Elizabeth? Lately, I get the feeling she don't like being married to me anymore. I know her heart is broke over Henry's death, but sometimes babies die."

He stood up straight and leaned against the gate, watching Pinky's piglets as they pulled on her teats.

Blackie came near him for a scratch, he leaned down to oblige, "You know, I've loved Elizabeth for a long time, and I were so happy when we wed. Then she lost Henry, her lover's child. But she's acting like she's the only one who's ever lost a baby."

He shook his head and stopped scratching the pig, climbed the gate and went to check the sheep.

~

Elizabeth looked up briefly from cutting beans when the front door opened. She was surprised to see Jane walk in. Returning her attention to the beans, she asked, "What brings you here?"

Jane sat at the table; her forehead puckered, "Ma said you might need some help."

Elizabeth didn't look up when she replied, "Unless you can give me my son, alive and healthy, I don't think there is anything you can do to help."

Jane leaned forward, saying, "The Lord must have had a good reason to take him."

Elizabeth slammed the knife on the table. "I'm sick and tired of people telling me, *The Lord must've had a good reason for taking him.* Well, I'm sorry, I don't believe that."

Picking up the knife she resumed her task. "I wake up every morning and remember that Henry's dead, and that it's not just a bad dream I had. Some mornings, I find it hard just to get out of bed."

Jane asked, "How's Sam? Sometimes I've seen him in the churchyard, looking at Henry's little grave. I think he's suffering too."

Elizabeth shook her head. "He's acting like he's the one who gave birth to him." Pointing at her chest, "But it was me, he was my son."

"I don't think Sam feels that way, he's lost a son too."

She looked up from the beans, tears streaming down her cheek as she spoke softly, "You have no idea of what it was like to hold him." Taking a deep breath, she continued, "Knowing he was going to die," Wiping her face with her hand, "And there was nothing I could do to stop it."

Elizabeth picked up the bowl and poured the contents into the cauldron over the fire. "The worst thing is, I keep wondering if I did something wrong." She put the bowl on the cupboard, and leaned on it with one hand, rubbing her eyes with the other. "Was it my fault? Was I being punished for being with child before we married?"

"You can't think that, look at Mrs. Pengelly. Richard didn't die, and he was born a week after she married, and look at him now, he's a healthy young lad. And Mrs. Pengelly certainly isn't the only woman who was with child before she wed."

Jane put her arms around Elizabeth, speaking softly into her hair. "You did nothing wrong." She stepped back but kept her hands on her shoulders, giving a half smile, "Remember that."

Elizabeth nodded, sat at the table, and cried again.

~

Elizabeth ignored the church bells as they rang, continuing to turn the handle of the stone grinder in rhythmic circles. Out of the corner of her eye, she saw Samson rush down the stairs in his Sunday best.

"Will you hurry up and get ready, bells have rung."

"I'm not going to church," she replied without looking up, pouring more wheat into the grinder.

He shouted in response, "Why not? You haven't been since Henry died, it's about time you did."

Wiping her hands on her apron, more tears flowed as she replied, "How can I worship a God who would take the life of a baby before he had a chance to live a full life?" Sobbing, she ran upstairs.

~

The straw broom fell from Elizabeth's hands when she heard the knock on the door. The last person she expected to see standing on the threshold was Reverend Ellacott.

Leaving the door open, she picked up the broom and continued sweeping. "Samson's out in fields."

Reverend Ellacott walked inside, standing near the door after he closed it. "It's you I've come to see."

Her cap fell on the floor as she turned her head. "What do you want with me?" Squaring her shoulders as she rested her hands on the top of the broom handle.

"I was quite disturbed when Sam told me this morning that you don't intend to come to church again."

Elizabeth retrieved her cap from the floor and threw it on the table. "I don't believe there is a God," She replied as she resumed her sweeping. "That's why I'm not coming to church again."

Keeping her focus on her work, she opened the back door and swept the dirt, dust, and flour outside. Ignoring the reverend, Elizabeth put the broom under the stairs, picked up her mixing bowl and began adding ingredients for bread.

Taking a few steps towards her, Reverend Ellacott put a hand on his chest, "Elizabeth, I'm worried about you. You need to find your faith again."

Holding her flour-covered hand over the bowl, her eyes narrowed as she looked at the reverend, "I lost my faith when my baby died." She resumed mixing, stating, "I don't know if I will come back to church." She added water from a jug to the mix. "Now, if you don't mind Vicar, I've got a lot to do today."

Reverend Ellacott stepped to the door and lifted the sneck. "I'll pray for you, Elizabeth."

She sprinkled flour on the table and replied without looking up, "Don't bother wasting your prayers on me."

He turned back to her, "Please remember Elizabeth, hate only hurts the heart in which it lives."

The door closed as she tipped the contents of the bowl onto the table.

~

After the warmth of Stokebridge church, Samson was eager to be inside the cottage, and out of the autumn chill. He heard hurried footsteps behind him and turned. He was surprised when Matthew Engels approached him.

"May I speak to you for a moment? I won't keep you long."

Samson wasn't in the mood for talking, he wanted to get back to Elizabeth. He chose to obey him, soon he would be the next Lord Trevelen. He touched his cap and followed him to the corner of the churchyard.

Samson lowered his eyebrows, "What can I do for you, Master Engels?"

"It's more of what I can do for you."

"What do you mean?" Samson stood up and folded his arms, he tried not to laugh as Matthew shifted uncomfortably on his feet.

"I understand Elizabeth hasn't been well since…" He glanced around before whispering, "Our son died."

Samson shook his head, "No, his death has affected her badly."

Matthew took a deep breath through his nose, letting it out quickly before he continued. "In a way, I feel somewhat responsible for your current situation."

Samson looked at him, not sure what to say and remained silent.

Matthew continued, "I was wondering if you would like to work at the manor as a gardener. Please don't feel you need to answer right now, you can let me know next Sunday, and I'll talk to the estate manager."

Samson scratched the back of his head while he thought about this unusual offer. "Are you asking me because you need a gardener or for some other reason?"

Samson sensed Matthew was startled by his boldness but replied, "I just want to help you and Elizabeth."

"So, this job offer is charity from you?" Samson confirmed.

"No, I wouldn't insult you like that. We do need another gardener, but I thought I would ask you. If I can assist in some small way, then at least I'll feel I'm doing something to make your lives easier."

A smile tugged at Samson's lips. "Hmm. I'm not sure I could be away from Elizabeth and my farm all the time, as much as wages would help."

Matthew nodded and replied, "What about if you work from Easter for about four months? They always need extra help then. We could arrange it so some of your wages would cover your rent." He tilted his head slightly as he looked at Samson, "That's if you want the job."

Samson hoped he wasn't blushing when he thought of what he called Matthew when Elizabeth told him of her situation. Deep down, he was a respectable man.

He looked up when Matthew spoke, "I want you to know I do still love Elizabeth, and it saddens me greatly that I didn't stand up to my father and give her the help she needed." He shoved his hands into his pockets. "In a way, I envy you."

Samson's jaw dropped. "Me?"

He nodded. "You had the strength to do what I was unable. I wanted to marry Elizabeth when she told me she was with child, but my father…" Shaking his head, "Wouldn't allow it. But you, you had the courage to do the right thing by her." He lowered his head. "Me. I was a coward."

Samson decided to end their conversation to save Matthew any further embarrassment, "Thank you, Master Engels, I think I will accept your offer."

"Very well, I'll talk to the estate manager. Would you be happy to start next Easter?"

Glancing towards the cottage, Samson agreed, "I think it would be best."

"I understand," He nodded, "Good day to you, Mr. Keslake."

"Thank you, Master Engels." Touching the peak of his cap again before Matthew left.

Walking towards Rose Cottage, Samson knew he should have told Matthew he could manage without his charity, but he bit his tongue. The truth of the matter was that he had to swallow his pride. A steady job at the manor, which would cover the rent, would make a big difference.

~

Lying in bed, Elizabeth watched as Samson threw more wood on the fire, rubbed his hands together and faced the palms towards the flames. Turning away from him as he climbed into bed, he kissed her neck and began lifting her nightgown.

She quickly turned to him, pushing him away. "Samson, leave me alone; I'm not in mood tonight."

He propped his elbow on the pillow, put his head on his hand, and asked, "When will you be in mood? It's been over three months since Henry died, and you haven't let me touch you since then."

In the light of the fire, she didn't care about the sad expression on his face. "I'll let you know when I'm ready, it's just not tonight."

"How will you let me know? You don't talk to me, and I haven't seen you smile for a long time."

"What's there to smile about? My son died." She responded, turning away from him again.

~

Speaking to the pigs after he threw food to them, "Elizabeth is really trying my patience lately, she's not same as she were before we wed. She won't let me touch her in bed, and it doesn't matter what I say to her, it's the wrong thing. And I can't remember last time she laughed."

He reached down to give Blackie a scratch. "Elizabeth's lucky I don't believe in hitting women; I want her to love me, not fear me. But some men in the village think nothing of giving their wives a backhander. Quite often, I see a wife come into church pulling her bonnet down a bit to hide a black eye."

Shaking his head at the memory, "My Grandda always said to me; *A man should do nothing he's not proud of, regardless of whether he's rich or poor,* and I know I wouldn't be proud of hitting a woman."

Grabbing one of Gutsy's piglets, Samson held it between his legs, ignoring its squeals as he examined him.

"I'll be able to sell you and rest of litter in a couple of weeks at Bradford markets, I should get a good price."

The piglet stopped squealing and turned his head to look at him. He laughed. "Did you think you were going to live out your days just eating and rolling in the mud?" He released his grip, and the piglet ran off as soon as he was free.

"Maybe Elizabeth would like to come with me, it might cheer her up a bit."

He climbed over the gate, and out of the corner of his eye, he saw Elizabeth coming out of the chicken run with her basket, but he continued to the sheep field. He wasn't sure what to say to her now.

When Elizabeth put bowls of porridge on the table, Samson asked as she sat opposite him, "Would you like to come with me to Bradford markets tomorrow? I'm taking all the piglets, except two. And lambs, of course, maybe some of the young chickens."

"Why are you keeping two piglets?"

Samson replied, "I want to keep a male for meat, and I'm swapping a female with Fred Pengelly. Gutsy's getting old now, and she struggled with her last litter. So we need another sow."

She put her head on her hand and closed her eyes when she answered, "Do I have to go?"

Samson picked up his spoon and put some food in his mouth while he thought about what to say.

"I'd be grateful if you could help with animals, an extra person would be useful to stop them running into woods and like."

Elizabeth half opened her eyes and sat up again, "Couldn't you ask your brothers to help?"

"They're already coming, Da has some piglets and lambs to sell too. I thought you might like to come. Have you been to Bradford before?"

Elizabeth shook her head, responding, "No, I haven't."

Hopeful, Samson encouraged, "You might enjoy it. There's also the yearly hiring fair this month, so there'll be a lot more people selling all sorts of things, you might find something you'd like for yourself."

Elizabeth leaned her left elbow on the table, put her chin in her hand and rubbed her cheek. She looked down at her food, sat up and yawned before replying, "All right, if you want me to come with you, I will."

Samson looked at his wife, "I'm sure you'll enjoy day out."

~

The sun had not risen when Samson awoke. Preparing for the day ahead at Bradford Markets, he nudged Elizabeth, "Come on, love, we've got a big day today."

He heard her groan as she opened her eyes. Pulling his braces over his shoulders, he saw she had pulled the bedclothes over her head. Samson sat on the bed to pull on his boots. He gave Elizabeth another shake, "Come on, I want to have some breakfast and be on the road before sun's up proper."

His feet thudded loudly as he stood up, "I'm going to feed animals."

He was about to close the door when he heard Elizabeth groan again, "Oh, all right I suppose I'd better get up."

Returning to the kitchen, Samson turned to the fire, rubbing his hands together. When his hands were warmer, he sat at the table as Elizabeth put a pot of tea, and four boiled eggs on a plate in front of him.

He cracked the eggs while he spoke, "All animals been fed, I've put chickens we're taking to market in wooden crate, it's sitting on handcart, ready for when we leave."

She poured a cup each and stood on the other side of the table, "I'm not coming with you today."

He slammed the spoon on the table and said through gritted teeth, "Why not?"

Elizabeth took a small step backwards. "There's going to be lots of people at markets, and I'm not in mood to be jolly."

Samson stood up and glared at her, he knew his face was red when he shouted, "You don't have to be jolly; I need you to help me with livestock."

Elizabeth stumbled backwards, her hand clutched at the front of her dress, tears ran down her cheek as she sobbed, "I'm sorry, Samson, but I can't come with you today." He barely heard the last few words as she ran up the stairs.

Samson sat down again and put his head in his hands while he thought of what to do next. He could hear Elizabeth sobbing in the bedroom above him.

"It'd be useless trying to talk to her right now," He said to the empty kitchen, turning his attention to the eggs again.

He finished his breakfast and walked up the stairs. She was lying on the bed, facing away from him when he opened the door.

"All right, if you don't want to come with me, I'll go on my own. I just thought you might like a change from being here all day, that's all." He continued as he turned to leave, "I won't be back till late this afternoon."

Picking up the two boiled eggs off Elizabeth's plate, he wrapped them in a rag. Scooping up his pipe and tobacco, he put everything in his jacket pocket before walking outside. Lifting the handles of the handcart, he walked to Lilac Cottage.

His father frowned when he asked, "Where's Elizabeth?"

Lowering the handles of the hand cart, Samson shook his head, "In bed crying again, where else."

"Never mind, we should be able to manage getting the livestock to Bradford with the six of us."

Samson raised his eyebrows, "Six?"

His father smiled, "Aye, Grandda's coming with us, and Fred has some calves he wants to sell."

"That's grand, can Johnny and Billy help me get the piglets and lambs from our cottage, then we can be on our way."

~

The sky was beginning to lighten in the east when the four men, two boys, thirty-seven piglets, three calves and nine lambs reached the crossroads half a mile from Stokebridge. The noise from the animals made conversation impossible.

On their arrival at Bradford, the little group herded the livestock towards the village green with its stone market cross in the centre. The market had a unique atmosphere, filled with bustling stall holders and patrons, a diverse array of goods on display and the noise and commotion of livestock.

Samson pointed to an area near the edge of the green. "Let's stop animals over there, next to that group of calves."

The animals didn't need much encouragement as they were heading towards the water trough. Samson lowered the handles of the handcart and looked around; it had been a year since he was last in Bradford. There were several carts and wagons selling a variety of wares. Tin pots, tobacco, food items and ale, just to name a few. Over to one side, he saw a salesman selling quack medicine. He also noticed other farmers selling sacks of wheat, oats, and barley.

George turned to Samson, "There're other lambs and piglets for sale, but I think our stock looks better, those ones look a bit thin."

"You're right Da. Hopefully, our livestock should fetch a good price."

Six-year-old Billy, who had never been to Bradford before, was looking around in fascination. He tugged on his father's sleeve and pointed, "What are those men doing over there?"

George looked to where Billy was pointing at the men standing in front of the cream sandstone church in their best clothes. Some held shepherds' crooks or farming tools, while others had tufts of wool or wisps of straw pinned to their coats. There were also young teenage girls carrying milking stools or mops and brooms.

"That's the mop fair."

Billy turned his head slightly and looked at his father with narrowed eyebrows. "What's a mop fair?"

"Those people are looking for employment for the next year, what they carry, or wear shows what work they can do."

George pointed to a man dressed in fine clothes and wearing a top hat giving a coin to a man carrying a shepherd's crook, "See that gentleman, he's just given the other man a shilling."

Billy looked at his father, "Why did he give him a shilling?" His eyes opened wide as he smiled. "Do you think if I went over there, he'd give me a shilling?"

George laughed and ruffled Billy's hair, "No, he won't give you a shilling. He gave *that* man a shilling because he wants him to work on his farm for next year."

Johnny grabbed Billy by the hand, "Come and help me with pigs, they keep trying to run away."

Samson and George laughed as they watched the two boys rounding them up. A few farmers approached them and began looking at their piglets, calves, and lambs, feeling their legs and bodies before looking into their mouths, and then moving on to look at other livestock.

A short time later, the man they had seen give the shilling to the worker, walked around inspecting other sheep. Eventually, he came towards them. He began feeling the fleece of the lambs, looking into their mouths, and feeling their legs.

"Good morning gentlemen, I'm looking for some new sheep for my flock, what's your best price for these?"

Samson looked at his father as he replied, "We were hoping to get twelve shillings each for them, they're from fine stock."

"Yes, I can see that, but I don't think they're worth twelve shillings. I'd happily give you ten shillings each."

George looked at Samson and he shrugged, "I'm happy with that price if you are."

Samson turned to the gentleman, a firm handshake sealing the agreement. "You have a deal, sir."

"Excellent, I'll fetch my sons and we'll collect them shortly." He pulled the money from his pocket and placed it in Samson's hand before walking off.

~

The clouds in the western sky were tinged with pink as the men and boys arrived in Stokebridge, Samson pushing the handcart with the empty chicken cage on top, while George carried Billy piggyback style. The walk home was made easier by having no livestock to manage. They waved goodbye to Fred before continuing to Lilac Cottage where Samson bid farewell to his father, grandfather, and brothers.

Pushing the handcart to Rose Cottage, he paused for a moment when he saw the candle burning in the sitting room. In the growing darkness, he continued around the side of the cottage and placed the handcart near the vegetable garden before walking through the back door. The light of the glowing fire revealed to Samson that the kitchen was empty, and the door to the sitting room slightly ajar.

"Elizabeth, I'm back," Samson called out as he sauntered to the fire to warm his hands.

Elizabeth walked out of the sitting room a moment later, carrying a candlestick, smiling at Samson. Placing it on the table, she walked to the pot over the fire, scooping some stew onto a plate for him.

"Did you do well at the market?" she asked as she put the plate on the table, turning around for the bread. "Sit down and eat your supper and tell me about it."

Samson turned towards the door, 'I've got to feed pigs first."

"You don't have to worry, I've already fed them, and chickens and checked on sheep," Smiling at him again. "The animals are happy."

He slowly moved to the table, not quite believing what she had said, and sat down. He was hungry, the two boiled eggs he ate at the markets were a distant memory. Elizabeth made a fresh pot of tea, pouring two cups before sitting opposite him, watching as he ate. Samson picked up the bread, dipped it into the stew and took a big bite, hardly tasting it as he followed it with a big spoonful. He swallowed the last from his plate and broke off another piece of bread and dabbed it round to wipe up the last of the gravy.

Wrapping his hands around his cup, he shared, "We did very well with our livestock, ten shillings each for lambs, a local butcher bought ten pigs for fifteen shillings each, and we sold rest for twelve shillings each."

"What about the chickens?" Elizabeth asked while leaning forward on the table. The smile on her face brought back fond memories of her before they were married.

"Got a shilling each, and Uncle Fred got two pounds each for calves. All in all, it was a good day."

"I am pleased for you," Elizabeth said, patting his hand.

"Once we pay our rent to Lord Trevelen and our tithe to church, we should have over ten shillings left."

"That's wonderful." Elizabeth collected his empty plate and placed it on the cupboard.

"I thought so; I need some new boots." He looked at his feet and lifted his left foot up towards Elizabeth exposing the beginnings of another hole in the sole, "I've repaired these so many times, I don't think I can do it again."

She nodded and returned to the table, "You deserve a new pair, you work hard."

Samson cocked his head towards her, "What were you doing in sitting room?"

Elizabeth glanced at the door, "I was spinning some of the wool, I need to knit more stockings for us." She looked at the table before saying, "I'm sorry, Samson, I should have gone with you today to Bradford, you needed help with animals."

"We managed; Grandda and Uncle Fred came with us."

He picked up the teapot and poured another cup for them both. While they sat drinking their tea, Samson picked up his pipe and began filling the bowl with tobacco, wondering what had caused this sudden change in Elizabeth. They sat in silence while Samson smoked his pipe.

Pulling his braces off his shoulders, he stood up. "I think I'll turn in now, it's been a long day."

Elizabeth blew out the candle and followed him up the stairs. The glow from the fire lit the way. The warmth of the bedroom was welcoming as they entered. Elizabeth walked around to her side of the bed and began undressing. Samson was pulling on his nightshirt by the time she had removed her chemise and reached for her nightgown. He walked behind her, put his hands on her upper arms and gently kissed her bare shoulders.

"You're a beautiful woman Elizabeth," He whispered into her ear.

She turned to face him, and he began kissing her again, working his way from her shoulders, up her slender neck before passionately kissing her eagerly waiting mouth. It was the first time in months she had let him touch her.

Samson was deliberately slow with his lovemaking, wanting to prolong their first intimacy since the baby's death for as long as possible.

Afterwards, Samson looked at Elizabeth while she slept with her head on his shoulder. He wondered if this change in her would be short-lived or if she had finally stopped grieving the loss of Henry.

10

The air in the room seemed to thicken as Samson exhaled a stream of pipe smoke, breaking the evening silence. As he leaned back, looking out the window, he said, "I was thinking, with warmer days coming, maybe we could do something with Grandda's garden out front of cottage, get some flowers growing."

Elizabeth looked up from her knitting, her brows slightly furrowed. "Flowers?"

Samson nodded. "Aye, you know, like your Ma used to have. It might brighten place up."

Elizabeth twitched her mouth and nose, a hint of hesitation in her voice, "I used to help her with that… but not right now."

Leaning forward, studying her, Samson said, "Everything alright Elizabeth? You seem a bit sad."

Looking away, Elizabeth replied, "I don't know. Just not in the mood for flowers, I guess."

Samson paused, choosing his words carefully. "It's not just about flowers, is it?"

Silent for a moment, then with a sigh, Elizabeth responded, "It's about a lot of things, Samson."

He didn't mention the garden again.

~

Samson threw the last corn cob into the hand cart, lifted the handles, and pushed it towards the food store.

Just inside the doorway, he watched as one of the resident cats pounced on a mouse, then pranced away with its prize in his mouth. He hoped the cat would kill a lot more, he had seen too many mice during the summer.

The last remnants of twilight remained as he shut the door, his feet dragging on the ground as he returned to the cottage. Flopping on the bench at the table, he put his head on his arms, only sitting up when he heard Elizabeth put a plate in front of him.

"You look tired."

He rolled his eyes, "That's because I *am* tired. I've been harvesting corn since I came home from manor, thankfully, I've finished." Resting his head on his hand, he continued, "I'll be finished at manor soon, then I can put all my energy into this farm."

"Do you really need to work at manor?"

He slammed his spoon on the table. "Of course, I need to work there, it's the only way I can pay rent for cottage." She backed away from him as his body tensed with rage.

He shook his head as he ate the stew.

~

Autumn was approaching when Elizabeth put two plates of food on the table and sat opposite Samson. "I have something to tell you," she said.

"And what would that be."

"I'm with child."

Samson could hear no delight in her voice. He reached to hold her hand. "That's wonderful news."

She pulled her hand away and looked down.

"Aren't you happy about having another baby?" Samson queried.

She lifted her head and faced him; her eyes shining as they filled with tears. "I'm scared."

He raced to her side of the table, wrapping his arms around her. "Why?"

"What if this one dies like Henry did. I couldn't bear to go through that pain again."

"I know you've been unhappy since he died, but this one may live, we can only pray it does," Samson reassured her.

Elizabeth stared out of the window and said softly. "Henry would be walking around by now if he hadn't died."

"I know."

She stood up and ran up the stairs.

The crying through the floorboards reached Samson. He had the unhappy feeling she was not as pleased about the baby as he was. He hoped that once it arrived, maternal instinct would take over, and she would find joy and be happy again.

11

November 1837

The winter was showing signs of being very cold. Carrying the wood in her apron, Elizabeth threw some on the fire to warm up the room.

She busied herself cutting meat and vegetables for a stew, scraping the cut pieces into the cauldron. After grinding some wheat, she began making a batch of dough, sprinkling excess flour on the table.

The dough landed on the tin plate with a clatter when the door opened. Jane walked in with no shawl around her shoulders. It was cold outside, why was she not wearing one?

Elizabeth immediately wiped her hands on her apron, put her arms around her sister, holding her close. "What's the matter? Did Da hit you?"

Jane nodded and sobbed on her shoulder for a few minutes. A kick from the baby made Jane step back, her sobs turned to laughter. "My goodness, I've never felt that before, maybe he or she is trying to cheer me up."

Elizabeth grabbed her hand and placed it on her left side where she could feel the baby stirring.

Jane's eyes opened wide, and her frown turn to a smile as she stood stock still, feeling her niece or nephew move in her sister's belly.

"The baby's been moving for a while; I didn't get to feel it much with Henry."

Elizabeth lifted her apron to wipe away her tears. "Let's have a cup of tea and you can tell me why Da gave you that bruise and why you've been crying."

Jane nodded and walked to the fire, moving the kettle over the flames, while Elizabeth covered the dough with a cloth. Jane filled the teapot and they both sat at the table.

"Now," Elizabeth said as she poured the tea, "What's troubling you?"

Jane slumped her shoulders. "I've started to walk out with Luke Parsons, but Ma and Da don't like him and want me to forget about him."

"Is it because of his brother who was sent to Australia?"

"Yes, but it was ages ago, Luke was only three years old when Ben was arrested for stealing."

"I don't know why Ma and Da would object."

The tears ran down Jane's cheeks again. "I love Luke, we want to get married."

"Did you tell Ma and Da this?"

"Yes, I did, but we ended up having a row, Da slapped me and I stormed out. As I shut the door, I heard Da say that if I continue to see him, they want nothing to do with me." She put her head on her arms and sobbed.

~

Samson walked in the back door a moment later and saw the head of his wife's sister bowed over, his eyebrows drew together as he looked questionably at Elizabeth.

"Hello Jane, what's troubling ye?"

Her eyes were red and teary when she looked at Samson. He sat beside Elizabeth, she poured him a cup of tea and explained Jane's dilemma.

Jane sniffed and shook her head. "Ma said if I live under their roof, I'm not allowed to walk out with him. I know he's not like his brother, they should know that too."

Samson nodded. "Luke's a good lad and his father's always telling me what a good worker he is on the farm." He glanced at Elizabeth and then turned back to Jane. "Do you think your Ma and Da will change their minds?"

"I hope so, Luke asked me to marry him."

Elizabeth put her hand on Jane's. "Why don't you live with us."

Samson nodded in agreement and said, "Who knows, maybe your Ma and Da will agree to you and Luke getting married later."

A smile returned to Jane's lips, "You wouldn't mind?"

Samson looked at Elizabeth and both shook their heads.

Jane sat up straight and the corners of her mouth turned up slightly. "And I can help you with the baby when it comes."

Samson picked up his tea and drained the cup, enjoying the smile which had returned to Jane's face. "Well, now that's settled. Where's my dinner?"

~

Elizabeth and Jane remained at the table after Samson had returned to the animals. Elizabeth turned to her sister. "I'll talk to Ma, explain that you'll be staying with us for a while. They're probably just as upset as you are now."

Jane nodded. "I don't want to defy them, but I love Luke and I don't want to marry anyone else."

Elizabeth took the dinner dishes to the cupboard and glanced at Jane. Tears streaming down her cheeks again.

Rushing over to Jane, she knelt on the floor, putting her arms around her shoulders, she whispered. "Might be best if I go and see Ma now, will you be alright until I come back?"

Jane nodded and wiped her eyes with the back of her hand. Elizabeth stood up, removed her flour covered apron and picked up her shawl. She pulled her shawl tighter around her as the cold November air hit, causing her to quicken her step to Bluebell Cottage.

Opening the front door Elizabeth immediately enjoyed the warmth coming from the fire. Emma was sitting in the corner of the room working some raw wool on the spinning wheel. She turned at the sound of the door, her eyes opened wide with surprise at the sight of her eldest daughter.

"Lizzie, I wasn't expecting you, I thought it was Jane coming back."

She moved closer to the fire, facing her palms towards the flames before sitting at the table. "I thought I'd better come and see you."

Emma stopped the wheel and waited for Elizabeth to talk.

"Jane came to see me this morning, she's very upset."

Her mother stood up and sat opposite Elizabeth. Taking a deep breath and letting it out before speaking. "I wish she'd forget about that Luke Parsons, he's a bad influence."

"Why would you think that?"

Emma sat up straight and simply said. "Ben, his brother."

Elizabeth shook her head and looked at the floor for a moment before saying. "Luke's not the same as Ben, Bill Parsons can't praise him highly enough, besides, everyone in the village knows Ben only turned bad after his mother died."

Her mother sat still, not saying a word. Elizabeth continued. "Luke was very young at the time; he was raised by his older sister Mary. He doesn't even remember Ben; he was sent to London as soon as he was arrested."

Emma remained silent.

Elizabeth stood up. "Anyway, Jane's going to stay with us for a while. I'll come back tomorrow to collect her clothes; can you have them ready for me please?"

Her mother stood up also, Elizabeth noticed the tense jaw, vertical wrinkles appearing between her eyebrows, while her nostrils flared. "I don't think any good can come from Jane seeing him."

Elizabeth stared at her mother and said firmly. "You don't know that, Jane loves Luke."

Pulling Jane's shawl off the hook near the door, she put her hand on the door sneck and lowered her voice. "I'll see you tomorrow, hopefully you and Da will have had some time to think about what's best for Jane."

~

When Elizabeth returned to Rose Cottage, she found Jane washing the plates from dinner. Jane turned towards Elizabeth when she heard her at the door. "What did Ma say?"

Elizabeth shook her head as she sat at the table, giving her swollen belly a rub. "Just the same as before, she thinks Luke will turn out bad like his brother."

Jane sat opposite her and slumped her shoulders. "I wish they'd forget about Ben, Luke's not like that."

"I'm going back tomorrow to collect your clothes, hopefully Ma and Da will have had some time to think about it."

Jane sighed. "I hope so."

~

When Elizabeth returned to Bluebell Cottage the following day, her father stood up, his arms folded as he faced her.

"Mornin' Da." His furrowed forehead made her think twice about smiling.

"Mornin' *Elizabeth.*" His tone was as icy as the wind blowing outside.

She picked up the cloth bag of clothes and turned to her father. "Why aren't you happy for Jane? She loves Luke and they want to be married."

He squared his shoulders, glaring at her. "I don't think he's right man for 'er, he might turn to stealing like 'is brother."

She lowered her head, gave it a shake before looking him in the eye. "Well, he hasn't done it yet, and if he was going to, he would have done it long before now. Give him a chance."

His expression softened as he put his hands in his pockets and gave a half shrug. "All right Lizzie, I'll talk to your Ma, and we'll think about it."

Elizabeth gave him a kiss on the cheek. "That's all Jane wants. Bye Da."

~

It was a week before Christmas when the front door of Rose Cottage opened.

Elizabeth stopped sweeping and Jane stopped scrubbing the floor when Henry and Emma Saunders walked in.

They both looked at each other as their parents slowly walked towards them. Elizabeth saw the anguish in Jane's eyes and took matters into her own hands.

"Mornin' Ma, Da, would you like a cup of tea? There's plenty in the pot," she said, whilst putting the straw broom under the stairs before fetching cups.

Jane stood up when her mother stepped towards her, giving her a kiss. Elizabeth was pleased when her sister relaxed and returned the hug. "Sit down Ma."

While Elizabeth busied herself pouring tea, Emma and Henry made themselves comfortable at the table.

Her father sat up straight and looked Jane in the eye. "Janie, we spoke to Bill Parsons t'other day." He turned to look at Emma who was staring at the cup in front of her. "Bill explained about Ben being his wife's son from her first marriage."

Emma looked up. "We didn't know that, the family moved to Stokebridge when Luke was a baby, and then Emily died when he was only two."

Taking a big mouthful of tea, Henry slowly placed the cup on the table before continuing, "Bill told us Ben always were a heller, and when his Ma died, well, that's when he started stealing." He took another mouthful and continued. "He said we shouldn't take any notice of what Ben did, because Luke isn't like him."

Jane straightened her shoulders and sat back. "No, he's not. He's a kind and caring man and I'll be proud to be his wife. I hope you'll be happy for me. Also, he's starting work as a gardener at Trevelen Manor in the spring."

Emma looked up at Jane and lowered her head again. "We've behaved very badly."

Henry walked to stand beside Jane with his arms open. Standing up, tears cascaded down her cheeks as she fell into his embrace.

He pushed her back but still held her arms. "We're so sorry Janie, we shouldn't have judged Luke the way we did. Will you forgive us?"

Jane wiped her eyes with the back of her hand and sniffed, "Of course I will."

~

The howling wind was determined to follow Jane inside after she had used the privy.

Pushing hard to close the door, she said, "I hope that wind isn't going to blow all the way through February." She brushed wisps of hair from her face, before flicking the snowflakes off her shawl, watching as they melted when they landed on the flagstone floor.

The shawl fell on the floor when she saw Elizabeth standing by the table, holding her back. "Are you all right Sister?" Rushing to her side.

In between quick breaths, she said, "Can you fetch Mrs. Bosley?"

Picking up her shawl, "I'll get Sam to fetch 'er, then I'll take you upstairs."

Jane raced outside, the wind blowing snow and loose strands of hair around her face.

"Sam! Sam!" She called out as she ran towards the barn. "Sam!"

Samson ran out of the barn with an empty bucket in his hand. "What's the matter?"

"Can you get Mrs. Bosley; Elizabeth thinks baby's coming."

Pulling his jacket tighter around his chest, he threw the bucket on the ground, running as fast as he could around the side of the cottage. Jane returned inside to tend to Elizabeth, who was still standing by the table.

"Let's get you up to bed, Sam's gone to fetch Mrs. Bosley, she should be here soon."

Jane guided Elizabeth up the stairs, helping her into her nightgown, and into bed. She put more wood on the fire, and the room was warming up nicely by the time the midwife arrived.

"Do you need my help?" Jane asked as she placed more blankets on the cupboard.

Mrs. Bosley grinned, "I'm sure Elizabeth would like you to hold her hand."

Jane quickly climbed on the bed. Mrs. Bosley pulled the bed clothes back, and began moving her hands around the bulge in Elizabeth's belly.

"How long have you been having pains, dear?"

"I had some mild ones yesterday afternoon and last night, but this morning they're really bad." Elizabeth grabbed Jane's right hand as another pain gripped her.

The midwife covered Elizabeth again and patted her on the arm. "I think before the day is over, you'll be holding your baby."

Jane gently squeezed Elizabeth's hand and said excitedly, "I'm going to be an aunty."

Elizabeth looked at her and smiled, then squeezed her hand when another contraction gripped her. Elizabeth's low moans were the only sounds to be heard over the howling wind outside the window. The three women grateful for the warmth of the crackling fire.

~

Samson walked inside after tending the livestock, it did not surprise him that Jane was not in sight. It had been over four hours since he fetched the midwife. Walking up the stairs, he could hear loud groans of pain as he stood on the landing.

He knocked on the door and Jane answered a moment later.

"Has the baby arrived yet?"

Through the doorway, he could see the midwife wiping Elizabeth's forehead.

"Not yet, Mrs. Bosley said it shouldn't be much longer." Jane turned back to him, gasping as she put her hand over her open mouth. "I haven't got anything for your dinner."

She raced down the stairs in front of him, calling out, "I think there's some stew left in the pot."

Samson smiled to himself as he followed at a slower pace. Jane was stirring the pot over the fire when he sat at the table. Scooping some onto a dish, placing it in front of him, Jane said, "I haven't made any bread today, but there's a bit left from yesterday."

She picked up the plate from the cupboard and placed it beside him. "Would you like a cup of tea?"

Samson nodded while he ate some bread dipped in the stew. Jane refilled the teapot and poured a cup for Samson and herself, sitting opposite him. "I'll drink this and take one up for Mrs. Bosley and Elizabeth."

Samson watched as Jane flexed her hand. "Have you hurt yourself?"

Jane looked at her hand, laughed and picked up her cup. "No, Elizabeth was squeezing it whenever the pains come."

A loud groan was heard, they both looked up at the smoke darkened ceiling.

She stood up quickly. "I'm going back upstairs, sounds like it won't be long now." She lifted her skirts and raced up the stairs, two at a time. Samson shook his head and laughed as she left the kitchen.

~

Elizabeth glanced at Jane when she walked in.

Mrs. Bosley looked up. "Just in time, your nephew or niece is about to arrive."

Jane took up her previous position beside Elizabeth and held her hand.

Mrs. Bosley said, "Won't be long Elizabeth, a couple of good pushes and this baby will be born."

Jane put her arm around her sister's shoulders and gave an encouraging squeeze. Elizabeth nodded, took a deep breath and pushed.

"Here comes the head, it's got a lot of dark hair."

The midwife looked up at Elizabeth's face. "Next push and it'll be all over, dear."

Jane sat and watched in fascination as Elizabeth gave one last push and Mrs. Bosley was holding the baby.

"It's a little girl," She shouted over the baby's cries.

Jane reached to pick up a blanket from the end of the bed, giving it to the midwife. She cut the cord and placed the baby in her mother's arms. "She's a beautiful healthy baby."

Elizabeth's gaze lingered on the small, delicate features of the newborn nestled in her arms. A rush of conflicting emotions welled up within her, and she fought to suppress the memories of Henry that threatened to surface. She traced the outline of her daughter's fingers with her eyes, a gesture that invoked bittersweet recollections. The room seemed to close in on her as the weight of the past pressed against her chest. The baby's innocent coos, a stark reminder of what was lost, echoed in her ears.

Elizabeth's tears began to flow. Her voice shaking, all she could bring herself to say was, "But she's not Henry." She sighed and looked away from her newborn daughter.

The midwife sat on the edge of the bed. "You need to forget about Henry." Pulling the blanket away from the baby's face, "This little girl needs you to be a mother to her, and take care of her, the way you would've taken care of Henry if he'd lived."

Jane stood up. "I'll go and tell Sam, shall I?"

Mrs. Bosley smiled and turned her head towards her, "Yes, yes, tell him the good news. Also, can you bring up a bucket of warm water, we need to get this little one cleaned up before she sees her father."

~

Samson stood by the bottom of the stairs when he heard the bedroom door open. His eyes wide when he spoke. "Well? I heard the baby crying."

"You have a beautiful daughter Sam." Jane was about to walk to the fire, she was taken by surprise when he picked her up, spinning her around before she had taken two steps.

"A daughter, how wonderful." He released her and looked up the stairs. He had put his foot on the first step when Jane called out, "Oh no you don't Sam Keslake."

He froze, glancing to the top of the stairs and back to Jane. "I want to see my daughter."

Jane turned and gently pushed him to the table, smiling as she said, "You can sit down for a while; she needs to be washed first."

"All right, you'll call me when I can see her?" His smile just about reached his eyes.

"Of course, I will." Returning to the kettle, she began pouring water into a bucket, checking the temperature, and adding some cold water from another on the cupboard.

"Now, I've got to get this bucket to Mrs. Bosley. Will you stay here until I call you?"

The corners of Samson's mouth turned down a little when he nodded and watched Jane walk up the stairs again.

~

Standing near the fire, the baby cried as Jane gently held her over the bucket, while Mrs. Bosley washed her. She was letting everyone know she wasn't happy about it. When Mrs. Bosley had finished, she carefully placed the baby on the bed. She glanced at Elizabeth, seeing more tears on her cheeks.

Jane rushed to sit beside her sister. "Elizabeth, what's the matter? You should be happy to have such a beautiful baby."

"I wish it was Henry." She said, as she rolled to face the window, not looking at them.

Mrs. Bosley dried and dressed the baby in the knitted garments Jane had made and placed her in the cradle near the fire where she lay quietly.

Jane looked at the midwife. "Shall I fetch Sam now? So he can see his daughter?"

Mrs. Bosley glanced at Elizabeth, shrugged and shook her head, and turned back to Jane. "Yes, tell Sam he can come and see the baby."

As soon as Jane had left the room, Mrs. Bosley sat on the edge of the bed, putting a hand on her shoulder. "Elizabeth, please try and cheer up, you have a beautiful baby."

She turned her head a little, tears ran down her face as she looked at the midwife. "Why can't it be Henry who's lying in that cradle?"

"Henry is dead, and you must accept that." Pointing to the cradle, "That little girl needs you to love her the way you would have loved Henry."

Mrs. Bosley stood up when Samson entered the room with Jane. He slowly walked to the cradle, looked at his daughter and smiled.

He turned to Elizabeth. "I was wondering if we could name her 'Louisa', after my mother, or would you like to call her 'Victoria', after our new queen? Unless you have another name chosen."

Elizabeth sat up, leaned against the bedhead and looked at him before looking towards the baby. "I haven't really thought about a name, you can call her Louisa if you wish." Elizabeth turned to gaze out the window.

Mrs. Bosley could feel the tension between Elizabeth and Samson and raised her eyebrows at Jane. Seeing this gesture, Jane began shepherding Samson out of the room, laughing as she gently pushed him in the middle of his back.

"All right Sam, you've seen your daughter, now you have to leave."

~

Jane shut the door behind them, Samson knew she wanted to talk to him.

As they stood on the landing, she whispered, "Sam, Elizabeth doesn't seem to be happy about the baby, do you know why?"

Samson lowered his head, deep in his heart he knew Elizabeth wished the child was Matthew's, not his, but he would never reveal his thoughts to Jane.

He simply replied, "I wish I did."

Jane glanced at the closed door. "I wish I did too, new mothers are supposed to be happy when they have a healthy baby, aren't they?"

Samson moved to the top of the stairs. "I'm going to tell Ma and Da about the baby, do you want to tell your Ma and Da?"

Jane smiled as she nodded. "Yes, I'll tell them."

~

Jane and Samson walked out the door of Rose Cottage. Samson pulled his collar up around his ears, giving a brief wave to her as he turned towards Lilac Cottage.

She pulled her shawl tighter around her shoulders as she walked briskly to Bluebell Cottage.

Jane opened the door and found her mother sitting in a rocking chair knitting, while her father watched her brothers work on the loom.

Emma Saunders put her knitting aside and stood up to greet her younger daughter. "What brings you here Jane?"

Spreading her hands in front of the fire, she rubbed them together before turning around. Jane smiled as she spoke, "I thought you'd like to know that you have a granddaughter, and she's been named 'Louisa'."

Emma hugged Jane. "Well, that is good news." Turning to her husband. "Did you hear that Henry; we have a granddaughter?"

Henry Saunders stood up to give Jane a hug. "Of course, I heard it, I ain't deef you know."

Emma turned to Jane, "Tell your sister; we'll come and visit soon."

"I will." Jane put her hand on the door sneck, and her father asked, "How's Luke?"

Jane straightened herself. "Luke is well, and when we get married, his father's going to move in with his daughter Mary and her family in Penstowe, so we can take over his farm."

Henry shook his head. "We did you wrong, young Janie, and we're sorry."

Jane looked over to her mother and saw her smile and nod her head. "He's a good man, and we'll be proud to call him son when you get married."

"Thank you, Ma, now I'd better get back to Elizabeth."

~

When Jane walked into the bedroom, she noticed the sheets had been changed. Mrs. Bosley was sitting on Elizabeth's side of the bed watching as she fed Louisa.

The midwife smiled as she observed the baby. "It'll take a day or two for you to get used to feeding her, then you shouldn't have too much trouble."

The baby closed her eyes and let go of her mother's breast.

Jane sat on the other side, reaching to take her while Elizabeth tied the ribbon at the neck of her nightgown.

Jane gently put the baby on her shoulder to burp her; she turned to Elizabeth. "I've just told Ma and Da about Louisa, Ma said she'll come and see you soon."

Elizabeth nodded. "Thank you." She lowered herself down the bed. "Would you be able to take care of her for a while? I'm very tired and I'd like to sleep." She rolled onto her side facing the window, pulling the patchwork quilt around her shoulders.

Mrs. Bosley stood up, picking up the baby blankets lying on the end of the bed. "Yes, you get some rest, I'll check on you later." Tilting her head to Jane, inviting her to follow.

Jane nodded and turned toward her sister. "I'll bring Louisa back when she needs to be fed again." There was no reply from the bed as Mrs. Bosley waited by the open door. Closing it behind them, Jane began to cry when she saw the midwife's eyes glistening too.

Samson was still sitting at the table when Jane walked downstairs with Mrs. Bosley.

The midwife sat on the bench. "Elizabeth's resting, giving birth is very exhausting for a woman."

Jane sat opposite him and continued rubbing the baby's back. A moment later, she was rewarded with a loud burp.

Samson stood up. "I'll go and check on animals." He smiled as he peeked at Louisa asleep in Jane's arms.

"Sam," Mrs. Bosley called out as he put his arms into his coat. "Do you have a spare box we can put the baby in while she's downstairs?"

Samson picked up his cap, "I think I have a spare one in tool shed; I'll fetch it for you now," Quickly closing the door behind him.

More tears cascaded down Jane's cheeks as she looked at the midwife. "Why do you think Elizabeth's not interested in Louisa?" Glancing at her niece. "She's beautiful."

Mrs. Bosley shook her head and wiped her own cheeks with the back of her hand. "I wish I knew. I thought she'd gotten over Henry's death, but maybe not."

Samson returned with a small wooden box about two feet by eighteen inches. "Will this one do? I do have another, but it's a lot bigger."

The midwife stood up. "Yes, this one'll be fine." Taking the box from him, putting it on the table.

Jane looked at Samson. "I might ask Mrs. Pengelly if we can borrow her cradle for a while."

Samson nodded, closing the door behind him. Mrs. Bosley put one of the blankets on the bottom of the box, and took Louisa from Jane, and covered her with the others.

Placing the box near the fire, she turned to Jane. "She'll be fine in here for a while."

Jane's shoulders shook as she sobbed. "I can't understand why Elizabeth is so uncaring about her own daughter."

Mrs. Bosley sat beside her, putting her arms around her shoulders. "I'm sure she'll learn to love her soon, in the meantime, I know you'll help her to see what a beautiful baby she is."

Jane nodded and sniffed as she looked towards the sleeping baby by the fire.

12

Elizabeth walked inside after visiting the privy when she heard Jane cooing to Louisa. Glancing at Jane as she stood near the fire, there was no doubt that she enjoyed looking after her niece. A week had passed since her daughter's birth, yet the warmth she expected to blossom in her heart remained elusive. She wished she knew why it wasn't there, but she could only think of Henry, and the sorrow of his loss. She returned to the bedroom.

Elizabeth did not realise she had fallen asleep, until she felt Jane gently nudging her awake. "Louisa needs to be fed."

Elizabeth sighed and sat up, she opened her nightgown, and took the crying baby from her. She put her to her breast, and Jane smiled as she watched the baby sucking hungrily.

"She's very greedy." Jane said as she put more wood on the fire.

Elizabeth's gaze fixated on the snowflakes pirouetting outside the frosty window, a delicate dance that mirrored the turmoil within. "I'll be glad when I don't have to do this anymore."

Jane swiftly turned to Elizabeth, standing with the piece of wood in her hand. "How can you say that? Ma always said she enjoyed feeding us when we were babies."

Elizabeth looked at the baby in her arms. As Louisa fed, each gulp resonated with the painful echo of Henry's absence, a haunting reminder etched in the quiet moments of motherhood.

With a sympathetic glance, Jane released the wood into the hungry flames, the crackling fire a backdrop to the silence between them. "Would you like a cup of tea?"

Elizabeth nodded and closed her eyes, listening to Jane's boots on the stairs. She cried as she looked at the feeding baby, whispering, "Why couldn't you be Matthew's child and not Samson's? I don't see why we couldn't have married, we'd have been so happy, and maybe your brother might not have died."

More tears cascaded down her cheeks, leaving wet marks on her nightgown. The occasional tear fell on Louisa's face. Hearing her sister return, she quickly reached down for the corner of the sheet to wipe her face.

Jane walked in the room with a cup and a plate. "Thought you might like a cold pork sandwich."

"Thank you." Putting Louisa on the bed beside her, she tied the ribbon at the neck of her nightgown. Jane placed the cup and plate on the crude homemade table beside Elizabeth, reaching to take the baby. She walked towards the fire, holding Louisa upright against her shoulder, gently rubbing her back. Within a minute she was rewarded with a resounding belch. "I remember doing this with our brother Jimmy when he was a baby."

Elizabeth reached for the sandwich and tea. "Will you be able to take care of her for a while? I might rest after I've finished this."

~

Samson wasn't sure if he could hear a baby crying, but when he walked out the church door, he knew immediately it was Louisa.

Elizabeth turned to him as soon as he opened the door, she was pacing the floor with Louisa upright in her arms.

"Where's Jane?" Elizabeth shouted.

"She and Luke have gone to Penstowe with Mary's family." He shouted back. "What's the matter with the little maid?" Walking towards his wife, and looking into his daughter's face.

Jiggling the baby slightly, she yelled. "She's got a pain in her tummy. I was hoping Jane could take her and get her settled, I can't stand this crying anymore."

Samson yelled back. "You're her mother, how come you can't do it?"

Elizabeth shook her head. "I guess she's used to the way Jane does it."

Samson had never held a baby before, and it distressed him to see his three-month-old daughter crying so fiercely. He threw his cap on the table, before putting his hands out to his wife. "Let me take her, see if she'll settle for me."

Elizabeth relinquished the baby to him. Handling her like a fragile piece of china, he gently put her upright on his shoulder, the same way he had seen his sister-in-law hold her.

He sat on the bench seat, slowly rocking Louisa back and forth. Eventually, she let out a loud burp. Her crying stopped and she fell asleep with her head on his shoulder.

Samson placed Louisa in the cradle near the fire. Elizabeth looked at the baby as she slept. "Why wouldn't she do that for me?"

"I just rocked her the same way I'd seen Jane do it, that's all." He picked up his cap and began walking up the stairs, "I'm going to change and get back to planting."

~

Samson glanced at the sheep field as he walked past. The last ewe to lamb was licking her newborn while another lamb sucked eagerly at her udder, tail swishing wildly.

Samson stopped by the gate and watched as the newborn lamb struggled to its feet. He never got tired of watching the new lambs after they were born, a sign the winter was over.

Before long, the second lamb was on his feet and soon, it too was sucking. The ewe was licking his rump, looking content with her offspring. He wondered why he didn't see that same look of contentment on Elizabeth's face. Shaking his head, he walked away.

~

Samson watched Jane as she carried six-month-old Louisa around the farm showing her the chickens, sheep, and pigs. He leaned his hoe against the hedge and briskly walked to the cottage, giving Jane a brief wave.

He opened the back door with a bang, Elizabeth flinched and froze as she looked at him. An opened pea shell in her hand.

Samson's nostrils flared as he stood in front of her with his arms folded, his heart and breathing in time as he shouted, "Other than feeding Louisa, you don't do much for her, you're her mother, why are you letting

Jane tend to her when you should be. Don't you love our daughter?"

Elizabeth dropped the pea shell on the table, put her head into her hands and burst out crying. "To be truthful, I don't know."

Samson's fiery temper vanished immediately as he unfolded his arms, leaned on the table, and looked at his wife. "What do you mean, 'I don't know'?"

She stood up, ran around him and up the stairs. "Exactly what I said, I don't know."

Samson shook his head as the last fleeting glimpse of his wife disappeared up the stairs.

~

Elizabeth looked at her sister as she played with her daughter on the floor of the kitchen. She kneaded the dough and wondered why she didn't feel jealous when Louisa snuggled into Jane's shoulder.

She couldn't even get excited when Louisa began walking, whereas Jane and Samson were so proud of her achievements. Was there something wrong with her?

13

November 1841

The smell of lamb stew hit Samson as he held the door of Rose Cottage open for Jane and Louisa. Elizabeth stood stirring the pot over the fire, glancing briefly as they walked in. Samson sat on the bench, snorting as he removed Louisa's shawl.

"You kept that quiet Jane, why didn't you tell me?"

Elizabeth turned at the sound of their laughter. "Tell you what?"

Jane smiled as she replied, "Reverend Ellacott called our banns today for the first time."

Elizabeth's eyes opened wide. "You and Luke are getting married?"

Jane nodded. "At the beginning of December." Pulling Louisa onto her lap, she began nuzzling her neck, causing her to giggle. "I'll miss you after Luke and I marry, will you miss me too?"

Louisa wrapped her arms around Jane's neck. "Yes, Aunty Jane."

Elizabeth turned back to the pot and muttered, "Well, I hope you'll be happy."

The bitterness in her voice made Samson look towards Jane and shake his head.

After putting Louisa on the floor, Jane reached for her hand. "Well, we'd better get you changed, we don't want your best dress to get dirty."

Samson followed them up the stairs, he wasn't surprised when he saw Jane usher Louisa into her room, saying, "Can you start taking your dress off; I'll be in to help you dreckly."

Closing the door, Jane whispered to him, "Why is Elizabeth angry with me?"

He rubbed his forefinger under his nose and let out a long breath. "Because now, she'll have to look after Louisa."

Jane nodded. "I see."

~

The howling wind swirled up loose leaves in the church ground. The guests attending Jane and Luke's wedding were glad to be inside out of the freezing squall. Reverend Ellacott began reading the vows, and Samson couldn't help smiling when he glanced at Jane. She radiated joy as she looked at Luke. His heart felt heavy when he remembered Elizabeth didn't smile at him the same way at their wedding.

Luke and Jane were cheered as they ran the one hundred yards towards Daffodil Cottage, their new home together.

~

Samson stood outside Stokebridge church wall, his eyes fixed on the departing figures of Bill Parsons, Mary, her husband, Thomas and their children. As the warmth of their familial bond enveloped the air, Samson's chest tightened with a mix of yearning and envy.

Holding Louisa in his arms, he felt the weight of her innocent affection. Her arms tightened around his neck, a gesture that both comforted and accentuated the void within him. In that moment, Samson pledged an unspoken promise to always protect Louisa's happiness. He adored his beautiful daughter, he only wished Elizabeth would love her too.

Louisa was nearly four years old, and he knew she would miss Jane terribly now that she was married. It was up to him to make up for the lack of affection from her mother.

~

Only three days of the new year had passed. Elizabeth was scrubbing the floor when Samson and Louisa entered the front door after church. She continued to scrub while Samson hung up his coat and Louisa's shawl.

Elizabeth glanced up, leaned back on her heels, brush still in her hand and asked, "Who died?"

He glanced at the black band on his arm. "His Lordship."

Elizabeth dropped the brush and stood up quickly. "Lord Trevelen is dead?"

Samson pulled Louisa beside him as he sat on the bench and sighed. "A few days ago, he were feeling poorly and went to bed, died next day."

"So, Matthew is now Lord Trevelen?"

"Yes, he is. His father is being buried in cemetery behind manor at midday tomorrow. All tenants must be there."

Elizabeth resumed her scrubbing. "Well, I'm not going."

She stopped when Samson placed his feet where she was making her circles. Elizabeth looked up and seeing his narrowed eyes, leaned away from him, causing her mop cap to fall behind her.

Looking down with steely eyes he hollered. "You *will* go to His Lordship's funeral, even if I have to drag you there kicking and screaming. Is that clear?"

Out of the corner of her eye she saw Louisa shuffle uncomfortably on the bench, confused by her father's outburst.

Her eyes darted left and right, wondering if he might slap her. She timidly replied, "Yes Samson."

"Good." Turning towards the stairs he stood on the bottom step. "I'm going to change now. Get Louisa changed and get our dinner ready." His loud footsteps echoed around the kitchen.

Elizabeth gingerly stood up, and reached for her daughter's hand. "Come Louisa, you heard what your father said. Let's get you changed."

Louisa asked, "Why was Da shouting?"

"Never mind, let's get you out of your Sunday best."

~

The black dress nearly reached the floor. Louisa had no idea where it came from, but it scratched her neck. She wanted to pull at the collar, but her mother held her hand firm as she fastened the buttons on the cuff.

"Why are we going to the manor today? It's cold outside."

Stretching her back as she stood up, Elizabeth replied, "Lord Trevelen died; we have to go to his funeral."

"Do I know him?"

"Of course, you did, he was the big man who always sat in the front pew at church."

Louisa pulled at the neckline. "Why do I have to wear this dress? I don't like it, it itches."

As Elizabeth sat on the bed, the timber frame creaked. "Sometimes child, you can be so annoying ," Her mother sighed.

Louisa rushed to pull on her arm. "Mother, don't break my bed."

Elizabeth stood up. "I don't think it would have broken. Now, *will you sit down* so I can put your boots on."

Louisa put her hand into the pocket on the front, pulling out a withered rose. Holding it in front of her mother, she asked, "Where did this come from?"

The boots fell from Elizabeth's grasp as she slowly reached for the flower.

Gently taking it from her, Elizabeth sat on the bed, twirling it slowly between her finger and thumb.

"Aunty Jane wore that dress to our grandmother's funeral; I didn't know she'd left this in the pocket."

Louisa saw a tear fall down her cheek. "Mother, why are you crying?"

Elizabeth gave a brief smile and wiped her face with her hand. "I was just remembering my grandmother, she taught me how to make bread." Standing up, she shook her head, threw the flower into the fire, and picked up the boots again. "Now, please sit down so I can put these on you."

~

Stokebridge in January emerged as a land of frosty desolation, a canvas painted in hues of wintry grey. The air, crisp and biting, clung to the villagers' every breath, weaving tales of the season's unyielding grip.

As the villagers embarked on their solemn procession, the landscape bore witness to winter's artistry; a delicate quilt, draped itself beneath the sheltering boughs of trees and hedges.

Elizabeth walked behind Samson as he carried Louisa. She held onto her cap with one hand, while holding tightly to her shawl with the other. Her dress billowed about in the freezing wind, occasionally flicking up the hem to reveal her boots. The icy wind was forcing the men to pull their jackets tightly closed and put their hands in their pockets.

The villagers gathered on one side of the open grave, Lord Trevelen's family on the other, sitting on chairs by the coffin. They were a little group, aloof, dressed in black. The servants standing not far away in their overcoats and shawls.

Elizabeth had only recently heard about Matthew's marriage to Victoria Parnell from Truro. Even from a distance, Elizabeth could see she was an attractive woman.

Matthew scanned the crowd, he gazed at Elizabeth for a moment before continuing to look at the other villagers. Did he sense she was watching him?

Elizabeth turned to glance at the ducks as they walked on the ice of the small lake, not far from the cemetery. She returned her attention to Lord Trevelen's coffin when Louisa spoke.

"Da, why is there holly on top of that box?"

Out of the corner of her eye, Elizabeth saw Samson bend to their daughter, put his finger to his lips and whisper, "Shush, you have to be very quiet."

Eventually, Reverend Ellacott began reading his service.

"We are gathered here today to farewell the ninth Lord Trevelen…"

The reverend's words were a noise in the background as Elizabeth stared at Matthew and his wife. Victoria was beautifully dressed in black with a veil covering her face. Why wasn't she the one sitting next to Matthew? The only person to blame for that, was the man in the coffin. She was glad he was dead. It was his refusal to allow her marriage to Matthew, which led to the misery she now endured as Samson's wife.

When Reverend Ellacott finished, the servants returned to the manor while the villagers spoke to the new Lord Trevelen. Elizabeth stood with Louisa while they waited for Samson to express his sympathy to Matthew. Louisa let go of her hand as she raced towards Jane, holding her arms out to her.

Elizabeth reached them as Louisa wrapped her arms around Jane's neck. "Aunty Jane, Mother said I'm wearing your dress."

Jane leaned back and looked. "Yes, you are, do you like it?"

Louisa shook her head and creased her nose. "No, I don't, it itches."

Jane laughed. "I had the same problem, never mind, you can take it off when you get home." Lowering Louisa to the ground, they waited for Samson and Luke.

~

Samson was not surprised to see Jane sitting at the table with Elizabeth when he walked in the back door with Louisa. Jane was a frequent visitor to Rose Cottage. Samson sat at the table as Louisa raced to Jane, putting her arms around her neck when she bent down to her, kissing her on the cheek many times.

"Aunty Jane. I've missed you."

Jane sat up, pulling her niece onto her lap, nuzzling into her neck. "I've missed you too."

Louisa giggled, pulling her head into her shoulders. "Aunty Jane, we've got three baby sheep and ten baby pigs."

Jane smiled, "Well, we don't have any baby sheep or pigs, but we do have some baby chickens. Would you like to come and see them?"

Louisa turned to Samson. "May I, Da? pleeaase"

Samson took off his cap, scratched his head and winked at Jane. "Well, if you go to Aunty Jane's to look at baby chickens, who's going to help me in fields?"

Louisa pleaded, "Please Da, I won't be long, honest."

Samson smiled at his daughter; he could never deny her anything. "All right, you can go. But only after you've had dinner."

Louisa slid from Jane's lap, nearly knocking Samson backwards off the bench as she rushed to give him a hug.

"Thank you, Da," and sat beside him.

Jane sat up straight. "I'm glad you're here together, I've something to tell you."

Elizabeth looked at her. "And what's that?"

Jane couldn't keep the smile off her face when she replied, "Luke and I are going to have a baby."

Samson stood up, rushing to the other side of the table, giving Jane a hug. "That's wonderful news."

Louisa had followed Samson, hugging Jane around her waist. In a voice devoid of any happiness, Elizabeth put a hand on Jane's arm. "Congratulations. I expect Luke is pleased." She stood up, fetching plates for dinner.

"Yes, he is." She replied to Elizabeth's back. Drawing her eyebrows together, she looked questioningly at Samson. He shrugged.

~

The clatter of bowls hitting the table echoed through the kitchen as a whirlwind of nausea gripped Elizabeth, forcing her to flee through the back door. Bent over the privet bush, the heaving sobs intertwined with her retches, each convulsion revealing a profound internal struggle.

Samson, seated at the table, spooned porridge into his mouth, concern etched across his face, he uttered the words, "Are you alright, love?" But the question lingered in the air.

Sitting opposite him, pushing some stray strands of hair from her face. She said firmly, "If you must know, I'm suffering the same condition as my sister."

Louisa looked up. "What's a dition?"

Elizabeth ignored Louisa and Samson's eyes opened wide as his spoon rattled when it dropped in his bowl. He stared at her. "Well I must say, I'm very surprised." He looked to Louisa. "Have you nearly finished?"

She nodded and asked again, "What's a dition Da?"

"Not something for you to worry about now. Would you be a good girl and feed chickens, and collect eggs?"

Putting the last spoonful in her mouth, she turned around on the bench, jumped down and skipped to the back door, closing it behind her.

Samson turned to Elizabeth. "As I said, I'm surprised you're with child."

She glared at him. "Why?"

Samson scratched his head as he paced the floor. "*Why?* You ask me *why?* I'll tell you why. You hardly let me touch you in bed, and now you tell me you're expecting another baby." He sat opposite her again; eyes open wide. "Am I the father?"

Elizabeth slid him a guarded look. "Well, I certainly haven't taken up with any other man, so you must be the father."

"Well, you don't sound very pleased about it." Reaching over to touch her hand.

She pulled it away and stood up, leaning on the oak mantelpiece, she stared at him with steely eyes. "Because I didn't want another baby, that's why."

"But babies bring so much joy, look at Jane and Luke, they're so happy about the baby they're expecting."

Elizabeth was about to speak but put her hand to her mouth instead. Opening the door, she rushed again to the privet bush.

Sitting at the table again, she said, "I don't want another baby because I find it hard to love the child I already have."

"Is it because she's my daughter, and not Matthew's?"

Elizabeth hung her head; she couldn't even look him in the eye.

"It's not Louisa's fault she's not Matthew's child."

Elizabeth's red and puffy eyes stared at him when she raised her head. "I don't understand why your child lived and Matthew's died."

"Some babies die, it's a fact of life."

In between sobs, she said, "If Matthew and I were married," Taking a deep breath, she continued, "Henry may not have died."

"You don't know that. Besides, I don't think he'd have married you even if his father had given permission."

"But he asked me," she wailed.

Samson scraped the bench on the flagstone floor as he stood up and began pacing the floor again. "He probably only said that so he could have his way with you."

Elizabeth's whole body shook as she sobbed.

He rubbed his hand through his hair before continuing. "Matthew shouldn't have led you on that way, and being the next Lord Trevelen, he should have known better."

She sobbed. "B... but, h... he, s... said he he loved me."

Samson threw his hands in the air and turned to face her. "He only pretended to love you, and you were fooling yourself if you thought he did."

Before he could go on, Louisa opened the door and walked towards Elizabeth.

Smiling at Samson, she said, "I found three eggs Da." Pulling them from her apron pocket and placing them on the table.

"Thank you, Louisa." Elizabeth stood up, placing them in the basket on the cupboard.

Samson said, "Would you like to visit Aunty Jane?"

Louisa jumped up and down. "Yes please."

He reached for her hand, turning to Elizabeth. "I won't be long, we can talk about this when I get back."

Jane looked up from her sewing basket when Samson and Louisa walked in the front door of Daffodil Cottage, her eyebrows raised.

"Jane, I hate to ask, but would you mind if little maid stay with you for a while?"

She picked Louisa up. "Of course, she can stay here," as Louisa nuzzled into her neck. Jane turned to him, "Is everything alright?"

He rubbed his hand through his hair. "Not really, but Elizabeth and I need to talk, and I don't want to do that in front of her." He gave Jane a quick peck on the cheek and walked out.

Returning to Rose Cottage, Samson pulled a bucket of water from the well, throwing it over the unpleasant sight clinging to the leaves of the privet.

Taking a deep breath, he entered the back door. He sat opposite Elizabeth and reached for her hand, and was happy when she didn't pull it away.

He gently rubbed his fingers over the back of her hand. "When you told me you were expecting Matthew's child, I was jealous."

She looked up. "Why?"

"I'd loved you for as long as I could remember. And when I realised he'd taken advantage of you, well, I wanted to punch him. Also, now he's Lord of the manor, he'd probably deny ever knowing you, other than you were once a servant."

She put her head down, tears dripping off her cheek as he continued. "I would have waited until we were married."

Elizabeth looked up again, her face glistening from tears. Samson realised despite everything that had happened, he still cared for her. The real question was, did he still love her?

She sniffed a couple of times before saying. "I think I could have been happy with you if Henry hadn't died."

Samson pulled his hand away and shouted. "Well, you should be happy regardless, you have a beautiful daughter, and now you're expecting another baby, and who knows, this one may be a boy."

Elizabeth stood up, banged her hands on the table. The anger on her face was unmistakable as she leaned forward and shouted back. "I can't love your child because the child I really want is buried in Stokebridge churchyard. I don't love you and I only married you because Matthew couldn't."

Samson stood up and leaned towards her, his face only inches away from hers as he yelled, "I married you because you were in a desperate situation, the least you can do is to show that you are grateful occasionally." He thumped his hand on the table before pacing around the kitchen.

He faced her and yelled again, "You only go through the motions of being a dutiful wife. When will you get it through your head that Matthew has forgotten about you, especially now he's married." Lowering his voice, he continued, "Yes, Henry died, but that doesn't mean you have to be miserable all the time."

Elizabeth shook as she sat at the table, put her head on her arms and began crying again. He knew it would be useless trying to continue talking to her now.

Samson's temper subsided as he picked up his cap and coat. "I'm going to fetch Louisa; will you be alright till I get back?"

She nodded as he walked out towards Daffodil Cottage.

~

Walking in the front door, Samson saw Louisa kneeling on the bench watching in fascination as Jane stitched some fabric.

Louisa jumped down and rushed to him. "Da." Holding her arms out, he picked her up. "Aunty Jane's making some clothes for her baby, and I was watching her."

He took off his cap and smiled at his daughter. "I could see that; I hope you were a good girl for Aunty Jane."

Jane walked to Samson and fiddled with Louisa's curly light brown hair. "No need to worry Sam, she was very well behaved."

Samson put Louisa on the floor and ruffled her hair. "I'm glad to hear that."

Jane squatted in front of Louisa. "Why don't you go and feed the chickens and collect any eggs you find."

Louisa raced to the side door, not shutting it behind her. Jane stood watching as her niece ran towards the chicken run before closing it. She turned to Samson. "What's the matter Sam? I can see it all over your face."

Samson sat heavily on the bench with his back towards the table, it tipped up a little causing him to readjust his position. Once he was settled, he said, "Elizabeth's just told me she's with child again."

Jane sat beside him and smiled, "That's wonderful." Her smile disappeared as she continued, "Isn't it?"

Samson shook his head. "She told me she doesn't want another baby because she doesn't love the child she has." Jane sat silent when he stood up and began pacing the floor. "If she doesn't love Louisa, what'll happen to this baby?"

He stopped by the end of the table, and Jane stood up and put a reassuring hand on his shoulder. "Don't worry Sam, I'm sure once the baby arrives, she'll fall in love with him or her."

The side door opened, and Louisa walked in.

"Aunty Jane, I found two eggs." Proudly holding one in her hand and pulling the other from her apron pocket.

Kneeling down, Jane gave her a kiss on the cheek and took them from her. "Thank you, Louisa, Uncle Luke and I might have them for supper tonight." Standing up, she placed them in a bowl on the table.

Samson reached for Louisa's hand and looked down at her. "Well, we'd better get home, we've got a lot of work to do in fields today."

Louisa turned around, smiled, and waved. "Bye Aunty Jane."

As they were about to walk out the door, Jane said, "Sam, I'm sure everything will be fine."

He nodded and waved as they left, wondering if Jane was right about her sister.

Time will tell.

~

Samson was harvesting wheat in the field behind the pig sty, while Louisa collected the cut pieces, placing them in stooks. A movement caught his eye, and he saw his father walking beside the sheep field. Sensing something was wrong, he dropped the scythe and ran to him. Louisa following as fast as her little legs could carry her.

"Da, what's wrong?"

"Grandda died last night."

Samson froze mid stride. "Died?" He didn't even feel Louisa when she wrapped her arms around his leg.

"Aye, your Ma took him a cup of tea this morning, went to wake him up, he were dead. Even with it being so hot, your Ma said he were cold as snow."

Samson didn't remember walking to the bench seat by the sheep field. He sat with his head forward, running his fingers through his hair.

He looked up at his father. "How's Ma?"

George sat beside him, pulling Louisa onto his lap. "She's upset, but she'll be all right." Gently putting a hand on his shoulder, George said, "I'm sorry Sam, I know how much you cared for him. I've just come from seeing Vicar, funeral's tomorrow morning in church ground."

Louisa turned to George. "Do I have to wear the black dress again?"

Samson gave a sad half laugh as he pulled her onto his lap. "I'm afraid so."

George stood up. "I'll leave now," putting his hand on his son's shoulder. "I'll see you in the morning."

"Thanks Da." Standing up. "I'd better tell Elizabeth." Reaching for Louisa's hand, his heart heavy as they walked to the cottage.

~

Within the confines of Rose Cottage, the kitchen unfolded as a sanctuary of warmth and flickering light. The fire, a dancing maestro of amber and gold, enveloped the room in a cocoon of comfort. Samson savoured his porridge in the gentle glow of the fire.

The rhythmic crackling of the logs provided a soothing backdrop as the front door swung open, unleashing a gust of frigid air. Luke, propelled by the chill outside, burst into the room, momentarily disrupting the tranquil ambiance with the urgency of the winter wind.

"Jane had a baby girl during the night."

Samson was up and shaking his hand in a moment. "Congratulations Luke, that's wonderful." He turned to Louisa standing on the bench seat. "You have a cousin, Louisa." Turning back to Luke, he asked, "What are you going to call her?"

"Hannah, after my grandmother." He walked to the fire spreading his hands in front of it.

Louisa rushed to Luke, jumping up and down in front of him. "Can I see my cousin?"

Samson quickly picked her up. "Not today, but maybe in a few days' time."

He turned to Elizabeth sitting at the table. "We have a niece, Elizabeth." He narrowed his eyes and glared at her.

Reluctantly, she stood up, giving Luke a hug. "That's wonderful news Luke, how's Jane?"

"She's wonderful, I don't think I've seen her look so happy before."

"Will you please tell Jane I'll come and visit her soon, and bring Louisa so she can see her new cousin."

Louisa rushed to Elizabeth to hold her hand, but her mother turned away to pick up the bowls off the table. Rage raced through Samson as his wife left his daughter standing opened mouthed. What was wrong with this woman?

Luke shook his head at Samson. "I'd better go now; I've still got to tell Jane's parents the good news."

Louisa tugged on her father's sleeve. "Can I go with Unky Luke to see Gran and Grandpa?"

Luke picked her up. "If it's all right with your Da, then you can come with me." Glancing at Samson, he said, "I'll bring her back on my way home."

Samson nodded.

Lowering her to the floor, Luke said. "Go get your shawl, then we'll go to Gran and Grandpa's."

Pulling Louisa's shawl from the peg, Samson placed it around her shoulders. He lowered his voice when he shook Luke's hand again. "When you come back, we might open a bottle of cider to celebrate."

Luke laughed, "Might do that."

Samson closed the door behind them, turned to face Elizabeth and glared at her when he said firmly, "Couldn't you be a bit more excited for Luke, your sister's just had a baby girl."

"I can't get excited about babies right now," Elizabeth said as she turned to sit at the table.

"But you're going to have a baby soon yourself." He said, moving closer to his wife.

She stood up quickly and shouted. "I've told you before, I don't want this baby."

Tenderly putting his hand on her shoulder, Samson said, "You might find by the time it's born, you'll love it."

Elizabeth pulled her shoulder back to remove his hand, shouting as she ran up the stairs, "I doubt that very much." Elizabeth disappeared behind the slamming bedroom door.

~

Elizabeth opened her eyes, but the sunlight streaming through the curtains was too harsh for her heavy heart. She quickly shut them again and groaned, the promise she made to Louisa the night before replaying in her mind. Since Hannah was born, Louisa had been insistent on seeing her new cousin.

As Elizabeth dressed, she realised she was dreading going to see Jane and her new baby. The thought of seeing them brought no joy, only a hollow ache. She glanced at her growing belly with a mixture of resentment and weariness.

While stirring the porridge, Louisa rushed down the stairs in her nightgown and began jumping on the spot. "Mother, we're going to see Hannah today, aren't we?"

Elizabeth pulled the pot away from the fire, her voice firm. "Yes, we are, but you need to get dressed first." She guided Louisa back up the stairs.

When Louisa was dressed, they returned to the kitchen, Elizabeth placed a bowl on the table. "Now, sit down and eat your porridge," she instructed, her tone leaving no room for argument.

Louisa reluctantly sat and began eating. "Can we go after I finish?" She asked between mouthfuls.

Elizabeth sat opposite her, managing a weary smile. "We'll go once I've washed dishes and started bread." She placed a bowl on the table as Samson returned from feeding the animals.

Elizabeth placed a cloth over the dough, and pulled her shawl from the peg. She forced a half-smile. "Ready to go to Aunty Jane's?"

Louisa's excitement couldn't be contained as she raced to the front door, standing on her tip toes to open the sneck. Samson laughed, giving Elizabeth a light kiss on the cheek. "I think she's ready. Give my love to Jane."

The wind howled as they walked to Daffodil Cottage, Elizabeth pulling her shawl tighter around her shoulders and drawing Louisa closer. The journey felt longer than usual, each step echoing the turmoil in Elizabeth's heart.

Upon entering the cozy warmth of Jane's home, they found her sewing at the table. Jane's face lit up with a smile as she stood to greet them. Louisa rushed forward, wrapping her arms around her aunt's legs. "Aunty Jane, I've missed you! Can we see Hannah now?"

Jane giggled, her eyes twinkling with affection. "Not just yet, she's still asleep." She turned to Elizabeth, her smile softening. "Sit down, Elizabeth. Would you like a cup of tea?"

Elizabeth nodded gratefully and sat opposite her sister, relieved to be able to take the weight off her feet.

Jane turned to Louisa. "Would you like to help me make the tea?"

The little girl jumped down and rushed to the cupboard, picked up the teapot, and emptied the used leaves in the bucket by the back door, just as she had seen her aunt do many times.

Jane laughed as she watched her niece before turning to Elizabeth. "She's such a lovely girl, I hope Hannah grows up like her."

Elizabeth looked at Louisa, wondering why everyone found her daughter to be so endearing.

They had just finished their tea when Hannah began stirring in her basket. Jane was up in an instant with Louisa following, standing on her tip toes trying to peer into the basket.

"Is that Hannah?" she asked, her voice filled with wonder.

Jane picked up the baby and knelt so Louisa could see. "Yes, this is Hannah, and she's your cousin."

Louisa stared in fascination at the infant wrapped in a blanket. "But she's so little," she murmured.

Jane laughed. "All babies are little when they're born." She stood up, the baby in her arms. "Let's take Hannah to meet her aunty."

Elizabeth took the baby, her arms instinctively cradling the small form. She looked down at her niece, searching for a spark of maternal instinct, but found only emptiness. She wondered again if something was wrong with her.

"Been a while since I've held one this small." Reaching for the little hand.

"You don't forget." Jane said with a grin as Hannah went red in the face and emptied her bowels.

Jane bent to take the baby from her sister as she began to cry. "I think we better change your napkin before I feed you." Turning back towards her basket.

Louisa followed and watched as she changed the baby's napkin, her nose wrinkling. "Aunty Jane, that smells."

Jane laughed. "It's no different from when you were a baby."

Louisa's eyes widened as she looked at her mother. "Did I smell like that?"

Elizabeth gave a brief smile. "Yes, you did." Holding her back as she stood up, she extended a hand to Louisa. "Now, I think we'd better go home so Aunty Jane can care for Hannah."

Louisa hugged Jane tightly around her legs. "Bye, Aunty Jane."

Jane, holding Hannah in one arm, knelt to kiss Louisa on the cheek. "Bye, my darling. I'll see you in church on Sunday."

Louisa gave one last enthusiastic wave before they left, her steps light with the joy of the visit, while Elizabeth's were burdened with the weight of her silent struggles.

14

The bang made Samson look at Elizabeth as she cleaned dishes after supper, her hands braced on the cupboard. She needed help.

He stood up quickly and put his arm around her. "Is it the baby?"

Elizabeth looked at the floor and nodded.

"I'll fetch Mrs. Bosley."

Grabbing his coat and cap, Samson rushed out the front door. He shivered as the snow fell down the back of his neck, so he pulled his collar up around his ears. He quickly ran past the church, knocking on the door of Snowdrop Cottage, his breath escaping in white plumes when Abe Bosley ushered him inside.

Mrs. Bosley looked up from her knitting. "Is it Elizabeth?"

Samson nodded and replied. 'Sorry to disturb your Christmas, but she were bent over in pain when I left."

"I'll fetch my basket." She knitted the last two stitches of the row before rising from her chair near the fire.

Samson stood by the door, slowly regaining his breath.

Abe Bosley laughed. "It's all right, Sam, I've seen many expectant fathers arrive in a similar state. Most of the time, there's no need for the rush," giving him a gentle pat on the shoulder.

Mrs. Bosley returned downstairs with her shawl around her shoulders and basket over her arm. Pulling her cloak from the hook near the door, she turned to her husband. "I don't know when I'll be back Abe."

He kissed her and laughed before saying, "I know, babies arrive when they're ready and not before. I'll manage."

Abe shook Samson's hand firmly. "Hope it's a boy this time."

Samson smiled, "A boy would be nice, but if it's another little maid, I wouldn't mind."

He followed Mrs. Bosley as she walked briskly to Rose Cottage.

Elizabeth was leaning over the table, her hands flat on the surface, when they returned. Louisa stood on the bench seat with a hand on her mother's shoulder; her eyes moist as she jumped down, rushed to Samson, and held his hand with both of hers. "Da, Mother's hurting. Can you help her?"

Mrs. Bosley leaned over and looked into her big hazel eyes. "That's why I'm here, to help your Ma." Standing up again, she turned to Samson. "I'll take Elizabeth upstairs, then I'll get Louisa ready for bed."

Samson nodded as he sat on the bench, pulling Louisa beside him.

Mrs. Bosley touched Elizabeth's back, encouraging her to stand up straight. "Let's get you to bed, shall we."

Samson watched as they walked up the stairs.

"Is Mother poorly?"

He smiled at Louisa, "No, she's going to have a baby."

"Just like Aunty Jane?"

He nodded. "Just like Aunty Jane."

Samson remained at the table after Mrs. Bosley put Louisa to bed. He felt the teapot, finding it still warm, he poured the last bit into his cup. He sat smoking his pipe, wondering what the new baby would be. Would it be another girl or maybe a boy? He smiled at the thought of another girl; he was sure he would love her just as much. Louisa surprised him every day with how bright she was. He had taught her how to tickle trout like his grandfather had taught him, and he was amazed at how many times she succeeded in flicking the fish out of the water.

What would it be like to have a son of his own, someone to inherit the farm and carry on the family legacy? He'd find out soon enough; he'd better get some sleep. Shivering as he walked into the spare bedroom at the front of the house, he pulled the straw mattress and blankets off the bed, placing them on the floor of Louisa's room. She didn't stir as he threw more wood on the fire. Listening to the sound of the crackling fire, he soon fell asleep.

Samson did not wake up until he heard the cries of his newborn baby. Sitting up, he rubbed the sleep from his eyes and looked out the window. A faint glow appeared on the horizon.

~

The tell-tale squeak of Louisa's door reached Mrs. Bosley. Walking out of the bedroom with the baby wrapped in a blanket in her arms, it didn't surprise her to find Samson waiting on the landing outside.

"You have a son, Sam."

"That's wonderful," he replied, looking at the bundle she held.

The midwife cocked her head and wiped her eyes with her upper arm, and spoke softly. "Elizabeth didn't want to look at him, and she's refusing to feed him."

Samson's face turned red as he threw the door open. Mrs. Bosley flinched when it hit the wall with a bang, hitting his shoulder when it rebounded.

Mrs. Bosley couldn't see Samson or Elizabeth, but their words carried to the landing.

"Why won't you care for our son?" Samson shouted, "I thought you'd be happy to have a son to replace Henry."

"He won't replace Henry, and he never will."

"But he's your child, you should take care of him."

"I've told you before, I didn't want the baby."

Samson stormed out of the bedroom, slamming the door behind him.

Mrs. Bosley stood waiting on the landing. "What are you going to do, Sam?" she whispered.

He rubbed his hand through his hair. "I don't know." He answered as he walked down the stairs. She followed, still carrying the baby.

Mrs. Bosley sat at the table, a ghost of a smile on her face as she looked at the baby. "He's a beautiful boy, Sam; reminds me of Louisa when she was a baby."

Samson threw more wood on the fire and leaned on the mantelpiece. After a minute or two, he turned to Mrs. Bosley. "I'll take him to Jane; at least she won't let the poor little fellow starve."

Mrs. Bosley replied, "Well, he needs to be bathed before you take him to her." Gently placing the baby on the table, she put the kettle on the hook over the fire to boil.

Samson picked up an empty bucket. "I'll get more water from well." He opened the door and quickly closed it behind him.

Mrs. Bosley shivered as the icy gust blew in the door; she rushed to the baby to protect him from the freezing wind.

"What's to become of you then? You poor little thing. I can't believe your mother doesn't want you." The baby looked around unfocused, taking in his new surroundings.

Another icy gust followed Samson inside when he returned with the water.

The baby let out several protest cries when Mrs. Bosley began to bathe him, she cooed. "Now then, there's no need for that noise; you'll feel much better when I'm finished."

Mrs. Bosley dried the baby and wrapped him in more blankets. Samson put on his coat, and she placed the baby into his waiting arms.

~

After the warmth of the cottage, the cold air outside hit Samson like a smack in the face. He couldn't imagine how the baby felt being exposed to such cold, but at least it had stopped snowing. He tucked the baby up against his chest and wrapped his coat around him, walking as quickly as possible.

He opened the door of Daffodil Cottage and walked inside, leaning on the closed door.

Luke stood up when Samson entered. "What's the matter, Sam, why are you out on such a cold day?"

Glancing around the room, Samson saw Jane putting Hannah into her basket. He turned to Luke. "Elizabeth had a baby boy this mornin'."

"Congratulations," Luke said.

Jane beamed. "How wonderful." Walking to kiss Samson on the cheek. Before she reached him, the baby stirred and gave a small cry.

Samson opened his coat to reveal him tucked up against his chest.

Jane stopped and looked at the baby in Samson's arms, her mouth wide open. Walking the last two steps, she took him and asked. "Why have you brought him here, Sam?"

"Elizabeth doesn't want him."

Jane was appalled at Elizabeth's rejection of her son.

"Oh, the poor little thing, I'll feed him in the bedroom. Sit down and have a cup of tea, Sam, then we'll talk about what to do next." Jane walked up the stairs with the baby.

Samson sat with his head hung low as Luke placed two cups on the table.

He looked up at Luke and sighed heavily, his shoulders slumped, as he ran his hand through his dishevelled hair. "I don't know what to do with Elizabeth anymore."

Luke replied, "After seeing Jane with Hannah, I find it hard to believe that any mother would reject her baby. Jane would rather die than let Hannah out of her sight, but don't worry, Sam, we'll find a way."

The crackling fire filled the room with warmth, its dancing flames casting flickering shadows on the walls as they sipped their tea in comforting silence. Samson put his empty cup on the table as Jane walked down the stairs. He looked up; his forehead puckered. "How's the baby?"

"I've fed him and dressed him in some of Hannah's clothes; he's sleeping now his tummy's full." Jane replied as she sat on the bench. "Have you any idea why Elizabeth doesn't want him? At least she would feed Louisa when she was a baby."

Samson slumped his shoulders. "She's still heartbroken over Henry. I thought she'd be happy to have another son, but no, I don't know what to do."

"Don't worry about the baby, Sam, I'll look after him, Hannah won't mind sharing. Have you decided on a name yet?"

"No, I haven't," He said, shaking his head.

Jane twisted her mouth as she thought. "How about we call him Sammy?"

"That'll be fine, and I can't thank you enough for taking care of him."

Samson stood up, kissing Jane on the cheek before shaking hands with Luke.

"It'll be all right, Sam." Luke nodded and smiled at his wife. "He's in good hands."

"I know Luke, and I'll be forever grateful." Samson left the cottage feeling heavy-hearted, but at least his son was being cared for. Now, he had to deal with his wife.

Returning to Rose Cottage, Samson found Mrs. Bosley sitting at the table with Louisa; she was dressed with an empty porridge bowl in front of her.

"How's Elizabeth?" he asked, taking off his coat and hanging it on the hook behind the back door.

"Everything's fine as regards the birth, but I can't understand why she wouldn't want the little boy."

"I don't think she's gotten over Henry's death, even though that were over six year ago."

Mrs. Bosley nodded in agreement. "Did you take the baby to Jane?"

"Yes, she said she'd look after him. I didn't know what else to do. I were worried if I left him with Elizabeth, she might hurt him."

"I think that was wise." Mrs. Bosley replied, "Jane's baby is about a month old, so she'll still have plenty of milk. I'm sure she'll be able to manage."

"I hope so, I couldn't bear the thought of losing him."

"Don't worry, Jane will be a wonderful mother to your son." Mrs. Bosley reassured him.

Samson nodded, turned, and walked up the stairs to confront Elizabeth. She was facing away from him when he entered the room.

Walking to her side of the bed, he shouted. "God will punish you for rejecting our son."

"I don't believe there is a God, or He wouldn't have let Henry die." More tears fell down Elizabeth's cheek. "Why did He let this baby live?"

Samson pulled his hands into fists, then released them. He was desperately trying to control the overwhelming urge to slap his wife. Samson could feel his heartbeat and breathing quicken. When he spoke, he said the words slowly and angrily. "When will you get it through your head? Some babies live, and some babies die; Henry was just one of those that died."

"It isn't fair," Elizabeth said through tears. She turned to face him. "Where's the baby now?"

Samson took a deep breath and said as calmly as he could. "Do you care? You don't have to worry about him. Jane said she'll look after him, and he's been named Sammy." He stormed out of the bedroom, slamming the door behind him.

Returning downstairs, the midwife stood up and rubbed her eyes. "I'd better go home now, I'm exhausted." She pulled her shawl off the peg behind the door, wrapping it around her shoulders. Samson held her cloak open, and she stepped into it. "If you're worried about Elizabeth, please come and see me, dear."

"Thank you, Mrs. Bosley, I will." He walked to the front door with her and said goodbye.

15

The following day, Samson and Louisa walked to Daffodil Cottage and entered the front door. Samson carried the cradle used by Louisa. Luke was putting more wood on the fire under the cooking pot.

"Mornin' Sam." Standing to shake his hand. He picked up Louisa, tickling her tummy as he asked, "And how's my little girl today?"

She laughed. "Da bought the cradle for my brother."

Samson placed it on the floor. "Aye, I thought you might need this for Sammy."

"Thanks, Sam." Lowering Louisa to the floor. "He slept in the wood box last night, but he was nice and warm. Jane's upstairs feeding the babies now. Sit down, and I'll pour you a cup of tea."

Sitting on the bench, Samson pulled Louisa beside him, slumping his shoulders, his head fell forward.

Luke put the cups on the table, sitting opposite him. "You look like the weight of the world is on your shoulders, Sam."

He raised his head, weariness etched across his face. "Maybe I do," he muttered, running his fingers through his hair, as if trying to shake off the weight pressing down on him.

Luke nodded as he glanced at Louisa. "And how is Elizabeth this mornin'?"

"I don't know, I slept on a mattress on the floor of Louisa's room last night." Turning to ruffle her curly hair. "I haven't spoken to Elizabeth since Sammy were born yesterday mornin'. I don't know if I can muster strength to face her."

Jane called from behind him. "'Allo me ansum. Is there any tea left in that pot?" Leaning down to kiss Louisa on the cheek. "I thought I heard your voice."

Luke, catching a glimpse of Samson's weary expression, lifted the pot and replied, "Aye, there's enough for a cup."

Jane fetched a cup from the cupboard and sat beside Samson.

Samson asked, "How's Sammy?"

Jane smiled, "He's fine and such a beautiful baby. Don't know why Elizabeth wouldn't want to care for him." She spied the cradle on the floor. "Thank you for bringing that by. Luke was going to make another one; now he doesn't need to."

Samson stood up. "I'd better get back to animals. Come, Louisa."

Louisa stood up on the bench. "But Da, I want to see Sammy."

Samson's eyes softened as he noticed her bottom lip quivering. "He's probably sleeping, and I don't think Aunty Jane would like it if you woke him up."

Jane picked up Louisa. "We'll go upstairs, and you can see him." Smiling as she looked the little girl in the face. "Will you promise me you'll be very quiet?"

Louisa nodded as Jane left the men, taking her niece to see her brother.

Samson sat again and turned back to Luke. "You're a lucky man."

"Yes, I am." Picking up the cup to hide his smile. Replacing his cup on the table, he asked, "What did you tell Louisa about Jane looking after Sammy?"

Samson let out a sigh. "I told her that her mother were too poorly to care for him. Which isn't far from the truth."

The stairs creaked as Jane returned, Louisa in tow. A breath of warmth followed her, briefly dispelling the heavy atmosphere in the room. "Da, I just saw Sammy; he's got no hair."

Samson pulled her onto his lap. "Not all babies have hair when they're born."

She turned to Jane and back to her father. "Really?"

Jane sat beside Samson, and fiddled with Louisa light brown curls. "That's right, but don't worry; Sammy's hair will grow soon."

Samson rose, a mix of gratitude and admiration in his eyes as he pressed a tender kiss to Jane's cheek. It was a silent acknowledgement of the support he found in her during these trying times. He shook Luke's hand, "Time to get back to animals," Samson said, a hint of sadness in his voice. "I'll see you in church on Sunday."

16

Avoiding the villagers' pitying stares and pointing fingers, Samson led Louisa into the church. His internal conflict mirrored the external judgements.

He knew what they were saying, echoing the questions that haunted his own thoughts. *"How could he love a woman who would abandon her baby?"*

Samson sat beside Jane and Luke. They each held a baby. Looking at Sammy asleep in Jane's arms, he wondered why Elizabeth couldn't love him. His eyes then fixed on the stained-glass window portraying Jesus on the cross, Samson sought solace, silently thanking God for Jane's presence beside him, cradling his son. His parents and Elizabeth's parents were horrified by Sammy's rejection, refusing to cross the threshold of Rose Cottage, taking pleasure in seeing their grandchildren at church.

Barely a word was exchanged between them after Sammy was born. If Samson walked outside to tend the fields or animals, Elizabeth would call out, "Take the child with you; she gets under my feet."

Looking at his daughter as she walked beside him, he wondered why she would consider Louisa a nuisance. She became his constant companion, always eager to learn about crops or looking after the stock.

~

Samson fed the pigs and checked on the sheep; his work at the manor finished for another day. Louisa rushed to greet him when he walked into the cottage.

Noticing a red mark on her cheek when he picked her up, he asked. "How did you get that?"

"Mother slapped me."

Quickly putting Louisa on the floor, he marched to confront his wife. "Is this true?"

Elizabeth slammed her knitting on the table. "Yes, I did." Elizabeth's voice carried an edge. "I'd just finished grinding wheat into flour, and she knocked the bowl off table. I was angry with her, that's all," she said, avoiding his gaze.

"Good God, Elizabeth, she's only a child. There were no need to slap 'er."

Standing up, she glared at him. "You weren't the one who spent all morning grinding that wheat; I had to sweep it out the door." Resuming her seat on the bench, she picked up her knitting, speaking as she looked at the needles. "Such a waste; she deserved the slap."

Samson shook his head and squared his shoulders. "You're lucky I don't believe in hitting women because right now, I would love to slap *you*." He turned to the stairs. "Don't bother about any supper for me. I'm going to bed."

Reaching the top of the stairs, Samson opened the front room door, slamming it behind him. He sat on the bed, wishing his marriage was better. But Samson married Elizabeth for better or worse. Right now, he didn't think it could get any worse. The villagers ostracised Elizabeth, and Samson could feel their pitying stares whenever he walked through the village. He took solace in his children and Luke and Jane's friendship.

The highlight of Samson's week was being in church, with Sammy sitting on his knee during Sunday's service—marvelling at how he was growing in Jane's care. Samson stood proudly in church holding Sammy when he and Hannah were baptised. Elizabeth refused to attend church, not even for such a special occasion.

~

Samson and Louisa sat in the pew the Sunday before Christmas, waiting for Luke and Jane.

Before long, Louisa called out. "Here they come, Da."

Samson stood up as they walked in the door, each carrying a child.

Jane stopped ten feet away, lowering Sammy to the floor. He took tentative steps towards his father in his little leather shoes.

Samson's mouth opened, then turned into a smile. Louisa jumped up and down and clapped. "Da, Sammy's walking."

Samson squatted when Sammy was close enough and picked him up, tickling his tummy. "What a clever boy you are." He turned to Jane. "When did he start walking?"

Jane smiled, "Hannah started walking three days ago, and he started walking yesterday. I think he was doing the same as she was."

Samson reached over and tickled Hannah under the chin. "Well, you're both very clever."

Louisa tugged on Samson's sleeve. "Da, can I hold Sammy's hand?"

Putting Sammy on the floor. "Yes, you can, but don't walk away; he's only learning."

Samson continued to smile as he stared at his children holding hands. He turned to Jane and beamed; no words could express how proud he felt at that moment.

~

Walking in the front door of Rose Cottage, Samson removed his coat and Louisa's shawl, hanging them on the back of the door. Louisa jumped up and down in front of Elizabeth while making bread. "Mother, Sammy's walking."

Elizabeth wiped a wisp of hair from her face with the back of her hand, replying without looking at her daughter. "That's lovely." Continuing to knead the dough.

Samson glared at Elizabeth's back before turning to his daughter. "Louisa, go into the sitting room. We'll do some work on the loom this afternoon."

Samson walked behind Elizabeth and said in a low and firm voice. "Aren't you the least bit interested in your son?"

Not waiting for an answer, he quickly followed Louisa.

17

Easter 1845

Samson and Luke stood by the church wall, each holding a child while waiting for Jane to finish talking to Luke's sister, Mary. Louisa played with the village children.

Luke asked, "How's Elizabeth?"

Samson shook his head. "I wish I knew; apart from going out to tend vegetable garden or feed chickens, she never leaves cottage and hardly talks to us. So, I have no idea how she is; I get feeling she don't like being wed to me anymore."

"It must be hard for you."

"Aye, but I put up with it. It's Louisa I feel sorry for."

"Elizabeth hasn't been to see Jane since Hannah was born. Has she ever asked about Sammy?"

Samson shook his head. "She don't seem interested in him or Louisa. If she didn't come with me to fields, I'm sure she'd ignore her."

"Louisa and Sammy are lovely children; you must be very proud of them."

"Aye, I am. Elizabeth doesn't realise what a joy they are. I wonder if later she'll regret not loving them as we do."

Jane walked towards them, taking Hannah from Luke. "What have you two been discussing while I was with Mary?"

"Just the gardens at the manor," Luke replied.

Jane nodded. "Mary was telling me she's learning to be a midwife. She helped Mrs. Bosley to deliver Mrs. Pengelly's last baby."

Luke grinned at his wife. "Do you want to tell Sam our good news?"

Samson tilted his head slightly. "And what's that?"

Jane kissed her daughter's cheek and smiled. "Hannah's going to have a brother or sister."

Samson kissed Jane on the cheek and shook Luke's hand. "Oh, that's wonderful news. Louisa will be happy to hear she'll have another cousin."

~

Samson and Louisa shivered in the chilly October winds as they separated the lambs from their mothers.

They both stopped when they heard Luke call out. "Sam! Sam!"

Racing to the gate, they reached it just as Luke leaned on the other side. Plumes of frosty air escaped as he tried to catch his breath.

"Why the rush, Luke?"

Louisa put a gentle hand on his. "Unky Luke, are you poorly?"

Luke ran a finger down her cheek. "I'm fine; I only came to tell you the good news."

Samson stepped closer. "Has Jane had the baby?"

Luke grinned from ear to ear when he answered. "Twin boys, Sam, two boys."

Louisa tugged on Luke's jacket sleeve, looking up at him. "Just like our sheep?"

Samson picked her up and smiled. "Yes, just like our sheep. A woman usually has only one baby, but occasionally she'll have two. Just like our sheep."

Her eyes widened. "So, I have two more cousins?"

"Yes, you have two more cousins. Do you want to go and tell your mother?" Gently lifting her over the gate to put her on the ground, watching as she ran to the cottage.

Samson leaned on the gate and turned to Luke. "What are you going to call them?"

"William, after my father, and Henry, after Jane's Da."

"Billy and Harry." Saying the names, enjoying the sound of them. "It's a shame your Da died before they were born."

Luke nodded. "He was looking forward to seeing the new baby, well, babies as it turned out."

Both men looked up when Louisa called; she was running towards them, with Elizabeth walking behind.

"Louisa tells me Jane had two boys. She kept babbling on about sheep."

The little girl jumped up and down for a moment. "I told you, Mother, Aunty Jane had two boys, just like our sheep."

Luke turned to Elizabeth. "Yes, Jane had twin boys this morning."

She smiled at Luke, "Well, that is a surprise." Elizabeth kissed him on the cheek before returning to the cottage.

Samson turned to Luke, "That's the first time I've seen 'er smile for a long time." The men shook hands. "Thanks for letting us know."

Later that evening, Louisa asked, "Can I see my new cousins tomorrow?"

With a heavy sigh, Samson laid his knife and fork on the plate, a momentary pause in the rhythm of their meal as tension lingered in the air. "I think we should wait until after we've been to Bradford markets." Taking a sip of his tea, he continued, "You can wait a few days, can't you?"

Louisa's shoulders slumped. "I think so." Taking a bite of her bread.

Elizabeth washed the plates from their meal after she tucked Louisa into bed. Samson sat at the table, smoking his pipe, thinking about Jane, Luke, and their two sons. He decided to fetch Sammy and bring him home to live at Rose Cottage. He could not impose on his in-law's good nature any longer. Besides, Samson wanted to get to know the son he had only seen at church on Sundays.

18

Samson and Louisa walked into Daffodil Cottage the day after the markets. Luke and Jane's twins were a week old.

"Hello, Aunty Jane, Unky Luke." Louisa rushed to Jane, as she held Hannah while rocking one of the cradles.

Looking at the sleeping babies one by one, her eyes opened wide with bewilderment as she looked at her aunty. "They look the same."

Jane laughed and put Hannah on the floor, crouching to Louisa's level. "Yes, they do look the same, but that's because they're twins." Jane put an arm around her waist and kissed her on the cheek. Louisa raced to greet Luke and Sammy. Jane checked both babies were asleep before joining them at the table.

Louisa kissed Luke and Sammy, shuffling her bottom to sit on the bench. "We've come to take Sammy home."

Jane looked at Samson as he leaned on the sitting room door frame.

He stood up straight. "That's right, Jane, I think the time has come for me to take this little fellow off your hands; you have enough with Billy and Harry. Besides, it's high time Elizabeth took care of her children."

A single tear trickled down her cheek. "I knew this day would come," glancing at Sammy sitting on Luke's lap. "At least I've had practice juggling two babies." Giving a half laugh as she pulled Hannah beside her. "I didn't think I would have two at a time of my own, but Sammy was never any bother."

Samson looked at Jane and Luke as they sat by the table. The debt he owed them could never be repaid. "Jane, I'll never forget what you and

133

Luke have done for Sammy."

Luke's eyes glistened as he looked up at him. "We're going to miss him, Sam." Lifting Sammy's hands. "He's such a lovely boy, very outgoing, and he can be cheeky." Nuzzling under his neck, causing him to giggle, Luke continued, "He's such a delight to have around. I think Hannah will miss him too." He glanced at Hannah sitting beside Jane, thumb in her mouth, twirling her hair with the other hand.

Samson picked Sammy up off Luke's lap, giving Louisa a gentle tap on the shoulder. After shaking hands with Luke, he turned to Jane, leaning down and giving her a peck on the cheek.

Jane's eyes glistened as he stood Sammy on her lap. She wrapped her arms around him and kissed him on the cheek before playing with his blond curls for a moment. "Be a good boy now," handing him back to his father.

Samson turned to look at his in-laws once more. Louisa and Sammy waved as he shut the door. "Come on, son, it's time to go home to your mother."

Returning to Rose Cottage with the children, Samson turned to Louisa. "Why don't you take Sammy to see the sheep while I talk to your mother."

Reaching for her brother's hand, they turned to the field.

Samson watched them walk away before he entered the back door. Elizabeth was sitting at the table, knitting. Slamming the door behind him, she physically jumped. Raising her eyebrows, she stared at him. Samson folded his arms, vertical wrinkles appeared between his eyebrows, and his nostrils flared as he spoke to his wife.

"Elizabeth, you'd better get over Henry's death and start looking after the two children you have; you can't keep expecting other people to do it for you."

Elizabeth, seemingly oblivious, continued her knitting. Ignoring his entrance, she put the wool and needles on the table, stood up and walked to the fireplace. Leaning on the mantelpiece as she stood in an old, stained dress, staring out of the window. Samson wondered if she could see the children, her features rigid and unmoved.

Samson exhaled noisily through pursed lips and banged his fist on the table. "Elizabeth, don't you care about your children?"

Her eyes quickly darted in different directions, and she trembled as she stepped backwards, catching her heel on a raised stone; she fell heavily on her bottom.

Samson stepped forward, leaning towards her as she lay on the floor and shouted. "Elizabeth, I've never hit a woman before, but you are pushing me into doing something I swore I'd never do. You've spent all these years moping over Matthew and Henry. It's time you accepted your life with me and forget about His Lordship. He's forgotten about you."

He stood up straight, pointing his finger at her. "You are my wife and the mother of those two children." Moving his finger towards the window. "It's about time you started acting like it."

Samson stared at her open-mouthed as she lay immobilised by fear, hands protecting her face. His fiery temper faded as he slowly sat on the bench. Regret etched Samson's face as he uttered, "I'm sorry, Elizabeth; I shouldn't have yelled at you like that," his fiery temper now replaced by a sense of remorse.

Elizabeth gradually rose from the floor, sitting opposite him, fiddling with the knitting on the table. Her voice quivered with realisation. "You're right; I've been pining over Henry's death for too long," she admitted, tears streaming down her face, a poignant moment of self-awareness.

Samson put a hand on hers as he replied softly, "Yes, you have. Henry is dead, but you have two other children who need you to be a mother to them."

She turned a tear-streaked face towards him. "I'm sorry; I should have been looking after the children; they're my responsibility and no one else's."

He patted her hand. "Glad you've finally realised that." With a gentle reassurance, Samson stated, "I'll fetch the children, and you can finally meet your son. Our son."

19

Samson and Louisa watched the new spring lambs frolicking in the field when the first church bells rang. Entering the back door, Samson turned Louisa to the stairs. "Go and change for church, there's a good girl."

Elizabeth was washing plates from breakfast, but his son was far from sight.

"Where's Sammy?"

She rolled her eyes. "In there," tilting her head to indicate the sitting room.

"Is he ready for church?"

Elizabeth's hands slammed against the cupboard, her eyes narrowing in annoyance. "I tried to get him ready, but he kept running away."

Samson, feeling a mix of determination and frustration, threw his cap on the table. "For the love of God, Elizabeth, can't you do a simple thing like dressing your son?" Striding to the sitting room door, Samson called, "Sammy, come on, let's get you ready."

Sammy stood up, trying to pick up the cotton reels he had on the floor. His blonde hair fell around his face whenever he picked one up, only to have another fall to the floor. Samson chuckled at his attempts, gently taking them from his hand and placing them on the rocking chair's seat.

"You can play with those later; it's time to get ready for church." Gently leading him towards Elizabeth. "Can you get him dressed while *I* change?" Samson asked, his eyes boring into hers. Turning on his heels, he raced up the stairs, two at a time.

Sitting on the church wall, Samson watched Louisa and Sammy play with Hannah and the other village children. Luke sat beside him, holding five-month-old Harry.

"How's Elizabeth coping with Sammy?"

"I know it's sad, but I think she finds him a nuisance." Shaking his head. "But most of the time, he's with me and Louisa in fields."

Luke took a deep breath and let it out slowly, "I don't think she realises what a delightful child he is."

Samson smiled, "They both are, and Elizabeth is missing out on their childhood. They're growing up so quickly." Turning to tickle Harry under the chin, Samson continued, "I mean, look at them."

January 1847

Samson put his pipe in his mouth and turned to Elizabeth. "I'd like the children to go to school."

Elizabeth looked up from her knitting; needles stopped mid-stitch. "What on earth for?"

Pulling the pipe from his mouth, he looked heavenward. "So they can learn to read and write."

"We can't read or write, yet we manage."

"I never had chance to go to school, and it would be good if they could learn. Being able to read might help us on the farm."

Elizabeth returned her attention to her knitting. "I don't see how, but if you want them to go to school, let them go. It'll be less time I have to look after them."

Samson banged his hand on the table and stood up, his nostrils flaring. "You don't look after them as it is. They're either with me or at Jane's."

Pulling his braces off his shoulders, he turned towards the stairs. "I'll ask Reverend Ellacott tomorrow about enrolling them in school." He stomped to the front bedroom he now shared with Sammy.

~

Louisa was collecting the eggs, holding them in her apron held by the corners. As she left the run, she saw her father and uncle outside the

138

rectory, shaking hands with the Vicar.

She stood waiting by the chicken run until he was closer. "Da, is something wrong? I saw you and Uncle Luke with Reverend Ellacott."

Stepping sideways from his purposeful stride, Samson let out a short breath. "Sorry, I didn't see you standing there." Reaching up to scratch his ear. "We've just spoken to Vicar about you and Sammy and Hannah going to school in Roweshorne."

"Really?" an egg fell to the ground when she released the corner of her apron, about to hug him. She quickly caught the apron again, preventing more from falling. "When do we start?"

Samson picked up the fallen egg, tossing it in the air before putting it with the others. "Next Monday. Are you happy about going to school?"

She smiled at him.

~

Louisa enjoyed the mile walk to Roweshorne school every morning with her brother and cousin. She loved to stop at the stone bridge, looking downstream.

The hypnotic sound of the water bubbling over rocks held her attention until she could force herself away.

If the weather was fine on their way home, Sammy and Hannah would follow her as she walked along the riverbank. Sitting on a grassy knoll, she removed her boots and stockings before walking in the stream. Some days, she successfully flicked trout out of the water, sometimes not.

Most afternoons, they walked to Jane and Luke's home, where they enjoyed chasing each other through the orchard. Their laughter and squeals filled the air.

One rainy afternoon, Louisa sat opposite her aunt, watching as she mended some of the children's clothes.

"Aunty Jane?"

"Yes, Louisa."

"Will you teach me how to sew?"

Jane raised her eyebrows. "Have you asked your mother to show you?"

"No, but I've noticed your work is much neater than Mother's."

Jane cupped Louisa's chin and smiled, "You're only nine years old, but if you'd like to learn, then I'll be happy to teach you."

Louisa raced to the other side of the table, put her arms around Jane's neck, giving her a big hug. "Thank you, Aunty Jane."

"Well." Jane laughed. "Let's start by showing you how to sew on a button; your Uncle Luke keeps losing them off his shirts." Louisa watched as Jane knotted the cotton and stitched the new button.

~

Louisa sat at the table practising her sewing, keeping the stitches of the seam as straight as possible. Her mother stood at the other end, kneading dough for the next day's bread.

She looked up when Elizabeth said. "You're doing a very neat seam, Louisa. Did Aunty Jane show you how to do that?"

"Yes, I asked her to teach me to sew."

"Well, Jane always was better than I was, I can't sew clothes as well as she can."

Louisa smiled, "Aunty Jane has been teaching me after school."

Elizabeth put the dough on a plate to prove, wiped her hands on her apron, and sat next to her daughter, a hint of a smile on her face.

Elizabeth gently took the fabric from Louisa, examining the work. "You've done that very neatly," handing back the fabric. "I'm sure Aunty Jane will teach you all she knows, which is a lot more than I do." Standing up, she covered the dough with a cloth and walked out the back door.

Louisa watched as her mother walked away, returning her attention to her sewing.

21

March 1849

Banging his cap on his leg as he walked to the cottage, Samson stopped when he saw Louisa standing near the chicken run, making lines in the dirt with a stick.

Flicking his cap on his head, he moved closer and stood watching her. "What are you doing?"

She looked up. "I'm practising my writing."

She rubbed out the previously written letters using her foot, making more with the stick. Pointing to each letter and saying them individually. "L.O.U.I.S.A, that's how my name's spelt."

Samson crouched beside her, putting his arm around her shoulder; he looked at the letters in the dirt. "That's very good, how clever you are. I was never given the chance to learn to read and write, but it's something I'd always wished I could do."

"Would you like me to teach you Da?" Smiling as she looked into his face.

Samson hugged her before standing up. "I'd like that very much."

Using the stick, Louisa again drew under her name. "That's the letter A, it's the first letter of the alphabet, and it's also the last letter of my name." Pointing at them. "See how they're the same."

Samson looked at the dirt again. "Yes, I do see."

~

Elizabeth looked towards the chicken run, standing up from tending the vegetable garden. Her curiosity heightened as she watched Louisa scratching in the dirt, wondering what she was doing that Samson found so fascinating.

Holding the corners of her apron, she called to Sammy, standing on the rail of the pig pen. "Can you fetch me that bucket near you for these beans."

Sammy raced to her, and she poured the beans from her apron into the bucket. "Now, can you help me pick the rest of these beans instead of spending time with the pigs."

"But I like the pigs," he whispered; the corners of his mouth turned down.

~

Putting plates on the table for their supper, Elizabeth asked Samson. "What were you and Louisa doing near the chicken run?"

Samson smiled at his daughter. "She was teaching me about reading."

Louisa said, "Da said it was something he always wanted to do, so I'm teaching him."

Elizabeth sat beside Sammy. "Surely you have better things to do with your time."

~

Most afternoons, after Samson had returned from working at the manor, Louisa and her father would spend time practicing writing letters in the dirt. Louisa would occasionally bring home a book from school; and they would sit in the tool shed, away from Elizabeth's disapproving stares.

During the lessons, Louisa would explain about the words and sentences in the book. She found her father to be a keen student, always eager to learn more.

22

August 1850

Sitting at the table with Louisa and Sammy, Samson slumped his shoulders as they waited for dinner. His work at the manor had finished for the year now summer was nearly over. He could devote his time to his farm.

He sat up as Elizabeth placed pasties on their plates. Although her mood had improved recently, he could tell she was still unhappy with their life. Therefore, he was stunned when, after they had finished eating, she said, "I've been thinking about what you said to me a few years ago."

Samson looked at Elizabeth; a faint smile on her face brought back memories from before they were married. "And what was that?"

"You suggested we grow flowers in the front garden. I think it would be nice to have lots of blooms with different colours."

Samson pulled his pipe and tobacco from his shirt pocket. "That would be pretty; I'll see if Luke can get some flower bulbs and seeds from the manor garden."

"Thank you, I know my Ma has some nice daffodils and other flowers. Maybe Louisa and Sammy can help with the planting, weeding, and watering."

Louisa looked up from sewing an apron. "I'd like to help; I sometimes help Aunty Jane with her herb garden."

Elizabeth smiled at her daughter. "Maybe we'll have a flower garden all the people from the village will admire."

Samson looked down as he packed tobacco in his pipe, hiding his grin. It was the first time he had seen his wife smile at their daughter for a long time.

He drank the last of his tea and picked up his pipe. He wanted to get back to the barley. They had a good crop this year; he wanted to get it harvested before the rains came. Louisa and Sammy had worked hard during the summer, but an acre still needed to be cut.

He turned to the children. "Come, we'd best get back to fields."

Standing up, Samson was startled by a knock on the front door, his pipe clattering when it fell on the table. Wiping her hands on her apron, Elizabeth answered the door. They were surprised to see Reverend Ellacott standing with Mr. Trevorrow, the schoolteacher.

Marching to stand beside his wife, Samson asked. "What can we do for you, Vicar?" Glancing at the children as they stood by the back door. Was that guilt on their faces or confusion?

The schoolteacher removed his cap. "I was wondering if we could have a word with you, Mr. Keslake," Nodding to the children, "In private."

Samson nodded, inviting them inside with his hand, closing the door behind them. "Sammy, Louisa, get back to that barley, I'll be down to help you dreckly."

He turned to the teacher, "Why have you come today? Have they done something wrong?"

Reverend Ellacott smiled, "No, no, they've done nothing wrong. May we sit down?"

Samson pointed at the table, "Please."

Elizabeth picked up the dirty plates and began washing them in a bucket on the cupboard.

The two men sat while Samson pulled a straw from the broom, putting it towards the fire to catch the flame. He sat opposite the Vicar.

Reverend Ellacott spoke, "Mr. Trevorrow told me you don't intend to send Louisa to school when it starts next week."

Samson picked up his pipe and lit it, taking a couple of puffs, sending plumes of smoke above the table. "To be perfectly honest, Vicar, she were upset when I told her we wouldn't be able to afford for her to continue her schooling."

Mr. Trevorrow leaned forward. "I wish you would reconsider Mr. Keslake; she's an exceptionally bright girl. A pleasure to teach, always wanting to learn more, and she loves reading."

Samson smiled, "Aye, I know she's clever; she taught me to read and write."

Mr. Trevorrow's eyes opened wide. "Did she really?"

He nodded. "Aye, even taught me to do figures."

The teacher leaned back. "To be truthful, Mr. Keslake, that doesn't surprise me. She's always helping the children struggling with their reading; usually, after sitting with them for a little while, their reading has improved. It would be a shame not to continue her education."

Samson pulled the pipe from his mouth and put it on the table, watching as it wobbled momentarily. "We'll find the money for Sammy, but Louisa." He shrugged.

Mr. Trevorrow leaned forward again. "Mr. Keslake, if it's the cost, I'm sure there are ways." Glancing at the Vicar sitting beside him, who gave a slight nod.

"But she'll be able to go into service after she turns thirteen."

Mr. Trevorrow scratched the back of his head. "Mr. Keslake, that's still a while away. In the meantime, she can learn so much more."

Samson picked up his pipe again. "You haven't said anything about Sammy."

The teacher smiled, "Your son is a delightful, curious, and outgoing child. And he's very bright, like his sister."

"I would like for Louisa to keep on with her schooling, but as I said before, we can't afford it."

Reverend Ellacott spoke, "Mr. Keslake, I think the church can pay for Louisa to continue at school."

Elizabeth turned from washing the dishes and wiped her hands on her apron as Samson leaned forward. Speaking around the pipe between his teeth. "Are you saying we won't have to pay for her to attend school?"

Reverend Ellacott nodded. "That's exactly what I'm saying."

Samson leaned back and removed his pipe. "Well, we thank you. I know Louisa will be happy to continue her schooling."

Mr. Trevorrow stood up, reaching to shake Samson's hand. "Thank you, Mr. Keslake. I'll look forward to teaching your children a while longer."

Reverend Ellacott also shook his hand. "I'll see you on Sunday."

Samson walked with them and nodded. "Thank you, both of you." He lifted the sneck and opened the door.

Closing the door behind the Vicar and the schoolteacher, Samson turned to Elizabeth. "Well, what do you think of that? The church offering to pay for Louisa to go back to school. I know she'll be happy."

"Waste of time if you ask me. Louisa should be here, helping you on farm, 'specially when you're working at the manor." Elizabeth responded.

Samson hid a scowl at Elizabeth's resistance as he picked up his pipe. Pausing at the back door, he muttered. "Education is never a waste of time," The weight of responsibility evident in his eyes. He slammed the door behind him.

~

Samson stood up and let the ewe go after he had finished shearing her, jumping twice as she ran off to join the others. He stretched his back while Sammy gathered the fleece, putting it in the handcart.

"Well, Sammy, we don't have to do that for another year."

Sammy looked down as he made circles in the dirt with his boot. "Da, I want to go to Australia when I'm old enough."

Samson was about to pick up the shears and stopped halfway, eyes wide open as he looked at him. "Really?" Quickly standing up again. "Why do you want to go there? That's where they send convicts."

Sammy looked up to him. "We've been learning about Australia at school, and they don't send convicts anymore."

Samson picked up the shears and took a deep breath, unsure what to say. He opened the gate and pushed the handcart outside. He sat on the bench and patted beside him for Sammy to sit. "Don't you want to stay in Stokebridge?"

"I want to see more of the world, Da. Eddie Penrose was telling me about his uncle who went there last year. He's found gold!"

"You're only seven right now. Do you think you'll still want to go there when you get older?"

"I'd like to. Mr. Trevorrow said some farms are so big, it can take two days of horse riding to get from one side to the other. I'd like to own a farm like that one day."

Samson smiled at him, "You can have this one when I'm too old."

Sammy laughed. "Da, I can walk across this farm in a few minutes. I want a bigger one."

"Have you told your sister you want to go to Australia?"

Sammy blushed. "Not yet, because she'll try to talk me into staying."

"Are you going to tell her?"

He screwed up his face. "I'll tell Louisa when I decide I'm going. I know she'll miss me."

Samson grinned. "Of course, she will, so will I."

Sammy turned to his father, his mouth twitching. "Please don't say anything to Louisa."

Samson patted him on the knee and stood up. "All right, I won't mention it to her."

Sammy stood up and wrapped his arms around his waist. "Thanks, Da."

Samson ruffled his hair and lifted the handles of the handcart. "Now, let's get this wool inside."

23

March 1851

Standing with the other villagers near the stone font as Lord Trevelen's infant son was about to be baptised, Samson looked past Lord Trevelen to his younger brother Robert, standing behind the proud parents. Samson could not help comparing the two brothers. He realised now that Matthew was a kind and caring man, while Robert was a sadistic bully.

Samson had occasionally seen him in the manor garden, walking around and sneering at the gardeners. Robert was letting them know he was superior, and they were nothing but peasants. The scowl on Robert's face made Samson wonder if he was angry he would no longer be the next Lord Trevelen. Secretly, he was glad Matthew now had an heir. There was no denying Robert would be a cruel Lord to the tenants.

~

Louisa stood beside her aunty during the baptismal, whispering as she tapped her arm. "Aunty Jane, do you think I could make something as beautiful as that christening gown?"

Jane moved eighteen-month-old Fran to her other arm, leaned closer to Louisa, and whispered, "I'm sure you'd be able to."

Louisa watched Reverend Ellacott take the baby from his mother and hold him in his arms. Scooping water from the font with a large oyster shell, he gently dripped a few drops over his forehead, causing him to cry.

"I baptise you 'James' in the name of the Father, the Son, and the Holy Spirit."

Louisa knew Reverend Ellacott was saying a prayer, but it was impossible to hear over the baby's cries. Lady Trevelen wrapped James in a shawl, gently rocking him as they walked outside.

After several congratulations from the villagers, Lord Trevelen put his arm around his wife, guiding her to their waiting carriage. Their coachman, John Holman, flicked the reins, and the horses trotted towards the manor.

24

Easter 1851

Reverend Ellacott stood in his pulpit, taking a deep breath after his sermon.

"Before we finish today, I'd like everyone to join me in welcoming Doctor James Hill and his family to our congregation. They have recently moved to Roweshorne from Devon."

Outside, all the villagers wanted to greet the new doctor and his family. Samson waited patiently with Louisa and Sammy to welcome them, too.

~

Samson drew in a deep breath, savouring the tantalizing scent of onions and turnips that enveloped Rose Cottage. As they stepped inside, the warm kitchen welcomed them with its rustic charm. The aroma, a symphony of flavours, tickled their noses, and Samson couldn't help but crack a contented smile. "Hmm, that smells good." He added as he hung up their coats.

"I've got pasties for dinner; go and change; they should be ready by the time you come back down." Elizabeth poured hot water into the teapot.

All three ran up the stairs, returning quickly in their farm clothes and sitting at the table. Pasties were a rare treat. Elizabeth placed a plate with a pasty in front of Samson and half a pasty on a plate each for the children before sitting down with her own. Samson took a big bite; cubes of meat, potato, and turnips landed on the plate with the pastry crumbs.

Licking his finger to pick up the last crumbs, he drank a big mouthful of tea.

He glanced towards Elizabeth. "We've got a new doctor in the district. Doctor James Hill. He and his family have just moved to Roweshorne."

Elizabeth sat up straight, a flicker of interest lighting up her eyes. "Oh."

"Had his wife and son with him." Samson shared the news, sitting up straight as he placed his cup on the table.

Sammy laughed, a mischievous sparkle in his eyes. "His son talks like a girl."

Samson shot a mock stern look at Sammy, reaching to playfully clip him through his hair. "Show some respect, lad. You never know how different folk might be."

Sammy ducked, his father's hand missing him. "But he does; he's taller than Louisa, and he sounds like a girl."

Elizabeth looked at Samson. "How old would he be?"

Samson thought for a moment. "I'd say he'd be about thirteen or fourteen."

Elizabeth, curious, tilted her head. "Is that so? I'd like to meet them someday."

~

Samson was surprised a month later when Elizabeth joined them at church. Picking some flowers from their garden, she placed them on Henry's grave before walking inside, her hand on Samson's arm.

Reverend Ellicott climbed into his pulpit; his gaze focused on Elizabeth sitting beside him. "Welcome back to our congregation, Mrs. Keslake."

He saw her nod at him from the corner of his eye.

Reverend Ellacott coughed to silence the steady murmur from the pews. "I think I might begin our sermon today by talking about forgiveness."

Casting his eye at all those assembled. "We have all made mistakes in life, and I ask that you please remember what Jesus said in the bible, 'Let he who is without sin, cast the first stone'."

Samson noticed some women putting their heads down. He saw Elizabeth glancing around during the service, wondering who she was looking for.

She whispered in his ear as they were about to walk outside. "Will you introduce me to Doctor Hill's wife?"

He lowered his eyebrows but walked towards Dorothea Hill, talking to Reverend Ellacott.

Waiting for her to finish, he spoke, "Good mornin' Mrs. Hill, lovely to see you again. May I introduce my wife, Elizabeth." Facing Elizabeth again. "Elizabeth, this is Mrs. Hill."

"Very pleased to meet you, Mrs. Keslake."

Nodding to Samson as he walked away. "Your husband tells me you are the keeper of the beautiful garden over there." Pointing towards Rose Cottage. "Every Sunday as we walk to church, I admire the lovely flowers; they seem to be thriving this spring. How do you get them looking so beautiful?"

Elizabeth glanced at the sea of red, yellow, white, pink, blue and green. "Once a week, Sammy scrapes the ground of the chicken run and sprinkles it around the stems."

Dorothea's shoulders slumped. "My flower garden's not doing very well at all."

Tilting her head a little, Elizabeth asked, "Would you like Sammy to bring you a handcart load of scrapings from our chicken run? He could take it to your home before he goes to school. Then your gardener can put it on your flowers."

Dorothea smiled, "That would be most appreciated, although our gardener leaves tending the flowers to me. It gives me great pleasure, but I doubt I'll ever get my garden to look as lovely as yours."

Elizabeth smiled, "I have a lot of help from Louisa and Sammy." Briefly looking at her children and back again. "Does your son help you with the garden?"

Dorothea shook her head as she glanced at her son standing beside her husband. "Only under sufferance, Phillip would rather spend his spare time reading. He hopes to become a doctor himself one day."

Elizabeth saw Samson, Louisa, and Sammy walking towards them. "I think my family would like their dinner. I'll ask Sammy to bring some scrapings in the handcart to your home next week. Goodbye Mrs. Hill."

"Thank you, Mrs. Keslake. I'll look forward to seeing you next Sunday."

~

Samson turned to her as they were about to enter the cottage. "You seemed to enjoy your talk with the doctor's wife."

She looked at him. "Yes, we discussed our flower gardens. She asked if Sammy could take a handcart full of scrapings from the chicken run to her home."

Closing the door behind them, Samson tapped their son on the shoulder. "Sammy, will you be able to get that ready for doctor's wife?"

Sammy turned around to face his father. "I'll do it this afternoon and take it tomorrow on my way to school."

Samson ruffled Sammy's hair. "Doesn't hurt to be appreciated by the doctor's family."

25

The hot July sun beat down on Samson as he talked to Luke after church. The sneer on Robert Engels's face made him stop mid-sentence. Following his gaze, he was horrified to find him staring at his daughter. Louisa moved behind her mother as if she sensed she was being watched.

Samson excused himself to Luke and gently grabbed Sammy's shoulder while he chased Eddie Penrose. "Come, it's time to go home."

Sammy drew his eyebrows together in question but followed his father regardless as he walked to Elizabeth and Dorothea Hill.

"Please excuse me, Mrs. Hill, we must return to fields. Louisa, would you like to come with us?"

Twelve-year-old Louisa let out a deep breath. "Goodbye, Mrs. Hill."

Walking beside her father as they marched towards Rose Cottage, Sammy stayed close behind.

"I don't like that man, Da, he frightens me," Louisa said when Samson closed the door behind them.

"Which man?"

"That man who was watching me. Lord Trevelen's brother, he scares me."

Sammy said, "I don't like him at all, he's always got that funny smile."

"Don't tell your mother, but I don't like him either," Samson confessed.

~

A soft shuffle of stones reached Louisa's ears, drawing her attention. Looking towards the church wall, Phillip Hill stood with his head down, casually moving his foot from side to side.

She walked towards him. "Are you feeling poorly, Master Hill?" Louisa inquired, concern in her voice.

"No." He looked at her with his dark eyes. "I miss Sidmouth."

"Sidmouth?"

"It's where we lived before we moved here."

"What do you miss the most?"

A smile graced Phillip's face as he shared, "I used to enjoy strolling to the seashore and watching the fishing boats. And of course, I miss my friends."

"Did you have many friends?" she asked as she sat on the wall.

Phillip sat beside her. "Just one I really miss."

"What's his name?"

"Jonathon, we were at boarding school together."

"Do you write to him?"

"Yes, I do, but it's not the same as sitting next to him in class."

"How come you didn't stay at the school?"

"Father thought it'd be best if I had a tutor when we moved to Roweshorne."

Louisa put her hand on the wall and leaned closer. "I can be your friend if you wish. I don't have a tutor, but I attend school in Roweshorne."

Phillip's eyes twinkled as he smiled. "I'd like that very much. Maybe we could talk for a while after you finish school."

"I walk home with my brother and cousin, but we could wave to you as we walk past."

"That would be nice, and we can always talk when we meet at church."

Louisa heard Samson calling and stood up. "I have to go, but I'll look for you on our way home tomorrow."

He smiled at her, "I'll look forward to that. Good day to you, Miss Keslake."

~

After school, Louisa, Sammy, and Hannah walked down the main street of Roweshorne. Phillip stood outside the largest cottage in the village.

Louisa called out as they ran towards him. "Master Hill, we thought you'd be inside, looking out the window."

"I was going to, but I heard the school bell, so I told my tutor I was going outside to see you before you left the village."

Louisa turned to the children standing behind her. "You remember my brother Sammy and my cousin, Miss Parsons, don't you?"

Phillip bowed slightly. "Please to meet you, Miss Parsons. Master Keslake."

Louisa heard a slight snicker from Sammy. He immediately stopped when she turned to him with her brows drawn together, and her mouth set in a hard line.

Turning to Phillip again, "We can't stay too long; we must help Da in the fields. Will we see you tomorrow?"

He nodded. "I'll be in my room." Pointing to the only window on the third floor. "I'll wave to you." Bowing slightly to them. "Miss Keslake, Master Keslake, Miss Parsons."

They waved goodbye while making their way to Stokebridge.

~

Phillip's eyes sparkled as Louisa settled beside him on the church boundary wall. "You seem happy today, Master Hill."

Phillip sat up straight and reached for her hand. "I wish you'd call me Phillip."

"If you like, why are you so happy…Phillip?"

"I received a letter from my friend Jonathon recently. He's coming to stay with us for the summer holidays."

"How lovely for you, when is he arriving?"

"The middle of next week, he's staying for a month."

A warm smile graced Louisa's lips. "I'll look forward to meeting him next Sunday."

Phillip nodded. "Yes, I'd like him to meet my only friend here."

~

The following Sunday, as Louisa sat in church, she gave a smile and a brief wave to Phillip and the boy beside him. She presumed it was Jonathon when she saw Phillip whisper to him, and then wave at her.

Later, Phillip and Louisa sat on the wall while Jonathon leaned on a moss-covered headstone.

Louisa turned to Jonathon. "How do you like Cornwall Master Northy?"

"I haven't seen much yet, but Phillip and I hope to go riding to Penstowe tomorrow."

"I hope you have an enjoyable day out. Maybe one day I can show you how to tickle trout."

Phillip stood up quickly and turned to Louisa, raising his eyebrows. "You can tickle trout?"

She nodded. "My Da taught me when I was very young."

Jonathon stood up in front of Louisa. "Where do you do that?"

"Sometimes I catch them in the stream at the back of our farm, but most of the time, it's on the road to Roweshorne, just below the bridge. I often look for trout on our way home from school."

Phillip turned to Jonathon. "Would you like to do that tomorrow instead of going for a ride?"

"Oh yes, I enjoy fishing with a pole, but I've never seen anyone tickle trout."

Louisa stood up. "I'll ask Da if we can go to the stream tomorrow."

Samson turned to her as she approached him. "Finished talking to Master Hill already, or don't you like his friend?"

A smile curved her lips as she spoke to her father, "Master Northy is quite nice." Glancing at the two boys by the church wall. "I'd like to take them to the stream tomorrow and show them how to tickle trout, if you don't need me to work on the farm."

Elizabeth turned and answered before he had a chance. "I'm sure the animals will be all right for the morning." Smiling at her husband. "Of course, Sammy must go with you."

Samson looked briefly at Elizabeth and back again. "I'll be leaving early to work at the manor, so you need to feed the animals before you go. You children enjoy yourselves fishing."

Louisa looked up, saw a smirk on her mother's face, and narrowed her eyebrows for a fraction of a second. "Thank you, Da."

She returned to Phillip and Jonathon a few minutes later. "Da says I can take you to the stream tomorrow, but my brother has to come too."

Phillip glanced at Jonathan. "That's wonderful. Shall we meet you there after breakfast?"

Louisa nodded. "Sammy and I will meet you then."

Phillip looked up and saw Samson and Elizabeth walking towards them. "I think your father is looking for you."

Louisa turned around. "Goodbye, Master Hill, Master Northy."

~

Beads of sweat trickled down Louisa's back as she walked towards the stone bridge with Sammy. Up ahead, Phillip and Jonathon were leaning over the wall, looking at the water. They stood up and waved when they saw the children approach them.

Phillip smiled, "Morning Miss Keslake, Master Keslake."

Louisa heard a slight giggle from Sammy and gently elbowed him in the ribs, whispering under her breath. "Stop that, he's my friend."

Jonathon had a fishing creel over his shoulder and a fishing pole held upright as they waited. "Where do you tickle trout Miss Keslake?"

Louisa pointed to the right of the bridge. "I usually go downstream, where the water runs over those rocks, just in front of the oak tree. The water's warm and not very deep; the fish like to swim there."

Sammy took the lead and began walking along the riverbank, occasionally stepping over tree roots and holding bushes aside so Louisa and the two boys could pass until they reached an open area covered in grass.

"This is where Louisa usually catches fish." Sammy said, pointing to the water bubbling over a collection of large and small rocks.

Jonathon put his fishing pole down, removed the creel from his shoulder and looked at Sammy. "Can you tickle trout too?"

"I've tried, but I never seem to catch any, unlike Louisa." Louisa turned to hide her blushing cheeks.

Walking towards the rocks, she held onto a small sapling, leaning over as far as possible.

"There are a couple of trout on the other side of those rocks." She said, pointing at the still water near the other bank.

Phillip asked, "Do you think you'll be able to catch those, Miss Keslake?"

"I'll try." Louisa sat on the bank and took off her boots and stockings, leaving them on the grassy knoll before taking cautious steps towards the water.

Phillip picked up the creel, put the strap over his shoulder and carefully followed her as she crossed the stream using the stepping stones. Walking along the other bank to where she had seen the fish, he placed the creel on the ground, stood still and waited. Gathering her skirts in her hand, she slowly stepped in the shin deep water, making as little splash as possible.

Sammy and Jonathan stood near the grassy knoll, watching as she stopped and reached with her free hand into the water. Louisa concentrated as she slowly put a hand under the fish, water splashed as she flicked it out of the water towards Phillip, standing on the bank. Picking up the flapping fish, he squealed in delight, holding it behind the gills.

"Well done, Miss Keslake."

Louisa called out. "Watch out Master Hill, they can slip out of your hand if you're not careful."

The fish gave another big flick, freeing itself from his grasp, flipping its way towards the water. Phillip fell to his knees, put both hands on the fish, quickly picking it up. Lifting the lid of the creel, he dropped it inside. Leaning back on his heels, he smiled at Jonathon and Sammy.

Louisa remained in the water, watching as Sammy and Jonathon crossed the stepping stones towards Phillip. He eagerly opened the lid of the creel so they could get a closer look at the trout.

Louisa took slow steps in the water, as Sammy called out. "Are there any more?"

She stopped briefly and looked upstream. "There's another just up here, I'll see if I can catch it too."

The three boys slowly followed her along the bank, watching her every move until she reached down again with her free hand. Within seconds, another fish was on the bank; Jonathon reached it first, quickly picking it up, and dropping it into the creel.

Sammy walked towards Phillip, and the three boys peeked at the latest fish flapping around inside.

Jonathon turned to Louisa as she walked slowly in the water. "Miss Keslake, will you teach me how to do that?"

She stood still. "If you want, but you'll need to take off your shoes and stockings."

Quickly removing them, he walked to the water's edge, taking careful steps towards her.

"Be careful; you don't want to fall in." When he stood beside her, she pointed further downstream.

"See along there, where the bank is washed out slightly, there's another one."

"Yes, I see. Can I try this time?"

"Of course, walk slowly, you don't want to scare it away."

Jonathon gradually stepped over the rocks, getting closer to the trout. Louisa a step behind. Phillip and Sammy watched from the riverbank.

When he was close enough, Louisa whispered, "Slowly put your hand into the water near the tail, then move towards the middle."

Keeping his eye on the fish, he nodded.

"Now curl your fingers so they go underneath and quickly flick it out."

Jonathon did as Louisa instructed, but instead of flicking the fish onto the bank, it ended up in the water again, but upstream.

Phillip clapped. "Bravo Jonathon."

Standing with his hands on his hips, he pouted. "But I didn't catch it."

Sammy took a step closer. "But you did flick it out the water, I couldn't even do that on my first try."

"Sammy's right, Master Northy, you managed to get it out of the water; maybe next time you'll get it on the bank."

"Do you think so?"

"I'm sure you will. Would you like to try again?"

He smiled, "Yes I would."

Louisa and the three boys spent the rest of the morning catching trout, but every time Phillip put his hand in the water, the fish would swim away. On Jonathan's third try, he managed to flick one onto the bank, where Sammy quickly picked it up.

Later, the four children sat on the grassy knoll enjoying the sunshine, when Louisa turned to Sammy. "We have to be going home soon for our dinner."

Jonathon lifted the lid on the fishing creel. "We have six fish, but I don't think we'll eat all of them. Would you like to take some home with you?"

Sammy stood up and found a stick. "Can we take four please, we'll give two to Aunty Jane."

Kneeling beside Jonathon, he reached into the creel, threading the fish through the lower mouth onto the stick.

Louisa turned to the two boys. "Are you going home now, or will you stay a while longer?"

Jonathan picked up his fishing pole and turned to Phillip. "We might try our luck with the pole before we go home."

"Well, I hope you catch some more." Tapping her brother on the shoulder. "Come on, Sammy, we'd better get home."

Sammy waved. "Goodbye Master Hill, Master Northy; I had a lot of fun. See you on Sunday." They turned to Stokebridge and headed home.

~

Louisa and Sammy walked into the back door of Rose Cottage, and Sammy called out. "Mother, we caught some fish for supper."

Elizabeth walked out of the sitting room. "Wonderful."

Taking the fish off the stick, she put them on a plate on the cupboard. Turning to face Louisa, "How did Master Hill and Master Northy enjoy themselves?"

Louisa lowered her eyebrows a fraction at the strange smile on her mother's face. "Master Northy managed to catch a couple, Master Hill tried, but the fish always seem to swim away."

Sammy said, "We caught six fish altogether, we gave two to Aunty Jane and brought these home for our supper; Master Hill took the others."

"Well, I'm glad you had a jolly time," Elizabeth said. "But after dinner, it's back to pulling weeds in corn field for both of you."

"Yes Mother." They said in unison.

The absence of Phillip from their usual place on the church wall stirred a sense of concern within Louisa. Jonathon was leaving in the morning for Devon; she wanted to say goodbye.

Navigating the path towards the rectory, looking for the two boys, she caught a glimpse of something unfamiliar among the Prunus bushes at the rear of the church. The air was thick with the scent of blossoms as she approached silently. A soft rustling of leaves greeted her ears as she moved closer to the dense foliage, hearing Phillip and Jonathon engaged in a private conversation.

"I'm so sad you're leaving tomorrow. I'm going to miss you." Phillip spoke softly.

"I'll miss you too. You will write to me, won't you?"

"Of course, I will, but it won't be the same as being with you. I've enjoyed our time together."

Louisa carefully moved closer, peering at them through small gaps in the foliage. They were holding hands, looking at each other. Phillip tenderly raised his right hand, stroking Jonathon's cheek, before putting his hand on his neck. Leaning forward, their foreheads touching, he kissed Jonathon on the mouth.

A gasp escaped Louisa's lips; a sudden intake of breath that seemed to hang suspended in the air. Her chest tightened as if the world had momentarily stilled. There, amidst the Prunus bushes, Phillip and Jonathon shared a moment that surpassed the boundaries of friendship.

Her eyes, widened in a mix of astonishment and bewilderment, were like windows to the storm of emotions brewing within. She sprinted around the side of the church, towards the chestnut tree growing near the Bosley's cottage. She tried to drag air into her lungs as she sat alone, thinking about what she had witnessed.

A moment later, Phillip and Jonathon were standing in front of her. They, too, were trying to catch their breath.

Sitting beside her on the church wall, Phillip's hand gently covered hers, his voice a delicate whisper laden with a mixture of fear and desperate pleading. "Louisa, please, you can't tell anyone you saw us," he implored, the weight of consequence heavy in his words.

Gazing at Jonathon, his eyes held an urgency that transcended the casual plea. "Pleeease," he added, as if the depth of their shared secret hung in the delicate balance of her response.

Louisa's heartbeat and breathing slowed. Turning to Phillip, she whispered, "I've only seen Aunty Jane do that to Uncle Luke. I was shocked when I saw you kiss Jonathon. I didn't know boys did that."

Jonathon moved closer, looking around; he spoke softly, "We're not supposed to; that's why we were *behind* the church. We didn't want anyone to see us."

Phillip put his hand on her shoulder, his touch light as he begged, "Please, can we keep this as our secret? If my parents found out..." Glancing at Jonathon, "They'll never let us see each other again."

"Please, Louisa, you can't say anything about us. I'd like to come back to Roweshorne to see Phillip again." Tilting his head slightly and giving a half smile. "And you."

Standing up, Phillip looked at her. "I don't have many friends, and if you tell anyone what you saw, then Jonathon won't be allowed to visit again." Glancing at him. "He's my best friend, I couldn't bear that."

Louisa understood the consequences for them would be severe if she said anything. She didn't want Phillip to lose his friend or for herself to lose his friendship.

Pulling up one side of her mouth, she promised, "All right, I'll keep your secret. Can we still be friends?"

Both boys smiled back at her; Phillip replied, "Of course, we can."

Helping her to her feet, he hugged her tightly, whispering in her ear, "Thank you."

~

Still haunted by the events of the previous Sunday, Louisa found herself mindlessly sewing a buttonhole at Jane's table. Her fingers moved with practiced ease, but her mind, entangled in the threads of secrecy, refused to let go.

As she worked the needle through the fabric, the weight of the unspoken secret pressed upon her. The events behind the church, now locked away in the recesses of her thoughts, demanded attention. With each stitch, she grappled with the promise she had made, unsure of the implications it held for her friendship with Phillip and Jonathon.

"What's bothering you, Louisa? You seem to be off with the pixies today."

Louisa, lost in thought, wrestled with conflicting emotions. Jane's words pulled her back, but the weight of secrecy pressed on her mind. "Sorry, Aunty Jane, I was thinking about something."

Jane leaned her elbows on the table, holding her sewing. "Do you want to talk about it?"

Louisa slumped her shoulders. "I can't. I promised I'd keep it a secret."

Jane pushed the needle through the fabric. "Well, if you must keep it secret. I understand." Knotting the cotton, she reached for her scissors and cut the thread.

Looking to the other side of the table when she had finished the buttonhole, Louisa said, "Aunty Jane?"

Jane looked up. "Yes?"

Louisa took a deep breath, slowly letting it out. "When two people kiss, it means they love each other, doesn't it?"

"It usually does, Uncle Luke and I kiss all the time." Lowering her eyebrows, Jane leaned closer. "Has someone tried to kiss you? You are thirteen." Dropping her sewing on the bench beside her. "Remember when I talked to you about what happens between a man and a woman and how babies are made? I wanted you to be ready for that sort of thing."

Louisa shook her head. "No, nothing like that, I just thought that's what it meant." Reaching into her basket for the buttons, Louisa hoped her face would not reveal the secret she promised to keep.

Jane resumed her sewing, made two stitches, and then asked, "Are you asking because you've never seen your parents kissing?"

Louisa kept her head down and nodded, threading more cotton in her needle. She suspected Jane wanted to know why she was asking these questions but was grateful when she let the matter drop. She regretted saying anything about what she saw, but something told her it wasn't natural. She needed to clarify things in her mind. Usually, she could talk to her aunt about anything, but somehow, she knew this was something she shouldn't tell anyone.

27

The summer was nearly over, the warm days not as frequent. After picking up the plates from their supper, Elizabeth turned to Louisa.

"The new dress you've made for Sunday best is lovely."

Samson picked up his pipe and tobacco, trying to hide his smile. Elizabeth rarely complimented Louisa's work; it was nice to hear.

"Thank you, I'm going to make a new shirt for Sammy next, he's grown out of his."

Elizabeth looked at her son. "Yes, he has, but you'll have to have your sewing lessons after school, now the holidays are over."

Louisa glanced at Samson. "That's if Da doesn't need me to help him in the fields."

Pulling the pipe from his mouth, Samson gave his daughter a wink. "I'm sure Sammy and I can manage; I think he needs a new shirt more."

~

Louisa stitched Sammy's new shirt while Jane mended the children's clothing, occasionally glancing at her daughter Fran, sitting on the floor playing with a rag doll. Both women looked up when the side door opened. Isaac Langdon ducked his tall, thin frame as he entered. He froze in the doorway.

"I'm s-sorry. Aunty Jane, I d-didn't know you had c-company." Regaining his composure, he closed the door. "Mornin' Miss Keslake."

Jane said, "'Allo me ansum, what brings you to Stokebridge today?"

"Ma asked me to bring a sack of taters for you; I've put them in the storage shed."

He reached to pick up Fran as she rushed to him. Squealing in delight as he lifted her above his head.

"Thank you, Ike, and please thank your Ma for me." Jane walked to the fire. "I'm sure we have some extra runner beans you can take home. Sit down, I'll make us a pot of tea."

Carrying Fran, his long legs reached the table in a few strides. Sitting opposite Louisa, he sat the toddler on his lap. Louisa sensed Isaac watching her; she looked down at the fabric in her hand for a moment until she knew the colour had faded from her cheeks. Glancing up again, she noticed the beginnings of a beard sprouting from his chin.

"Nice to see you again, Ike," she said.

Placing the fabric on the table and sitting up straight on the bench, she pushed an imaginary strand of hair behind her ear. Her heart raced with a mix of excitement and nervousness bubbling within her.

Jane put the pot of tea on the table, turning as the side door opened; Sammy walked in with Billy and Harry. The twins were excited, each holding an egg in their hand. Jane crouched to their level and kissed each boy on the cheek before taking the eggs from them and placing them in a bowl on the table. Their laughter echoed as they ran outside again.

Louisa said to her brother when he sat beside her. "Ike's come to visit Aunty Jane."

Sammy tilted his head slightly, asking, "Did Elijah come with you?"

Isaac laughed, "No, he's still at home."

Hannah walked in the side door with a basket containing about a dozen eggs. "The chickens have been busy today, Ma."

Spying Isaac at the table, she blurted, "Ike, I didn't know you were here." Putting the basket on the cupboard, she raced towards Isaac, wrapping her arms around him, planting a sloppy kiss on his cheek before sitting near him.

Jane placed the cups on the table and fetched four apples and a knife from the cupboard, then sat beside Hannah.

As Jane poured the tea, she said, "There's a small sack on the cupboard with runner beans for you to take home. Do you need any eggs? We have plenty." Putting the pot in the centre of the table, Jane continued,

"I'm sorry I haven't got any mushrooms to give you, but I only picked enough for us earlier today."

She began cutting the apples into small pieces. Isaac lifted Fran from his lap, and she ran to her mother. Her rag doll dragging on the floor as she held it by the foot.

"That's all right, Ma gathered some this morning. And we have plenty of eggs, too."

Jane pulled Fran onto her lap; throwing her doll on the table, Fran took the piece of apple offered to her.

The room was filled with chatter. Louisa folded the fabric in her hand and put it in her basket. "I'll finish that later," she declared.

Sammy turned to Isaac, "Louisa's making me a new shirt."

She turned to ruffle his hair. "Aunty Jane's been giving me sewing lessons."

Jane laughed, "I haven't had to teach her very much; she has a natural gift when it comes to sewing."

Billy and Harry shrieked as they rushed in the side door, pushing each other as they fought for the empty seat beside their mother. Hannah rolled her eyes and moved beside Sammy.

Isaac finished his tea and stood up, gently patting the twins on the head as they chewed on pieces of apple. Picking up the sack of beans, he glanced at Louisa. "I'll see you at church unless I have to bring more vegetables for you."

Jane laughed, "You can come any time, Ike, you don't have to bring vegetables to visit us." Jane gave her niece a wink.

Louisa knew she was blushing as she looked into Isaac's pale blue eyes. Was this going to happen every time she saw him?

"I might do that, Aunty Jane; if not, I'll see you Sunday," he said as he exited the cottage.

~

As Isaac briskly walked to Penstowe, he could only think of Louisa. Her light brown hair, highlighting her beautiful hazel eyes, defined her oval face. He loved the cute dimple that appeared on her cheek whenever she smiled. He had seen her at church most Sundays, but he had never really taken much notice of her before. She was only that little girl who ran around the church grounds with his younger brother and sister. Why had he not noticed she had blossomed into a beautiful young woman?

When she smiled at him, Isaac knew he was in love. There was no denying there was a spark between them; he was sure Louisa felt it, too. He decided that next Sunday, he would talk to her again. He wanted to get to know her better.

~

Isaac walked around the church grounds, looking for Louisa. Eventually, he spotted her sitting on the wall near the chestnut tree, talking to the doctor's son. Not wanting to intrude, he stood still, but she beckoned him to join them.

"Morning Ike." She said when he was closer. "Have you been introduced to Master Hill?"

"Not formally," Isaac replied, extending his hand to Phillip.

"Pleased to make your acquaintance, Master Hill. My name is Isaac Langdon, but please call me Ike."

Phillip shook the offered hand, Isaac noticing no firmness in his grip. "Pleased to meet you, Ike. And I'd be happy if you'd call me Phillip."

Isaac coughed to hide the giggle when Phillip talked. "How do you like Cornwall, Mast... Phillip?"

"I'm beginning to feel welcome." Turning to Louisa, he smiled, "Miss Keslake has been a wonderful friend since I arrived."

Isaac tried not to look at Louisa as she blushed. To save her any more embarrassment, he asked, "Have you seen some of the other villages around Stokebridge?"

"When my friend was visiting from Devon, Father took us to Bradford. We enjoyed our time there." Phillip replied.

"Bradford is much bigger than Stokebridge, Penstowe, and Roweshorne. Of course, Callington is our nearest big city. Have you been there yet?" Isaac asked.

Isaac desperately wanted to talk to Louisa alone; the last thing he wanted was to make small talk. He was grateful when Phillip stood up.

"No, I haven't. I'll go and ask Father if we could make the journey one day." Tipping his hat, "Good day to you, Ike." Striding towards his parents.

Isaac sat next to Louisa. "I hope I didn't drive him away," glancing as Phillip strolled away. "Are you walking out with him?"

Louisa smiled, "No, Phillip and I are just friends."

Isaac grinned, "I'm glad to hear that."

Her smile disappeared as she looked at him directly. "Why?"

"Because I would be deeply honoured if you would walk out with me." Taking a deep breath, he added quickly, "That's if you'd like to."

Her smile returned as she put her hand on his. "I'd like that very much, but I'd like to talk to my Da first. Can I let you know my answer next Sunday?"

"Next Sunday will be fine."

Louisa shivered, and she quickly looked up; Isaac followed her gaze. He saw the scowl on her mother's face. Louisa released his hand quickly.

"I'm sorry, Ike, but I'd better go. I'll see you next Sunday."

~

Elizabeth grabbed Louisa's arm when she was within reach. The force made her cry out in pain.

"What were you doing talking to that Langdon boy?" Elizabeth questioned.

Failing to free herself, she cried out, "Mother, let go, you're hurting me."

Elizabeth said firmly, "I'll hurt you a lot more if I see you talking to him again." She released her grip and pushed her, forcing Louisa to step back to regain her balance.

Louisa rubbed her arm. "What's wrong with talking to Ike?"

"Never mind, I don't want to see you talking to him again."

"But I see him every Sunday."

"Yes, you do, and I'm going to make sure you don't talk to him again. Do you understand?"

"Hmph." She glared at her mother before turning towards Phillip, rubbing her arm as she walked.

Phillip had seen the confrontation with Elizabeth, and when she reached him, he asked, "Are you badly hurt, Louisa? Why did your mother grab you like that?”

“No, I’m not hurt,” Letting go of her arm, “Mother was angry because I was talking to Ike.”

“I don’t see why she would be angry about that.”

“Neither do I.” Turning her back to her mother, she whispered to Phillip, “Ike asked me to walk out with him.”

He grinned. “I wondered if that’s why he came to join us this morning. Are you going to?”

“I’d like to, but Mother doesn’t want me to talk to him again.” Louisa briefly glanced at Elizabeth.

“Why don’t you talk to your Da, tell him about Ike. He may be able to convince your mother to reconsider.”

“I will talk to Da, but I don’t think Mother will change her mind. She can be very stubborn sometimes.”

“I hope for your sake, she will.” Phillip turned when his father called him. “I have to go now.” Putting a hand on her shoulder, “Promise me you’ll talk to your Da?”

Louisa nodded before he walked away.

~

After dinner, Louisa helped Samson pull the dead corn stalks from the field, Sammy not far away.

Louisa approached her father. “Da, can I talk to you?”

Samson stood up, “You know you can talk to me about anything. What’s troublin’ ye?”

She glanced at Sammy walking towards them.

Samson called out, “Sammy, can you do that field near the stream for me?” He turned back to her. “Now, what’s troublin’ ye?”

“This morning, Ike Langdon asked me if I’d walk out with him.” She confessed.

“Do you want to?” A hint of a smile on his face.

“Yes, I do, but Mother doesn’t want me to talk to him again.” Telling Samson what had happened in the churchyard.

“She shouldn’t have said that.” He took off his cap and ran his fingers through his hair. "I'll talk with your mother tonight."

"Thanks, Da." She said, hugging him.

~

During supper, Samson tried to think of the best way to broach the subject of Louisa and Isaac with his wife. The children had gone to bed, and Samson and Elizabeth sat at the table, enjoying a cup of tea.

"I saw you grab Louisa roughly in the church grounds this morning; what did she do for you to hurt her like that?"

Elizabeth picked up their empty cups, putting them on the cupboard. "She was talking to Master Hill, then sent him away so she could talk to that Langdon boy."

"I don't think there's anything wrong with Louisa talking to him." Pretending he did not know the reason for the incident, "Which one was she talking to?"

"I think she said it was Isaac." Picking up a piece of wood, she threw it on the fire.

Samson asked her, "Ike's a good lad, so are his brothers. Why would you object to the maid talking to him?"

She picked up the fire poker and moved the fresh piece of wood amongst the coals. "I don't want her to ruin her friendship with Master Hill so she can be friends with that Langdon boy."

Samson stood up. "I don't think you need worry; Louisa's very fond of Master Hill, and I know she wouldn't do anything to hurt his feelings."

"I've told her she's not to talk to that Langdon boy again, and that's that."

Samson shook his head; he would be wasting his time trying to convince her otherwise.

~

The following Sunday, Samson tapped Isaac on the shoulder as they walked out the church door. He whispered, "Come with me, young man, let's talk."

Samson grinned at Isaac's fearful look as he led him to the boundary wall near Rose Cottage. Elizabeth's eyes watched him, but thankfully, she could not hear them.

They sat on the wall; Samson turned to Isaac and took a deep breath before saying. "Ike, you do realise Louisa will be going into service soon?"

He nodded. "Yes."

Samson looked at him. "I'm sorry, but I can't remember how old you are?"

"Jacob and I turned seventeen last August."

Samson rubbed his finger under his nose. "And are you just friends with my daughter?"

Isaac said shyly to Samson, "I've known Louisa all my life but never really noticed her. I saw her at Aunty Jane's two weeks ago; she smiled at me that day, and in that moment, I knew I was in love." Isaac threw his arms in the air briefly. "I know that sounds stupid, but there's no other way to describe my feelings for her."

Samson chuckled, "My father said the same thing about my mother, and Louisa is like her in so many ways." The tension left Isaac's body as Samson continued, "My daughter is a very headstrong and determined young woman. Once she decides she wants something, there's no stopping her. She told me last Sunday she'd like to walk out with you." The smile returned to Isaac's face, as he continued, "Problem is, my wife doesn't want her talking to you."

Isaac's eyebrows lowered, and his smile vanished immediately. "Do you know why?"

Samson shrugged. "I'm not sure, she hasn't told me the reason."

"Mr. Keslake, do you have any objection to your daughter walking out with me?"

Samson patted Isaac on the knee. "No, I don't."

"Then how can we see one another if we're not allowed to talk when we're at church?"

Samson looked at Isaac sympathetically; he liked the young man. "May I suggest you arrange to meet her at your Uncle Luke's home? That way, my wife won't know you're spending time together. I'll talk to Louisa and suggest she has a lot more sewing lessons with her Aunty Jane."

"I don't want to sneak around. What if Mrs. Keslake finds out about us walking out together?"

"We can only pray that doesn't happen. If it does, then I'll deal with my wife. I only want Louisa to be happy."

"Thank you, Mr. Keslake," Isaac stood up and offered his hand, "I don't think I could imagine my life without Louisa."

Samson smiled as he shook his hand. He was in love once and could understand how he was feeling. Samson darted a glance at Elizabeth; the smirk on her face hinted at a scheme in the making, casting a shadow over the budding romance between Louisa and Isaac. He wished he knew what it was.

~

Louisa and Samson were separating the lambs, ready for the upcoming Bradford Markets.

"Da, I noticed you talking to Ike after church today."

He leaned on the gate and gazed at her. "Your mother thinks I told him he's not allowed to talk to you, but I told him I was happy for you to walk out together."

Louisa's eyes widened as she shook her head. "But how?"

Samson grinned, "Well, maybe you should have more sewing lessons with Aunty Jane." He put his hand on her shoulder, "Just promise me you won't do anything you'll regret."

"I won't Da."

"Good." Winking as he patted her shoulder, "Now, let's get these sheep ready for market."

~

Louisa sat at the table opposite Jane, sewing the shirt for Sammy. The side door opened, and Isaac walked in.

Jane looked up. "Nice to see you, Ike," laughing softly, "Or have you come to see Louisa?"

Louisa tried not to laugh as Isaac's face turned pale. "Mr. K-Keslake said to m-meet her here."

Jane stood up and smiled at him, "Sam told us about Elizabeth refusing to let you talk to her." Turning to Louisa, Jane continued, "Why don't you leave that shirt for now? I'm sure you'd prefer to go for a walk with Ike."

Louisa put the sewing in her basket and stood up. "I wish we didn't have to sneak around like this."

Jane placed her hands on Louisa's shoulders. "I wish you didn't have to either, but if you and Ike want to see each other, then this is the only way." Kissing her forehead, "Now go and enjoy your walk."

"Thank you, Aunty Jane."

Walking out the side door, Isaac asked, "Where would you like to walk?"

Louisa smiled, "We could go to the stream and see if we can catch some trout. You may be able to take some home for your supper tonight."

"I'd love to."

They followed the public footpath behind Luke and Jane's farm to avoid walking past Rose Cottage, where Elizabeth could see them. Louisa led the way as they walked along the bank, pausing occasionally to look for trout. Stopping at the grassy knoll, they removed their boots and stockings.

They could see the stone bridge from where they were sitting, but it was only if someone walking across it looked in their direction, could they be easily seen, reassuring Louisa her mother may not find out about her meeting Isaac.

Watching Isaac as he rolled up his trousers, she asked, "Can you tickle trout, Ike?"

"I've tried a few times, but I'm not very good."

"Never mind," smiling at him, "We'll have fun trying."

Standing up, they walked to the water's edge. Isaac crossed the stream on the stepping stones, turning around; he offered his hand to help her over the final couple of steps.

She pointed downstream, "There's a spot near that bend where I usually find fish. We'll try there."

Isaac stayed on the bank as Louisa gathered her skirts, carefully stepping into the water.

She turned to Isaac after taking two steps, "The water feels like a winter's breath, it's freezing!"

The crisp chill of the water sent shivers down Louisa's spine as she waded through the stream. Not seeing any fish, she moved further downstream. Isaac followed her along the bank. Louisa stopped and slowly reached into the water with her free hand. She flicked a fish out of the water which landed two feet from where Isaac was standing.

"My goodness." Laughing as he bent to pick it up, he held the fish by the head. "One of us has supper tonight."

Louisa stepped out of the water, pulled a small branch off a sapling, and gave it to Isaac. He threaded it through the fish's lower lip before placing it on the ground.

"I might see if I can catch one." Turning to face Louisa after one step, he said, "You're right, the water is cold."

Giggling as he carefully stepped into the deeper water, being careful to keep his trousers dry; he strolled to a fish near the other bank. Louisa watched as he lowered his hand into the water, but the fish swam away before he could catch it.

Isaac splashed his hand on the water's surface, his trousers dotted with wet patches. Louisa stood on the bank, hand on her waist, her laughter echoing along the stream, dancing like gentle ripples in the water.

Climbing out of the water, he stood before her and scowled, "Maybe you'll have to catch another if we both want fish for supper."

Louisa coughed, trying to stop her laughter as she stepped into the water again, eventually spotting another fish. In a flash, it landed on the bank.

Isaac picked it up, threading it on the stick. "I've never seen anyone so skilled in tickling trout. Who taught you to do that?" Offering his hand to help her climb up the bank.

"My Da." Her whole body shivered, "That water's too cold to catch anymore. Let's sit on the grass in the sun."

Isaac removed his jacket, "You're cold, wear this," placing it around her shoulders.

"Thank you."

Isaac picked up the stick, following her over the stepping stones.

Louisa leaned back on her hands, turning her face to the sun. "This is a lovely spot. I love listening to the water and the birds."

Isaac lay on his side, propping his head on his hand as he looked at her. "Yes, it is."

Louisa sat up and wrapped her arms around her knees. "Do people get you and Jacob mixed up?"

He laughed as he sat up. "Sometimes, but I always say I'm the better looking one."

"I wish I had other brothers and sisters, but I've only got Sammy."

"There were eight in Ma's family; she was the eldest girl. Just after she turned fourteen, her Ma died, Uncle Luke was only two." Ike responded.

"That must have been hard for her."

"She never complained. She always said that the world didn't stop just because her Ma died, so she raised her brothers and sisters. Grandda used to call her 'His Angel'."

"I know this sounds terrible, but if my mother died, I don't think I would be very sad. But if Aunty Jane died, I'd be heartbroken. I love her more than I love my mother."

Isaac looked to the western sky and stood up. "We'd best be getting back; we've been here a while."

Extending a hand to help her stand, "Shall we meet here again next Saturday?"

Smiling as she looked up at him, "I'd like that very much."

~

Louisa waved to Isaac when he left Daffodil Cottage, carrying the two trout. She resumed her seat at the table, continuing with Sammy's shirt.

Jane sat opposite her and asked, "How was your time with Ike? I told him he had to behave like a gentleman, did he?"

"It was lovely, and yes, he did. Although I'll see him at church tomorrow, it's going to be hard not being able to talk to him without Mother getting angry."

Louisa's mind raced with conflicting thoughts, torn between the thrill of newfound love and the fear of her mother's disapproval. She threaded more cotton through her needle, and without looking up, she continued sadly, "I wish I knew why."

28

Sitting on the wall beside Phillip, Louisa turned her head so her mother could not see her smile at Isaac as he walked with his family towards Penstowe.

Following her gaze, Phillip whispered, "Did you meet Ike at your Aunty Jane's yesterday?"

His eyes sparkled, making her feel like she was the only person worthy of his heart. She giggled like a joyous child, "Yes. We went to the stream to tickle trout," smoothing down her skirt. "But the water was so cold, we sat on the grass and talked about our families."

He leaned over, gently putting his hand on top of hers. "I'm so happy for you."

"It was lovely, being able to spend time with him, without Mother getting angry," she said, smiling. "We're going to meet again next Saturday."

Phillip patted her hand and sat up straight. "I'm glad your Da approves of Ike."

Hearing sadness in Phillip's voice, she asked, "Have you heard from Jonathon?"

He lowered his head. "No, but I'm hoping a letter will arrive this week."

Louisa turned to him and whispered . "You miss him, don't you?"

"Yes, I do." Raising his head, a half-smile on his lips, "You know, you're the only person I can talk to about him."

"We both have secrets to keep." She tilted her head slightly as she spoke, "And your secret is safe with me."

Phillip gazed at her. "Rest assured, yours is safe with me too."

Louisa took a deep breath. "Now Edith Pengelly's banns have been called, Mother will take me to the manor tomorrow. Hopefully I can get a position as a servant."

Pushing a stray strand of hair from her face, he replied, "That will be different from working on your farm."

"Yes, it will." Louisa stood up when her father called to her. "I have to go."

Phillip stood up and reached for her hand. "I'm so grateful to have you as my friend. Thank you."

Louisa smiled, "And *I'm* grateful to have you as my friend too."

Slowly, she let his fingers slip from her grasp as she walked away. "Goodbye Phillip, I'll talk to you again next Sunday."

~

Isaac and Louisa were collecting the eggs at Jane and Luke's home. Isaac asked, "Doesn't your mother wonder about how much time you spend at Aunty Jane's?"

Louisa giggled; a bittersweet smile touched her lips. "Not really; if Sammy and I are with Aunty Jane, then she doesn't have to look after us; it's a sad thing to say, but she isn't a very good mother."

Tilting his head, he queried, "Why's that?"

Curiosity lingered in his eyes as Louisa, now holding a basket of freshly collected eggs, opened up about her family. "I asked Da about it one day, he said she's still moping about my brother Henry, who died before I was born. Aunty Jane's a better mother to me and Sammy than she'll ever be." Reaching into another nesting box.

"Is that why you call her Mother and not Ma?"

"I think so." She put the egg into her basket.

Isaac decided to change the subject.

"Louisa, would you like to come to our home for dinner next Saturday?"

She faced him and beamed. "I'd love to."

~

After washing the breakfast plates, Louisa picked up her sewing basket and walked to the sheep field, where Samson was checking a ewe.

"Bye Da, I'm going to Aunty Jane's to meet Ike. Then we're going to Penstowe for dinner with his family."

Samson walked to the gate and leaned on it. "Just make sure you're back in time for supper," winking at her, "We don't want your mother to find out about these meetings with Ike."

Louisa stood on her tiptoes, kissing Samson on the cheek. "I'm so lucky to have a wonderful Da like you, but don't worry, I'll make sure I'm back in time."

Louisa briskly walked to the road, calling out to her mother, who was working in the flower garden. Without looking at her, Louisa said, "Bye, Mother, I'm going to Aunty Jane's. I'll be back for supper."

~

Swinging her basket, Louisa opened the front door of Daffodil Cottage. Jane was shelling peas at the table.

"Mornin' Aunty Jane." Squatting as Fran ran to her, Louisa picked her up, carrying her on her hip. She placed her basket on the table and sat opposite Jane, making Fran comfortable on her lap.

Jane continued with the peas, "Mornin' Louisa. Would you like a cup of tea?" dropping the peas in one dish, the shell into another.

Putting Fran on the floor, Louisa stood up. "I'll get it." Seeing Jane's cup empty, she asked, "Would you like another?"

Watching Fran as she played with her rag doll on the cloth rug, Louisa poured two cups and returned to her seat, pulling the pieces of Sammy's shirt from her basket.

She began sewing, turning to Jane. "I'd better do some work on this, or Mother may suspect something."

Jane took the bowls of peas to the cupboard, turning around to face her. "She hasn't said anything about the time you spend here?"

Louisa cut the thread and replied, "Nothing."

Dropping the fabric on the table, she rested her head on her hands and burst into tears. Jane rushed beside her, putting her arm around her as she sobbed.

"I wish we didn't have to sneak around like this." Sitting up, she pulled her handkerchief from her pocket, wiping her eyes before looking directly at Jane. "What has Ike done for Mother to hate him so much?"

"I wish I knew."

Wiping her eyes again, Louisa sniffed, "Mother has no objections to me talking to Phillip, why won't she let me talk to Ike?"

Jane looked heavenward and laughed ironically. "Ahh, of course."

Louisa narrowed her eyebrows. "Of course, what?"

Jane smiled, "I think I know why." Brushing a stray hair from Louisa's face, "Can you remember when your mother started attending church again?"

Louisa's head tilted slightly. "I think it was a few months ago. Why?"

Jane nodded, "Yes, that's right. It was just after Doctor Hill moved to the district and started to attend Stokebridge church. She's hoping Phillip would make a suitable husband for you; she doesn't want Ike getting in the way."

It was Louisa's turn to smile. "Phillip's just a friend, but he'll never be a suitable husband for me."

Jane cocked her head. "Why not?"

Louisa looked around the room, trying to think of an answer that would not reveal his secret. She was saved by Isaac walking in. Louisa wiped her face and smiled at him.

Isaac stopped, asking, "Is everything alright?"

Jane stood up. "No need to worry, we were just talking."

Louisa put the fabric in her basket and stood up. "It's lovely to see you again, I'm looking forward to our day together."

Isaac tilted his head slightly. "Are you sure about coming for dinner today? We can go another time if you want."

She smiled at him again. "No, we'll go to Penstowe today. As planned."

"Only if you're sure."

Linking her arm in his. "Yes, I'm sure. Shall we go?"

Isaac turned to the door. "Goodbye, Aunty Jane." Both waving as they left.

There was an uneasy silence between them as they walked to the crossroads.

Turning towards Penstowe, Isaac asked Louisa, "Do you want to tell me why you were crying at Aunty Jane's."

Louisa hesitated before answering, "I was upset about Mother not wanting me to talk to you, that's all."

He stiffened, "Do you know why?"

It was Louisa's turn to give an ironic laugh. "Aunty Jane thinks it's because she wants me to marry Phillip Hill, she's worried you may be a threat."

Isaac stopped suddenly. "Do you want to marry Phillip?"

Louisa stepped back and looped her hand through his arm, urging him to continue walking. "Phillip is a dear friend, but he's not the man I want to marry."

Isaac stared ahead. "Who do you want to marry then?"

Louisa leaned on his upper arm. "Someone who loves me."

~

Louisa gazed at the cottages in Penstowe, seeing them for the first time. An ivy-covered cottage caught her attention, the stonework entirely hidden. A handcart covered with fallen leaves stood underneath a lemon tree near the front door. Isaac gently guided her towards it.

"Is this your home?" She asked.

"Hmm."

The aroma of freshly baked bread and roasting pork greeted them as they walked inside; Louisa breathed deeply, enjoying the smell.

Mary kissed Louisa lightly on her cheek. "Please sit down Louisa, dinner shan't be long."

Louisa looked around as she sat on the bench, noticing that the layout resembled Jane's cottage. With the sitting room to the left of the front door, stairs against the back wall, and a door leading outside in the side wall.

Only Jacob could have made the tables and cupboards dotted around the kitchen. His repair of the broken pew in Stokebridge church proved he was a skilled Craftsman.

Mary placed plates on the table in front of Thomas and herself.

Louisa stood up. "Let me help."

Mary turned around. "You're our guest, Louisa, Martha will help."

She looked at the food on the plate; the vegetables had been cooked together, but the pork had been roasted in suet, not boiled. It was delicious. She wished she didn't have to keep secrets from her mother, or she would suggest cooking freshly killed pork like this. The meal was eaten in silence, and Mary poured a cup of tea each once it was consumed. An easy conversation began.

Thomas said, "Louisa, Ike says you'll be going into service soon."

Louisa put her cup on the table. "Yes, now Edith Pengelly is getting married, I'll be starting there in two weeks." Glancing at Isaac, she continued, "Ike was telling me Grace has been working at the manor for a while, how does she like it?"

Mary laughed, "She's so frightened of knocking an ornament over; she says there's so many. Other than that, she says it's no different to cleaning here at home."

Louisa relaxed a little; the fear of what to expect when she began working at the manor had been dispelled.

Louisa turned to Thomas as they were about to leave. "I want to thank you, Mr. Langdon, for allowing Ike to spend Saturdays with me, it's the only time we can spend together."

Thomas laughed. "He works hard every other day; I can't deny him that."

Louisa kissed him on the cheek.

~

Walking back to Stokebridge, she mentioned the items Jacob had made.

"We both learnt carpentry at the same time, but his work is always better; I don't know why. Da says he has a gift from God."

Wrapping her hand around his arm. "That's what Aunty Jane says about my sewing."

When they reached Jane's home, it was mid-afternoon; Louisa held Isaac's hand. "I had a lovely time today; it was nice to see where you live finally." She giggled. "But I didn't think your home would be covered in ivy."

Isaac laughed, too. "Ma likes it, she says 'if it's good enough for gentry to have ivy on their homes, then it's good enough for me', but she's not the one who has to hang out the window cutting it back."

Opening the door, Jane looked up from kneading dough. "You two sound happy."

Louisa's hair swished as she turned to him. "Ike was just saying about cutting the ivy from the windows of his home."

One side of Jane's mouth pulled up. "I remember Tom saying how happy he was when the boys could take over doing that."

Wiping her flour-covered hands on her apron, she walked to the cupboard. "Would you like a cup of tea?"

Isaac shook his head. "I'd better get back to help Da." Turning to Louisa, "Shall I see you next Saturday?"

Louisa reached for his hand. "Even though I'll see you tomorrow at church, I would love to see you next Saturday. But once I start working at the manor, I'll only be able to see you on my Sundays off."

"I'll look forward to those Sundays," giving her a brief smile.

"Goodbye Ike." Reluctantly releasing his hand.

She stood staring at the closed door, only being brought back to her surroundings when Jane asked, "Do you want this cup or not?"

Louisa nodded, sitting at the table and accepting the tea.

"How was dinner?"

"It was lovely, and it was nice to see Ike's family other than at church." Taking a mouthful from her cup, Louisa confessed, "I hope Ike will ask me to marry him one day."

Jane smiled, "I'm sure he will; I know he feels the same way. Meanwhile, you need to work on Sammy's shirt, or your mother might wonder what you've been doing while you're here."

Louisa pulled her sewing basket from the other end of the table and reached inside for the fabric. She was grateful to have her father, Jane, Sammy, and Phillip as allies. Being able to talk to them about Isaac was such a blessing.

Looking at the material as she sewed. "I wish I could talk to Mother about Ike the way I talk to you."

Jane looked up from the dough, stopping in mid-knead. "Don't get me wrong, Elizabeth is my sister, and I love her dearly, but sometimes she can be so stupid. This problem with you and Ike is one of those times."

Jane reached over, putting a floured hand on Louisa's. "She'll see it one day; we can only pray she'll understand."

~

Enjoying a talk with Phillip the following day, she hid her smile at Isaac as he left the church. She dared not risk Elizabeth's wrath.

Her friend was attuned to her moods and kept his voice low. "I know how much you want to talk to Ike, but I can feel your mother's eyes watching us."

"I know, she watches me like a hawk when we're at church."

Phillip put his hand on hers. "She'll find out sometime about you and Ike." He grinned. "But hopefully not too soon."

Louisa giggled. "Isn't it funny, I've known Ike all my life, saw him every Sunday at church, even used to play with him after services, but it wasn't until I saw him at Aunty Jane's recently that I fell in love with him. I hope he feels the same way."

Phillip smiled, "I've seen the way he looks at you, I have no doubt he does." He leaned over and whispered, "How was your dinner with his family yesterday?"

Smiling at the memory, "It was lovely, just being able to talk to his family without rushing. Mrs. Langdon was telling me about Grace working at the manor."

"You'll be working there soon, won't you?"

Louisa sighed, "I start in just over a week. But it also means I won't be able to see Ike as often as I do now."

Leaning towards her, "I'm sorry, I didn't mean to upset you."

"You didn't. I've enjoyed my times with Ike; I wish we didn't have to sneak around." Louisa threw her head back and laughed.

Phillip sat back. "What's so funny?"

"When I was at Aunty Jane's yesterday, she said she thinks she knows why Mother doesn't want me talking to Ike."

"Hmm, why's that?"

Louisa straightened up and smiled. "She doesn't want me to talk to him because she's hoping you and I might get married. That's part of the reason she started going to church again."

It was Phillip's turn to laugh. "Well, we both know that won't happen."

Louisa's days were filled with leaving Rose Cottage at dawn, sweeping floors, dusting ornaments, cleaning fire grates, and polishing silverware at the manor. She didn't return until the early evening.

Each day spent working at the manor was another day closer to when she would see Isaac again. He was constantly in her thoughts. As she worked alongside other servants cleaning the many rooms, she couldn't help but daydream about their next meeting. On her Sundays off, she usually met Isaac at Jane and Luke's home. Once the weather warmed up, it was at the stream.

Her only fear was her mother finding out; it was constantly on her mind. If villagers knew about their meetings, they had not told Elizabeth.

Time spent with Isaac was precious. When sitting at the stream, they would talk until it was time to return to Jane's home, but after he had left to return to Penstowe, she couldn't remember what they had talked about, but she didn't care; it was being in his company that mattered the most.

It saddened her that she could not talk to her mother about Isaac. She would love to have the same relationship with her mother that her cousin Hannah had with Jane. In many ways, she considered Jane, her mother, and it would not surprise her if Jane thought of her as another daughter.

~

At the end of each month, Louisa would bring home her wages of fifteen shillings, giving them to her mother. Samson insisted she be allowed to keep a shilling; Louisa kept this money in one of her father's old tobacco tins, hidden in the drawer with her undergarments.

Louisa enjoyed working at the manor; her only worry was being watched by Lord Trevelen's brother, Robert. As she dusted the ornaments, the hairs on the back of her neck would tingle, she knew he would be there, a strange expression on his face before he walked away.

She mentioned her concerns to Grace one afternoon as they walked to the crossroads, "He does that with all the girls. You've only been working at the manor for three months; he's been doing that to me for nearly two years, I wish he'd stop. He scares all of us."

"Hmm." Louisa nodded in understanding but didn't feel any better.

~

Louisa was hanging up her shawl when Mrs. Tremaine gathered the staff in the servants' hall.

"We have a new footman starting tomorrow, his name is John Warren. I hope you'll all make him feel welcome."

A collective "Yes, Mrs. Tremaine" was heard before they left for their assigned duties.

Louisa was returning to the servants' quarters in the afternoon to help Bessie polish the silverware. Walking down the stairs, she stopped two steps from the bottom, and burst out laughing.

A man stood near the table, struggling with a livery suit that seemed a size too large. He clutched the trousers to prevent them from falling, and the jacket sleeves hung awkwardly over his knuckles. She presumed it was John Warren, the new footman Mrs. Tremaine had mentioned earlier in the day.

The housekeeper glanced at Louisa and explained. "Mr. Warren, this is one of our domestic servants, Miss Keslake." Mrs. Tremaine could no longer contain herself, her giggles turned into full-blown laughter too.

John glanced at Louisa and blushed as he shook his head. "Please don't laugh, this is the only suit Mrs. Tremaine had, and I'm supposed to wait on the family for breakfast tomorrow." He looked down and threw his free hand into the air. "How am I supposed to do that when I need at least one hand to hold me trousers up?"

The housekeeper turned her laughter back to a giggle. "I don't know what we're going to do about it, we have no sewing maid at the manor right now."

Louisa finally controlled her laughter as she walked down the last two steps. "Mrs. Tremaine, I may be able to help. Can you fetch me a needle and thread from the sewing room? I should be able to alter the suit this afternoon, then Mr. Warren won't embarrass himself while serving the family at breakfast."

The housekeeper glanced at him again and burst out with laughter once more. At the table in the corner of the room, Bessie giggled.

"That would be wonderful." Mrs. Tremaine's laughter echoed down the hallway when she left the room.

Louisa cleared her throat as she looked at the blushing footmen. "Don't worry, Mr. Warren, I'm sure I'll have it fitting like a glove before the day is through."

Still holding onto his trousers, John rolled his eyes as he slumped on the bench. "I hope so; I'd like to make a good impression on my first day."

Soon, Mrs. Tremaine returned with a needle pushed through the thread of a reel of black cotton, a pin cushion full of pins, and a pair of scissors, handing them to Louisa. "Do you think you can have them altered in time?"

Louisa nodded. "I should be able to, but I won't be able to help Bessie with the silverware."

Waving her hand in dismissal, Mrs. Tremaine said. "Never mind about the silverware, I'll find someone else to do that, I'll leave you to alter Mr. Warren's suit."

Louisa spent the rest of the day sewing in the servants' quarters. She was taking in the back seam, shortening the length of the leg, and taking up the jacket sleeves. When John tried on the suit again at the end of the day, it did, indeed, fit like a glove, just as Louisa had promised.

Mrs. Tremaine walked around the new footman, running her eyes up and down. "Louisa, you've done wonders with this livery suit, it's a much-improved fit."

Louisa giggled again as she recalled what it looked like earlier in the day.

"I agree, you've done wonders, Miss Keslake." John held out both hands. "And I don't need to hold up my trousers anymore. Thank you."

Louisa handed the cotton, pins, and scissors back to the housekeeper, "I best be going home now, Da will wonder why I'm late."

Mrs. Tremaine quickly turned a worried face to Louisa. "He won't beat you, will he?"

She smiled and shook her head. "No, Da would never do anything like that. He worries, that's all."

"Very well Louisa, you must go home." Turning to look at John again. "Thank you for your work this afternoon, you've saved Mr. Warren from major embarrassment at breakfast tomorrow."

Louisa smiled as she collected her shawl and walked to Rose Cottage.

~

A month later, Louisa was dusting in the library when she heard the familiar rustle of silk. Turning around, she saw Victoria Engels approach her.

She curtsied to the tall, slim, elegant woman before her. Her warm smile pushed aside any nervousness.

"Louisa, Mrs. Tremaine tells me you're very skilled with a needle and thread."

"Yes, M'lady." Bobbing to curtsy again. "I altered the suit for the new footman, that's all."

"How would you like to work as our sewing maid?"

Louisa's eyes widened in surprise. "Sewing maid, M'lady?"

The beautiful smile on her employer's face made her relax.

"Yes, our previous dressmaker finished two months ago, and I haven't found anyone to replace her yet."

"Would you like me to make dresses for you, M'lady?" Louisa replied, still somewhat surprised by the request.

"Yes, and for my daughter, Emily, and little James. Would you be able to do that? We have all the patterns in the sewing room."

"Certainly, M'lady."

"Very well, I'll tell Mrs. Tremaine you'll only be working with her on special occasions."

Curtsying, Louisa expressed her gratitude. "Thank you, M'lady."

After taking a step, Victoria Engels turned around. "Can you come to the sewing room tomorrow morning? I'll be able to show you what I'd like made. Also, you'll be paid two shillings extra a week."

Louisa watched her employer walk away. When she was out of sight, she ran on the spot a couple of times while silently clapping her hands, then covered her mouth to smother a squeal of delight. Being the sewing maid would give her a rise in status of the household staff. Smiling to herself, she thought, her Aunty Jane had taught her well.

~

Arriving home that afternoon, Louisa rushed to tell her father the good news; she found him feeding the pigs.

"Da, Lady Trevelen asked me to be her sewing maid."

"That's wonderful, my girl; I always said you were clever. I couldn't be prouder of you."

"And I get two extra shillings a week." Smiling as she bounced on her toes.

Samson's smile vanished. "Have you told your mother about the extra wages?"

Louisa immediately stopped moving. "I came straight to tell you; I haven't told her yet." Glancing to the cottage and back to her father with questioning eyes.

He breathed a sigh of relief. "Tell your mother about becoming the sewing maid, and then tell her you get an extra shilling a week."

"Why, Da?"

"If you tell her you get two shillings extra, she'll expect you to give it all to her; I want you to keep a shilling for yourself. You've earned it."

"Thank you, Da," hugging him. Walking to the cottage, Louisa decided she would buy her father a tin of pipe tobacco with her first extra shilling.

30

Louisa arrived at the manor early, walking up three levels of stairs. She went straight to the sewing room; she knew where it was, she had cleaned it often.

Ellen, the previous sewing maid had been a widow for many years and recently remarried, now living in Bradford. Louisa never dreamt she would be the new sewing maid.

She opened the sewing room door at the southern end of the manor, specks of dust floated in the air; it had been over two weeks since she had cleaned the room. Louisa looked around, remembering the times she had spent with Ellen while she cleaned. One particular day, she was admiring the half-finished dress on the wicker dummy and asked Ellen about the stitches she had used around the edge of the collar, the detail was exquisite.

On the wall opposite the door was a sizeable cross-lead window nearly as wide as the room. Up against the oak-panelled sidewall, in the right corner near the window, was the cutting table, about eight feet long and four feet wide. The top was the same height as her waist, making it the perfect height for cutting fabric. A smaller table covered in dress patterns was in the other corner to the right. Louisa lifted the top piece, and more dust particles flew into the air.

The wicker dressmaker's dummy behind the door, was also covered in dust. Louisa decided that she would have to give the room a good clean before she began working on any garments.

To her left was a large wooden cupboard with rose details carved into each door. She had never seen inside it but her curiosity peaked as she ran her hands over the carvings. Louisa cautiously opened the doors and the smell of lavender floated around the room. Bolts of fabric, lace, and ribbons covered the shelves. She delicately ran her fingers along the beautiful silks and fine brocade fabric, comparing them to the flaxen linen of her own dresses.

Closing the cupboard doors, she turned her attention to the table in the other corner near the window. There was several bowls with an assortment of reels of cottons, buttons, toggles, bits of boning and other items.

The sewing table was positioned in front of the window, making the most of the natural light. It was lower than the cutting table, four feet long by three feet wide. On it were more bowls with needles, thimbles, more cotton, a pin cushion, and a small pair of scissors.

Louisa stood with her hands on the back of the chair, absorbing the ambience of the sewing room – dust dancing in the sunlight, the scent of lavender lingering in the air. She looked at the garden through the window and spied her Uncle Luke trimming a hedge.

Returning her attention to the cutting table, she spotted a large pair of dressmaker shears. Leaving a scissor shape in the dust, Louisa judged their weight, enjoying the feel of them in her hands. Hearing someone approach the room, she returned the shears to the table.

"Good morning, Louisa," said Lady Trevelen.

Louisa bobbed to a curtsy, responding, "Good morning, M'lady."

"Do you think you will enjoy working in here?"

"Yes, M'lady."

Smiling briefly, "Very well."

Her silk skirts rustled as she walked to the cupboard and opened the doors. Pulling a bolt of pale blue cotton fabric from the shelf, she placed it on top of some emerald green silk.

Patting the blue cotton, she turned to Louisa, "I think we'll use this fabric for the first dress you make, something simple that you feel you would be able to manage."

Louisa nodded, "Thank you, M'lady. I would hate to ruin such fine silk."

Lady Trevelen's lips curved into a warm smile, her eyes sparkling with genuine kindness. She stepped over to the wicker dressmaker's dummy. "I've had this made to my size; Ellen would use it whenever she made dresses for me."

Louisa brushed some dust from the dummy's shoulder, sending more dust particles into the air.

"I've always admired the dresses Ellen made for you. Sometimes, she would show me how to do the beautiful stitches she used to decorate them."

Lady Trevelen tilted her head as she smiled, "Sounds like you'll manage very well. I've asked Ellen if she would come today to explain things to you; she should be here soon."

"Thank you, M'lady," She released a breath she didn't realize she was holding, her nerves easing under Lady Trevelen's encouraging gaze.

Just then, there was a knock on the door, and Ellen walked in, bobbing to a curtsy before greeting Lady Trevelen and smiling at Louisa.

Lady Trevelen turned to Ellen, "Thank you for coming today, I'm sure Louisa will be grateful for your advice." Facing Louisa again, she continued, "For the first dress, take your time; there is no need to rush."

"Thank you, M'lady. I'll do my best," Louisa replied, dipping into a graceful curtsy that mirrored her gratitude.

"I'll find Mrs. Tremaine to send someone to clean the room."

Louisa and Ellen listened to the rustle of Lady Trevelen's silk dress fading down the corridor. Turning to Louisa, Ellen asked, "Well, how do you feel about becoming the sewing maid?"

Louisa's heart raced with excitement, yet a hint of nervousness lingered in the back of her mind. "Excited but scared," she replied.

Ellen patted her on the shoulder, "Of course you are, but I'm sure you'll be an excellent sewing maid; all you need is a bit of encouragement."

Glancing to the door to ensure no one was listening, she continued, "Lady Trevelen is a lovely mistress. She may come from gentry, but she's a caring woman and kind to all classes of people. Now, did Her Ladyship say what style of dress she wanted you to make?"

Louisa shook her head, "No, she only showed me what fabric to use."

Walking towards the cupboard, she opened the doors, showing Ellen the pale blue cotton fabric.

Ellen smiled, "I'm sure you can make a lovely dress with this."

Louisa followed Ellen to the pattern table, scattering more dust into the air as she lifted the pattern pieces.

"Her Ladyship has a simple dress pattern, but I'm sure you could add some flounces and frills. They suit her slim figure," Ellen suggested.

Louisa and Ellen were sorting through the pattern pieces, both turning when Bessie and Grace knocked on the door.

"Mrs. Tremaine said we have to clean in here." Grace announced as they entered the room.

Ellen responded, "Thank you. The whole room needs a good clean. Grace, can you start by dusting the cutting table? We need to work there soon." Turning to Bessie, she added, "The patterns are very dusty. Can you begin with them and then move onto the sewing table?'"

~

Once the room was clean, Ellen and Louisa worked together to create the beginnings of the blue cotton dress. Engrossed in their work, they didn't hear the footsteps coming down the corridor and were startled when Bessie poked her head in the door.

"Mrs. Tremaine wants to know if you're coming down for dinner?" she said.

Louisa suddenly realised that the sun was high in the sky outside. "Good heavens," she exclaimed.

Ellen turned to Bessie, "Please tell Mrs. Tremaine we'll be down shortly."

As they left the room, Ellen commented to Louisa, "You've done very well this morning, Louisa. I'll go home after dinner, but I'll come again tomorrow, and maybe one day next week. But I don't think you'll need my assistance for much longer," leaving a sense of expectation.

~

When Ellen arrived the following day, Louisa had the bodice nearly completed. Ellen inspected the seams, commenting, "You've done exceptional work. Your stitches are so neat. Who taught you to sew?"

Louisa smiled, responding proudly, "My Aunty Jane."

"Well, she's an excellent teacher." Walking to the cutting table, she said, "Let's make a start on the skirt pieces."

~

When Ellen returned a week later, Louisa was putting the bodice on the wicker dummy. Ellen gently touched the lace around the neckline, nodding as she admired the tiny daisies in a neat row below the lace.

Ellen smiled at Louisa, "I'm very impressed with what you've done. These are the stitches I taught you, aren't they?"

Louisa let out a deep sigh. "Yes, I thought it might brighten the plain fabric."

"Well, it certainly has."

By the end of the day, the dress had been stitched together; all that remained was for Louisa to hem the raw edges, make the buttonholes, and sew on the buttons. They both looked at the dress as it hung on the dummy.

Ellen said, "Louisa, for the first dress you've made for gentry, you should be proud of your efforts. It may be plain fabric, but you've decorated it beautifully."

"Thank you. I hope Lady Trevelen likes it."

"I'm sure she will."

~

Louisa and Ellen admired the completed dress on the dummy a few days later. Ellen stepped closer, examining and inspecting the embroidered daisies around the bottom of the flounces and the cuffs of the sleeves.

Ellen turned to Louisa. "I think you've made a lovely dress for Her Ladyship. Are you ready for her to try it on?"

Nervously, Louisa agreed. While Ellen went to fetch Lady Trevelen, Louisa unfolded the screen against the wall and stood it in the corner.

Soon, Ellen returned with Lady Trevelen, her maid a step behind.

"Ellen tells me you've finished my dress?" She said to Louisa.

Louisa curtsied, replying, "Yes, M'lady. I hope you like it."

Lady Trevelen walked to the dummy and examined the embroidery before running her fingers delicately over the lace around the neckline. Louisa wanted to say something; the people moved around her, but she could not move.

Ellen spoke, "Would you like to try it on M'lady?"

The lady's maid and Ellen helped Lady Trevelen change into the dress before she walked to the oval mirror near the cupboard.

Lady Trevelen beamed at Louisa, "You are a very talented seamstress, Louisa. I'm so glad Mrs. Tremaine mentioned your skills to me. I'm delighted with this dress. It may be a plain colour, but the little daisies you've sewn on it make it look so elegant."

Louisa curtsied, "Thank you, M'lady."

Once changed again, Lady Trevelen said to Louisa, "I'll have to think about what I would like my next dress to be, so in the meantime, could you make a new dress for Emily? That girl is growing up so quickly!"

Delighted, Louisa replied, "Yes, M'lady."

Lady Trevelen and her maid exited the room. Ellen guided Louisa to a chair, giggling, "I think you'd better sit down. I knew Her Ladyship would be happy."

31

February 1854

Bitter cold seeped through the walls of Jane's kitchen, the fire's warmth struggling to combat the winter chill. Isaac didn't join in the chatter at the table; he was spellbound by Louisa's expertise with a needle and thread.

He shook his head when Jane asked Louisa, "Is that another shirt for Sammy?"

Louisa nodded, "He's nearly as tall as Da, he's growing up so fast."

Jane laughed, "So are Billy and Harry; I'm forever making new shirts for them."

Jane turned to Ike, "Your Ma would understand, especially having four boys."

He nodded, a shadow of concern crossing his face. "She always seems to be sewing something for us, but I don't know what Jack's going to do when he goes to Australia."

Jane stopped stirring the pot over the fire. "Australia? Jack?"

The ladle trembled in Jane's hand, droplets hissing on the hot coals as her eyes widened in surprise. Quickly returning the ladle to the pot, she walked to the end of the table, wiping her hands on her apron. "What made him decide to do that?"

Isaac looked up, "He were at the hiring fair in Bradford last year and said there were broadsheets everywhere advertising for people to build houses in Brisbane, Australia. He ended up talking to the Emigration

Agent; he said they were looking for tradespeople of all occupations, so he applied.”

“Won’t you miss him?” Jane asked Isaac.

“Of course, I’ll miss him.”

Louisa looked up from her sewing, “I remember learning about Australia in school, from when it was a penal colony.”

“Jack said they don’t send convicts there anymore, more people are emigrating, and that’s what he’s doing,” added Isaac.

“When’s he leaving?” Asked Jane.

Isaac put his head down slightly, “Just before Easter.”

“That’s not very far away.” Louisa said, as she turned her attention back to her sewing.

32

Louisa's hands trembled, and a shiver ran down her spine as she sat at the table beneath the window. She immediately stopped her needlework, turned, and caught a fleeting sight of Robert Engels's back as he walked down the corridor. Puzzled by his presence on the third floor of the manor, she couldn't shake the feeling that he was once again watching her.

~

The following morning, assisted by Grace, they dedicated an hour to rearranging the furniture. The cutting table was moved, placing its long side beneath the window, while the sewing table claimed the room's centre, its short side facing the window. Louisa now had unhindered access around it.

Ensuring the cutting table was on her right side, Louisa positioned the chair, affording her the advantage of the natural light filtering through the window. This adjustment allowed her a discreet view of anyone passing by the door with just a slight turn of her head.

After the furniture reshuffling, Louisa observed Robert pacing the hallway, slowing down as he fixed his gaze on her. Following the third pass before dinner, she decided to address the matter with the housekeeper.

"Mrs. Tremaine, do you think Her Ladyship would object if I locked the door while I'm working?" she inquired, alluding to Lord Trevelen's brother.

The housekeeper hesitated. "I don't know if Her Ladyship would approve."

"He's doing it deliberately. I used to find him watching me when I cleaned downstairs. Once I became the sewing maid, I thought it would stop."

"He's always hanging around the kitchen, watching the girls in the scullery. I'm forever having to chase him out. I'm a bit concerned about his intentions."

"That's what frightens me."

"Just keep the door closed for now. Let's hope that'll stop him from bothering you."

"Thank you, Mrs. Tremaine."

~

Louisa felt more secure behind the closed door during her work. A few weeks later, Robert burst into the room, the swinging door nearly toppling the wicker dummy. He demanded, holding a tweed jacket, "Miss Keslake, this coat has a missing button. Replace it for me. *Now.*"

Louisa flinched, her heart racing as she stood up, ready to flee if he made any improper advances. Maintaining composure, she pretended not to be petrified. "I'm sure I have a suitable replacement. Please leave the jacket, and I'll return it shortly."

"I'm going riding, and I need to wear it immediately. I'll wait." He replied.

Louisa's hands shook as she accepted the jacket, keeping a vigilant eye on his movements. The smell of rancid cheese wafted to her nostrils; the foul stench intense. Realizing it was Robert, she breathed through her mouth to prevent nausea.

The metallic taste in her mouth was a strange sensation, she knew it was from the fear that ran through her. The sound of her heart pounding in her ears drowned out all other noise, but Louisa was determined not to let him see she felt threatened as she resumed her seat.

Putting his hand on the tabletop, he leaned forward, his head almost touching hers, oblivious to the fact he was sitting on a half-sewn dress for Lady Trevelen.

Willing her hands to stop shaking, she picked up the jacket. Summoning up courage to keep her voice steady, she said. "Master Engels, I can't see properly, you're blocking the light, will you please move."

She wished he would get off the table, but he only leaned back.

Louisa prepared to push the needle through the fabric, noticing the thread from the old button had been cut. It wasn't frayed. He had purposely cut it off, putting a small hole in the fabric.

"You liar," She thought, *"I doubt you're even going riding."*

Anger had overridden fear, she now had to darn the hole. Could she stand him sitting near her while she mended it?

Pricking her fingers occasionally as she sewed, she clenched her jaw, fighting back tears, determined not to let fear overpower her resolve. The needle pricks were minor compared to the rage she felt about his deliberate damage to the jacket.

Her eyes darted around the room, how would she escape if he tried to attack her, she was certain this was his intention. Out of the corner of her eye, she spied the handle of the dressmakers' shears under a pattern piece on the cutting table to her right. A glimmer of hope.

Louisa darned the hole, stitched on the button, and knotted the thread. Pulling the shears from their hiding place, she clumsily cut the cotton.

Louisa kept a firm grip on the shears in her hand as she lowered them onto the table. She hoped she had the nerve to use them if he made any indecent advances towards her.

As she finished, Louisa handed the repaired jacket to Robert. "I hope you have an enjoyable ride, Master Engels," she said, keeping her voice steady.

He looked down at her disdainfully, snatched the jacket, and left.

Louisa, in response, slammed the door shut, leaning against it to regain composure. Through the closed door, she heard Robert mutter, *"Bitch.* One day, I'll have you right where I want you."

Once his footsteps faded, Louisa slid down the door, still trembling, her face in her hands. It was the most terrifying experience of her life.

Later, she tearfully recounted the incident to Mrs. Tremaine, expressing her fear of Robert.

"I'll talk to His Lordship about this. I don't think it's the first time he's behaved this way," the housekeeper reassured her.

"Thank you, Mrs. Tremaine. I don't want to leave my employment here."

"I'll walk with you to the sewing room, and then I'll find His Lordship. This behaviour of his brother's has to stop."

~

When Grace came to clean the sewing room two days later, Louisa shared the incident with Robert Engels.

"He's still at it," Grace remarked, dusting the windowsill. Her words hung in the air, a chilling reminder that Robert's unsettling behaviour was far from over. "We servants work in pairs now to avoid being alone with him."

"That's terrible," Louisa sighed. "Last night, I had a nightmare about him and woke up in a cold sweat."

"I'm not surprised," Grace responded. "He tried something with me once in the drawing room while I was cleaning the fire grate. Fortunately, his mother walked in, and I hurried out."

"My goodness, has he tried again?"

Grace shook her head. "Thankfully no." Tilting her head slightly. "Did you know he attacked one of the kitchen maids in the scullery?"

"No, I didn't. Was she badly hurt?"

"I've heard she's with child."

"Poor girl," Louisa sympathised. "I think I may have been lucky."

Grace laughed, "Maybe he won't bother you again, especially after seeing you were prepared to use those shears."

~

Louisa and Isaac basked in the warm sunshine, sitting on the soft, grassy knoll overlooking the stream. Louisa was making daisy chains, and as she did, she asked Isaac. "When did Jack leave for Plymouth?"

Isaac shook his head. "A week before Easter."

"Is that what's been on your mind?" she inquired.

He snorted. "How did you know I was thinking of him?"

Tossing away the daisy chain, she propped her head on her hand. "What else would you be thinking about? "

Isaac sat up, wrapping his arms around his knees. "He's been gone three weeks now, and it'll be months before he arrives in Brisbane, and even when he writes to tell us he's arrived, it could be another three or four months before we get the letter."

"All we can do is pray he arrives safely."

Looking through the weeping willow branches hanging low, she listened to the water bubbling over the rocks, the occasional plop as a fish broke the surface to catch an insect, and a sheep bleating in the distance.

Pulling a long piece of grass from the ground, she began tickling his ear.

Isaac laughed, grabbed her around the shoulders, pulling her onto the grass. Rolling her onto her back, they began kissing, and he placed his hand on her breast.

Quickly sitting up, he breathed rapidly, while raking his fingers through his hair.

Louisa sat up. "What's wrong Ike?"

"We'd best be getting back." He stood up, offering his hand to help her.

She leaned back on her hands, giving him a frosty look. "Are you angry with me?"

He shook his head. "No, but I think we'd better leave before we do something we'll both regret."

She accepted his help, and looked up at him. "Ike, I know what you're talking about, and I wouldn't mind at all."

"I know, but I love you too much to ruin your reputation like that."

Not a word was spoken as they walked to Daffodil Cottage.

~

Walking to Penstowe, Isaac thought about what had nearly happened by the stream. Kissing Louisa, he was beginning to swell, it took all his will power to stop before they did something they would regret.

He recalled the conversation he'd had with Jacob only yesterday. They were working side by side in the fields. "Have you done anything more than kiss Louisa?"

Isaac was surprised by the question but answered honestly. "No, but there have been a few times when my cock wants to do more, I have to be strong and think about something else." Looking for understanding from his twin, he continued. "Louisa trusts me, and I don't want to break that trust. I'm not going to take advantage or force myself upon her." Driving the digging fork into the ground, he pushed it with his foot. "I want to marry Louisa one day and that can wait till then, and we'll have the rest of our lives together to do that."

Jacob laughed. "You always were the more sensitive out of the two of us, Louisa's a lovely girl, I can see why you want to save yourself."

~

Louisa and Sammy had turned the corner at the crossroads to Penstowe. It was early July, and Isaac's family were in the middle of harvesting barley. Louisa understood Isaac could not leave the farm during such a busy time.

Sammy was in front of Louisa, turning around, walking backwards as he spoke. "I hope Mother doesn't find out we're going to Ike's today."

"I hope so too, but if the mountain won't go to Mohammad." She laughed.

Sammy turned around, skipping a few steps, saying. "Mohammad must go to the mountain."

Wiping the sweat from her brow, Louisa joined Sammy as they walked behind Pine Cottage, pausing to survey the bustling activity in the fields. Isaac's brothers and father were cutting the barley, while his mother and sister were picking up the cut pieces.

Sammy picked up a hand scythe, rushing towards Elijah and began cutting. Louisa quickly stepped towards Mary, picking up cut stems, tying them in small bundles, adding them to stooks around the field.

The sun was high when she looked at Isaac. The barley shimmered behind him as he worked shirtless, giving him a god-like appearance.

Watching his arm and chest muscles ripple with each cut of the scythe, she felt a strange sensation between her legs, she wasn't sure what it was. Louisa felt her face heat up as a blush coloured her cheeks.

She remembered feeling that same sensation when they were at the stream, just after Easter. It was a complete mystery to her then as it was now. She turned her attention back to the barley.

~

Jane stirred the pot over the fire, and Louisa, sitting at the table, stared out the window as the sun dipped below the horizon.

"What's bothering you? The pixies more interesting?" Jane asked.

Louisa shook her head, turning to her aunt. "Something happened today."

Jane moved the pot away from the fire, sitting beside her. "It can't be too bad, or Sammy would have said something."

Louisa looked at the tabletop. "He didn't know about it."

Jane brushed some hair away from her face. "The children are outside; do you want to tell me?"

Louisa gave a half-smile, explaining the strange sensations she felt while helping with the barley.

Jane put a finger under her chin, lifting her head gently and smiled. "My darling girl, it's completely natural for you to feel that when you're with the one you love."

Louisa reached into her apron pocket for her handkerchief, wiping her nose, giving a half-laugh. "I wasn't sure if I should feel ashamed."

Jane put her arm around her shoulders, pulling her closer. "It just means that you're growing up, and it's all part of how babies are made. And you should never feel ashamed."

Louisa's eyes glistened with gratitude as she said, "Thank you, Aunty Jane," her heart feeling lighter with the weight of newfound understanding.

33

February 1855

It was Louisa's Sunday off, and Isaac sat at the table with her, their aunt, and cousins. He announced, "Ma and Da got a letter from Jack the other day."

Jane's eyes lit up with joy. "That's wonderful news!"

Louisa looked up from her sewing. "How's life in Australia?"

"Just grand, he's working for a Londoner by the name of Bill Spink, and they're building houses in Brisbane. He said in his letter that they build the houses on high stumps, sometimes the stumps are nearly twelve feet high."

Jane looked up from pulling Fran onto her lap. "Twelve feet!"

Hannah asked, "Why are the houses so far off the ground?"

"Jack says it helps keep the house cool in summer; if they're not built on the ground, the breeze can come through the floorboards, and the ceilings are also high."

Jane asked, "How do they manage in winter; wouldn't it get cold inside with all the snow around?"

"Jack said he arrived in July, it was the middle of winter then, and there wasn't any snow. By September, it was starting to get hot again."

Hannah was fascinated. "No snow at all?"

Isaac nodded. "He wrote the letter in October, and he'd only been there three months, but he likes it."

34

August 1855

Louisa and Isaac found solace on their cherished grassy knoll, surrounded by the gentle hum of nature. It was a beautiful sunny day after several miserable cold rainy days. They talked as melodious birds chirped in the trees, and a gentle breeze carried the scent of blooming daisies and buttercups growing amongst the grass.

"Do you feel any different now you've come of age, Ike?"

He laughed. "No different from the day before."

"Well, you don't look any different," Louisa teased with a playful grin.

Louisa picked a buttercup, twirling it in her fingers for a moment, before throwing it away. Turning back to Isaac, "Dotty had fifteen piglets yesterday, Da's hoping he can get a good price for them as weaners at Bradford market."

"Will he keep one or two for bac—" Isaac's eyes and mouth open wide, instantly he was on his feet, picked her up, quickly moving up the bank.

"Ike, put me down, Ike!" But he took no notice of her cries. He stopped ten yards from where they'd been sitting, gently lowering her to the ground.

"Ike, what did you do that for?" She wasn't angry, just curious.

He pointed to where they had been sitting. "Look over there." Louisa saw the patterned brown adder slithering in the grass, its shiny scales reflecting the sun like a rainbow. "I'm sorry, I didn't have time to warn you, I could only grab you and run."

"Ike, you saved my life. Thank you." Reaching to hold his hands, she stood on her tiptoes to kiss him.

Louisa welcomed him as he wrapped his arms tightly around her, kissing her with more passion than ever before. Her heart pounded in her ears, almost blocking out the sigh of the breeze. Thinking, *"If this is what love feels like, I want more."*

Louisa felt a twinge of rejection as Isaac swiftly released his hold and walked away, leaving a lingering uncertainty in the air. She called after him. "Ike, what's wrong? Where are you going?"

He stopped, slowly returning. "Louisa, I had to walk away, or I may have done something I shouldn't have."

Her body ached for his touch. "Like what Ike? Like what tups do to ewes, and what boars do to sows?"

Reaching for her hands, he said. "Yes, exactly like that, I desperately wanted to take you under the oak tree." He lowered his head. "Then I was ashamed of what I was thinking."

"Ike, I think about that too." She giggled. "And if Da knew, I doubt he'd ever let me see you again."

"Louisa, you are a beautiful young woman, I want us to get married one day, and that's only supposed to happen after we're wed." Lifting her hands to his face. "Will you marry me, Louisa?"

She looked into his pale blue eyes. "Of course, I'll marry you. I've loved you for a long time, but I don't know what Mother will say when she finds out we've been seeing each other."

"I know your mother doesn't want you to talk to me, but I hope she'd accept me if you told her we want to get married."

Louisa shrugged with a hint of uncertainty, "I guess I'll find out when I tell her."

~

Later that afternoon, upon returning home, Louisa spoke with Samson as he worked in a field, turning the soil. "Da, Ike asked me to marry him."

Samson stood up and smiled. "I wondered when he was going to ask you, did you say you'd accept?"

"Of course, I did, I've loved Ike for a long time. Telling Mother might be difficult."

Leaning on his digging fork, he tilted his head slightly. "Do you want me to talk to her?"

Louisa's gaze dropped as she contemplated the delicate balance between her feelings and her mother's expectations. "I think I'd better; Aunty Jane thinks she's got her heart set on me and Phillip getting married."

Samson drew in a deep breath, exhaling it rapidly as if trying to make sense of the situation. "I see. She's never said anything to me." Banging his palm on his forehead. "*That's* why she didn't want you talking to Ike." He threw his hands in the air. "It all makes sense now."

A line etched between her brows. "I'll try to explain to her that Phillip and I are good friends, nothing more."

35

Louisa had finished washing the supper dishes when the back door closed after her father and brother walked outside, making the most of the twilight to tend to the animals before going to bed. Sitting at the table, her mind was on Isaac's proposal instead of mending the seam in her brother's trousers. Putting the sewing in her basket, she looked over to Elizabeth, tending the fire under the kettle.

Louisa took a deep breath before breaking the news, "Mother, Ike proposed to me today."

"Isaac!" Still crouching, she turned around. "Have you been seeing that Langdon boy, even after I forbid it?" Her whole body shook as her mother stared at her with unmistakable rage.

Summoning up all her self-control, she sat up straight and glared back. "Yes. And we're going to ask Reverend Ellacott to call the banns next Sunday."

Elizabeth stood up, a piece of firewood still in her hand as she marched towards her. Slamming it hard on the table in front of her daughter, Louisa jumped and slid back on the bench seat. Pointing the wood at her, Elizabeth shouted, "If the banns are called this Sunday, and the good Reverend asks if anyone has any objections, I'll get up and say that I do, then you and Isaac will be the laughing-stock of the village. How do you think it would look to the congregation that your own mother doesn't want you to marry *that* boy?"

Leaning back further, Louisa replied, "Ike's hardly a boy; he's just come of age. And what's so wrong with me and Ike getting married?"

Elizabeth threw the wood towards the fire, the force sending sparks onto the stone floor. The slap her mother gave Louisa caught her by surprise when she shouted, "Because I want you to marry Master Hill when he's old enough."

Louisa held her cheek as her mother continued. "What about Master Hill? Does he know you've been seeing this Isaac behind his back, and all this time you've been toying with his affection?" She folded her arms, frowning at her. "Did it ever occur to you that Master Hill might propose to you?"

Still holding her cheek, Louisa replied, "It was Phillip who encouraged me to see Ike."

Elizabeth's brows drew together, hooding her eyes. "Why would he do that? I thought you'd be the perfect girl for him."

Louisa walked to the other end of the table, shaking her head. "Phillip is a dear friend, but he won't propose to me."

Elizabeth glared at her, leaning on the end of the table; she shouted again. "And why wouldn't he?" Standing up, she lowered her voice. "He'd be a fine catch for any young girl, and friendship can turn to love."

"I'm sorry Mother, but hell will freeze over before Phillip and I get married."

A line etched between Elizabeth's brows. "You must be mistaken; you spend so much time together."

"Yes, we do, and he talks about the person he really cares for. And it isn't me." Rushing to the front door, Louisa slammed it behind her.

As she ran to Daffodil Cottage, the image of Phillip and Jonathon kissing behind the church popped into her mind. Opening the door, Jane sat at the table, cutting up apples by candlelight. Hannah and Fran were beside her, helping.

Jane looked up, turning to her daughters; she said, "Girls, will you take yourselves to bed please; Louisa and I need to talk privately."

Hannah's eyes opened wide as she looked at her mother. "What about the apples?"

Jane put a gentle hand on her shoulder as she smiled. "The apples can wait 'til tomorrow. Now, get yourselves to bed." They all stood up; Jane put a cloth over the apple pieces before giving the girls a kiss on the cheek. She looked up the stairs, making sure Hannah and Fran were in their room.

Louisa caught her by surprise as she wrapped her arms around her, crying on her shoulder. "You were right about mother. She wants me to marry Phillip."

Pushing her niece away gently, looking into her red and swollen eyes. Guiding her to the bench. "Let's sit down and talk about it."

Louisa explained about Isaac's proposal and her mother's response.

Jane smiled, "I presume you said 'Yes' to Ike."

"Of course, you know how I feel about Ike, but Mother was furious when she found out we'd been seeing each other," wiping her eyes with her handkerchief.

Jane shook her head. "She can be very narrow-minded sometimes; she can't see what's in front of her."

Louisa put her head in her hands. "Oh, Aunty Jane, what am I going to do?" Looking up again. "I love Ike, but I don't think I could bear the humiliation of Mother objecting when Reverend Ellacott calls the banns."

"Is your Da happy about you and Ike getting married?"

Louisa sniffed, giving a small laugh. "Da wanted to know why it took him so long."

The side door opened, and Luke and the twins walked in.

"Evenin' Louisa." Turning to the boys, "Billy, Harry, get yourselves to bed; you've got school in the morning."

The boys spoke as one, "Yes Da." Turning to the stairs.

Luke sat beside Jane, looking at Louisa. "What brings you here at this time of night? And I assume your mother gave you that bruise."

She nodded, giving Luke the details of what happened.

He shook his head. "Elizabeth can be so stupid sometimes. But threatening to object to the banns would be so...so...?"

"Spiteful?" Jane added for him.

"Yes, that's the word." He reached over, putting his hand on hers. "Does Sam know what your mother said?"

Louisa shook her head. "No, I was so upset; I came straight here to see Aunty Jane."

Luke snorted. "He may have heard Elizabeth yelling at you, and I wouldn't be surprised if they're arguing about it now."

Louisa stood up. "I'd better go home. Sometimes Mother throws things when she's angry."

Giving her aunt and uncle a quick hug, she rushed out the door towards Rose Cottage.

By candlelight, Louisa saw Sammy's silhouette in his bedroom window at the front of the cottage, obviously waiting for her to return. Holding his hands over his ears, a signal that their parents were arguing.

She nodded to him, quietly walking to the front door, stopping when she heard her father shouting.

"What's wrong with Louisa marrying Ike?"

"She could marry much better; she's a very smart girl and would be a fine catch for any young man."

"I'm glad you realise how clever she is, but surely it's her choice to marry who she wants."

Louisa opened the front door with a bang. "Yes Mother, it is *my* choice to marry who I want."

"You're not of age yet, so it's up to your Da and me to make sure you don't make a foolish choice for a husband."

"But I'm the one who has to live with that choice, not you. And I don't think I'm making a bad choice with Ike."

Elizabeth turned on her heels, stomping up the stairs. "Hmph."

Louisa and Samson watched Elizabeth disappear; her father turned to her. "I'm sorry, she should never have said those things to you. We could hear her down by sheep field."

Louisa put her arms around his waist. "Oh Da, do you really think she'll object to the banns?"

Wrapping his arm around her, talking into her hair, he replied, "She might; we'll just have to find a way to make sure she doesn't."

Louisa stepped back. "Do you think you can talk to her?"

Samson exhaled. "I'll try, but you know your mother. Once she gets an idea in that silly 'ead of 'ers, it's hard to shift it."

"Hmm." Louisa sighed. Scattered on the floor near the stairs was her sewing basket and its contents. Her mother obviously knocked it off the table.

"I'm too upset to think right now. I'll talk to Ike next time I see him." She bent down, picking up her basket, putting everything back.

Samson picked up two cotton reels near his feet, handing them to her. "I'm sorry, I wasn't close enough to stop 'er from knocking it off table."

"That's all right Da, I know what she's like when she's angry, and nothing got broken." Standing up, she gave her father a hug. "Goodnight, Da." Picking up the basket, she walked up the stairs.

~

A fortnight later, Louisa and Isaac were sitting on their favourite grassy knoll; she recounted the turmoil of the past weeks.

She looked at the grass near her feet. "Oh Ike, I wish I knew what to do."

His mouth twisted. "Does your Da have any ideas?"

She shook her head. "I know he's been trying to talk to her about it, but he hasn't said anything to me yet."

Pulling his knees up to his chin, he wrapped his arms around his legs, staring ahead.

After a while, Louisa asked, "What's bothering you, Ike? There's something else worrying you, isn't there?"

He took a deep breath through his nose. "I'm not sure how to tell you about it."

"Try saying it; it might be a good way to start." While waiting for Isaac to speak, Louisa watched a dragonfly as it flew down and landed on the surface of the water.

"We got another letter from Jack the other day; he said Bill has offered him a partnership in the business, and they've employed more workers."

"I'm glad to hear he's doing well, but why is that upsetting you?"

She was shocked by the words he said quickly. "Because Ma and Da are thinking about moving to Australia too."

Louisa's mind reeled, she managed to utter, "All of you?" Her thoughts heavy with the weight of impending change.

"Yes, all of us. Da went to see the agent in Bradford the other day and mentioned it after supper."

The only thing Louisa could say was "Oh." Pulling her knees to her chin also, she added. "What if some of you don't want to go?"

Isaac turned to face her. "We all want to go. Including me, but only if I can take you as my bride."

"That changes everything." Bumping her chin on her knee.

"Yes, it does. I couldn't bear the thought of being parted from you if we can't get married before we leave. Da said I could stay with Uncle Luke and Aunty Jane and remain in Cornwall, but I don't want to stay here without my family."

Louisa reached to hold his hand. "We'll just have to think of something, but it's hard when I only get the chance to see you every other Sunday."

Pulling her closer to him, he kissed her hair. "I want to go to Australia, and I want you to come with us."

"I love you, Ike. I'll go wherever you go."

They sat a while longer without speaking before they left.

Not wanting to face her mother, Louisa walked to Daffodil Cottage. She needed her aunt right now.

Walking along the road, she wished Jane was her mother. Her aunt was so kind and caring; it was no wonder she loved her more.

She was about to open the door when she heard Jane's voice in the garden.

Jane was picking apples with Fran but stopped when she saw her walking toward her. Throwing the apple from her hand into the basket on the ground, she rushed to her. "What's wrong?"

Louisa buried her face on Jane's shoulder, tears streaming down her cheeks, the weight of uncertainty bearing down on her.

Jane turned to Fran. "Can you pick a few more apples for me; I'm going inside with Louisa."

"Yes Ma."

Once they were settled at the table, Louisa blurted it all out. "Ike and his family may be going to Australia. I love Ike, and I want to go with them. As his wife."

Jane sat back. "I didn't know about that, when did Tom and Mary decide they were going?"

Louisa shrugged. "They haven't made up their minds yet, but they've been talking about it a lot apparently. Ike told me before ; he said he doesn't want to go without me." Wiping her eyes with the back of her hand, she continued. "If they do decide to go to Australia, I want to go with them, but we have to be married before they leave Cornwall. But how can we be married if Mother's going to object when Reverend Ellacott calls the banns?"

"Have you told your Da about Ike's family yet?"

Louisa shook her head. "I came straight here, Aunty Jane. I needed to talk to someone who understands."

Jane patted her hand gently. "Talk to your Da; he may be able to change Elizabeth's mind."

Louisa gave a small smile. "You really think so?"

"He might, but if he can't." Tilting her head slightly, giving a brief smile, "There may be another way." Jane's cryptic suggestion lingered in the air, leaving Louisa curious about the alternative solution.

Raising her eyebrows. "How?"

"If you were with child, Elizabeth would have no choice but to allow your marriage to take place. Unless she wants her grandchild to be born out of wedlock."

Louisa shook her head. "Ike and I want to stay pure till our wedding night."

Jane smiled as she cupped her hand under her chin. "You're such a beautiful young lady; I wish my sister could see what everyone else sees. Let's hope Sam can convince her to let you and Ike get married."

Louisa sprang to her feet, enveloping Jane in a tight hug, seeking comfort in her aunt's warmth. "I hope so. I'll talk to Da right now." She rushed out the door.

36

Louisa, determined to talk to her father about the pressing matter, walked towards the sheep field, hoping to find Samson there. The scene before her, with ewes and lambs grazing peacefully under the serene sky, offered no sign of her father. Turning her attention to the field behind the pigsty, she spotted Sammy cutting wheat.

Approaching Sammy, he said, "Louisa, I thought you'd still be with Ike."

"I was, but I need to speak to Da. Do you know where he is?"

"I think he went to field near stream."

"Thank you," she replied, marching purposefully towards the back of the farm.

Approaching the willow tree, Louisa noticed her father's stockings and boots lying under it. Samson stood in the stream, scanning the water. A trout landed not far from her as she reached the tree. Picking up the fish, she held it at arm's length.

Samson smiled as he stood in knee deep water. "That's grand, I thought we'd enjoy some trout for supper. Care to join me?"

Shaking her head, Louisa said, "Da, I need to talk to you. It's important."

His smile vanished as he walked out of the stream, the splashing water leaving wet dots on his shirt and trousers. Taking the fish from her, he threw it back into the water, saying, "Maybe I'll catch it another day."

Sitting near his boots, Samson patted the ground beside him. "Now tell me, what's so important?"

Louisa sat beside him, putting her head on his shoulder, and burst into tears again, recounting what Isaac had told her earlier. Sniffing and wiping her face, she said, "If Ike's family do go to Australia, we have to be married first."

"No wonder you're upset." Putting his arm around her, he continued, "Remember t'other day I said we'd have to find a way to stop your mother objecting to banns?" She nodded. "I think I may have a way."

"Really?"

Brushing the dirt from his feet, he put on his stockings and boots. "It'll mean breaking a confidence, but let's see if we can convince your mother to allow you and Ike to marry first. Don't tell her about Australia until you know for sure." Standing up, he held out his hand. "Ready for battle?"

Elizabeth was using the stone grinder when they walked in the back door. She stopped when she saw the serious look on Samson's face.

"Sit down, Elizabeth, we have to talk about Louisa and Ike."

Frustration etched on Elizabeth's face, she wiped her hands vigorously on her apron, her eyes meeting Samson's with a mix of defiance and curiosity.

Samson turned to Louisa. "Tell your mother what you just told me."

"Ike and I would like to get married; we're going to ask Reverend Ellacott to call the first banns next Sunday." Glancing at Samson. "Da is happy for us to be wed."

Elizabeth jutted out her chin. "Well, I've already told you what I'll do if your banns are called."

Louisa glanced at her father and sighed. "It's because you want me to marry Phillip, isn't it?"

"Yes, you'd be the perfect wife for him."

Louisa shook her head and laughed softly.

Elizabeth stood up, yelling at her. "What's so funny?" Glaring at her.

Louisa shouted. "Because he..." Shutting her mouth quickly. The fear of saying something that would reveal her friend's secret was very real.

"Because what?" Elizabeth stood with her hands on her hips and shouted. "Well?"

Louisa thought for a moment before replying. "Phillip is a dear friend, but he's told me more than once, he doesn't want to get married, to me, or anyone else."

Louisa jumped when Elizabeth banged her hand on the table. "Why on earth not?"

She looked up at her mother, her heart pounding in her ears. "Phillip doesn't want to get married. That's all."

Elizabeth stared at Louisa, shouting again. "Even if you don't marry Phillip Hill, you can do so much better with your choice of husband. Isaac is nothing but a common farmer, that's why I didn't want you to have anything to do with him." Turning around, she stormed out the back door.

Louisa sat with her mouth open. If her mother had slapped her, it wouldn't have hurt any more than her spiteful words.

Watching as Samson followed immediately. "Get back inside Elizabeth. Right now."

Her mother stopped and turned around, hands on her hips, she stared at him defiantly. When he reached her, he put his hand between her shoulder blades, giving her a shove. *"Get inside."*

Her father's tone and thunderous look made her mother relent, allowing herself to be guided inside. She resumed her seat.

Samson stood at the end of the table, arms folded as he glared at her. "Elizabeth, when Reverend Ellacott calls the banns next Sunday, you will not object."

Elizabeth stood up, Louisa could see she was determined to win this argument one way or another and moved closer to her father. "Yes, I will, I don't want Louisa to marry *that* boy."

Samson forcefully pushed her back onto the bench, leaning on the table, his face only inches away from hers. "You will not object to the banns because if you do, I'll get up and tell everyone in church that Lord Trevelen was Henry's father, not me." Standing up straight, he refolded his arms as he glared at her.

Louisa sat with her mouth open, watching as the colour drained from her mother's face.

After a moment, Elizabeth spoke, hardly more than a whisper. "Y-you w-w-wouldn't do t-that?"

Samson leaned on the table again, looking directly at Elizabeth. "Yes, I would. I know I told you when we wed, I'd never give your secret away. Well, I will if you do anything to prevent Louisa and Ike getting married."

Beads of sweat appeared on her mother's brow, and her hands shook. Eventually, she said. "How c-could you s-say that in front of our daughter? I didn't want anyone to know about Henry."

"And we can keep it that way if you let Louisa and Ike get married. If you saw them together, you would see how much they love each other."

Elizabeth simply stared ahead.

Samson put a hand on Louisa's shoulder. "Get Sammy to go with you, fetch Ike, then ask Reverend Ellacott to call the banns next Sunday; your mother isn't going to object." Turning to Elizabeth, he shouted. "*Are you?*"

Her mother's face was blank as she hung her head, replying softly. "No Samson."

"Good."

Louisa stood up, wrapping her arms around his neck. "Thanks Da," rushing out the door.

~

After Louisa left, Samson walked to the field, and his mind wandered as he watched the sheep. His life had not turned out as he hoped. When he married Elizabeth, he thought he would be happy with her. But God had other plans.

Henry died, and Elizabeth fell into a well of self-pity; he could feel himself falling out of love with her. When she rejected Sammy, whatever remaining love he felt for her disappeared.

He moved into the front room, and there had been no intimacy between them since Sammy's birth, and he couldn't help but wonder if confronting Elizabeth and threatening her would be a turning point in their strained relationship.

He accepted his life now; his only wish was for his children to be happy with theirs.

Louisa was about to be married to Isaac, and if his family did go to Australia, he would ask Thomas if Sammy could go with them. He may get his wish too.

The daylight was fading, moving to the pigsty, he threw more food to them before returning to the cottage.

Opening the back door, he saw Louisa and Sammy had returned. Elizabeth put their plates on the table as he sat down.

She was silent, Samson knew she was still angry with him for revealing her secret to Louisa; he hoped she would forgive him in time.

Wiping his plate with a piece of bread, Samson asked Louisa. "Did you and Ike see Reverend Ellacott?" Popping the bread into his mouth.

Louisa could not contain her excitement as she fidgeted on the bench. "Yes, and he's going to call the first banns next Sunday."

"That's grand, did he give you a date for the wedding?"

Louisa nodded as she picked up her cup. Taking a mouthful, she looked at him. "Twenty-ninth of September, and Da?"

"Hmm?"

"Would you be my witness? Jacob is going to be Ike's."

Placing his hand on hers. "I'd be happy to."

Sammy sat quietly, his body tense. Samson glanced at Elizabeth; she was off with the pixies. How he wished he could see into her mind and understand what she was thinking.

She eventually stood up and collected the dirty plates, taking them to the cupboard. Louisa joined her to help wash them.

When they had finished, Samson watched as Elizabeth tended the fire.

Louisa stacked the plates and faced her mother, hands on her hips, she blurted. "Mother, aren't you happy for me?"

Not looking at anyone, Elizabeth replied, "I'm going to bed."

Samson, Sammy, and Louisa watched as she walked up the stairs, listening as she stomped along the landing, followed by the slamming door.

Samson let out a long loud breath. "I hope she'll get used to the idea soon."

Sammy stood up. "You're lucky Louisa, you're working at the manor. Da and I have to be here with her all day."

A guilty look shrouded her face. "Oh, I feel terrible now."

Samson stood up, saying firmly. "You have no reason to feel terrible." Touching her cheek gently. "Your mother will soon realise that you and Ike getting married is what God wanted."

Louisa hugged him. "Thanks Da."

37

Louisa walked into the servants' quarters the following morning and found Mrs. Tremaine talking to Bessie. When the housekeeper finished, she turned to her. "Mornin', Louisa. What can I do for you? Do you need the sewing room cleaned?"

"No, the sewing room is clean enough. I'd like to speak to Her Ladyship if possible. It's important."

Concern shadowed her face. "Your Da or Ma haven't died, have they?"

Smiling as she shook her head. "No, I'm getting married soon, that's all. I'd like to tell Her Ladyship."

"Very well, I'll ask Her Ladyship when it would be convenient for you to talk to her."

"Thank you, Mrs. Tremaine," turning to the stairs.

Putting her foot on the first tread, the housekeeper called out. "Congratulations, Louisa. Who's the lucky man?"

Stopping in mid-step, she replied, "Ike Langdon from Penstowe."

Mrs. Tremaine smiled. "I wish you all the best."

"Thank you."

Entering the sewing room, Louisa looked at the half-finished dress on the dummy and the cut pieces on the cutting table. A pang of melancholy enveloped Louisa as she surveyed the sewing room, realizing these unfinished dresses marked the end of her tenure as the sewing maid at the manor. Picking up the sleeve from the sewing table, she began sewing. Pushing the needle in and out of the silk, Louisa's thoughts wandered to the dresses she had made for Lady Trevelen during her three years as the sewing maid. Her skills had improved dramatically. Why had she not realised how much she had taught herself since she began making dresses for gentry?

Footsteps coming down the corridor reached her. Turning to the door, the housekeeper walked in. "Louisa, Her Ladyship will see you in the drawing room."

Placing the fabric on the table, she stood up, "Thank you, Mrs. Tremaine." Following her downstairs.

Louisa paused at the entrance to the drawing room, her hand lingering on the doorknob, a moment of anticipation hanging in the air. She straightened her dress before knocking.

"Come in." A voice called from inside.

Louisa took two steps after she entered and curtsied, a mixture of nervousness and respect in her demeanour. "Mornin', M'lady."

Lady Trevelen smiled and stood up. "Ah, Louisa, do come in. Mrs. Tremaine said you wished to speak to me." Walking towards her. "I believe you intend to marry soon?"

Bobbing another curtsy. "Yes, M'lady. Our first banns will be called this Sunday."

Smiling as she tilted her head slightly. "And when is the happy day?"

"Twenty-ninth of September, M'lady."

"Well, I shall be sorry to lose you as our sewing maid. I've been very happy with the dresses you've made for myself and the children."

Giving her employer another curtsy. "Thank you, M'lady, would you like me to finish the dresses I've already started?"

Lady Trevelen's eyes sparkled with genuine delight, her gratitude evident as Louisa offered to finish the dresses, a silent acknowledgment of their shared bond. "Oh yes, please. How long do you think it will take?"

Thinking for a moment before replying, "Probably a couple of weeks. That'll give me a little time afterwards to make myself a new dress for the wedding."

Lady Trevelen sighed as she sat in her chair. "Thank you for offering to finish those dresses, although how I'll find someone who can sew as well as you do, I'll never know."

"I'm sorry to be leaving too, M'lady."

Taking a deep breath. "Don't be sorry." Giving a half-smile. "I hope you are very happy with your husband."

Louisa was about to turn to the door but hesitated.

"Is there something else?"

She bobbed again. "Yes, M'lady." Shifting her weight from one foot to the other. "I was wondering if you would write me a letter?"

Standing up quickly, her skirts rustled as she stepped towards her, she replied, "Of course, why didn't I think of that. Yes, I'll write you a letter and give it to you later."

"Thank you, M'lady."

~

The air in Rose Cottage hung heavy with tension after the clash with Elizabeth, leaving Louisa torn between relief at escaping to the manor and a lingering concern for Sammy and her father.

On the next Sunday, Louisa sat with the rest of the servants at the back of the church, looking towards the front. Isaac was sitting with his family a few rows in front of them. He turned around, smiled at her. How she wished she could be sitting with him, holding his hand when their banns were called.

Reverend Ellacott stood in his pulpit, giving his sermon, and after he had finished, he announced. "I am authorised to publish the banns of marriage between Isaac Langdon of Penstowe and Louisa Keslake of Stokebridge. This is the first time of asking. If any of you know cause or just impediment why these two persons should not be joined together in Holy Matrimony, you are to declare it."

Louisa looked towards her mother sitting in the pews on the other side, hoping she would keep her promise and not object to the calling of the banns. Relief flooded through her when she saw her lower her head and sit subdued beside her father.

~

The congregation walked outside, Samson waved to Louisa as she and the other servants returned to the manor. He looked around, seeing Isaac standing with his father. He walked to Thomas, tapping him on the shoulder. "May I have a quiet word, Tom?" Gesturing with his thumb to the corner of the churchyard.

Thomas leaned against a headstone. "What can I do for you, Sam?"

Samson stood in front of Thomas, shoving his hands in his pockets. "Louisa mentioned that your family may be going to Australia."

"We're still trying to make up our minds, but I think we'll go. Jack's already there, and there's more opportunities for the children, than here in Cornwall." Tilting his head slightly. "Are you worried about Louisa leaving?"

Samson grinned as he shook his head. "I know Louisa will be safe with Ike, although I'll miss her, of course. No, it's Sammy."

Thomas narrowed his eyebrows a fraction. "Sammy? What about Sammy?"

Samson pulled his hand from his pocket and scratched his head. "I know it's a lot to ask, but if you do decide to go to Australia, would you consider taking him with you?"

Thomas stroked his beard thoughtfully. "Don't you need him to help you on your farm?"

Samson smiled, "He's a very good worker, and I'll miss him too, but ever since he learned about Australia at school, he's wanted to go there."

Thomas lifted an eyebrow. "I didn't know that."

Samson grinned. "Well, he's only told me; he hasn't even told Louisa. They're very close, and he knows how much she'd miss him. He has every intention of going to Australia as soon as he's old enough. If he travels with your family, I know he'll be safe, and he'll be with Louisa. That would mean so much to her."

Thomas nodded. "I see." The corners of his eyes crinkled as he smiled. "So instead of traveling with my wife, five children, and daughter-in-law, I may be traveling with her brother as well." Scratching his head, he asked, "How old is the lad? So I can tell the agent when I see him."

"He'll turn thirteen the day after Christmas."

"I'll see if it can be arranged." Smiling as he shook Samson's hand.

"Thank you, Tom," putting his hand on top of his. "I won't say anything to Sammy until you know for sure."

"That may be wise, but I'll let you know as soon as we make a decision."

Samson patted Thomas on the upper arm, a silent plea for a favour that could shape Sammy's future. "Thank you."

~

The next Sunday, it was thrilling for Louisa to sit with Isaac and his family during church services. Her parents and Sammy were in the pew behind them with Luke, Jane, and their children.

After the sermon, Reverend Ellacott called their banns for the second time. Reaching for Isaac's hand, Louisa resisted the urge to turn around. Smiling at him when there was still no objection from her mother.

For Louisa, holding Isaac's hand as they walked out of the church felt so natural. Smiling when she spied Phillip waiting on the wall in their usual spot. His face nearly split in half by his grin.

Turning to Isaac, he smiled as he let go of her hand, indicating with his head to go to him. Dodging around people nearby, Phillip stood up as she approached, wrapping his arms around her, releasing her a moment later from his embrace.

"I'd like to congratulate you on your forthcoming wedding."

"It's nice not having to sneak around anymore," hearing Isaac stop next to her, glancing at him as she reached for his hand.

"I'm very happy for you both." Phillip reached to shake Isaac's hand, placed his other hand on top, looking him in the eye. "Will you promise to look after my dearest friend for me?"

"Of course I will, and Louisa and I hope you'll attend our wedding?"

Phillip beamed. "Nothing would prevent me from being there."

~

Samson stood talking to Luke; out of the corner of his eye, he saw Elizabeth standing alone, crying as she watched Louisa and Isaac talking to Phillip. He bid farewell to Luke and walked towards her, smiling as he crooked his elbow. "Let's go home."

She nodded, put her hand on his arm as they walked to Rose Cottage. All afternoon Samson noticed a tremendous change in Elizabeth's attitude, like a great weight had settled on her heart. He wondered if it was guilt. As Louisa returned from Penstowe, a hesitant smile flickered across Elizabeth's face, a subtle indication of shifting emotions, leaving Samson pondering the complexities within his wife.

38

Louisa wondered if her feet were touching the ground as she walked to the manor. Their banns had been called twice; soon she would be Mrs. Isaac Langdon. She flinched when Mrs. Tremaine approached her as she entered the servants' quarters. "Louisa, will you help cook today? Polly's attending her grandfather's funeral."

Putting her hand to her chest, she caught her breath and replied, "Of course." Pulling an apron off the peg, she tied it around her waist and walked to the kitchen.

Louisa was alone in the scullery, washing the last of the dinner dishes when the sound of unfamiliar footsteps made her turn around. Robert Engels stood in the doorway. Her heart skipped a beat at the sight of his snarling dog impression.

Doing her best to steady her voice, Louisa asked. "What can I do for you, Master Engels?" She was in the corner of the scullery; the only way out was beside him. Then she remembered what Grace had told her of how he enjoyed catching the kitchen staff alone.

"I think you know why I'm here."

His sneer frightened her. She looked to see if there was anything she could use to fight him off. Unfortunately, the plates were out of her reach, or she would have smashed one over his head.

"I heard your banns being called in church yesterday."

Louisa's heart raced; her breath caught in her throat as she faced Robert Engels. She felt a mixture of fear and disgust, the room closing in around her. Moving to step around him, he blocked her way. Trying to sound relaxed, she replied, "Yes, I'm getting married in two weeks."

Turning to walk the other way, he sidestepped in front of her again.

It was a dance of power and vulnerability, and Louisa found herself trapped in the corner, her only way out blocked by the looming figure before her.

"Well, maybe I can show you what'll be expected of you on your wedding night." Robert taunted, each word a menacing growl that echoed through the scullery.

A sense of helplessness washed over Louisa as he quickly grabbed her shoulder and pushed her hard against the bench, trying to kiss her. As Robert forced himself upon her, his breath reeking of ale, Louisa's mind raced. The scullery, once a haven of warmth, now felt like a claustrophobic nightmare.

Using his body weight to hold her against the bench, she could feel his erection against her hip. She yelled. "Get off me, you pig, I'm not a hedge-creeper."

"You will be after I'm finished, you bitch, I've finally got you where I want you. And this time you don't have your scissors." Robert hissed, lifting her dress and groping her breast.

Louisa continued to turn her face away from him, at the same time she was trying to push his hand off her breast and push her dress down. Realizing he was standing on one foot, as he tried to force her legs apart, she kicked out, hoping he would release her. But it was all in vain.

His strength surprised her, and even though her efforts were futile, she continued to fight and screamed as loud as she could.

"Shut up, you bitch." Robert hissed, slapping her on the left side of her face, while increasing his efforts to push her legs apart.

The force of the blow sent shockwaves through Louisa as white dots danced before her eyes, but she continued to fight like a wild cat possessed to prevent his bestial assault on her innocence. The confrontation unfolded, each passing second etching a traumatic memory into Louisa's mind. Robert's sneer transformed into a mask of malevolence, and the scullery walls seemed to close in on her.

The sudden intrusion of Mrs. Tremaine's voice provided a lifeline. "Master Engels, leave that poor girl alone *right now*. And get out of my kitchen this instant."

Louisa felt a brief reprieve as Robert released his hold, her legs buckling underneath her. Falling to her hands and knees, she sobbed uncontrollably. *Was this horrible ordeal finally over?*

The black ribbon from Robert's hair was under her hand. She brushed it away as far as she could.

Mrs. Tremaine ran to Louisa, helping her to her feet. She didn't think it was possible, but she sobbed even harder into the housekeeper's ample bosom.

"Are you all right, lass, did he hurt you?"

Shaking her head. "No, yes." She replied, her voice raw from screaming. "He was forcing himself on me; he did slap me, but-but if you hadn't wa-walked in when you did, he—he … I couldn't have fought him for much longer…"

The housekeeper held Louisa's arm as she struggled to reach a chair near the table. Her fingers trembled as she tugged at her clothes. She could barely look in the direction he had sauntered.

Louisa flinched in pain as Mrs. Tremaine touched her bruised cheek.

"That brute. Stay here; I'll fetch a damp cloth for the bruise."

Louisa's eyes opened wide with terror, as she clawed desperately at the housekeeper's arm. "Please don't leave me. I'm scared he might come back again."

Mrs. Tremaine knelt beside her.

They both froze a moment later when the door to the garden opened, relieved when Mrs. Gilbert walked in, carrying a basket full of eggs.

"My goodness, what on earth happened here?" Mrs. Gilbert cried, dumping the basket on the table, rushing to Louisa's side.

The housekeeper drew herself up from the floor. "Master Engels, that's what. I caught him attacking Louisa in the scullery."

"That scoundrel! I thought he'd have learnt his lesson when I caught him in here tormenting Polly. She was yelling at him to leave her alone, so I hit him on the head with my rolling pin. Poor Polly was terrified for weeks after."

The housekeeper turned to the cook. "Will you stay with Louisa while I get her a drop of brandy? Then I'm going to tell His Lordship about his brother's unsavoury behaviour; the servants are not here for his pleasure."

Mrs. Gilbert squatted beside Louisa, putting a gentle hand on her shoulder. "I'm going to make sure the girls are not alone in the scullery again." Looking up to the housekeeper. "I agree with you, Mrs. Tremaine, this can't go on."

Before the housekeeper left, she fetched a wet rag from the scullery, placing it in Louisa's hand. "Hold that on your face; it'll help with the swelling."

Holding the rag to her cheek, Louisa could feel pain throb with each beat of her heart. A pounding reminder of what Robert Engels had tried to do to her.

Mrs. Tremaine returned shortly with a small glass of amber-coloured liquid, handing it to Louisa. "Take a few small sips; brandy is very good after an experience like this." Concern filled her kindly face. "I'm going to see His Lordship now; will you be alright with Mrs. Gilbert until I get back?"

Louisa nodded as she took the glass in her free hand. The liquid sloshed slightly as she allowed a small amount to enter her mouth.

Dropping the wet rag, she opened her mouth and fanned her hand to cool the fire in her throat.

Picking up the rag, Mrs. Gilbert put it in her hand, smiling as she patted her shoulder. "I looked like that the first time I had some brandy. Try some more; you'll feel better soon."

Taking another sip of brandy, the feeling wasn't such a surprise, now she was aware of what to expect.

"Thank you," Louisa said gratefully.

Mrs. Gilbert studied the girl as she sat on the chair. "Do you feel a bit better now?"

Placing the empty glass on the table, Louisa held up her hand. "I'm still shaking." Letting the rag fall again, she put her head in her hands. "Why did he think he could do that to me?" Looking up at the cook again. "I'm getting married soon."

Mrs. Gilbert knelt beside her and whispered. "I know I shouldn't say this about gentry, but he's a beast."

Louisa snorted.

Mrs. Gilbert stood up. "I'm sorry to ask this after such a horrible experience, but we've got to get supper ready. Do you think you could peel some potatoes for me?"

Louisa nodded. "Yes, I think so." Trying to stand, she grabbed the table to steady herself.

Mrs. Gilbert gently pushed her back on the chair. "Sit down my girl. That brandy's makin' your legs wobble. I'll get the potatoes and a bucket, you can sit here and peel them, it'll take your mind off it."

Her eyes darted to the scullery. "But what if Master Engels comes back?"

Mrs. Gilbert laughed. "I'll be able to see you, so if he does come back, I'll hit him on the head with the bucket this time," smiling as she added. "And nothing would give me more pleasure."

Louisa gave a nervous laugh. "I'm sorry Mrs. Gilbert, but I l-looked in there, and all I could see was his evil grin."

"Nothing for you to be sorry about, he had no right to force himself upon you like that. You stay here, I'll get that bucket." Mrs. Gilbert gently stroked her hair. "That's my girl. I'll be back in a moment."

Placing a dozen or more potatoes on the table, Mrs. Gilbert returned to the scullery.

Listening to the sound of the pump handle being pulled up and down, the water running into the bucket, Louisa began to relax, safe in the knowledge there were people who would protect her. Or maybe it was the brandy making her feel that way.

Louisa's heart skipped a beat at the sound of footsteps. Trying to stand, her legs refused to hold her up, she fell on the chair again.

Selecting a large potato from the table, she was ready to throw it if necessary.

Relief flooded through her when the housekeeper emerged from the corridor with Lord Trevelen.

"M'lord, Mrs. Tremaine." Returning the potato to the table. "S-sorry, I thought it was Master Engels coming back."

Lord Trevelen pulled a chair from the table, sitting in front of Louisa. She lowered her head as he examined the emerging bruise on her face.

"Is that what my brother did to you?"

She looked up into his kind face, wondering how two brothers could be so different. Not trusting herself to speak, she simply nodded.

Mrs. Tremaine spoke, "I heard Louisa scream and guessed what was happening. I raced into the scullery and found Master Engels leaning over her, trying to force his will upon her in the most violent way. I told him to get out before he did anything else."

"Thank God." Lord Trevelen stood up, pushed the chair back under the table. "Rest assured Miss Keslake, I'm going to have a strong word with my brother about his deplorable behaviour. I've spoken to him before about it, but this time." His hands tightened into fists. "This time, I'm going to make him listen."

"Thank you, M'lord."

Lord Trevelen turned to the housekeeper. "Mrs. Tremaine, I think it would be best if Miss Keslake was escorted home. Would you be able to arrange that?"

"Yes, M'lord."

Turning on his heels, he was gone. Anger echoing in his heavy footsteps as he marched down the corridor.

Louisa pulled her head back as Mrs. Tremaine reached out to gently touch the purple colouring on her cheek. The housekeeper checked Lord Trevelen was out of earshot and whispered. "I'm so sorry you had to go through that. Just because Master Engels is gentry, doesn't mean he can do that sort of thing. I'm so thankful I heard you scream when I did."

Louisa let out a long breath. "So am I."

Mrs. Gilbert returned with the bucket, placing it on the table.

The housekeeper stood up straight, addressing the cook. "Mrs. Gilbert, His Lordship asks that Louisa be escorted home, who do you think would be the best person to do that?"

Tilting her head slightly. "Her Uncle Luke works in the garden; she might feel safer walking home with him."

Louisa grabbed Mrs. Gilbert's hand, giving a half smile. "Thank you."

Attempting to stand up, her legs buckled once more, narrowly avoiding the table as she fell into the arms of the housekeeper.

Mrs. Tremaine helped her sit, as Mrs. Gilbert said. "Brandy's good for shock, but not the legs. I don't think she'll be able to walk home."

Mrs. Tremaine straightened up. "No, she won't. I'll fetch Old John to take her home in the dog cart." Squatting down to Louisa, "Would you mind if John took you home?"

Louisa thought of the old coachman who worked in the stables. A kindly little white-haired man approaching eighty, he looked after the horses like they were his children. His shoulders hunched from age, but he still drove Lord and Lady Trevelen to church every Sunday in their carriage.

She nodded.

"Very well, I'll fetch him right away."

With Mrs. Gilbert's help, she climbed into the dog cart. John glanced at the bruise on her cheek, she was thankful when he said nothing.

John slowly walked the horse along the road, Louisa was still shaking as she sat beside him. Halfway to the crossroads, John glanced at her again.

Louisa touched the side of her cheek. "Mr. Holman, what do you think my Da's going to say about this?"

His voice deep and gravelly, he replied, "You won't be able to hide it from him, that's a nasty bruise." He loosened the reins and the horse slowed even more. "I know it were His Lordship's brother who did that to you."

She softly replied, "How did you know?"

He took a deep breath, avoiding her eyes. "Because he did the same to my niece's daughter over two year ago."

"Oh no. Is she alright?"

Tears shimmered in his eyes as he sniffed. "She's dead." He fiddled with the reins, as he kept his eyes on the road ahead.

Her throat clenched with sadness. "Dead? How?"

Anger thundered through him. "She were a sixteen-year-old girl, and after what he did to her, she became with child. She couldn't bear the shame." His voice began to shake as he continued. "One day she walked to Bradford, jumped off the bridge into the river, killed herself. They f-found her the next day."

Louisa shook her head slowly. "Oh Mr. Holman, I'm so sorry."

"Don't be, it weren't you that did it to 'er." Glancing at her briefly, he said, "Philippa may have killed herself, but Robert Engels drove her to it." He took a deep breath through his nose. "My sister never got over her granddaughter's death, it killed 'er not long after."

Reaching the crossroads, he turned left towards Stokebridge. "He always were a heller, his mother pampered him too much." John continued. "Robert Engels only uses his strength on women and young girls because they can't fight back. He's nothing but a coward."

"He was too strong for me."

John turned to Louisa as he stopped the horse. "I've met men who use their fists on their wives and children, but as soon as a man confronts them, they run."

"He did walk away when Mrs. Tremaine told him to leave me alone. I was lucky she heard me scream."

John flicked the reins, the horse walked on. "Aye, you were, no girl should have to suffer like that."

Guilt flooded over her. "I suppose I should be grateful he didn't do to me what he did to Philippa."

He nodded as he looked ahead. "Every father who has a daughter working at the manor worries about Robert Engels, he's raped at least two girls that I know of, heaven knows how many more. There's also a lot of men who won't let their daughters work there because of him, even though the wages they'd earn would help."

"Maybe that's why Uncle Luke said my cousin Hannah's not going to work there when she's old enough."

"Probably." He turned to her as they passed Snowdrop Cottage. "What do you think your Da's going to say?"

"I don't know, but I'd hate for him to confront Master Engels at church." Putting her hand to her cheek again. "And I hope this bruise goes away before next Sunday, I *don't* want Ike to know what happened."

John clicked his tongue. "Your Ike's a strong lad, I'd hate to see what he'd do to him if he found out."

Rose Cottage was in sight when Louisa said, "I think I'll tell Da not to say anything to Master Engels when he sees him at church. And His Lordship did say he would speak to his brother."

John pulled the horse to a stop outside the front door and turned to her. "You tell your Da that Master Engels isn't worth hurting his hands on. One day, he'll get what's coming to him. I just hope I'm around to see it." Jumping from the cart with more agility than she thought possible, he turned to her. "Wait here while I knock on the door."

Elizabeth answered a moment later, her hands covered in flour and pastry mix. She rushed to Louisa as she climbed from the cart, putting a hand on her cheek, leaving creamy coloured smudges on her face. "My goodness, what on earth happened to you?"

John returned to Louisa's side, helping her walk to the door, Elizabeth hovering by their side. "What happened?"

Crossing the threshold of her home, Louisa's legs began to tremble once more. "Please Mother, I need to sit down."

Elizabeth helped her to the table while John stood by the door. "Mrs. Keslake, I think you'd better get your husband."

Elizabeth's eyes darted from Louisa, to John, and back again. "Will someone please tell me what happened?"

Louisa looked up with haunted eyes. "Please Mother, go fetch Da."

Wiping her hands on her apron, Elizabeth raced to the back door, and shouted. "Samson! Sammy! Come quickly!"

John coughed from the front door. "I'll be leaving now, Miss Keslake, you'll be safe with your family."

Louisa gave him a half smile, "Thank you, Mr. Holman. For everything."

Elizabeth returned to sit beside her, patting her on the arm. "Will you please tell me what happened?"

Louisa let out a sigh, "I'll wait till Da gets here, I'm only going to explain it once."

Soon, Samson and Sammy rushed in the back door. Samson saw the bruising on her face, knelt beside her, putting a gentle hand on her shoulder, Sammy, one step behind.

"What happened to you?" Samson asked.

"Who did this to you?" Sammy asked at the same time.

Louisa explained what had transpired in the scullery, when she finished, she watched both her parents stand up. Her father's face turned deep shades of red and purple, her mother stood opened mouthed.

"That *bastard*!" Samson bellowed.

Elizabeth stared at him. "Samson Keslake! I'll not have that sort of language in this house."

He turned to face her, the veins pulsating in his neck as he shouted. "Honestly Elizabeth, you really make me mad sometimes."

She backed away two steps.

Samson pointed in the direction of the manor, shouting again. "That *bastard* tried to violate our daughter, and you're worried about my language! You should be angry at him for what he did to Louisa, not at me." Throwing his hands in the air, he sat next to Louisa, his elbow sitting in the pastry mixture. Putting his head on his hand, he began running the other through his hair.

Sammy stood near their mother, he was clenching, and unclenching his fists. Louisa knew he would be outraged by the violence inflicted on her.

Louisa moved closer to her father, putting her arm around his shoulders, speaking while her own tears flowed. "Da, I d-don't want you to say or do anything to him, Lord Trevelen is going to s-speak to him, and *please*, don't tell Ike." She sniffed loudly. "Besides, I'm going to be finishing in a couple of days, so I won't see him at the manor anymore." Sniffing again, she touched her cheek. "This will heal, and thankfully, that was all he did to me."

Samson put his arms around her, burying his face in her hair. Louisa felt moisture on her neck, realizing her father was crying too.

~

Louisa was peeling potatoes in the kitchen of the manor when Robert walked in, sneering at her. "Did you think I would leave you alone? *You bitch!*"

She threw the potato at him, but he only laughed. It was the sort of laugh she would expect from the devil. She ran towards the door leading to the garden, but the handle came off in her hand. She turned around, throwing it at him. He laughed again.

She stood frozen with terror, as he walked towards her, with an evil grin, and eyes the colour of a furnace. Reaching out, he grabbed her shoulder, her skin burning from his touch.

"Get off me!" She shouted.

She banged her fists against his chest, but they seemed to go right through his body.

"Leave me alone!" She shouted again.

She looked up as he laughed. "I'm going to finish what I started this afternoon; *you bitch!*" Leaning forward he tried to kiss her.

Putting her hands in front of her face, closing her eyes, Louisa screamed as Robert shook her.

Opening her eyes, she realised she was in her own bed. By the dim light of the coals, she saw it was her mother who was shaking her.

"Louisa, are you alright? You were shouting and screaming."

She sat up, looked around as relief flowed through her. Flopping back on the pillow, she pulled the feather quilt over her head. "I'm sorry if I woke you Mother." Her voice muffled.

"Did you have a dream about what happened?"

Louisa flipped the quilt back and said firmly, "It wasn't a dream; it was a nightmare."

Elizabeth sat on the edge of the bed, the framework creaking. "Do you want me to stay with you?"

Louisa put her hand on her mother's arm. "No, I'll be all right, thank you."

Elizabeth stood up. "If you're sure."

Even though there was very little light in the room, she smiled, "I'm sure. Good night, Mother."

The door closed and Louisa lay in the darkness, trying to forget about the nightmare. She wondered how often she would have them. Her thoughts drifted to Philippa who took her own life, unable to endure the shame of what Robert Engels had done to her.

She recalled the words Grace had said, just after she became the sewing maid. Was the kitchen maid Robert attacked Philippa? Did he even care how his actions had affected her or any other girl he attacked?

Closing her eyes briefly, she thanked God Mrs. Tremaine heard her scream.

Louisa rolled onto her side, pulling the quilt over her shoulder, wondering if she could sleep. Putting her hand to her cheek, it was tender and swollen. She said a brief prayer. "Please God, can you make this bruise go away by Sunday? I don't want to keep secrets from Ike, but I think you'll understand why I need to keep this one."

Closing her eyes, she had a vision of her Aunty Jane hugging her. Maybe it was her mother wanting to make her feel safe, preparing to sit with her till she fell asleep. The last thing she remembered was a tiny flickering flame in the fire.

39

Louisa was tidying up the patterns in the sewing room the following morning when she heard footsteps along the corridor. Picking up the cutting shears; she was ready to protect herself.

Hearing the familiar rustle of silk, she let out the breath she didn't realise she was holding. As Lady Trevelen walked in the door, an envelope in her hand, Louisa replaced the shears on the table.

Lady Trevelen stopped when she heard the clunk of the scissors. "Oh Louisa, I'm so sorry. My husband told me what happened to you yesterday."

She bobbed to a curtsy, burst into tears, and began hiccupping. "He said." Hic. "He was going to turn me into a..." Hic. "*A hedge-creeper.*"

Putting her hand out for the chair, she only managed to get half her bottom on it.

"May God forgive me, M'lady." Fumbling for her handkerchief, wiping her nose. "But if Master Engels comes near me again, I'll use whatever weapon I can find to protect myself."

Lady Trevelen squatted in front of her. "You don't have to worry about him anymore. My husband told him he'd throw him out without a penny if he touches any of the servants again. In the meantime, I'll permit you to keep the door locked while you're working."

Louisa sniffed and wiped her eyes with shaking hands. "Thank you, M'lady."

"I'm so sorry," she said again. "I can see how much his behaviour has affected you. He had no right."

Lady Trevelen glanced at the dress on the wicker dummy and stepped towards it, lifting the sleeve of the dress to examine the embroidery on the cuff, delicately running her fingers over the daisies. "You've created a wonderful gown for me, Louisa; I think I'll wear it for Christmas."

Louisa stood beside her, fiddling with the collar. "I've only got to sew the lace on the bodice, then this dress is finished."

"It's beautiful." Letting the sleeve fall, she handed the envelope to Louisa. "Here's the letter you asked for."

Bobbing again. "Thank you, M'lady." Turning it over, she recognised the seal of Trevelen Manor—a letter 'T' sprouting from the top of an acorn.

"There's a pound in there from me; I felt you deserve it for your service. Also, another from my husband for what his brother did to you."

"T-thank you, M'lady. I don't know what to say."

Lady Trevelen smiled as she put her hand on Louisa's arm. "No, thank *you*."

~

Louisa walked out the door of the servants' quarters at the end of the day and was surprised to see her uncle leaning on a tree.

"Uncle Luke! Are you waiting for me?"

"Aye, I thought we could walk home together," offering his arm.

"Thank you."

They had been walking a few minutes before Luke spoke, "Old John told me what happened yesterday."

Louisa shook her head. "I was lucky Mrs. Tremaine heard me scream."

"So John said. He suggested I walk you home to make sure you were safe."

Louisa saw him glance at her face, and she touched her cheek. "He did that when I screamed; thank goodness, that was all he did."

"When Hannah asked me about working at the manor, I told her she didn't need to as I was earning a good wage. The truth is, I didn't want her working there because of him."

"M'lady told me His Lordship said if he does it again, he'll throw him out without a penny."

"Serve him right. Have you told Ike?"

"No, and I don't want him to know. If Ike found out what he'd done, he might confront Master Engels, which could end badly. I don't want to be responsible for that."

Luke stopped, smiling as he put his finger under her chin, "My darling Louisa, you are wise beyond your years; no wonder Ike loves you so much."

~

Louisa was relieved when her father said on Sunday morning that the bruise was nearly gone; only a tiny patch of purple and yellow remained on her cheekbone. She could laugh it off if Isaac asked her about it, saying the wicker dummy fell on her.

Louisa entered the church, her eyes scanning the congregation. Lord and Lady Trevelen occupied their privately owned pew, and Robert lingered next to his brother. An unsettling sensation twisted in her stomach as his narrowing eyes locked onto hers when he turned around. Her heart began to race as he held her gaze, but a stern word in his ear from Lord Trevelen made him turn to the front quickly.

Glancing at her father, he put a reassuring hand on her arm. She smiled at him, knowing he would lay down his life to protect her. She sat beside Isaac.

~

Samson noticed Lord Trevelen hastily ushering his brother into their carriage after services. It rocked slightly as he sat down heavily. Lord Trevelen pointed his finger at him. "You stay there until we're ready to leave." Bunching his hand into a fist and holding it before his face, he added. "And don't you dare get out." Robert pouted as he folded his arms and flopped back in the seat. Matthew turned on his heels.

Lord Trevelen glanced around, apparently looking for someone.

Samson breathed easier; Louisa was safe with Isaac's family. Lord Trevelen walked towards him.

Samson was pleased that His Lordship had swiftly removed his brother from the church grounds. If Robert Engels was standing around with the other congregation members, he may have confronted him. The memory of what he had done to his daughter was still raw.

Shaking his head, Samson waited until he reached him. "M'lord."

Lord Trevelen spoke, "Mr. Keslake, may I have a word in private, please?"

Samson walked away from the crowd, indicating to Lord Trevelen to follow; his good mood vanished as he removed his cap. "What can I do for you, M'lord?"

Lord Trevelen floundered with embarrassment, "Firstly, let me tell you I am deeply ashamed of what my brother did to your daughter the other day." Glancing at the carriage. "I've spoken with him about his behaviour, and he knows what will happen if he attacks another servant."

Samson nodded, his face stern. "Well, I *hope* it doesn't happen again."

Lord Trevelen continued. "Mr. Keslake, Sam. Can you please forget for a moment that I'm lord of the manor? If you wish to say something to me, please say it."

Samson looked him in the eye, raking his fingers through his hair, deciding whether to continue. He rarely got the chance to speak to Lord Trevelen; he settled on telling him everything he knew.

"From what Louisa's told me, it's not the first time he's tried to force himself upon her."

The veins pulsated in Lord Trevelen's neck as he breathed quickly through his nose.

Samson wondered what was going through His Lordship's mind as he shifted his weight from one foot to the other. He continued. "Louisa told me he raped another girl two years ago?"

Lord Trevelen's eyes widened, and his nostrils flared. "What!"

Samson added. "That poor girl became with child. She killed herself because she didn't want to bring shame to her family."

Lord Trevelen's face reddened even more as he pulled his hands into fists. "I didn't know that." Glancing at the carriage. "How many others have there been?"

"I don't know; Louisa said the servants do their best not to be alone with him. They're terrified of what he might do. Louisa's no longer working for Her Ladyship so I can breathe easier. It's the girls still working at the manor I worry about."

Lord Trevelen simmered with rage when he spoke. "His behaviour is unforgivable; I don't want the servants living in fear. I feel ashamed." He lowered his head. "Our father never taught my brother respect, and his mother indulged him too much." Reaching to shake Samson's hand. "Thank you for telling me." He turned towards the carriage.

Samson remained by the chestnut tree as Lord Trevelen ushered his wife and children into the carriage and glared at his brother. He wondered what Matthew would say to Robert when they returned to the manor.

Turning around, he saw Elizabeth standing alone, crying.

Walking towards her, he gently put his arm around her shoulders. "Come on, love."

She walked with him to Rose Cottage.

By the light of the fire, Samson and Elizabeth sat at the table after Louisa and Sammy had gone to bed. Elizabeth rested one elbow on the table, banging the palm of her hand on her forehead before looking up at him.

"Oh, Samson, what have I done to our daughter." Wiping her eyes with her apron. "At church this morning, I saw her with Isaac; any fool can see how much they love each other. Why didn't I just let them walk out together? Instead of trying to push her onto Master Hill." Putting her head on her folded arms.

"Phillip will always be her friend; it's just that she loves Ike."

Her voice muffled as she talked. "I've driven her away, and Sammy too. I don't think they'll ever love me as much as they love you or Jane."

Samson put his hand on hers. "You did the best you could."

Lifting her head. "They don't even call me 'Ma'; they always call me Mother."

"They've always heard Jane and me say, 'Go and see your mother'."

Softly, she replied, "I haven't been a good mother to them, have I?"

Her tears fell on the table, and Samson's heart went out to her. He struggled, unsure how to comfort her. She was right; she hadn't been a good mother to their children, but he wouldn't voice those thoughts when she was so vulnerable.

Wiping her eyes with her apron once more, she looked at him. "Jane is a much better mother to them than I ever was." More tears flowed down her cheek. "They must hate me so much. Will they ever know that I do care about them?"

Samson kissed her cheek, tasting the salt from her tears. "I think they know." Standing up, he reached for her hand. "Come on, love, it's time for bed."

She nodded, accepted his hand, and walked up the stairs with him.

Samson turned when he didn't hear Elizabeth walk along the landing. "What's wrong?"

"Samson, will you sleep in our room tonight? I don't want to be alone." Extending her hand to him.

Removing his hand from the door handle of the front room, he reached for her hand, following her to the room they used to share.

He was still holding her hand when he closed the door. Elizabeth put her head on his chest and cried again. Shaking with every sob.

Samson had no idea how long they stood there. Eventually, he sensed she had no tears left to cry. "Are you all right, love?"

She looked up at him, her face and eyes red. "I'm so sorry." More tears fell down her cheek.

"Don't worry about that now; let's get you to bed." She stood looking like an abandoned fawn; his heart went out to her again. "Are you sure you want me to stay?"

She smiled slightly, stood on her tiptoes, and kissed him in a way he had almost forgotten. "Does that answer your question?"

Kissing passionately, he hurriedly pulled his braces off his shoulders as she pulled his shirt from his trousers.

Soon, clothes lay scattered on the floor. Naked under the blankets, they embraced as if there were no tomorrow.

Afterwards, as they lay in the darkness, Elizabeth's head in the curve of his shoulder, she whispered, "I have a lot to be thankful for; I should have realised it before now." She kissed him once more, and soon, they were making love again.

~

Sunlight streaming through the window stirred Samson awake. At first, he needed to figure out where he was. Glancing around the room, he smiled as he remembered the night before.

He was lying against Elizabeth's back, his arm around her waist. Both were still naked.

Reaching up, he fondled her breast while kissing her slender neck.

She turned to him and smiled, "I'd forgotten how much I enjoyed being with you."

He kissed her on the forehead. "I enjoy being with you too." Very soon, they were aroused again.

~

Samson smirked, savouring the puzzled expressions on the children's faces. Elizabeth lifted one side of her mouth whenever she looked at him. *Let them wonder*, he thought.

Louisa finished her tea, rising from her seat. "I'm going to Aunty Jane's," She said, giving Samson a peck on the cheek. "Bye, Da."

Elizabeth stood up also, putting a gentle hand on her daughter's arm. "Louisa, I want you to know I'm so sorry. For everything." Kissing her before she walked to the front door.

The crisp morning air seeped in the back door when Elizabeth walked outside to feed the chickens, and Sammy turned to him. "Is Mother alright? You didn't sleep in my room last night."

Samson nodded as he remembered the night before. "She's grand." Hiding his smile in his cup.

Sammy finished his porridge, saying no more.

Elizabeth returned inside, eggs held up in her apron. Samson turned to Sammy. "Can you feed pigs and start harvesting corn in bottom field? I'll be down to help you dreckly."

Sammy drank the last of his tea and left.

Samson walked over to Elizabeth as she put the last egg in the basket on the cupboard. He kissed the back of her neck, causing her to giggle.

She turned around, playfully hitting him on the chest. "Haven't you got corn to harvest?"

He picked her up and began walking towards the stairs. "The corn can wait." They laughed all the way to the bedroom.

~

There were three days until her wedding; Louisa sat at the table in Rose Cottage, sewing the buttons on her dress.

Elizabeth walked down the stairs, sitting opposite her daughter. "Louisa, I'm so sorry about everything. Your father made me realise the other day that I haven't been a good mother to you and Sammy; you deserve an explanation."

Louisa looked up when her mother began talking; she had been so different the last few days that she wasn't sure how to react. She put her sewing on the table.

Elizabeth began with the story of her love for Matthew and that the previous Lord Trevelen would not allow them to marry.

"When I told your father of the mess I was in, he said he would marry me so at least the child would have a father; I was pleased he would do that for me. I was very fond of him, and he was a good friend, but I didn't realise how much he loved me then."

Louisa was shocked by her mother's admission. "Why did you marry Da if you didn't love him?"

Briefly wringing her hands together, she continued. "I thought if I couldn't marry Matthew, I could have his child. Samson was giving me the chance to keep the baby, so I married him. I want you to know that I do love your father, just not like I loved Matthew."

Louisa shook her head. "You need to tell Da that."

"I think he knows, but I'll talk to him later, but right now, you need to hear the rest of the story." Breathing deeply through her nose, she resumed. "When Henry arrived early and died after a couple of hours, I was heartbroken. Everyone kept saying, '*You can always have another baby.*' yes, I could, but not Matthew's. I was angry at everybody; I realise now it was from the pain of losing Henry."

Elizabeth looked down and shook her head. "Henry was my only link to Matthew. I'd lost the man I loved, and then I lost his child." Looking up at Louisa, she rubbed her temples for a moment. "I began to think there was no God because if He did exist, He wouldn't have taken Henry from me."

"Aunty Jane told me you weren't interested in me when I was a baby."

"I'm sorry to say that's true; I kept cursing God because He let you live but took Matthew's son; it wasn't fair."

"What about Sammy? Aunty Jane said she had to feed and look after him because you didn't even want to look at him; why was that?"

"When Mrs. Bosley told me I had a healthy son, all I could think about was Henry; I cursed God again for taking him. Henry was the son of the Lord of Trevelen Manor, and Sammy was the son of a farmer."

Elizabeth hesitated a moment, trying to find the right words. "I realise now I should have rejoiced at yours and Sammy's birth, but I was still grieving over Henry, and it was wrong; you both deserved better than that."

"Is that why you don't love us? Because we're the children of a farmer?"

"That's the strange thing; it wasn't until the other day that I realised how much I do love you and Sammy. When you were younger, I pushed you both onto Samson and Jane; I was too miserable to look after you as I should have. There's no going back, and unfortunately, it's too late for us to be close now."

Louisa looked at her mother sadly as she continued. "I'm pleased you and Sammy spent a lot of time with your father. He taught you well, and anyone can see he adores you both. Jane and Luke deserve some of the credit; they did a good job raising you, too."

Elizabeth's gaze shifted to the dress on the table. "I'm glad Jane taught you to sew," she said. "She's much better than I am; it's a good skill to have."

Louisa smiled, "Lady Trevelen was pleased with the dresses I made for her."

Her mother smiled back, "I saw some she wore to church; they're beautiful. She *should* be pleased."

Elizabeth walked around to Louisa's side of the table. Louisa stood up, and they hugged each other. When Elizabeth pulled away, she stood holding Louisa's hands. "I should never have objected to Isaac courting you; he's a good man, and I can see that now. I hope you both have a wonderful life together."

"I'm sure we will."

Elizabeth wiped her eyes with her apron, a bittersweet smile playing on her lips. "I'm going to miss you after you're married; I know Sammy will, too."

"We're only going to live with Ike's family until a farm becomes available." Deciding not to mention Australia until she knew for sure. "I'll come and visit at least twice a week. And you'll always see us at church on Sundays."

The morning of September twenty-ninth unfolded with a bright, cloudless sky, and a gentle warmth graced the early autumn day. The soft breeze danced, caressing strands of Louisa's hair, as Isaac guided her towards the entrance of Stokebridge church.

Walking down the aisle, Isaac caught the delighted gasp escaping Louisa's lips. Glancing to his left, Phillip stood in the pew, accompanied by a young man - he assumed it was Phillip's friend, Jonathon. Both received a radiant beam from Louisa before she turned to smile at Isaac once more. At the altar, Reverend Ellacott stood in his immaculate white cassock.

Isaac smiled, captivated by Louisa, adorned in a new dress she had made for the occasion. The buttercup yellow accentuated her hazel eyes and wavy brown hair. She had never looked more beautiful.

Exchanging vows at the altar, surrounded by their families and friends in the pews, Isaac couldn't help but watch Louisa. Her focus on Reverend Ellacott, she sensed his gaze, shifting her attention to meet his. In that moment, no one else existed; they were the only two people in the world.

Isaac's heart swelled as he thought of the day he fell in love with Louisa. She smiled at him again, showing the cute little dimple on her cheek that he loved so much. They were about to start a new life together as husband and wife.

Reverend Ellacott interrupted his thoughts when he said. "Isaac and Louisa, you have declared your love before the church. May the Lord, in His goodness, strengthen your love and fill you both with His blessings. What God has joined; men must not divide. Amen."

Walking back down the aisle, they encountered numerous family members eager to offer congratulations and express their joy. When they reached Phillip, Louisa embraced him before hugging Jonathon.

"What a wonderful surprise to see you here today. I'm glad you were able to make the trip from Devon."

"When Phillip told me about your wedding, I was determined to be here to share your special day."

Louisa glanced at Isaac and Phillip. "I'm so glad you did."

~

Walking outside, loud cheers and warm sunshine greeted the newly married couple. The ladies from the village had tables outside the church wall weighed down with pasties and apple pies. At another table, stood several jugs of Mrs. Bosley's apple cider.

Isaac was shaking hands with his father, brothers, Samson, and Uncle Luke; so many people were demanding their attention.

Walking to the cider table, he poured himself a tankard. He stood and waited when Elizabeth approached him.

Looking at him thoughtfully, she confessed. "Isaac, I'm so sorry for what I did to stop you from marrying Louisa; if I had looked at you both properly, I'd have seen you were in love. I realise now you're the man who makes my daughter happy."

Isaac looked at Elizabeth and saw a softer side to her, one he thought he would never see. "Thank you for your honesty, Mrs. Keslake. I love your daughter, and I'll look after her the best I can."

Quickly hugging him, he wondered if it was to hide her blushing face. She spoke into his upper arm, "We only want her to be happy." Releasing her hold, she walked away swiftly, leaving him slightly bewildered as he picked up his tankard.

~

Louisa hugged the well-wishers standing on the road and tried hard not to cry as she hugged her Aunty Jane and Sammy, but failed. A pasty appeared in her hand as she hugged Isaac's sisters, Grace and Martha.

Realising she was hungry; she took a bite. That was all she needed to determine that her mother made it. As pastry crumbs fell from her hand, sparrows flew to the ground, collecting them to return to their nests.

She brushed the crumbs from her hands after eating the last piece when Phillip and Jonathon walked up to her. They, too, were wrapping their mouths around giant pasties.

Crumbs fell from Phillip's mouth as he spoke. "I've never had a Cornish pasty before; they're delicious."

Jonathon nodded as he finished his mouthful. "I agree, they're wonderful."

Louisa laughed. "Don't forget to have an apple pie; I think Aunty Jane made them."

Isaac walked towards them, smiling as he carried a tankard of cider.

Phillip said. "Ike, I'd like to introduce you to my friend Jonathon Northy."

Putting the tankard into his left hand, Isaac shook the offered hand. "So pleased you could attend our wedding today, Jonathon." Grinning as he glanced at Louisa. "Seeing you here today has brought great joy to my wife."

"Then I've not wasted my journey," smiling at Louisa. "I wish you both happiness in your new life together."

"Thank you, Jonathon." Taking a mouthful from his tankard. "Have you tried the apple cider yet?"

Both men shook their heads. "Don't drink too much, or they'll have to take you home in a handcart," Isaac laughed. "I don't know what Mrs. Bosley puts in it, but I'll only have a couple." Giving Phillip a wink.

The sound of a violin being tuned caught their attention; turning to the sound, Louisa clapped her hands. "How wonderful, Mr. Pengelly's going to play for us."

He began playing the Flora dance. Isaac put his tankard on the church wall and reached for Louisa's hand, "Shall we dance?" He turned to Phillip and Jonathon. "Are you going to join us?"

Phillip shook his head. "I've never seen this dance before; you enjoy dancing with your bride."

Isaac and Louisa joined the line of couples as they danced to the music. They were stepping forward, stepping back, turning around on the spot before changing partners and continuing up the road. Once the line of dancers reached Snowdrop Cottage, they danced their way back to the church.

Fred Pengelly put his violin on the table near the cider, picked up a tankard and drank deeply. He was grinning as he let out a deep sigh.

The crowd called out. "More, more, more."

"You'll have to wait until I've quenched my thirst." Wiping the back of his hand over his mouth, beaming as he lifted the tankard towards Mrs. Bosley. "And I hope you don't mind if it takes another drink or two of this fine cider to do it."

Mrs. Bosley blushed and flicked her hand at the wrist. "Get away with ya, you ol' rascal."

~

The afternoon unfolded in a symphony of conversation, laughter, and dancing. As twilight cast its gentle glow, guests began to meander back to their cottages or village.

Isaac and Louisa strolled hand in hand towards Rose Cottage. Samson, Elizabeth, and Sammy bid them farewell, heading to Daffodil Cottage to spend the night with Luke and Jane. This generous gesture left the newlyweds with the solitude of their first night together.

Isaac and Louisa walked in the front door and stood near the table. She seemed to glow in the light of the fire. He held her hands. "I don't think I have ever seen you look so lovely." Bending to kiss her. "Are you nervous?"

Louisa giggled softly. "A little."

Isaac joined her amusement. "Good, I didn't want to be the only one."

His hand found the nape of her neck, fingers playing with her hair as it cascaded down her back. Pulling her closer; their foreheads were touching. Their kissing quickly became frenzied.

Isaac's hand ventured to her breast, seeking to undo the buttons down the front. Louisa playfully pushed him away when a determined tug pulled off the third.

Laughing, she picked up the button, placing it on the table. "Ike, I don't want you to ruin my new dress. Besides, there's no need to rush. Shall we go upstairs?"

Reaching for his hand, she led him to her parent's bedroom, where the glow from the fire bathed the room in a comforting light. Isaac suggested, "I'll go outside while you change into your nightgown," turning towards the door.

"No, please stay." Louisa's plea halted him in his tracks.

Standing by the end of the bed, Louisa undid the buttons and shed her dress. Eventually, the layers of corset, petticoat, chemise, and bloomers, leaving her standing completely naked before Isaac.

His gaze wandered from her head to her toes as he slowly walked towards her. "You're such a beautiful woman, Louisa. I count my blessings daily that you've fallen in love with me."

"I count my blessings too."

Reaching up to pull the braces off his shoulders, she pulled his shirt from his trousers and began undoing the buttons. Isaac pulled her closer, kissing her bare shoulders and neck. She shivered as his beard tickled her skin.

After removing his clothes, they stood by the fire. Tracing a finger from her cheek, down her neck and over her breast, Isaac kissed her again. Grabbing his hand, Louisa led him to the bed.

Looking at each other as they lay on their sides, Isaac kissed her neck, slowly moving towards her breast, kissing her nipples. She shivered again. Was it from anticipation?

She stopped kissing his shoulder to let out a small groan, wrapping her arms around his neck.

Moving over her upper body, he gently pushed her onto her back, and their kissing intensified. Feeling him harden, she opened her legs, and Isaac entered her.

Letting out a small cry of pain, he paused, turning to her. "Did I hurt you?"

She shook her head and smiled, "No, it's all right; Aunty Jane told me it would hurt the first time. Don't stop."

"Only if you're sure?"

She kissed him on the shoulder and neck, saying between kisses. "Yes, I'm sure."

Their rhythmic movements intensified, and Isaac groaned, eventually collapsing on top of her before rolling off.

Under the feather quilt, they lay gazing at each other. Louisa nestled with her head in the crook of his shoulder. Isaac gently ran his fingers down her cheek and neck. "I'm sorry I hurt you."

"Don't be sorry; it won't hurt next time." Smiling in the diminishing firelight.

Isaac chuckled. "There's going to be a next time?"

"Of course, there is." Propping herself onto her elbow, she kissed him passionately, instantly reigniting his arousal.

~

In the morning, Louisa made breakfast while Isaac tended the pigs and chickens. As the aroma of cooking filled the cottage, they discussed their plans to move to Penstowe.

"Where are we going to sleep in your home?"

"Ma said we can have my room, Jacob and Elijah are sleeping in the crog loft." Isaac laughed. "They're not sleeping with us."

"Doesn't it get cold in the loft?"

"Yes, it does. But if we go to Australia, it won't be for long."

Louisa put plates of bacon and eggs on the table, sitting opposite Isaac. Picking up her knife and fork, she hesitated. "Mother and I had a good talk a few days ago."

Isaac looked up, wiping egg yolk from his mouth. "What about?"

"She told me about her life, Da, and my brother Henry, who died." Cutting a piece of bacon, holding it above her plate before continuing. "She also said she was sorry for not being a good mother to me and Sammy," putting the food in her mouth.

Isaac stopped mid-chew and gaped at her, his expression turned serious. "She came up to me yesterday, saying she was sorry for everything she'd done to keep us apart. It's a pity she didn't explain all this before." He finished the last piece of his bacon.

Wiping a small tear from her eye, Louisa said, "She's so different and even admitted it was too late for us to become close," finishing the last bit of egg.

Taking the kettle off the hook over the fire, she refilled the teapot. Feeling Isaac's arms around her, she turned to kiss him. He nuzzled her neck. "I don't want to talk about your mother right now; we have better things to do." Waggling his eyebrows suggestively.

Louisa grinned. "Yes, we do." Taking his hand, she led him up the stairs.

When the first church bells rang, Louisa sat bolt upright, holding the quilt over her breasts, "We'd better get dressed for church."

Isaac gently pulled her onto the pillow. "What's the hurry." Grinning at her. "The church is next door; we've got plenty of time." He kissed her again, making her forget about getting ready.

~

Isaac and Louisa held hands, giggling as they rushed in the church door, sitting next to Jacob as the organ began to play.

Jacob elbowed him in the ribs and teased him. "I gather you were too busy in bed to get ready for church."

Isaac grinned as he pushed him playfully with his shoulder. "One day, you'll have the same problem."

The organist stopped playing as Reverend Ellacott stepped up to the pulpit. "Before we begin today, I'd like you all to join me in welcoming Mr. and Mrs. Isaac Langdon to our congregation. Some of you may have attended their wedding yesterday." Smiling as he nodded in their direction.

Louisa and Isaac walked to Penstowe after church; he carried her few belongings in a borrowed carpet bag.

Isaac put his arm around her shoulder as they strolled along the road; she looped the handle of the sewing basket over her arm.

"Have your parents made up their minds about Australia yet?"

Isaac removed his arm from her shoulder, putting the bag in the other hand. "Da's going to see the agent on Tuesday, then we'll know if we're going." He stopped for a moment. "Are you worried about leaving your family?"

She took a deep breath through her nose. "Of course, I'll miss Sammy, not just because he's my brother, he's also my best friend. And Da, I'll miss him terribly, even Mother." A tear fell down her cheek.

Louisa's heart wrestled with conflicting emotions; the idea of the daunting sea journey to the other side of the world stirred a mixture of fear and excitement within her, but staying in Cornwall wouldn't give them the opportunities of a new country.

But Isaac was her husband now; she would go wherever he went. "What do you think it will be like in Australia?"

"I can only say what Jack's told us. He said the seasons are opposite to Cornwall, and it gets hot in summer, and there's no snow in winter." Isaac laughed. "Jack said last Christmas, he went swimming in the river because it was so hot."

"It's going to be a completely different way of life from what we know here."

"There's lots of strange animals and plenty of land." Shifting the bag to his other hand, Isaac felt the weight of their uncertain future together. "It would be nice to own some land, not having to pay rent to the manor."

She looped her arm through his. 'Well, we'll just have to wait and see, won't we?" she said, a brave smile masking the uncertainty in her voice.

~

Isaac was eating his porridge when his father said, "Ike, I'm going to see the agent today in Bradford. Would you come with me?"

Holding his spoon over the bowl, he replied, "I was going to help Jacob pull corn stalks in the lower field."

Gulping a mouthful of his tea, Thomas placed the tin mug on the table. "Elijah can help Jacob; I'd like you to come with me because you can read; and we have to tell the agent you've married."

Casting a quick glance at Louisa by his side, he replied, "All right, Da," before resuming his meal.

Isaac kissed Louisa, grabbed his cap, and followed his father out the door.

Trevelen Manor was an imposing sight before them when they reached the crossroads.

Turning left towards Bradford, Thomas asked, "Do you want to go to Australia?"

Isaac considered the question. "I think we'd have a better life there." Facing his father, "Have you changed your mind?"

"No, I don't think so. I was thinking if we do go, and Louisa wants to stay in Cornwall to be with her family, maybe you could take over the tenancy of Pine Cottage."

Eventually, Isaac replied, "I don't want to stay here if you leave, and Louisa's happy to go to Australia. If you decide to go, Louisa and I will go with you. Of course, she'll miss her family."

Thomas chuckled, a mischievous twinkle in his eye. "Maybe she won't miss them all," he teased, a playful grin playing on his lips.

Isaac grabbed his father by the arm, making him stop. "What are you talking about?"

Thomas grinned. "Sam asked me if we could take Sammy with us."

"To Australia?"

Thomas nodded. "Sam said the lad has always wanted to go to Australia. That's part of the reason I wanted you to come with me today."

Isaac stood stunned momentarily, taking in what his father had said, sprinting to catch up with him. "That'll make Louisa very happy."

"I think Sam's hoping if he can travel with us, he'll be safer than if he travels alone."

Cobbled streets replaced the rutted tracks as they approached Bradford. Isaac followed his father to the bank opposite the church.

He stopped momentarily to admire the large, three-storey building made of multi-coloured stone, with two large bay windows on either side of the wooden door.

Opening the door, the tellers sat at desks straight ahead. To the left of the door, a balding man was seated at a separate desk, writing in a ledger—a painting of a thoroughbred horse adorned the wall behind him, casting a sophisticated atmosphere within the bank.

He looked over his half-moon glasses at the two men walking towards him. Closing his book, he quickly stood up, extending his hand to Thomas.

"Ah, Mr. Langdon." Gesturing for him to sit on the chair in front of his desk.

"Mr. Stanbury, may I introduce my son, Isaac."

Isaac reached to shake his hand.

"Pleased to make your acquaintance, Mr. Langdon. Sit down." Indicating the chair beside Thomas, returning to his own.

Cyrus Stanbury placed his elbows on the desk, briefly rubbing the bridge of his pointed nose. "I presume you wish to find out if your family can emigrate to Australia?"

Thomas nodded.

He began shuffling papers, eventually finding what he was looking for. "Ah, here we are." Taking off his glasses, he looked at the two men. "Have you any experience with sheep?"

"Yes, we do; we have sheep of our own."

He nodded. "Very well, there's a sheep farm north of Adelaide in South Australia, who want families to work there. Would you be interested?"

Thomas smiled as he looked at Isaac, "What do you think Ike?"

His eyebrows narrowed. "But Jack's in Brisbane."

Thomas turned to Cyrus. "Jack's our eldest son." Turning back to Isaac. "I'm sure we'll see him again; we must get to Australia first."

Cyrus coughed, and both men turned back to him. "If you accept this offer, the South Australian Government will pay your passage to Adelaide."

Thomas quickly sat forward. "You mean we don't have to pay anything?"

Cyrus nodded. "One of the conditions is that you work for at least two years before you leave the state. There's an incredible labour shortage as many men have gone looking for gold. Families like yours will be most welcome."

Thomas sat back in his chair, raising his eyebrows as he looked at Isaac. "That's a very tempting offer indeed," turning back to the agent, "I must tell you that Ike is newly married, so his wife will be joining us. And if possible, her brother."

Cyrus replaced his glasses and sat forward, nibbed pen poised, ready to write. "May I ask the name and age of your wife, Mr. Langdon? Also, her brother."

"My wife is Louisa, seventeen, turning eighteen in February. My brother-in-law is Sammy Keslake; he'll be thirteen the day after Christmas."

The agent nodded, writing the details. "I think it can be arranged for your brother-in-law to be included with your family; he's a good age. Landowners do prefer young men."

Opening a drawer, Cyrus pulled out a little light brown book. Isaac saw the cover as he opened it. *'The Emigrant's Friend.'*

Looking through the pages, he read for a moment before saying. "Farm servants receive an average yearly wage of twenty-five pounds, which includes food and lodging." He removed his glasses, looking at Thomas. "Do you think you'll be able to earn that much money in Cornwall, Mr. Langdon?"

Isaac's cap fell on the floor as he sat forward. "Goodness, we can earn that much?"

Cyrus nodded, sitting back in his chair; he rested his hands on his ample stomach, smiling as he twiddled his thumbs. "Australia is a new country, and there are many opportunities for young men and their families. I'm sure you'll make a good life for yourselves over there." He leaned forward. "This is a huge decision, Mr. Langdon, and one I don't expect you to make right now. Why don't you discuss it with your family? Come and see me in a couple of days?"

Isaac turned to his father. "That's a good idea, Da. We can talk after supper tonight."

"Yes, yes." Thomas nodded as he stood up. "We'll talk tonight and tell you our answer very soon." He reached over to shake Cyrus's hand. "Thank you for your help, Mr. Stanbury."

Thomas and Isaac turned towards Penstowe, silently walking until they reached the outskirts of town.

"You're very quiet, Ike."

He chuckled. "I'm trying to imagine what Louisa will say when she finds out Sammy's coming to Australia with us."

"Don't say anything to her yet; we must talk to Sam first."

"When are you going to see him?"

"We might go tomorrow after we discuss it tonight. Don't want to get the lad's hopes up."

~

Supper was finished, and Isaac wondered when his father would mention their trip to Bradford.

The plates were washed, and the family were seated at the table. The women and Elijah were drinking tea; he joined his father and Jacob as they enjoyed a tankard of cider.

"Children." Thomas began. "Your mother and I had a good talk today. There's a sheep farm in South Australia looking for families to work for them, and we've decided that if you agree, we will emigrate to Australia."

Grace looked up. "To be with Jack?"

"Not right away; we can join him later. Ma and I think it'll be a better life there than staying here in Penstowe."

Elijah and Martha smiled with delight as they looked at each other. Martha excitedly clapped her hands. "We're all going to Australia."

Jacob asked, "How will you pay for it, Da?"

Thomas replied, "The South Australian Government will pay for our passage. There's a shortage of workers; many men are looking for gold, so this is one way of getting people into the country."

Jacob inquired, "Do you know when we'll be leaving?"

Thomas shook his head. "Ike and I have to go to Bradford the day after tomorrow, and we hope to find out then."

Jacob turned to Isaac. "You want to go, don't you?" He put his hand on Louisa's. "We both do. We hope you'll come too." Isaac studied Jacob thoughtfully. Being parted from his twin, his other self, was too much to bear. He hoped his brother felt the same way.

Jacob nodded, turning to his father. "I've been thinking about Australia since you first talked about it." Shaking his head. "Truthfully, I don't want to stay here without my family, so I'll go with you."

Thomas turned to Grace. "What about you?"

Grace sat up straight. "I don't want to be working at the manor all my life, and like Jacob, I don't want to stay here without you. So, I'll go, too."

Thomas leaned back. "So, we're all agreed?"

Isaac watched as his father's eyes moved slowly across each member of his family, searching for any hint of doubt or hesitation. With a nod from each, relief washed over him like a warm embrace.

"Well, it looks like we're going to Australia." Thomas said and reached out to hold Mary's hand, smiling at her.

43

Thomas turned to Louisa as she helped Mary prepare breakfast. "We need to speak to your parents and let them know of our decision. I also want to see Luke and Jane to let them know. Will you and Ike come with me?"

She nodded. "Da knows you've been thinking about it, but Mother doesn't."

Isaac winked at his father; Louisa wondered what it was about.

Louisa opened the front door of Rose Cottage. Finding it empty, the trio walked out the back door; Elizabeth was working in the vegetable garden.

"Mornin' Mother."

Elizabeth dropped the handful of peas in the bucket when she heard her daughter's voice—rushing to hug her, holding her hands when they moved apart.

"How lovely to see you both." Glancing at Isaac, seeing Thomas standing beside him, she gave a brief nod. "Mr. Langdon."

Thomas asked, "Can you tell me where to find Sam? We need to talk to him."

Elizabeth frowned as she jerked her head toward the sheep field. "He's separating lambs from mothers."

Louisa slowly released her mother's hand, following Thomas and Isaac. "We'll be back later."

Samson and Sammy were putting willow fence panels in the corner of the field. Her father threw the panel against the hedge, narrowly missing Sammy. He jumped the gate, hugging Louisa.

"What brings you here today?" Turning to Thomas, he added, "I gather you have news for us?"

"Yes, we do. Do you want to talk here, or would you prefer to go inside?"

"I think I know what you're going to say, so how about we do it over a bottle of cider?" He turned to Sammy, indicating with his head. "Come on."

Louisa sat at the table, Isaac beside her, Thomas on his other side. Sammy sat opposite Thomas, her father opposite Isaac. Elizabeth put two bottles of cider on the table and sat next to Samson.

Elizabeth asked as she poured the cider. "You have something to tell us? Have you been given a farm to rent?"

Louisa waited until she passed mugs to everyone. "Yes, but not a farm, something else, but I'll leave that for Ike to tell you."

Elizabeth looked to Isaac, picked up her mug and waited.

Isaac cleared his throat. "Da and Ma have been thinking about going to Australia for a while now."

Elizabeth took a tentative sip from her mug, but the news hit her like a sudden storm. She spat most of it onto the table, shock and disbelief etched across her face. Wiping her mouth with the back of her hand before saying. "Au...Australia, why do you want to go to that God-forsaken place? It's full of convicts and savages."

Thomas shook his head. "No, it isn't. Our son Jack went there last year. We've got letters from him saying what a wonderful country it is, full of opportunities, which is why we're going there."

Sammy sat up, smiling as he drummed his hands on the table. "Australia! I want to go there when I'm old enough."

Louisa and Elizabeth looked at him. Louisa, surprised by his statement, asked, "Would you? You've never said anything to me about that."

"Da knows how much I want to go there." Glancing at Samson. "Whenever Mr. Penrose got a letter from his brother, he'd tell me about it. In his last letter, he said that he's just bought a farm, and it's over a thousand acres!"

Samson raised his eyebrows at Isaac.

Thomas saw this signal from Samson and asked, "Sammy, would you like to come with us?"

Elizabeth stared at Thomas open-mouthed, "But he's too young."

Samson put a hand on hers, the other round her shoulders. "He's nearly thirteen. Yes, he'd be too young if he travelled by himself, but if he travels with Ike's family, he won't be. It'll be a great opportunity for him, and he did tell me how much he wants to go there."

Elizabeth was close to tears and turned to Samson. "Why didn't you say anything to me before?"

Samson shook his head. "I didn't see the need as it would be a few years before he hoped to go. When Louisa told me recently that Ike's family were considering going, I asked Tom if they'd take Sammy too."

Thomas explained, "Ike and I saw the agent in Bradford yesterday; that's when we asked about Sammy. A sheep farm in South Australia is looking for families like ours, and willing to pay our passage."

Isaac put his arm around Louisa. "Mr. Stanbury said Sammy could come as part of our family."

Louisa looked at her brother. "You really want to go to Australia?"

Sammy's grin stretched from ear to ear as he eagerly nodded several times.

Louisa smiled as she playfully hit Isaac on the arm. "Why didn't you tell me Sammy was coming too?" Her mind raced with the joy of having her brother by her side in the journey ahead.

He laughed as he rubbed his arm, pretending he was seriously hurt. "I wanted you both to hear it at the same time." His forehead puckered. "Aren't you happy about Sammy coming too?"

She leaned on his shoulder. "Of course I am." Sitting up, she looked at Samson. "Da?"

"I won't lie; I'll miss you a lot, and so will Aunty Jane and Uncle Luke and their family. I know your mother will, too." Putting his arm around Elizabeth, pulling her closer.

Tears ran down Elizabeth's cheek; Louisa put a hand on hers. "We're going to miss you too."

Sammy turned to his father. "Are you really going to let me go to

Australia with Ike's family?"

Samson removed his arm from around Elizabeth, putting the other around Sammy, pulling him closer; their foreheads briefly touched. "I don't want to stand in the way of your dream; if it means you'll leave us a few years earlier than I hoped, I'll wish you Godspeed. I know you'll be safe with Louisa and Ike." He turned to Louisa. "You will write to us, won't you?"

"Of course we will." Louisa laughed. "It's fortunate I taught you how to read and write."

Samson snickered and turned to Thomas. "Do you know when you'll be leaving?"

He shook his head. "Ike and I hope to find out tomorrow."

Samson reached to shake his hand. "Thank you, Tom."

Sammy stood up and rushed around the table, putting his arms tightly around Thomas, nearly knocking him backwards. "Thank you, Mr. Langdon."

His voice and laughter muffled as he tapped him on the arm. "You're welcome, lad. Now, will you let me go so I can breathe?"

Standing up again. "Sorry." Smiling as he danced around the table. "I'm going to Australia; I'm going to Australia."

Isaac stood up and straddled the bench, gently touching his shoulder. "I hope you're not going to be like this all the way?"

"Sorry, Ike, I'm so happy." The excitement in the room buzzed like static in the air.

"We won't be leaving for a while yet; as soon as Da and I find out when, we'll let you know."

Thomas rose from the bench. "We'd best be going; we want to see Luke and Jane before we go home."

Samson stood up. "I'll see you sometime in the next few days."

Louisa hugged Samson. "Bye, Da." Linking her hand through Isaac's arm, she waved as they walked out the front door.

~

Sammy stared at the door as it closed behind his sister, turning to Samson. "I'm not dreaming, am I? You're really going to let me go to

Australia?"

Elizabeth approached him; at twelve, Sammy had outgrown his mother. "I didn't know it was something you wanted to do." She sniffed. "But as your father said, we won't stand in the way of your dream." Wiping her face with the back of her hand.

More tears fell down her cheek. Sammy looked at his father; he didn't know what to do or say. A moment later, he hugged Elizabeth. "Thank you, Mother."

~

Samson and Elizabeth sat at the table later that evening.

Elizabeth wiped her face for the third time. "I've driven our children away, haven't I?" Standing up, she walked to the fireplace, turning back to her husband. "To Australia, of all places."

Samson was by her side instantly. "You didn't drive them away. Louisa is following her husband, and Sammy, well, he's always wanted to go to Australia. It's just a little earlier than I thought he would go."

Overwhelmed, Elizabeth collapsed onto his shoulder. He led her to the table a minute later, encouraging her to sit beside him.

He held her hand, rubbing his thumb over the back of her hand. "Sammy's always been fascinated by Australia since he learnt about it at school. When Bob Penrose's brother went there, Sammy would always ask him if he'd received a letter from him. Same with Ike, as soon as they got a letter from Jack, Sammy was keen to hear about life in Australia."

Elizabeth looked up. "I'm going to miss them."

"Of course you are; we both will. But if they stay in Stokebridge, what future would they have? They'd either work at the manor or work hard on a farm, paying rent to the manor. In Australia, I'm sure they'll have a better life."

Putting her head on his shoulder. "I hope you're right, but I'll still miss them."

Samson kissed the top of her head. "Come on, love, it's time to go to bed." He gently reached for her hand, and together, they ascended the staircase, their quiet footsteps echoing through the empty house.

Thomas and Isaac walked the three miles to Bradford, mostly in silence.

Upon entering the bank, Isaac saw Cyrus Stanbury at his desk, reading a letter to an older man. He looked up when he saw the two men.

"Please take a seat, Mr. Langdon; I shouldn't be long."

Sitting in chairs near the bay window, they waited. Isaac's ears caught the hushed murmurs uttered by the bank tellers and Cyrus, the ambient sounds blending with the scent of ink and polished wood. But Isaac wasn't listening; he had other things on his mind; he wondered what life would be like in Australia and questioned if they were making the right decision.

Cyrus shook hands with the older man, who promptly left. He removed his glasses and pointed his hand to the empty chairs before his desk. "Please sit down, gentlemen." Cyrus put his elbows on the desk and steepled his fingers. "I presume you have made a decision?"

Thomas exchanged a quick glance with Isaac before confirming, "Yes, we'd like to work on the sheep farm in Australia."

Replacing his glasses, Cyrus sat back and shuffled his papers, eventually finding what he was looking for. "That's wonderful; I'll make arrangements for you." Dipping his pen in the ink well, he began writing.

Isaac leaned forward, a mixture of anticipation and apprehension etched across his face. "Do you know when we'll be leaving Cornwall?"

Looking up from the paper, he shrugged, "You'll have to be examined by Doctor Bartlett first; if you are deemed fit for the colony, it could be before Christmas or just after."

Isaac's eyes just about popped from his head as he sat forward. "That soon?"

Cyrus smirked, "As I told you two days ago, Mr. Langdon, there's a severe labour shortage in South Australia."

Turning to Thomas, "You have three healthy sons, and now Isaac's brother-in-law will be travelling with you; your family is just what they're looking for."

Thomas grinned at Isaac. "Well, it looks like we're going to work on a sheep farm in Australia."

Cyrus wrote on his sheet of paper before looking up, "I should find out today or tomorrow when you need to present yourself to the doctor. Once you've been examined, I'll know when you'll be sailing. When I have that information, I'll send it to you by messenger."

Pen poised over the paper, he said, "Now, may I confirm your family's names and dates of birth for the application?"

Cyrus looked at Thomas when he had finished writing, "Mr. Langdon, I must tell you that Miss Langdon will have to travel in the single ladies' quarters as she's over fourteen years of age. She'll have no contact with any other passengers during the voyage."

Thomas sat forward; his eyes opened wide. "We won't be able to see her at all?"

"I'm afraid not; this is to protect the women from the men. Your wife may be able to visit her, but only at the matron's discretion. Also, your two sons and Master Keslake will travel in the single men's quarters."

Thomas nodded, "I see." Standing up, he shook hands with Cyrus. "Thank you. We'll wait to hear when we have to be examined by the doctor."

"Good day to you, Mr. Langdon."

Walking out of the bank later, Isaac turned to his father, "We're going to Australia; we're really going to Australia!"

"Yes, we are. At first, it was an idea, but now it's going to happen. How does that make you feel?"

Isaac put his hands on his head and let out a big sigh, "Excited and scared at the same time," letting his arms fall. "Silly, isn't it?"

Thomas walked on, "No, not really."

~

The following afternoon, a rider arrived at Pine Cottage with an envelope for Thomas. Mary stood at the table kneading dough so Louisa answered the door, accepting the envelope. Turning it over to read the sender's name, she looked to her mother-in-law, "This is from Mr. Stanbury in Bradford."

Mary wiped her floury hands on her apron. "I'll call everyone from fields."

The family sat at the table as Isaac read the letter.

Bank of England
Church Street,
Bradford

5th October 1855

Dear Mr. Langdon,

> *You and your family are now requested to present themselves to Doctor Bartlett's surgery in Bradford on Monday morning, 8th October.*

> *Once you have all been examined and are deemed fit for the colony, I will advise you of your departure date. From the advice I have received so far, I can only speculate, but it could be as early as December or January.*

> *I will send the exact date once I receive that information.*

Yours faithfully,
Cyrus Stanbury

Jacob blew out a long, loud breath, "That's only two or three months away."

A knowing smile played on Thomas's lips as he placed his hands on the edge of the table and leaned back. "After we've tended to animals on Monday, we'll go to Bradford," he declared, a sense of anticipation lingering in the air.

"Elijah's eyes opened wide with excitement, "We might be leaving for Australia before Christmas!"

Mary looked up, "Martha won't be able to go to school that day, and Grace won't be able to work at the manor."

Isaac held up the letter. "This is more important."

Thomas agreed, "Yes, it is." Standing up, he headed to the back door. "Come, lads, let's get back to work." Isaac, Jacob, and Elijah followed.

Louisa looked at her mother-in-law. "Well, it's happening." Seeing her brow furrowed, she asked, "Have you changed your mind?"

Mary picked up the teapot, pouring another cup each, "I'm not sure."

Louisa swallowed a mouthful, "I know Ike is excited about going to Australia." Leaning forward, she lowered her voice, "Please don't tell him, but sometimes I feel like I'm about to walk into a dark room and have no idea what to expect."

Mary patted her hand, "I know exactly what you mean."

~

The following morning, Louisa had barely sat with the rest of the family for breakfast when there was an urgent knock on the door. Jacob opened it, and their neighbour, Ted Whitehall, rushed in. He stood with his hands on the end of the table for a moment, recovering his breath.

Jacob returned to his seat, "What's the rush about Ted?"

"Haven't you heard about the murder?"

Isaac's brows rose as he looked at him, "What murder?"

Ted stood up straight, "Lord Trevelen's brother. He's been found murdered in woods near manor."

Louisa's fork was halfway to her mouth; it landed on the tin plate with a loud clatter, "When?"

"From what I heard; it were yesterday afternoon."

Holding his fork of food in front of his face, Thomas asked, "How?" shoving the bacon in his mouth.

Elijah moved along the bench; Ted sat down with a grateful nod, "Apparently, he were knocked off his horse; as he lay on the ground, he were hit several times. Whoever did it made sure he were dead."

Louisa's head spun; voices buzzed around her, but she wasn't listening. The words John had said to her when he took her home were ringing in her ears; *'One day, he'll get what's coming to him.'* She wondered if he was responsible for his death.

She shook her head when Ted said, "Whoever did it must've been very strong."

Swallowing, she breathed a small sigh of relief, safe in the knowledge it couldn't have been John. She doubted a man his age could inflict such injuries as Ted described.

Ted stood up, "This'll be talk at church tomorrow," and let himself out the front door.

Isaac's hand gently found its way to Louisa's arm, a silent gesture of concern. "Are you alright? You've gone very pale," he inquired.

"I-I've never known anyone who was murdered before. I wonder how Lord and Lady Trevelen are?"

Thomas pulled a piece of bread off the loaf before him, putting it in his mouth, "I don't think many people will mourn his loss; he were a nasty man." Crumbs fell from his mouth as he talked.

Isaac reached for his mug of tea, "I wonder if they'll find out who did it?"

Thomas picked up his fork, waving it around as he talked, "I doubt the authorities will try very hard. Oh, they'll put on a show for His Lordship's sake, but deep down, I'm sure they don't care if his killer's found. No one liked the man."

Isaac looked at his father, "Why would you say that, Da?"

Thomas took a deep breath, "Because whoever killed him had a very good reason."

Jacob looked at him curiously, "What reason is there for taking another man's life? Murder is a sin."

Thomas turned to his youngest daughter, "Martha, will you see if there're any eggs? Elijah, you can help." The ten-year-old stood up, collected a basket, and skipped out the side door.

Fourteen-year-old Elijah gave his father a frosty look, "She doesn't need my help."

Thomas placed his elbow on the table, leaned forward and stared at his son, "*Go.*"

He was up and followed his sister, but not before poking his tongue at his father's back as he opened the door.

Thomas looked at his son, "You say murder is a sin, well, so is rape."

Jacob stared at him, "Rape?"

Thomas put his fork into another piece of bacon, holding it above his plate, the meat held on one tine of the fork, threatening to fall off.

"Haven't you heard rumours 'round villages?" Putting the food in his mouth, he continued while chewing. "The man were very fond of having his way with the servant girls, whether they were willing or not. I've always worried about Grace working there, but we need her wages; that's why I haven't told her to stop."

Louisa clasped her hands together under the table, fearing Isaac would see them shake. Realisation dawned on her as to how close *she* had come to being raped by Robert Engels in the scullery three weeks ago.

Thomas picked up his mug, looking at the stunned faces watching him, "I'd be very surprised if his killer wasn't the father of a servant he attacked." Swallowing a mouthful of his tea, he added, "If you ask me, whoever killed him did every girl in the district a kindness."

Louisa had her arm on Isaac's as they walked to Stokebridge. Isaac asked, "Is something troubling you? You're very quiet."

She shook her head, "I was wondering how Lord and Lady Trevelen are; losing his brother like that," she trailed off.

"You don't work there anymore, so why are you worried?"

"Lady Trevelen was very good to me while I worked for her; she's a lovely lady. This must be quite a shock for them."

He patted the hand looped through his arm, "They may not even be at church today."

She smiled at him briefly as they walked. Isaac was right; His Lordship may not be at church. Pity. She was hoping to have a word with John.

Sammy was standing with her parents outside the church. As soon as he saw them, he rushed to meet them. Picking her up and swinging her around, "Have you heard anything yet?"

Louisa laughed, "Put me down, then I can tell you."

Isaac said, "Go fetch your Da, then I can tell you both at the same time."

They laughed as Sammy raced to Samson standing with Elizabeth, nearly pulling him off his feet as he dragged him to join them.

Samson ruffled his son's hair, then hugged Louisa, "I gather you've heard something?"

Louisa nodded while Isaac spoke, "We have to go to Doctor

Bartlett's surgery in Bradford tomorrow to be examined. Can Sammy meet us at the crossroads after breakfast?"

Sammy jumped on the spot for a moment, "I'll sleep there tonight if you want me to."

Samson laughed as he put his hand on his shoulder, "No need for that; you can leave after breakfast."

Isaac laughed at his impatience. "Once we've had the examination, they'll tell us when we'll sail."

Samson ruffled Sammy's hair again, "Well, lad, looks like you'll be going to Australia soon."

Louisa laughed as she knew nothing would wipe the smile off his face at that moment. The organ began to play, and Samson turned to Isaac and Louisa, "We'd better go inside."

Standing in his pulpit, Reverend Ellacott spoke of the death of Lord Trevelen's brother after the sermon, "Let us pray for the soul of our lost brother, Robert Engels. He was a good man whose life was taken too soon by a callous murderer."

Louisa thought she heard someone say, "Hmph!" Wondering if it was her father. Although there were murmurs around the pews, she doubted any were sympathy over his death.

Milling outside the church afterwards, the murder of Robert Engels was on everyone's lips. Louisa was standing with Isaac when Phillip asked, "You're very quiet, Louisa. Are you alright?"

She forcefully shook her head, attempting to banish the persistent memory of John's words. "Master Engels's murder is all anyone can talk about. Surely there's other things."

Phillip was surprised by her statement; a smile tugged at his lips, "It's not every day we have a murder in the district."

Louisa felt a shiver go down her spine, "Can we talk about something else, please?"

Isaac looked at her, "Are you feeling poorly?"

She shook her head and said firmly, "No, but everyone's saying how sad it is that Master Engels was killed. To be truthful, he was a horrible man, and I'm not sad. Even Lady Trevelen didn't like him."

Isaac smiled as he put his arm around her, "How about we tell

Phillip our news?"

Phillip looked with interest. "What news?"

Louisa smiled and nodded, "Ike and I have to go to Bradford tomorrow to be examined by Doctor Bartlett and the rest of Ike's family." Looking up at Isaac. She continued, "If we're classed as fit, we're going to Australia. We haven't told the rest of the village yet until we know if we're going."

Phillip shook hands with Isaac, then hugged Louisa, "Australia! How wonderful." Standing back, he looked at them. "Do you know when you'll be leaving?"

"It could be sometime in December or January; we'll know more after we've been to Bradford tomorrow."

Phillip turned to Louisa, "Your family are going to miss you, especially Sammy."

Louisa's face lit up, "Sammy's coming with us."

"Really?" Glancing at Sammy as he talked to Samson. "No wonder he's got a smile on his face."

"Da asked Ike's Da if Sammy could come with us. He was planning to go to Australia when he was old enough anyway."

Phillip hugged Louisa and shook Isaac's hand again. "I'm going to miss you both very much. Church on Sunday won't be the same without spending some time talking to you both."

Louisa spied Jacob, walking towards them, "I think everyone's ready to go home." Turning to Phillip, "We'll let you know next Sunday if we hear anything." Giving him a final hug, "Goodbye, Phillip."

They turned to walk to Penstowe.

~

While Grace swept the floor, Louisa helped Mary wash the dishes after breakfast; occasionally looking out the window, watching the steadily falling rain. The day appeared miserable, with a relentless downpour turning the once cheerful sky into a sea of bleak, ominous grey. Louisa jumped when the front door opened, Sammy walked in, brushing raindrops off his jacket onto the stone floor.

Louisa put her hand to her chest, "Sammy! You scared me; we were meeting you at the crossroads."

"I know, but I was up before sunrise. Mother could see how eager I was to get going; she made me breakfast and I left afterwards. Besides, I didn't want to stand in the rain, so I thought I'd come here and wait."

Louisa faced her brother, "The men are tending to the animals; once they're finished, we'll leave."

Mary turned to him, "Sammy, sit in front of fire to dry off a bit. We don't want you catching your death before we get to Bradford."

Sammy sat on a stool, warming his hands in front of the fire. A moment later the side door opened and Martha walked in with a basket of eggs, placing it on the table. Pulling her shawl off her shoulders, she shook raindrops onto the floor, leaving wet dots where Grace had just swept.

"Mornin' Sammy," Smiling at him.

He smiled as he stood up, "Mornin' Martha, you're all wet. Come and sit with me by the fire and dry off a bit."

Louisa shared a knowing look with Mary, silently acknowledging the blossoming connection between Martha and Sammy.

~

The rain fell down Thomas's neck. He pulled his jacket collar up in a futile effort to prevent more from falling down his back. He looked at his family; his sons and Sammy were doing the same, the women pulled their shawls over their heads. The mud splashing under their feet dotted the hems of their skirts.

By the time they reached Bradford, they were soaked to the skin. Thomas held the door of the doctor's surgery open for his family, all thankful to be out of the pouring rain and in a warm room.

One by one, they were each examined, Doctor Bartlett checked their general health and teeth. Thomas was called into his consulting room afterwards. "Sit down, Mr. Langdon. I've examined all of your family, and I can see you've all been vaccinated against smallpox, so therefore, I can see no reason why you shouldn't be allowed to enter Australia. My only concern is your daughter-in-law."

A torrent of thoughts surged through Thomas's mind, each one carrying the weight of potential outcomes for Louisa. He fiddled with his cap. "Louisa? What's wrong with Louisa?"

"I believe she only recently married your son?"

Thomas nodded, "Just over a week ago."

Doctor Bartlett grinned, "It could be possible, by the time you leave for Australia, she may be with child. Sea voyages can be risky for women in that condition."

His throat tightened. "Risky? How risky?"

"If she miscarries, it could be fatal. I've examined your daughter-in-law; she is very healthy, and the chances of that happening are slim."

Thomas thought for a moment, taking a deep breath through his nose. "My wife is a midwife; I'm sure she'll keep an eye on her."

Seeing the concerned look on Thomas's face, Dr Bartlett chuckled softly, "Then she'll be in good hands, and a surgeon will be on board. Don't worry; if she is with child when you embark, I'm sure she'll give you a healthy grandchild soon after you arrive in Adelaide."

"So, Ike and Louisa will be able to join us?"

Doctor Bartlett's nod carried a weight of unspoken concerns. "Yes, they will join you, but be aware, challenges may await them on the turbulent seas."

"I see."

Doctor Bartlett picked up his nibbed pen, dipped it in the ink bottle and smiled. "Don't worry, I'll write my report to Mr. Stanbury saying you're all fit and healthy. I'll send it to his office this afternoon."

"Thank you, Doctor Bartlett," thinking he must tell Mary about Louisa so she can be prepared.

~

After bidding farewell to Sammy at the crossroads, the warmth of the fire in Pine Cottage was welcoming; each taking turns to warm their hands.

After supper, Thomas took a mouthful of cider and addressed his family. "Well, we're all going to Australia soon. Before we leave, we must sell everything we can't take and give away whatever's left."

Mary said, "I'll give my mother's rocking chair to Luke and Jane; I know Jane will appreciate it."

Thomas nodded, "The stock can be sold at Bradford markets at the end of the month; I'll use that money to buy the farming tools to sell in Australia."

Louisa said, "I can make cloth bags to put some of our clothes in."

Thomas nodded, "Thank you, Louisa; there will be much for us to do. Until we know when we're leaving, we'll prepare as best we can."

Mary looked up from her cup of tea, "Hopefully, we'll hear from Mr. Stanbury soon."

Under the morning sun, Louisa's steps echoed along the path to Stokebridge, her thoughts tangled in the lingering shadows of Robert Engel's death. Reaching the crossroads, she stood momentarily, deciding whether to see John before visiting her family. Looking at the manor in front of her, she glanced at the Stokebridge church bell tower to her right. There was only one way to rid herself of the nagging thought racing through her mind. She walked ahead.

Louisa inhaled the sweet aroma of hay, the scent embracing her senses as she ventured into the dimly lit stable. The soft sounds of shuffling hooves and the occasional whinny added to the ambience. Walking along the row of horse stalls, the occupants, with their ears forward, looked at her over the half doors.

She found John sitting on a stool in the cluttered tack room. He smiled at her as she carefully stepped around the bucket containing brushes and a hoof pick. Avoiding the folded-up blankets and a coil of rope, she reached the upturned wooden box near him and sat on it.

He continued cleaning a bridle using a cloth stained with harness soap. "Mornin' Mrs. Langdon. What brings you 'ere today?"

"Morning Mr. Holman." Looking around, she spoke softly, "Are we alone?"

He nodded as he pulled the reins through the folded material in his hand. "Aye, young Fred's taken His Lordship to Bradford in the carriage, won't be back for a while."

Her basket gently settled on the cool cobblestone floor, Louisa delicately smoothed the folds of her skirt, her fingers tracing absent patterns in the fabric, a silent prelude to the weighty question hanging in the air. With her back stiffly erect, she stared into his questioning blue eyes, and took a deep breath. "There's no simple way to ask this. Did you kill Master Engels?"

He slowly turned, placing the bridle and cloth on the bench behind him; he briefly rubbed the back of his neck. "I've known your Da since he were a lad, and I've known you all your life, so I know you won't tell His Lordship if I said I did."

Louisa leaned forward and shook her head, "No, I wouldn't say anything. If anyone deserved to die, it was him."

John rested against the bench. "Aye, he did. I didn't like what he tried to do to you, and he deserved to be punished."

Louisa sat up straight, "But M'lady told me His Lordship threatened him, said he'd throw him out if he attacked another servant."

John leaned in; his gaze unwavering. "Well, he probably thought his brother wouldn't carry out that threat." The weight of conviction in his voice hinted at layers of history and unspoken truths.

"How do you know?"

Louisa watched as John trembled with fury and spoke through gritted teeth, "Because he attacked someone else."

She put her hand over her mouth, "Oh no, not again." Letting her hand drop to her chest, "Who?"

His expression sobered, "Are you sure you want to hear this?"

Her shoulders slumped, and she nodded in reluctant agreement. "I think I need to."

"Aye, I think you do too." Leaning forward again, he placed his hands on his knees and began his story.

"A day or two after your wedding, I noticed young Fred had become quiet. He weren't his usual jolly self. Usually, he were always smiling and laughing, making a fuss of the horses. Then, a few days later, I caught him hitting one of them. Fred never did that before; he were always gentle.

"I had my suspicions, so I brought him in here, and after a bit of coaxing, he eventually told me Robert Engels had trapped him in an empty stall." John shook his head and breathed deeply through his nose. "Fred's only a sixteen-year-old lad, and that...that..." He turned slightly and banged his fist on the bench. "*Bastard* forced himself upon him."

Louisa flinched at the word he'd used but ignored it and put her hand to her mouth again. "The poor boy."

John nodded, "You said His Lordship would talk to him, and I've no doubt he did. But he took no notice, and after what happened to you and Philippa, and then young Fred, I knew nothing would stop his evil ways."

Louisa sat transfixed as he spoke.

"If he moved to another town, he'd only inflict more misery on other young girls, maybe boys there. I felt I had to do something.

"I knew he rode in the woods most afternoons, so I took one of the hoes from the gardeners' shed, walked into the woods and waited. I were standing behind the big chestnut tree near the washout. The path's uneven from the tree roots, and I knew he'd have to slow and walk his horse until he were past it. It were the perfect spot to ambush him.

"I'd been waiting a while, beginning to think he weren't riding that day, and then I heard hoofbeats slowing down the path. He couldn't see me, but I heard him coming closer; I could see his horse's head, no more than a yard from where I stood. I swung the hoe towards him with all the force I could muster." Using his hands to give her a visual description of swinging it to his right.

"It hit 'im on the shoulder, and he fell off his horse, landing on his back. I jumped down beside him; he were lying on the ground, trying to get his breath back. He saw me standing over him with the hoe ready to hit him, and he started cryin', *'Please don't kill me, please don't kill me,'* like the coward he were. I said, *'This is for Philippa'* and hit 'im on the head. I could hear his skull cracking, and his eyes rolled back, and blood started to spill on the ground. I did a proper job to make sure he were dead."

Louisa stared at the coachman as he spoke so matter-of-factly, not sure what to say as she listened to the rest of his tale.

"I were walking through the woods to the manor and found a spot just off the path where the fern grew quite thick, I buried the hoe there before I went back to the stables, I don't think anyone saw me. I were cleaning one of the stalls when I heard his horse walk back. I put him in it and ran to the manor to raise the alarm."

"Didn't the authorities ask you questions about it?"

"Aye, they did, but I only said his horse come back without 'im. Then they questioned young Fred, but he could only tell 'em he'd saddled his horse for Master Engels before he went for his ride, then he went home.”

Louisa leaned forward to put her hand on his, “Oh, Mr. Holman, what if they find out it was you?”

“I’m not worried about being punished for killin’ ’im; I’m an old man; I’ve lived my life. I only wanted the people living around the manor to feel safe again, and that couldn’t happen while Robert Engels drew breath. To be truthful, I don’t think the authorities believed that at my age, I’d be capable of killing ’im. They only asked me about his horse comin’ back riderless.”

He leaned forward, his forehead puckering. “Am I sorry for what I’d done? No. He were an awful man who did awful things. I know I’ll not meet Robert Engels in hell because the Good Lord will forgive me for saving other young people from the same fate Philippa, you, young Fred, and his other victims suffered.”

He leaned back again, “Yesterday, young Fred came to me and said he wanted to thank me. When I asked him what for, he said, ‘You know’. I didn’t say anything, and I know he won’t either. I sleep better at nights knowing he’s not going to hurt anyone else, but you, young Fred and all the others have to live with what he did.”

A weight settled heavily in Louisa’s chest, an unyielding stone. In a hushed voice, she confessed, “I’m struggling to forget, but I doubt if not remembering what he did to me is even possible. May the Lord forgive me for saying this, but I’m glad he’s dead, and I hope no one finds out it was you who killed him.”

John cocked his ear, stood up and whispered, “Sounds like young Fred come back. Don’t say any more.”

He indicated with his head to walk with him, they found Fred undoing the harness on one of the horses. He beamed as Louisa approached.

“Mrs. Langdon, and what do we owe the pleasure of this visit?”

Louisa smiled at him, “I was telling Mr. Holman, my husband’s family are going to Australia. Ike and I are going with them.”

John offered her a conspiratorial wink.

The corners of Fred’s eyes crinkled. “I’ve thought about emigrating, but who’d look after me Mam, if I left Cornwall?”

Louisa saw a flash of fear in his eye as John touched his shoulder affectionately. She understood why.

"Lad, you've got a good job here with the horses. Who knows, maybe when you're older, the chance will come."

Louisa turned to go. "I'll leave you to tend the horses. Goodbye Mr. Holman, Fred." Giving a wave as she left.

The gravel crunched beneath Louisa's worn boots as she headed toward the crossroad, her thoughts absorbed by John's confession. No good would come from him being sent to prison or being hanged for his crime. He was a kind man who had saved more young girls and boys from the terror she, Philippa and Fred had experienced.

Louisa couldn't shake the chilling thought of what might unfold if the truth ever saw the light of day. She turned toward Stokebridge, away from the weight of John's confession. A silent oath to guard John's secret echoed in her steps.

Nearly a week later, a letter arrived by messenger from Bradford. Accepting the letter, Louisa gripped it tightly, warding off the wind's attempt to snatch it before she could secure the door. Thomas was sitting in the chair by the fire, so she handed it to him.

"No good giving it to me; call Ike from the barn, then he can read it."

Mary opened the side door, calling out to Isaac and Jacob before making a fresh pot of tea.

Isaac strode into the room, his twin shadowing his every move. They stood in front of the fire, warming their hands. Louisa handed the letter to Isaac. "Da said for you to read it."

Mary poured mugs of tea and placed them on the table. Isaac sat at the end next to Louisa. She watched him break the seal, open the letter, and began reading.

Bank of England
Church Street,
Bradford

15th October 1855

Dear Mr. Langdon,
    Approval has been granted for your family to emigrate to Australia.

Isaac handed Thomas the letter across the table. "Well, looks like we'll be spending Christmas on board a ship."

Thomas looked at his two sons and daughter-in-law. "Are you sure you want to go to Australia? It's not too late to change your minds."

Laughter bubbled up within Louisa, as she shared a look with Isaac. "Do you think Sammy would forgive me if we stayed in Cornwall?"

Isaac joined in her laughter. "I doubt it; I guess we'll have to go." He turned to his twin. "Jacob?"

He smiled and said, "I'm excited about going to Australia," turning to his father. "Besides, could you disappoint Elijah and Martha?"

Thomas shook his head. "No, those two have been so excited; some nights, I don't think they sleep."

Jacob stood up. "The markets are less than two weeks away; we have a lot to do before then."

Thomas placed his hands on the table, pushing himself up; he looked at Louisa. "Will you tell Sammy?"

She nodded and grinned, "I'll visit Da and Mother tomorrow and tell him. He's as excited as Elijah and Martha." Glancing briefly at Mary, a fleeting look of fear in her eyes. Giving a slight nod to let her know she was feeling the same fear. "Do you want me to tell Aunty Jane and Uncle Luke?"

Thomas chuckled, "You might as well; I doubt Sammy will keep quiet for long."

Isaac stood up also. "Do you want me to write to Jack and tell him we're coming to Australia?"

Thomas nodded, "Yes, please; I'm sure he'll be happy to hear the news."

"I'll write it tonight."

Mary called to the men as they were about to walk outside, "Tom, Ike, I've just thought of something."

Isaac turned, "What is it, Ma?"

"Will you be able to take Louisa and me to Bradford? We need to buy a couple of trunks for our clothes."

Thomas turned to his wife, "Would you like to come with us on market day when we take the stock?"

Mary turned to Louisa, raising her eyebrows as she silently asked the question. Louisa nodded, "Market day will be good."

~

Isaac sat at the table, writing a letter to his brother. He struggled with his spelling but continued, excitedly sharing his news.

Pine Cottage,
Penstowe,
Cornwall,
England

17th October 1855

My dearest brother Jack,

This is to let you no we'll be sailing for Adelaide in December. We are going to work on a sheep farm in South Australia.

We received a letter today saying we must be in Plymouth by the 11th of December and sailing two days later.

Unfortunately, it'll be a while before we see you in Brisbane. Because the South Australian Government is paying our passige, we must stay there for at least two years. But I'm sure time

291

~

Louisa pulled her shawl tighter around her shoulders, and her mop cap was blown off her head. She gave up when it landed in a puddle, holding it in her hand with one end of her shawl. Turning the top of her head to the wind, she walked to the crossroads, quickening her pace to Stokebridge. Louisa closed the door of Rose Cottage, leaning against it, hoping the wind would not follow her inside.

Elizabeth looked up from cutting apples, "Louisa!" Rushing to greet her daughter, guiding her to the fire. "Come and warm yourself; I'll tell Da and Sammy you're here."

Louisa stood facing her palms to the flames, feeling them tingle as they warmed. Hearing the door sneck as her mother walked outside, she concentrated on holding her cap in front of the flames.

She had sufficiently warmed up when her family returned; placing her cap on the hearth to dry, she greeted her father and brother. It warmed her even more.

Elizabeth busied herself making tea while Samson and Sammy sat at the table with Louisa. Sammy could not contain his enthusiasm, leaning over the table towards her, "Have you heard anything yet?"

Placing the teapot and cups on the table, Elizabeth sat beside her daughter and poured tea.

Accepting the cup, Louisa gave a lopsided grin, "Yes, we have; a letter arrived yesterday."

Excitement raced through him, "When do we leave?"

Her eyes gleamed. "We have to be in Plymouth by the eleventh of December, ready to sail two days later."

Sammy sat back, grinning and drumming his hands on the table. "December." Turning to his father. "Da, I'm leaving for Australia in December."

Samson tried to hide his sadness by taking a mouthful of tea and lowering his cup. "Well, lad, it's happening." Putting his hand behind Sammy's neck, he pulled him slightly closer. "Your mother and I are going to miss you."

His shoulders slumped. "I'm going to miss you too, Da."

Elizabeth asked, "Do you know the name of the ship you'll be sailing on?"

Louisa put her cup on the table. "Not yet."

Elizabeth turned to Sammy, "Well, you might need more clothes before you sail; I'll ask Aunty Jane if she can help me make some for you." She winked at Louisa, "At the rate you're growing, your sister might have to make more on-board ship."

Sammy snorted good-heartedly, "Hmph!!"

Samson turned to Louisa, "If we can help in any way, you only need to ask."

"Thanks, Da. There's lots to be organised. We discussed some things last night."

Sammy looked at Louisa, "How are we going to get to Plymouth?"

Louisa shrugged, "That was one of the things we discussed; we're not sure yet."

Samson stood up and looked out the front window to Crocus Cottage. "I might ask Fred Pengelly if he wouldn't mind taking his cart."

Louisa stood beside her father, following his gaze, "We will have a lot of luggage; the cart would be useful. Would you like me to come with you?"

Samson smiled as he patted her on the shoulder, turning to fetch his jacket. "Grab your cap and shawl; we'll ask him now."

As they rushed across the road, pulling their warm clothes tighter around them, Annie Pengelly opened the door as they were about to knock.

"Come inside; that wind blows right through to bones." She quickly closed the door behind them and returned to the table with her daughters to resume the fruit preservation. The smell of burning peat was welcoming as Fred limped to Samson, shaking his hand, nodding briefly to Louisa. "What can I do for you, Sam?"

Samson glanced at his daughter, "Louisa and Ike's family are leaving in December to sail to Australia." Running his hands through his hair before shoving them in his pockets. "Would you mind taking them and their belongings to Plymouth in your cart?"

"I don't know if my bad foot will take me all that way, but I'd happily loan you Bobby and the cart; you'd have to get someone else to take you."

Louisa turned to Samson. "Would Uncle Luke know how to drive a cart?"

Fred nodded, "I'm sure he'd manage the trip there an' back." Turning to Louisa and smiling, "Australia's a long way; it's going to be very different to Stokebridge."

She returned the smile. "Very different. Sammy can't wait to get there."

Fred turned to Samson. "Sammy's going too, is he?"

Samson nodded, "Aye, he's wanted to go since he were a young lad."

Annie stood up, returned to Louisa, hugged her, and smiled, "You'll be sadly missed in the village; we wish you and Ike all the best in Australia."

"Thank you, Mrs. Pengelly, and we appreciate the loan of the horse and cart."

Samson shook hands with Fred, turning to leave. "Thank you for your help."

Louisa waved as she followed her father, "Goodbye."

As Louisa stepped outside, the wind wrapped around her, prompting her to tighten her shawl. The noise of the wind was deafening. "Da, I'm going to see Aunty Jane and Uncle Luke. Then I'll go back to Penstowe."

Putting his hand behind his ear, "What?"

Leaning closer, she shouted, "I'm going to see Aunty Jane."

He nodded as he pulled his collar up around his ears, running to Rose Cottage, giving her a brief wave.

Opening the door of Daffodil Cottage felt like coming home for Louisa; she took off her shawl, preparing herself for the collision as Fran ran towards her like she had the devil behind her.

"Louisa!" The force from Fran crashing into her caused her to step backwards. "I've missed you." The six-year-old wrapped her arms around her cousin's waist.

She looked down into her face and smiled, "I've missed you too."

Louisa saw Jane move the kettle over the flames before she asked, "Why are you out on a wretched day like today?"

Louisa sat at the table, letting Fran snuggle next to her. "I had to come and see Sammy; let him know when we're leaving for Australia."

Jane turned around as she stood by the cupboard, holding a tea container. "When are you leaving?" She put fresh leaves in the pot before sitting opposite her niece.

She felt numb at the thought of leaving her aunt, uncle, and cousins. It took all her willpower to hold back the tears building up.

"We must be in Plymouth by the eleventh of December, sailing two days later."

Jane turned to Fran, "Go and fetch Da and your brothers from the barn." She jumped to the floor, running to the side door. Jane called out, "Get your shawl; we don't want you catching your death." Fran stopped to pull her shawl off the peg, wrapped it around her shoulders and left.

Jane laughed as she watched the door being closed. "That girl will be the death of me." Turning to Louisa again. "Are you excited about going to Australia?"

Louisa reached over to hold her hands. "If you want the truth, I'm terrif—"

Hearing the side door open, she leaned back when Luke walked in as he carried Fran, followed by the twins. He grinned as he lowered the six-year-old to the floor, "We were about to come in when Fran told us you're sailing soon?" Hanging his jacket and Fran's shawl on the peg.

Louisa nodded, "In early December, we must be in Plymouth by the eleventh."

Luke sat next to Jane, giving her a sad smile, "I know we'll miss you, and so will the children." He looked to the twins sitting at the end of the table, nodding, and Fran sitting beside her.

Jane filled the teapot, put it on the table, returned a moment later with mugs and began pouring.

Louisa lifted her mug, enjoying the warmth on her hands as she held it. "Da spoke to Mr. Pengelly; he said he's happy for us to borrow his horse and cart, but he won't be able to make the journey." Taking a mouthful of tea, she continued, "Can you come with us to Plymouth and bring the horse and cart back?"

"Yes, I can do that; December's a slow time at the manor garden." Luke gritted his teeth in sympathy and frowned. "Poor Fred, his foot's never been the same since the horse stepped on it."

"When I get home, I'll tell Ike's Da we've got a cart to take us to Plymouth. Thank you, Uncle Luke."

Luke turned to Louisa. "Is there anything else you need help with before you leave Cornwall?"

Drinking the last of her tea. "I'll ask Ike when I get home."

Louisa stood up, collected her shawl, and leaned to kiss Jane. "I'll see you next time I visit Da and Mother."

Jane smiled, "I'll look forward to it."

~

Later that evening as the wind howled outside, Isaac and Louisa lay in bed, contemplating the uncertainties that lay ahead in the vast unknown of Australia.

"Louisa, you were quiet during supper. Are you feeling poorly?"

She pondered momentarily before answering, "I was just wondering about sailing to Australia; it's a complete unknown."

Isaac pulled her towards him and kissed her, "Whatever happens, we'll face it together."

"I guess we will." With that, she nestled into his shoulder, finding solace in the warmth of their shared dreams as they drifted into a night filled with the distant echoes of a howling wind.

48

Two weeks later, Louisa finally had the opportunity to visit her parents and Jane. Preparations for sailing to Australia took up so much time. Thankfully the rain had stopped, and although there was a cold wind blowing, she wasn't soaked when she opened the door of Daffodil Cottage. Jane walked out of the sitting room when she heard the door open, smiling when she saw her visitor.

"Louisa. How lovely to see you. Come sit by the fire and warm up; I can hear your teeth chattering."

Louisa looked at the rocking chair which had been at Isaac's cottage. "Can I sit in that?"

"Of course you can. It was lovely of Mary to give it to us." Watching as Louisa put her hands closer to the fire.

Jane sat on the bench and resumed her knitting at the table. "I gather you've been busy getting things ready for Australia."

Louisa nodded, her gaze dropping to her hands as she sat opposite her aunt. "There's so much to do," she admitted softly, feeling the weight of impending departure settling heavily on her shoulders. "I'm beginning to wonder if we'll ever be ready to leave on the eighth."

Jane put her knitting on the table and leaned forward, "I can see something's bothering you. Have you changed your mind about going?"

She shook her head, "No, I haven't, but the thought of leaving you and Uncle Luke..." She stopped as a tear ran down her cheek.

Jane tilted her head slightly, "I know you too well, Louisa; I can see there's something else; what is it?"

She looked into Jane's face, "I'm worried about sailing to Australia; they say it can take up to four months to get there."

Jane pulled her eyebrows together. "Is that all you're worried about?"

Louisa put her head down as she wrung her hands. "I'm not sure, but I think I may be with child."

Jane reached for her hands, holding both, she asked, "Are your courses late?"

She looked up and nodded, "A couple of weeks."

"Then there's a good chance you are."

Louisa bit her bottom lip, trying to prevent herself from bursting into tears.

Jane quickly sat beside her. "Aren't you happy about having a baby?"

Sniffing a couple of times before she answered, "If we were staying in Penstowe, I'd be delighted." She shook her head and gave a half smile. "I'm a bit frightened of what's going to happen."

Jane put her arm around Louisa, giving her a gentle squeeze. "Of course you are; your life is going to change dramatically. Not only with travelling to Australia, but having a baby as well."

Louisa looked into Jane's face. "When will I know for sure?"

"If your courses haven't come in another week, then I'd say you're going to have a baby." Smiling, she gave Louisa an affectionate shake. "I'm certain of it; I can see a difference in you."

"Really?"

"Really. And there's something else I can tell you, that feeling you get when you meet your baby for the first time. There are no words to describe it; it's a moment you'll treasure forever." Patting Louisa on the arm briefly, "But you'd better leave it for another few days to be sure before you tell Ike."

Louisa put her head on Jane's shoulder. "Thanks Aunty Jane."

Walking across the road to Rose Cottage, Louisa thought about what her aunt had said. Maybe she was right; it might be best to leave telling Isaac until she was certain. Opening the door, she was greeted by the smell of baking bread. Her mother was making pasties, flour all over the table with sprinkles on the floor.

"Louisa, I wasn't expecting you today." Elizabeth said, wiping her hands on her apron before hugging her.

"I thought I'd come today as it wasn't raining." Walking to the fire to warm her hands.

Elizabeth poured her a cup of tea. "I'm glad you've come to visit; I've got something to give you."

Louisa turned as she sat at the table, catching a glimpse of her mother walking into the sitting room. She returned a moment later with a beautiful new wicker basket, placing it on the table before sitting beside her. "You might like to use this for your sewing things. The one you've been using is just about falling apart."

Louisa was entirely surprised by the gift; her mother was not known to spend money on such extravagance. It was a lovely big basket with two lids hinged in the centre under the handle, and it would easily hold all her sewing items. "I don't know what to say, Mother, it's lovely, and you're right; my old one won't last much longer."

"I bought it when your Da and I went to Bradford markets a week ago; I also bought some soft cotton fabric and buttons so you can make baby clothes for when you and Isaac have children."

Louisa glanced at her mother before opening the lid. Did she suspect she might be with child?

"Thank you, Mother," Kissing her on the cheek.

Elizabeth touched the edge of the basket. "There's also something else in there I want you to have."

Looking inside, Louisa found a small black leather pouch under the material; picking it up, she could feel the weight of the coins. She loosened the drawstring and peeked into the dark interior of the bag. "Mother, where did you get this money?"

"Your father doesn't know about this, but I've been saving it for years; it's some of the money I got from selling flowers; you never know when you might need a few shillings." Giving her a grin.

Louisa looked at the coins. "There must be eight or nine shillings here."

"Ten shillings. I still have some more put away in case your father and I need some money, but you and Isaac may be able to use this more than we can now."

Louisa looked at Elizabeth again and saw the mother she had always wanted and started to cry; she wrapped her arms around her mother's neck, her voice quivering when she spoke into her hair. "I wasn't expecting this, thank you."

~

Louisa couldn't put it off any longer. With still a month until they were due to sail, she had to tell Isaac.

Lying in bed that night, Louisa turned to him, "Ike, I've something to tell you."

Isaac smiled, "I know you love me; what else can you tell me?"

She kissed him, "I'm with child."

Isaac's smile widened, his eyes alight with joy at the news. "That's wonderful," he breathed, leaning in to kiss her forehead tenderly. "I'm going to be a father."

She laughed, "Yes, *we're* going to have a baby."

Isaac lay on his back and pulled her on top of him, kissing her again. "Have you told your parents yet?"

"Of course not; I had to tell you first." Rolling onto her side, Louisa looked at him in the light of the fire. "I'll tell them tomorrow."

He pulled her closer, her head in the curve of his shoulder; he let out a happy sigh. "Wait till I tell Jacob."

She sat up quickly, playfully hitting his chest. "What about your Ma and Da?"

He laughed, "Of course, I'll tell them."

She lay down again. "Good, I'll tell Aunty Jane as well."

~

At breakfast, Louisa helped Mary serve porridge. She had put a bowl in front of Thomas when Isaac reached to hold her hand as she stood beside him. "Ma, Da, Louisa's with child." His voice laced with excitement as his grin reached from ear to ear. Mary stopped with the ladle in mid-air, a small drop of porridge plopped on the floor.

Thomas's eyes lit up with pride as he reached over to clasp Isaac's hand warmly. "That's grand, great news," he declared, a hint of paternal pride evident in his voice as he regarded his son with a mixture of admiration and affection. He looked at his wife near the fire.

Martha jumped up and down. "I'm going to be an aunty."

Jacob slapped him on the back. "Well done, brother."

Mary placed bowls in front of Isaac and Jacob, then turned to Louisa, leaning in to press a gentle kiss to her cheek. "That's wonderful news, my dear," she said, her eyes sparkling with genuine warmth. "And have ye been feelin' any sickness yet?" she added, her tone filled with concern as she reached out to squeeze Louisa's hand.

Louisa giggled, "Not yet, but I'm not looking forward to that."

Mary put a reassuring hand on her shoulder. "No one looks forward to that."

~

Gravel crunched under Louisa's feet as she made her way to Stokebridge, her shawl billowing in the brisk wind that swept down from the hills. She wondered what her parents' reaction would be to her news. Jane knew already and was happy for her. Louisa lifted the sneck of the front door, stepping inside out of the wind; Elizabeth sat at the table, peeling apples.

"Apple pie for supper?" Louisa asked.

She smiled and nodded, "You know how much your father loves it; I thought I'd give him a treat."

Louisa sat opposite her mother. "Where's Da and Sammy?"

Elizabeth cocked her head towards the back of the cottage. "In the barn, should be back soon."

Louisa smiled as she listened to her mother's tone; there was so much joy in her now that it radiated from her. She even noticed it in her father, the same atmosphere that oozed from Jane and Luke. The tension she had lived with all her childhood had disappeared.

Louisa lifted the teapot, seeing it was nearly empty, she asked, "Would you like me to make a fresh pot?"

Elizabeth nodded as she focused on the apples. As if they could smell the tea, Samson and Sammy walked in as she put the pot on the table. Samson rushed over to hug her. "Hello, love. It's nice to see you."

Elizabeth put the apples aside to pour tea. Pushing a cup before everyone, Louisa smiled, "Da, Mother, Sammy, I want you to know,"

Letting out a quick breath, "I'm with child."

Elizabeth's cup slipped from her hand, landing on the table with a clatter, spilling tea on the wood. Standing up quickly, she wiped the liquid with her apron. Turning to her husband, "Samson, we're going to be grandparents!"

Louisa looked down, sighing as she ran her finger around the rim of the tin cup. "I'm sorry you won't get to meet him or her." Tears fell as she picked up her cup.

Sammy put his arm around her shoulders, giving her a gentle squeeze. "I'll be there; I'll be its uncle."

Samson reached to place his hand on hers. "We'll be sad too, but Australia will be a better place to raise young children."

Elizabeth removed her wet apron and sat down. "At least your baby will have Isaac's parents to love it."

Louisa wiped her face with the back of her hand. "But I wanted my parents to love it too."

She thought about the chain of events that had led to her child being born in a country on the other side of the world. It all started with Isaac's brother Jack emigrating to Brisbane and his parents wanting to follow him. She assumed they would live in Stokebridge or Penstowe when Isaac began courting her. She would never have imagined five years ago; she would be sailing to Australia to work on a sheep farm with his family.

Time passed quickly; Louisa left for Daffodil Cottage.

Jane stood up, racing to hug her, a huge smile on her face. "How wonderful to see you," releasing her hold. "Have you told Ike you're with child?" Guiding her to the table, pushing aside the fabric and scissors to make room for her.

Sitting on the bench, she replied, "Yes, I told him last night, and we told his Ma and Da this morning."

Jane sat opposite. "Do Sam and Elizabeth know?"

She nodded, "I've just come from there."

Jane tilted her head as she looked at her. "How are you feeling? Not sick yet?"

Louisa laughed, "Not yet."

"Well, I hope you'll be lucky like I was; I was only sick with the twins, not the girls."

Louisa tried hard to keep the tears from escaping but wasn't successful.

Jane quickly moved beside her. "What's wrong, my darling?"

Putting her head on her shoulder. "You won't be able to hold my baby when it's born."

"Your baby will have plenty of people to love it." Reaching to wipe the tear from her cheek, "You're going to have the most wonderful life in Australia, so please don't be sad I won't get to hold your baby. And you know how much I love holding babies."

Louisa sat up and laughed, thinking of all the times her aunt would ask new mothers if she could hold theirs.

Jane's face sobered. "I always hoped Luke and I would have more children."

Louisa saw her pained expression. "I thought you would, too; why didn't you?"

"Just after Fran turned two, I lost a baby; I was about four months pregnant. Since then," She shrugged, "It seems the Good Lord doesn't want me to have any more."

"Oh, Aunty Jane, I'm so sorry."

"Don't be." She laughed, "I'll have grandchildren one day."

Louisa wiped her face with her hand. "I'm going to miss you so much."

Jane smiled, "You can always send me a letter occasionally."

Louisa snorted as she laughed, "That won't be the same."

"You'll have Ike's family, and I know life there will be different to Cornwall, but whatever happens, I know you'll be happy with Ike."

"I'm happy with Ike now; I'm worried about being with child while we sail."

Jane hugged her briefly again. "I wouldn't worry about that. Ike's family, Sammy and the Lord will look after you."

Fran walked in after finishing school. "Louisa!" Rushing to wrap her arms around her cousin's neck. "Mr. Trevorrow said I'm the best-behaved child in school."

Louisa reached up to hold Fran's slender arm. "Of course you are; you're always so well-behaved at home." Lightly tapping the tip of her upturned nose.

Time passed quickly for Louisa as she talked to Jane and Fran; but soon, she had to leave. It was useless trying to keep her mop cap on her head; she didn't feel like chasing it again. Clutching her shawl, she walked quickly to Penstowe, arriving as the light faded.

Louisa considered how much she would miss her aunt, uncle, and children when they sailed for Australia. Now she was expecting a baby; she found travelling to a new land terrifying. Hiding her fears from Isaac would be her greatest challenge.

~

A few mornings later, Louisa woke to a hundred butterflies in her stomach. The dryness in her mouth didn't help. Isaac snored beside her; she was going to be sick but was too scared to move lest she vomited when she sat up. She gave Isaac a shake. "Ike, Ike, wake up."

He snorted and rolled away from her.

"Grr," she said between clenched teeth and pushed him as hard as she could. He fell out of bed, taking most of the bedding with him.

He knelt on the floor and stared at her. "Ow, what was that for?"

Fumbling around, she found the corner of the feather quilt, pulling it over herself. "Ike, can you get me a bucket? I'm going to be sick."

Scrambling to his feet, he rushed out the door, shirttail flapping as he ran.

She shouted, "Hurry!"

Louisa lay on her back and looked at the ceiling, swallowing several times, hoping Isaac would return in time. Soon, she heard hurried footsteps as he raced to her side of the bed. When Louisa leaned over, she immediately vomited, splashes of bile landing on the floor. The odour of food scraps wafted from the bucket, causing her to vomit again. He watched as she hurled a third time. "Sorry, it was the first bucket I saw."

Eventually, she sat up, pushing her hair over her head. "I hope that doesn't continue until it's born."

Isaac picked up the bucket, moving it nearer to the door. He sat on the bed beside her and held her hand. "I hope so, too. But look on the bright side; in the end, we'll have a beautiful son or daughter."

She leaned her head on his shoulder. "Yes, we will."

305

On their last Sunday before leaving Cornwall, the Langdons were walking quickly to Stokebridge, trying to keep warm in the howling wind.

Louisa nearly bumped into Thomas as he stopped abruptly under the chestnut tree, his gaze fixed on the ancient church.

Mary asked, "What's the matter, Tom?"

The family gathered around him as he replied, "I'm taking a long last look at the church; we're never going to see it again."

Isaac put a hand on his shoulder. "Have you changed your mind about going?"

Thomas shook his head. "No, nothing like that; I was wondering if we'll see another church like this one?"

Louisa laughed. "I doubt that very much; this church is over four hundred years old. They only settled in Australia late last century."

Mary tugged on his arm. "Let's go inside and enjoy our final service."

As they sat in their pew, the organist began to play. Sammy turned and beamed at his sister and Isaac's family.

Reverend Ellacott took a deep breath after his sermon and announced. "I know you will join me in wishing the Langdon family and Master Sammy Keslake a safe journey to Australia." Murmurs were heard from the congregation before he continued. "The journey they are about to embark on is fraught with perils, but they go knowing God will protect them. Let us pray," he said, lowering his head.

"Oh, Lord, we ask you to look after our flock during their voyage to a new land and way of life. Amen."

~

Everyone stood up to leave, but the cold kept the congregation from milling outside as usual. Everyone seemed to gather near the wooden door, wanting to say their goodbyes to the travelling family.

Louisa's eyes lit up as she spotted Phillip leaning against the stone font. With a quick squeeze of Isaac's hand, she darted toward him, enveloping him in a tight embrace before pressing a kiss to his cheek. "I'm going to miss you so much," she whispered, her voice filled with genuine affection.

He smiled at her, "I'm going to miss you too, but maybe not for long." His dark eyes twinkled with mischief.

"Please don't tease me; what are you talking about?" asked Louisa.

He glanced at Isaac as he joined them. "Jonathon and I are considering emigrating to Australia once we qualify. So, there's a good chance we'll see you again."

Isaac shook his hand, saying, "That's wonderful news. It'll be grand to see you in Australia."

Phillip tilted his head a little. "It won't be for a few years. I won't become a doctor for at least five years, and Jonathon has only begun his law studies."

Louisa squealed with delight, stood on her tiptoes, and kissed his cheek again. "Just knowing we'll see you again is so exciting."

Isaac shook his hand a second time. "I agree; it will be good to see you in Australia." Glancing at Louisa, he added, "We'll both look forward to it."

From the corner of her eye, Louisa noticed Lady Trevelen walk towards her. She curtsied. "M'lady."

She smiled as she stopped near her. "Louisa, I wish you and your family all the best for the future. Australia will be so different from Cornwall." Pulling her cloak tighter around her neck, she continued, "I would like it if you would write to me and tell me all about your new life."

Louisa curtsied once more. "If you would like me to, M'lady."

Lady Trevelen put her hand on her arm before leaving. "I'd like that very much. Goodbye, Louisa." She turned and followed her husband out the door.

307

50

Jacob held the hammer over his shoulder, preparing to nail the box lid, when Thomas rushed and knelt on the floor, lifting it again, peering inside.

Jacob shook his head, letting his hand holding the hammer fall beside him. "Da! You've checked these boxes several times; you don't need to do it again."

"I know, I'm just worried," Thomas replied, "I keep thinking I've forgotten something."

Isaac pounced on his father's words, "Da, I'm sure that everything that should be in there is there. What are you so worried about?"

"I'm worried about what it will be like on the ship to Australia and what it'll be like once we get there." His knee creaked as he stood up. "I know Jack said it's a grand place, but it's still another country and so different to what we know here in Penstowe."

Grace spoke, "Da, we're all willing to go with you and Ma. You did give us the chance to stay in Stokebridge with Uncle Luke and Aunty Jane if we didn't want to go. We're all going because we want to."

Isaac said, "Da, Louisa and I are coming with you because there are more opportunities in Australia. I'm sure we'll have a good life there, much better than we could ever hope for here in Penstowe or Stokebridge."

Jacob looked at his father. "I agree; now, can I finish nailing these shut? We're leaving tomorrow morning."

Thomas nodded, and Jacob expertly nailed the lids of the first two boxes. Walking to the hearth, he picked up a sturdy piece of wood, placed his hammer in the last box, and used the wood to nail it shut.

Isaac looked at the boxes Jacob had made. The rope handles were secured into the ends, and he had beautifully chiselled 'Langdon' into each lid. Two boxes held the farming tools; the other contained Jacob's carpentry tools and other belongings not needed for the voyage, which would be loaded into the cargo hold.

After the final nail had been driven into the box, Thomas said, "I know we're taking a risk going to Australia." Looking at the faces watching him, he added, "But I don't think I could be any prouder of you right now."

Elijah said, "We can't wait to begin our big adventure."

~

Louisa stood by the window; her gaze fixed on the ivy-obscured view outside. Despite the chilly December morning, a faint smile graced her lips as she watched Elijah and Martha playing outside, her eyes tracing their joyful movements.

When Isaac opened the door, cold air rushed into the cottage. Louisa pulled her shawl around herself and followed him to greet Luke and Sammy when they arrived with the cart.

Isaac and Jacob carried the boxes and two trunks to the cart; Luke secured them with ropes while Sammy, Elijah, and Thomas loaded the bundles of bedding, clothing, and other items.

The men looked around outside, while Louisa followed Mary and Grace to check inside the cottage.

When they were satisfied that nothing had been left behind and everything had been loaded onto the cart, Thomas said, "Well, we'd best be on our way."

Mary closed the door; Luke tugged on Bobby's lead rope. It was time to walk to Stokebridge and say goodbye to Samson, Elizabeth, Jane, and the children.

Louisa was walking beside Isaac. She smiled at Martha who stopped her skipping when they had passed the last cottage, turned around, and waved, "Goodbye, Penstowe." Turning back, she ran to catch up with Elijah and Sammy.

When they reached the crossroads, Trevelen Manor stood on the hill before them. Louisa stopped while everyone else turned right towards Stokebridge.

Isaac stepped back to her side. "What is it?"

She turned to him, knowing her eyes were glistening. "I was thinking about my time working at the manor."

He looked at the grey stone house. "Hmm, they still haven't found out who killed His Lordship's brother."

She wondered if he could read her mind. "Perhaps they never will, " she said. She linked her arm through his, and they turned right. This was the beginning of a very long journey.

~

When Luke stopped the cart outside Rose Cottage, Samson was waiting with Elizabeth, Jane, and the children.

He stood with Elizabeth, watching Jane say goodbye to Louisa and Isaac. Jane gave Isaac a big hug, her head hardly reaching his shoulder. "You look after yourself and Louisa, and make sure you let us know when the baby arrives and tell us all about Australia."

Isaac nodded. "We'll try to write as often as we can; we're both going to miss you all very much, " he said, kissing her on the cheek.

Jane embraced Louisa; Samson could see she was becoming quite teary as she let her go. Reaching into her basket, she pulled out a parcel wrapped in brown paper. "Louisa, I have a little going away present for you, something I know you'll appreciate."

Louisa looked at the package in her hand for a moment. Jane asked, "Well, aren't you going to open it?"

Louisa looked up and nodded, her eyes beginning to glisten, but when she unwrapped the brown paper, the tears fell. Inside was a beautiful pair of dressmakers' scissors, wrapped in white cotton fabric. "I thought you might find them useful when you start sewing in Australia, much better than my old ones you've been using."

Louisa hugged Jane so tightly that Samson thought she would never let her go. "Thank you, Aunty Jane." Louisa released her grip. "I'll treasure them. I can't thank you enough for everything you have done for us over the years, and we'll never forget you and Uncle Luke."

Samson turned and walked towards Sammy as he hugged Hannah. Pulling his handkerchief from his pocket, Samson wiped his face before wrapping his arms around his son.

"I'm going to miss you, young man. Make sure you take care of yourself and look after your sister; I won't be there to help either of you anymore."

Sammy replied with a grin. "Don't worry about me, Da. I can look after myself. It's the convicts who need to watch out."

Samson smiled as he tousled his hair. "I almost forgot." Reaching into his pocket. "I have a small present for you." He placed a penny knife into his hand.

Sammy looked at the pale wood handle. Using his fingernail, he pulled out the blade and replaced it again. He smiled at his father and said, "Da, thank you so much. I'm sure this'll be very useful in Australia. I'll think of you every time I use it." Samson hugged him once more and walked to Louisa and Isaac.

Samson shook hands with Isaac and wrapped his arms around Louisa. She reminded him so much of his late mother. "Your mother and I will miss you very much, and we wish you all the best for the future."

Isaac replied, "Thank you, Mr. Keslake. I want you to know I'll do everything possible to care for Louisa and Sammy."

"I know you will, Ike, and that's a great comfort." Samson turned to Louisa. "Will you try to write as often as you can, and tell us all about the baby and Australia? I'm interested to hear all about it."

Louisa nodded, kissing her father on the cheek. "I'll try my best to write at least once a month, but I don't know what the mail will be like returning to Cornwall so you might get several letters at once."

"We don't care; as long as we hear from you, we just want to know you're safe."

Samson pulled a package wrapped in brown paper from inside his jacket and gave it to Louisa. "I thought you might like to have this."

She took the parcel and slowly opened it, finding a notebook with a speckled black and white cover and black binding—a nibbed pen, spare nibs, and ink powder inside.

Louisa stood staring at the gift for a moment. "Da, this must have cost you a lot of money. I can't accept this."

He gently placed a hand on her shoulder. "You can, and you will. I know you've already got writing paper and envelopes, pen, and ink bottle, but I thought you might like to keep a journal of the voyage to show the baby." Giving her a wink. "I had a few shillings saved your mother didn't know about; I bought them in Bradford last time I was there." Samson tapped the book. "In the back, you'll find something special."

When Louisa opened it, she found the pressed flower still showing signs of its previous brilliant red. Tears flowed as she twirled the stem between her fingers.

"When you told us you were going to Australia, your mother picked the last rose from the garden; she pressed it in an old apron under a stone. *'A rose to remind you of Rose Cottage.'* She's sorry there wasn't a daffodil to press as well."

Louisa nodded, replaced the rose, and handed the package to Isaac before wrapping her arms around Samson's neck. "I love you so much, Da. Thank you." Her voice trembled as she spoke.

Reaching into his pocket, he placed ten shillings in her hand. "Five shillings for you and the other five for Sammy. I'm giving it to you as I know you'll look after it for him."

"Thanks, Da; I'll put it with the money Mother gave me."

Samson laughed. "When you told me about that, I was surprised, but I'm glad she gave it to you."

Elizabeth and Sammy walked toward Samson, her arm around his waist, stopping when they reached them. Elizabeth gave Sammy one last hug and quickly stepped back. "Please take care of yourself and Louisa when you get to Australia; Stokebridge will be so quiet without you here." She flicked back a stray strand of sandy hair from his forehead. "I'm sure Reverend Ellacott will say some prayers tomorrow for a safe journey."

Sammy laughed. "I hope the Good Lord hears them; we'll need all your prayers."

Elizabeth hugged him once more, keeping hold of his hands. "I want you to know I do love you."

He nodded. "I love you too, Mother."

She kissed his cheek and turned towards Louisa.

Reaching out to hold her hand. "I'm going to miss you and Sammy." Turning to Isaac as she wiped a tear from her eye. "Please take care of my daughter for me."

"I'll do everything in my power to keep her safe."

Elizabeth nodded, linking her arm through Samson's. "Thank you, and take care of our grandchild, too."

"Of course I will," Isaac replied.

~

Luke picked up the lead rope and asked, "Would anyone like to sit on the cart? It's going to be a long way to Plymouth."

Louisa glanced at Mary and Martha. "I'm happy to walk."

Both shaking their heads, Mary replied. "We'll walk too."

Isaac tapped her on the shoulder. "Maybe you should ride on the cart; you are in a delicate condition."

She laughed softly as she playfully pushed him. "I'm only having a baby; I'm not crippled. Besides, walking will help keep me warm."

Luke grinned. "Let me know if you change your mind." He slightly tugged the rope, and the horse walked towards Roweshorne.

They all turned to wave at the family they were leaving behind. There were several calls of "Godspeed" as the cart pulled away from Stokebridge.

As the cart rounded the bend in the road, the figures of their loved ones waving goodbye dwindled into mere specks in the distance, prompting a collective forward gaze from everyone.

Louisa turned to Isaac and cried. "After seventeen years, I've finally found the mother I've always wanted. Now I'm leaving her forever."

"I know, Love, I know." He pulled her closer as they walked.

Louisa stopped at the bridge, leaning over the stone wall, looking at the stream as it flowed underneath. The trees bare as they waited for the return of spring, their favourite grassy knoll, brown from the heavy frost. A lone holly bush near the oak tree, the only greenery to be seen.

Isaac stood beside Louisa, enveloping her in a comforting embrace as he pressed a tender kiss to her cheek. "I often think of our times spent sitting beside the stream," he whispered, his voice filled with warmth and nostalgia.

"So do I," turning to kiss him. "We'd best catch up with the others."

Upon reaching Roweshorne, Phillip waited outside Robin Cottage with his parents. Louisa rushed to hug him.

"I'm going to miss you, my darling Louisa." Freeing her from his hold, he shook hands with Isaac. He glanced at his parents standing behind him. "We hope you have a safe journey, and please write to me as often as you can. I want to show your letters to Jonathon when I see him."

"Of course I will."

Dorothea Hill hugged Louisa. "I wish you all the best, my dear. Phillip always talks about you, and I know he will miss you." She glanced at her husband. "We hope you have a good life in Australia."

"Thank you."

James Hill approached, kissing Louisa on the cheek. "Thank you for being Phillip's friend. He was very lonely after we moved to Cornwall; your friendship has given him great joy." The look he gave her confirmed he knew Phillip's secret. "We look forward to hearing all about Australia."

More tears fell as Louisa hugged Phillip once more.

Hearing the cart moving through the village, Isaac tapped her shoulder. "We really must be on our way."

Louisa stepped back but still held Phillip's hand for a moment, wiping her face with her free hand. "Goodbye, Phillip." More tears fell as she hugged him again.

"Godspeed, my friend." He spoke into her hair before releasing her.

Isaac put his arm around her shoulders, gently guiding her in the direction Luke and his family took, waving as they walked.

When Phillip was no longer in sight, she burst into tears again, putting her head on Isaac's shoulder. "I'm going to miss him so much."

"I know you are, but hopefully, we'll see him again in Australia."

51

Isaac looked at the milestone, only two miles to Callington. Although it was December, it was cold, but a lovely bright day. He held Louisa's hand as they walked; Luke led the way with the horse and cart.

The pace could have been faster but there was only three and a half miles from Callington to St Mellion, their planned stop for the night.

Isaac stole a worried glance at Louisa, his mind filled with doubts about their decision to leave Cornwall. He could have taken over the tenancy of Pine Cottage and farm, and stayed in Penstowe. Louisa could have remained closer to her family; she would miss their Aunty Jane very much. Was it fair to ask her to leave them?

Roweshorne was a mile behind them when Louisa wrapped her hand around his upper arm. "What's the matter, Ike? You have a worried look on your face."

Walking a little behind the others, he knew their conversation would not be overheard.

He let out a deep sigh. "Are we making a big mistake? Should we have stayed in Penstowe, where you could be near your parents, instead of taking a big risk of travelling to the other side of the world, to a completely unknown country?" He searched her eyes for reassurance.

"It's not an unknown country, Ike. Your brother Jack's there. He said in his letters that you could become a landowner. Don't you want that?"

"Yes, I do, but I'm still worried about what I'm asking of you, especially with the baby coming." Isaac stopped and turned to face her, holding her cheeks. "If you have any doubts before we get on that ship, please tell me. If it's what you want, we'll return to Stokebridge to live with your parents, or with Uncle Luke and Aunty Jane."

"Ike, I'll not change my mind; I'm going to Australia with you and the rest of your family," Louisa added with a smile. "And I couldn't disappoint Sammy, could I?"

Isaac pulled her closer, wrapping his arms around her. "It wasn't until we left this morning that I realized how much I was asking you to give up, especially now that your mother has accepted me." He kissed her again. She was a strong woman but not domineering. Maybe that's what he loved about her.

"Of course, I'm going to miss my parents, Aunty Jane and Uncle Luke and their children, and Phillip, but my place is with you, and if you're going to Australia, then I'm going too."

Smiling as he reached for her hand, they continued walking, eventually catching up with the others.

Isaac laughed as he watched Sammy running ahead with Elijah and Martha. "I don't think Sammy can wait to get to Australia."

Louisa laughed, too. "No, he can't." She shouted, "Sammy, slow down and wait for us. You won't get to Australia any quicker by running."

The three children slowed, and Isaac could see Sammy's shoulders slump as they stopped.

Isaac heard his father say, "I hope they don't get tired before we get to St Mellion this afternoon."

His mother laughed, "They'd better be able to walk there. Those three are a bit too big to carry."

~

It was near Callington's outskirts when Bobby walked towards a big puddle.

Mary said, "Can we rest for a while? We can have some of Jane's bread and cold pork."

Thomas nodded. "Yes, I know I'm hungry."

Luke put hay in the feedbag for Bobby, securing the handle over the top of his head.

Thomas sat heavily on the ground, Isaac and Jacob sitting beside him. He laughed at the children as they ran around. Mary, Grace, and

Louisa searched for the bundle of food and ceramic bottles of water.

Mary said, "Take your time; I think we all need a rest before we continue our journey."

Thomas called out, "Sit down, children. You might want to keep going, but your mother's right. We need a rest."

The three children reluctantly sat down. With a mouthful of bread, Sammy asked, "Mr. Langdon, when does the ship sail from Plymouth?"

"Mr. Stanbury said in his letter that it's due to leave on the thirteenth of December, but don't worry, we'll be in Plymouth in plenty of time. We should be there the day after tomorrow, and then we'll have a day or two to look around the town before we board the ship."

Isaac smiled. "Sammy, we're not going to miss boarding the ship, and arriving early in Plymouth isn't going to make it leave any sooner. It'll leave when the captain is ready and not before."

"But I can't wait to get to Australia."

Thomas chuckled at Isaac's fatherly tone. "Well, you're going to have to wait. It'll take nearly four months before we arrive in Adelaide, and then we'll have to make our way to the sheep farm. We'll get there in the end; the journey has only just started."

Sammy's shoulders slumped. "All right, Ike."

Elijah finished his food, reached over, and pulled Sammy's cap off his head, running off with it. Sammy was up immediately, chasing him; Martha stood up, her hand clenched around bread as she joined in the fun and games until Luke called them back.

"Well, it's time we continued on our way. Mary, Louisa, do you want to ride on the cart?"

Mary replied, "I'm happy to walk." Louisa nodded in agreement.

"Right, let's go to St Mellion." Luke gave the rope a slight tug, and Bobby walked beside him, white plumes of warm air escaped every time the horse exhaled.

~

As they neared Callington, the village bustled with activity, the air alive with the sound of merchants hawking their wares and children's laughter echoing from the schoolyard.

Bobby's hooves changed from soft thuds in the dirt to the clip-clop of hooves on cobbled streets. The cart began to vibrate, and Thomas turned to check that the boxes were secure and would not move with the constant bumping. Thomas was admiring St Mary's church's square tower, with the clock on each side—the once cream sandstone, now grey, weathered with age. As they continued walking, they found the well in the middle of the main street; the church bells rang as they refilled their water bottles.

Martha turned to him. "Why are the bells ringing?"

Thomas laughed. "That was the church clock; it's midday." He looked to the sky. "Come, we'd better keep moving if we want to reach St Mellion this afternoon."

Leaving Callington, they saw chimneys and engine houses of mines scattered not far from the road. There were some men with picks, their backs stooped as they walked.

Thomas heard Jacob say, "I'm glad I'm not a miner. By the time they've turned thirty, they're hunched over like old men. And most are dead by the time they're fifty." He shook his head. "I'd rather be a farmer; at least we enjoy the fresh air rather than being stuck in a dusty mine all day."

Isaac nodded in agreement.

~

As the weary group approached the Travellers Rest in St Mellion, the setting sun cast long shadows across the narrow building, its bay windows glinting in the fading light, promising warmth and respite from the day's journey. To the right of the inn was an arched entrance big enough for coaches to drive through. They could see the stables at the back of the building through the arch.

Thomas walked in the main door and inquired about lodgings, his family following; Luke and Sammy waited with the horse and cart.

He approached the innkeeper. "Do you have any rooms for the night, please?"

"I have four rooms vacant, each with a double bed." The innkeeper surveyed the crowd before his desk and held out his hand. "Arthur Pendragon at your service."

Thomas could hear the smile in his voice as he shook hands with the portly gentleman. "Tom Langdon. Thank you. There are ten of us all together; we'll take them all." He asked, "Would it be all right if we put some of our bedding on the floor for the children?"

Arthur replied, "I have some spare mattresses; they might be more comfortable for them."

"Thank you." Thomas sorted through his coins to pay.

"The room cost also includes an evening meal and breakfast in the morning."

"That's grand; I know everyone's hungry," Thomas replied. "We also have a horse that needs to be stabled for the night. Is there an extra charge for him?"

"A penny."

Thomas found a penny and handed it to Arthur.

"Where have you travelled from today?"

Thomas chuckled softly as he looked down at his dust-covered clothes. "We've walked from Penstowe; we're going to Australia."

"Well, you've had a long walk, and a long journey ahead of you. Do you need any help with your belongings?"

"Thank you very much, but my sons should be able to manage if you could just show me where the rooms are."

Arthur led the way up the stairs, showing him the rooms. As he opened each door, Thomas could see the room had a fireplace, and they were clean, and the linen was fresh—an ewer and basin sitting on a small table in the corner.

"Thank you very much. I'm sure we'll be comfortable. Can we bring our boxes and trunks into the rooms?"

"Of course, but you're welcome to leave anything you don't need on the cart in the stables; they're at the back of the inn."

"Thank you very much; we might do that."

"You'll have to get hay from the loft and water from the well for the horse."

Thomas shook his hand and walked down the stairs to his waiting family. "I'll tell Luke where to take the horse and be right back."

Cold air seeped in as he opened the front door of the inn, closing it behind him with a soft thud. "Luke, they have four rooms available for the night, and there's a stable out back for Bobby. Do you need help with getting him settled?" he asked, rubbing his hands together to ward off the chill.

"Sammy's offered to help; you just worry about getting everything inside so we can all get out of the cold."

Thomas nodded and stepped back into the warmth of the inn. He turned to his sons. "Take our bags of clothing up to the rooms; the boxes, trunks, and bedding bundles can stay on the cart. We'll work out who'll be sleeping where once we get everything upstairs and the horse seen to."

Isaac, Jacob, and Elijah climbed onto the cart and began unloading the bundles of clothing, handing them down to Mary, Grace, and Martha. Louisa reached to take a bundle of clothing from Elijah, but Mary put a hand on her arm. "Don't give Louisa anything to carry." Turning to her. "You're not to lift anything heavy; we don't need any problems with the baby this close to leaving Cornwall."

She nodded and asked, "Can I at least carry my sewing basket?"

"I'll allow you to carry that." Mary smiled as she passed it to Louisa.

Thomas picked up two of the bundles of clothing, turning to his daughter-in-law. "Come, I'll show you to the rooms." He briskly walked inside and up the stairs.

When Thomas opened the first door, he was pleased to see the fire had been lit. "You and Ike can have this room. I'll put our clothing in the next room for Mary and myself, and then I'll help bring the other bundles inside."

~

Sammy and Luke led Bobby to the stable after the cart was unloaded. Once unharnessed, Luke put him in an empty stall, and Sammy climbed up to the loft and threw down some hay.

Climbing down, he said. "I'll get some water."

Luke nodded as he put the hay in the manger.

Satisfied the horse was settled, Sammy and Luke returned inside and walked upstairs.

They found Thomas helping Arthur put mattresses on the floor of a room. Luke said, "I assume this room is for me and the boys?"

Sammy spoke, "I don't mind sleeping on the floor."

"I can sleep on the floor also; Jacob and Elijah can share the bed."

Arthur said, "I'm sorry there aren't enough beds for you all; this is the best we can do."

Luke replied, "The room is starting to warm. We'll sleep well; we're all very tired."

As he was about to walk out the door, Thomas turned to Arthur and said, "Thank you. We'll see you later for the evening meal."

~

Thomas walked into the room with his and Mary's belongings; he lay on the bed, arms outstretched, looking at the ceiling.

Mary followed him and smiled, "You look like you couldn't even raise an eyebrow, Tom."

Thomas didn't move but replied, "And we still have another two or three days of walking before we reach Plymouth."

Mary sat beside him on the bed and held his hand. "Just think of all the days on the ship when you won't have to walk," she said.

Thomas sat up, looking at his wife. "Are we making a big mistake, Mary?"

"I don't think so; the children will have a much better life in Australia than in Cornwall."

"I know Jack says it's wonderful in Brisbane, but what if he just wrote that, and things aren't as good as he's saying in his letters? Besides, we're not going to Brisbane; we're going to South Australia."

"I know Australia is a different country, but we'll have to make the best of what we're given. Do you want to turn around and go back to Penstowe and disappoint the children?"

"No, I couldn't do that to them, especially those three young ones; I get tired just watching them." They laughed.

~

Louisa sat alone at a table in the dining room, the notebook her father gave her open in front of her. Isaac smiled at her but remained at an adjoining table. She smiled back; he must have realized she wanted privacy while she wrote in it.

She looked at the pristine blank page, wondering where to begin.

Louisa looked at the date she had written, holding the pen over the page. Leaning back to prevent her tears from falling onto the paper, she found her handkerchief, wiped her eyes, and continued writing.

> *It was sad leaving Stokebridge today, knowing we will never see it, or our families again. Waving goodbye to the people we love was the hardest part of the journey. We're going to miss them so much.*
>
> *Saying goodbye to Phillip was also difficult. I will miss him, too, but hopefully we'll see him and Jonathan again when they go to Australia.*

Louisa sat beside Isaac as they ate their evening meal. "Are you settled into your rooms?" Arthur asked as he put more wood on the fire.

"Yes, thank you very much," Thomas replied.

"I'm pleased to hear that." Standing up, he added, "We start serving breakfast before sun up; just let me know if you want it earlier."

"Thank you, but I'm sure there'll be no need. We'll probably be up early; we still have a long way to travel tomorrow, and by the time we finish putting everything on the cart, it might be just in time for breakfast." Thomas replied, yawning. "I think we'll have an early night. I don't know about the young ones, but I'm very tired; it's been a long day."

Louisa and Isaac climbed into bed and were talking. "With the money I've saved from working at the manor, the two pounds Lady Trevelen gave me, and the money Da and Mother gave us, and the few shillings you had, we have nearly seven pounds. Plus, I've got Sammy's five shillings."

"I'm sure it'll be needed once we reach Adelaide, but where shall we put it for safekeeping 'til we get there?"

"I thought I might make a pocket in the lining of my sewing basket, and hopefully, it won't be found."

"You think of everything." Isaac said, kissing her lovingly.

52

As he predicted, Thomas was up early. He dressed, walked out onto the landing, and banged on doors to wake everyone.

He stood and waited as each family member emerged from their rooms. His sons, and Luke and Sammy, stood near him.

"We'll leave the women to get dressed. Let's take the bags downstairs, then we can have breakfast and be on our way."

The men returned to their respective rooms and began piling bags on the floor outside their doors.

The lantern lit the stall while Luke and Sammy loaded the bags and harnessed Bobby. Thomas had thrown the last bag on the cart when Luke pulled out a piece of tar-coated sailcloth from under the bundles of bedding.

He turned to Thomas and said, "Looks like it may rain later. We don't want everything getting wet."

As Sammy helped Luke secure the sailcloth, a loud rumble was heard from Elijah's stomach.

Isaac laughed. "I think we'd better go inside and eat."

Sitting near the fire, Thomas enjoyed breakfast and steaming cups of tea. He grinned as he watched Elijah and Sammy eat an extra bowl of porridge, followed by several slices of bread.

Picking up the final baskets and bags, they were ready to depart. "Do you have any fresh bread to spare?" Thomas asked Arthur.

"Aye, we might have a couple of loaves you can have; I'll fetch them for you."

He returned soon with two loaves wrapped in a linen cloth. "They're still warm; they've not long come out of oven."

Thomas paid Arthur, "Thank you for your help yesterday and this morning. I hope everyone else we meet is as kind as you've been."

"It's all part of being a good innkeeper," he grinned. "I hope you have a good journey to Australia." Arthur shook hands with Thomas before following the family outside.

Thomas looked at the sky, which was utterly different from the previous day. The weather was gloomy, and no blue sky could be seen. The dark grey clouds were an undeniable indication of approaching rain.

The travelling group followed the cart; every time Thomas breathed, he felt like he had swallowed a mouthful of snow. He wished there was some warmth from the sun, but the dark clouds kept it hidden from view. The wind seemed to blow right through him as he walked. The only reprieve was from the high hedges by the side of the road.

They had only travelled a mile from St Mellion when light rain began, and it showed no sign of giving up soon. Thomas pulled his collar up and adjusted his cap; his sons and Sammy did the same. The women pulled their shawls over their heads.

As the rain drizzled down, Thomas watched the powerful Clydesdale as he pulled the cart, plodding along the muddy road. His head bobbing, steam rising from the thick mane that covered his strong, arched neck. The mud-covered thick hair glued itself to his giant hooves, not floating as it had been the day before.

He heard Mary cry, "Oh no," as the rain turned to sleet, stinging their faces.

Luke stopped Bobby under a tree, pulling out another piece of tar-coated sailcloth. He placed it over the horse, securing it to the traces.

Louisa and Martha climbed onto the cart, their feet hanging over the side. Using another piece of sailcloth, they held it over themselves in a futile effort to keep dry.

The sloshing of water as the cart went through puddles made Thomas miserable. He did not doubt that everyone else felt the same. His toes felt like ice from the cold mud on his boots. Mary and Grace's dresses were dotted with mud around the hem.

Thomas grimaced as Bobby's tail lifted, leaving behind lumps of manure, adding insult to injury amidst the miserable weather. He glanced at Louisa and Martha, who wrinkled their noses in disgust.

~

The quaint town of Hatt was a welcoming sight. Mary was weary and wondered how the rest of the family felt. Luke moved Bobby under a tree near an inn, filling his feed bag and looping the handle over his head.

Once inside the Inn, they were shown to a room next to the main bar. Mary pointed to a large table in the corner, the children were jostling for the chair closest to the hearth. Soon, jackets and shawls were draped over chairs in front of the blazing fire. The relentless wind howled as it whipped down the chimney, sending shivers down their spines and ruffling the flames dancing in the hearth.

Mary glanced at the miserable faces of their group after they sat down; they were wet and cold. If they stayed at the inn for a short while, they could warm up while they rested.

She was worried about Thomas, who looked very fatigued. She turned to him and said, "Tom, why don't you treat yourself to a glass of ale? I'm sure Luke would like to join you."

Luke stood up. "That sounds like a good idea, Tom. Why not?" Thomas wearily followed his brother-in-law.

Isaac sat beside Mary. "Are you worried Da won't be able to walk to Plymouth?"

"Yes, nineteen miles is a long way to walk in three days. He keeps forgetting he's not young anymore. He may be used to working in fields all hours of the day, but walking to the port?" She shrugged. "He told me last night he's worried we're making a big mistake."

Isaac looked at her thoughtfully. "What do you think? Are we making a big mistake?"

"I don't think so. Jack's letters are full of what a wonderful country Australia is, and I don't think he'd lie to us."

"I don't think he would, either. Maybe we should stay in Hatt tonight and not worry about reaching Saltash, it's still another five miles away.

Mary nodded. "I'll talk to your father and Luke when they come back. Then we'll discuss whether we stay or go on. Meanwhile, let's see if we can get something for everyone to eat."

Mary and Isaac purchased some bread and beef from the bar. They could hear murmurs as people talked, and the unmistakable smell of ale and strong tobacco wafted through the door. There was also a strange clicking sound, which was puzzling.

Martha cocked her head. "What's making that noise?"

Mary tilted her head to listen. "I don't know, I've never heard that before."

Jacob stood up. "I'm curious too. I'll see if I can find out what it is." He said, walking into the next room.

He returned shortly, a curious glint in his eyes. "That noise is coming from a game the men are playing," he explained. "It's called dominoes; they match little blocks of wood with dots together."

When Thomas and Luke returned, Mary asked Thomas, "Do you want to continue to Saltash, or would you like to stay in Hatt tonight? We still have plenty of time to get to Plymouth."

He slowly shook his head. "We'll keep going to Saltash; we should be in Plymouth by tomorrow afternoon. We can rest for a couple of days at the emigration depot. I want to get to the port as soon as possible, and Luke can't be away from the manor for too long."

Mary nodded and pushed the remaining bread and beef towards him. "Well, have some food, and we'll leave."

53

Several Friesian cows and Cotswold sheep huddled in fields under bare-branched oak and chestnut trees.

Sammy stopped walking with Elijah and Martha and waited until Isaac caught up with him. As they walked, he asked, "Ike, do you think they'll be the breed of sheep we'll have to look after in South Australia?"

"I don't know what breed of sheep they'll have on the farm; we'll find out when we get there. The agent did say the farm is quite large, so I can only assume there'll be many sheep to look after."

"I can't wait to get there, Ike."

"We'll get there in time, and then you'll have the rest of your life in Australia unless you're thinking about returning to Cornwall," Isaac said with a grin.

"Oh no, I've wanted to go to Australia for a long time. I'm staying there."

"Well, we should get to Adelaide around Easter if you can wait that long." Isaac ruffled his hair, before he ran to join Elijah and Martha, jumping over puddles.

~

Sammy found the milestone indicating there were only three miles to Saltash. The rain and sleet had finally stopped, but it was still cold and cloudy. He put his hands deep into his pockets.

Sammy was walking ahead with Elijah and Martha when he heard the wind rushing towards them. He started running, and his companions joined him, but they couldn't outrun the rain that fell from the bare

327

branches.

Martha shook herself. "Brr!" Pulling her shawl over her head.

A short while later, Sammy saw a slight movement in the woods out of the corner of his eye. He immediately stopped, and Elijah and Martha stood beside him.

"What is it?" Elijah whispered.

"Look over there." Sammy pointed. Not far from the road were six deer, one big stag, three does and two nearly grown fawns.

Luke stopped the horse, and the family carefully walked closer.

Grace looked at the deer and whispered, "I doubt we'll see any of those in Australia."

Jacob replied softly, "You might be right, but we'll see some very different types of animals. Remember what Jack said in his letters."

Luke pulled Bobby's lead rope and the deer bounded off.

~

In the clearing sky, the sun dipped toward the horizon, casting an orange glow over the landscape, they finally arrived in Saltash, the weary travellers' faces illuminated by its fading light. They found a small Inn, and Thomas led them inside to escape the cold. Sammy had volunteered to stay with the horse and cart.

When Thomas inquired about staying for the night, he was happy to hear that the innkeeper had enough beds for everyone. At least Sammy and Luke wouldn't have to sleep on the floor again.

Thomas approached the group, his voice filled with relief. "Good news, everyone. We've got enough beds for the night and there's one room with four beds, so Luke, Jacob, Elijah, and Sammy can sleep there. And another three that have double beds."

Luke said, "That's good. Let's get our stuff off the cart, so we can get the horse stabled and Sammy can come inside."

While Thomas paid the innkeeper, the men walked outside and began unloading their belongings, dropping them inside the door.

Grace and Martha picked up their bags, following the innkeeper up the stairs to the rooms. As Thomas picked up two bags, he heard Mary reminding Louisa she could only carry her sewing basket.

Luke and Sammy joined them as their evening meal was being served. Luke said, "I've just spoken to the innkeeper. He said it's only half a mile to the ferry crossing at the Tamar River. Once we reach Devon, we should only have another four miles to get to Plymouth."

Thomas looked at his brother-in-law. "How's the horse faring?"

"He's grand, probably enjoying the change from ploughing fields all day," Luke replied.

Thomas looked at his family. "We still have to walk again tomorrow, so we should all get to bed."

~

Louisa sat up in bed, writing in her journal by candlelight while Isaac tended the fire.

> *It was a miserable journey from St Mellion. The rain, wind and sleet seemed determined to make us miserable. We were cold when we reached Hatt, and sitting inside the inn by the fire warmed us up. However, when we went outside to continue walking, we got wet again. I didn't think it was possible, but we were even colder.*
>
> *I'm sure by the time we reached Saltash, we resembled drowned rats.*

Closing her notebook, she put it on the side table when Isaac said, "Louisa, it's not too late if you want to change your mind about going to Australia."

"Ike, I'm not going to change my mind." She looked at him as she pulled the blankets over herself. "I'm looking forward to seeing Australia for myself."

Isaac nodded. "I want to go to Australia too; I just want to make sure you won't regret your decision not to stay in Cornwall."

He threw another piece of wood on the fire and climbed under the covers. "I won't ask again, but please tell me if you have any second thoughts."

Louisa's voice was firm but gentle as she reassured him, her eyes reflecting determination. "I'll not change my mind; our baby will be born in Australia, and so will any other babies we have." She blew out the candle and cuddled into him.

54

Luke shivered while he and Sammy waited outside with the horse and cart, waiting to load the bags before leaving.

Thankfully, the rain had stopped, and thick grey clouds veiled the sun, casting a sombre hue over the landscape as they trudged forward. They had only been walking for a short while when the river appeared in the distance.

Jacob stopped walking and asked no one in particular, "Do you realise that once we cross the Tamar River, we'll have left Cornwall for good?" Glancing around, he added, "Except Uncle Luke, of course."

Isaac stood beside him, his eyes reflecting a mix of excitement and uncertainty. "And we're about to embark on a new life in Australia; who knows what the future will hold for us there?"

Luke said, "Let's hope it's a good future for you all." He tugged on Bobby's rope and continued towards the ferry bay.

As Luke approached the river's edge, he saw plumes of smoke from the steam ferry crossing the river. He stopped to watch it come towards their side of the river, but the buildings soon hid it.

"I've never seen a steam engine before," Luke said as they walked on.

Isaac looked at him. "Neither have I; I've only heard about them."

The ferry steamed towards the riverbank as they rounded the last corner to the landing site.

Luke glanced at Sammy and Elijah, who stood with open mouths as they watched; they were both captivated.

"It looks like a floating bridge," Sammy remarked, his eyes wide with wonder.

Martha's voice showed a slight tremble when she asked, "Da, do we have to get on that?"

Thomas put a reassuring hand on her shoulder. "This ferry has been running for many years; I'm sure we'll be quite safe crossing the river."

They all watched the ferry as it slowly appraoched the landing bay.

Looking at the people waiting to cross the river, Luke noticed many were peasants like themselves, carrying bundles of goods for sale. He glanced at two well-dressed men standing holding the reins of their horses. No other carts were waiting to cross the river.

There was a loud bang as the wooden platform was lowered. Luke kept a firm grip on the rope when Bobby began throwing his head up and down after being startled by the steam engine.

Two horses pulling a carriage moved off, and other passengers followed. The ferryman was ready to take the waiting people on board.

"All right folks, let's get the horse and cart on first."

Luke began leading Bobby towards the ferry, but as he got closer, he refused to move any further, throwing his head up and down again. No calming words from Luke would encourage him to walk on.

The ferryman marched towards Luke. "Turn him around and start walking away, then stop after about twenty yards. We'll put a blindfold on him; once he can't see what's happening, he won't be a problem." Pulling an old shirt from a wooden box on the end of the ferry, he said, "Use this."

With Sammy's help, Luke did as the ferryman said. Bobby still threw his head up and down and gave a few whinnies, but after soothing words from Luke, he walked onto the ferry.

Luke was about to remove the shirt when the ferryman called out, "Keep the blindfold on him till we get to the other side; we don't want him to panic once we start moving."

Luke kept talking to Bobby and rubbing his neck while Thomas and his family walked on board, along with the other people and two men leading their horses.

The ferryman walked on, instructing the crew to raise the platform behind them. Slowly, the engine increased its power, and the ferry moved away from the Cornwall side of the river.

Luke smiled warmly as he watched Martha reach for her father's hand, a silent gesture of trust and reassurance amidst the unfamiliarity of their journey. The ferry moved towards the middle of the river.

Luke would have joined Sammy and Elijah as they leaned over the side, looking at the water washing up against the vessel's side, but he needed to keep the horse calm. The two boys turned their attention to the smoke from the chimney; they were fascinated by the engine.

Half an hour later, the ferry reached the Devon side of the Tamar River, and the platform at the other end was lowered.

Luke and the cart walked off first. After twenty yards, Sammy held Bobby while he removed the blindfold.

Luke returned the shirt to the ferryman and shook his hand. "Thank you for your help with the horse. I'll be back this way in the next day or two, so we may have to do the same thing again."

"You're welcome; the blindfold is usually the best way to deal with skittish horses, especially when they're not used to the ferry."

Luke was about to return to the waiting group when the ferryman called him back. "Are you going to Plymouth?"

"Yes, we are; my sister and her family are sailing to Australia in a few days. How did you know we were going there?"

"I've seen a lot of loaded carts coming this way, all going to Plymouth. Just be careful when you get there; you'll probably find lots of street urchins begging for money; the best thing you can do is ignore them; don't even look at them."

"Why's that?" Luke asked, very curious.

"Sometimes they have bigger friends waiting behind buildings; if you stop, they may come out and rob you."

"Good heavens, thank you for the warning." He waved farewell before returning to the others.

As they neared Plymouth, Elijah, Sammy, and Martha ran ahead, looking for the milestones. "Only three more miles to Plymouth, Uncle Luke," Sammy called out.

Thomas said, "I think we can stop for a while and have something to eat before we continue. Don't you agree, Luke?"

"That's a good idea; Bobby will enjoy a rest, too." Luke lifted the bucket hanging from the rear of the cart. "Sammy, can you get some water for him?"

Mary got the remaining food from the cart and called the children to sit. When Sammy returned with the water, Luke offered it to Bobby. After the horse had quenched its thirst, Luke put the handle of the feedbag over Bobby's head and sat next to Thomas.

Thomas asked, "It shouldn't take us long to get to Plymouth now. When do you think we'll arrive there, Luke?"

"We should arrive by early afternoon, which will give us plenty of time to find the emigration depot."

Thomas glanced at his family. "Then we'll have a few days to rest before we board our ship and say farewell to England."

~

After they had eaten, they started walking again towards Plymouth. Thomas noticed a renewed vigour in their steps, realising how close they were to the port.

The closer they were to Plymouth, the fewer fields they passed. Several cottage roofs, buildings, and spires seemed to take their place. Thomas was fascinated by them and smiled as his family admired them, too, especially Louisa.

The pot-holed, rough gravel road was replaced with cobbled streets, busy with carts loaded with commercial goods and carriages carrying private passengers. This was so different to the villages they had left behind.

Occasionally, a boy rolling a barrel hoop would run past.

Thomas was walking behind the cart, feeling very weary. He was reassured when Jacob occasionally looked over his shoulder to check on him.

A boy, about six years old dressed in ragged clothes, ran up to Thomas, walking backwards in front of him as he spoke. "Please, Mister, have you got a spare farthing?"

Thomas ignored the boy and was relieved when Jacob returned to walk beside him. "Are you all right, Da?" he asked, darting a glance at the rascal.

"I'll be glad when we reach the depot." He increased his pace, wanting to get away from the urchin.

The boy stopped and shouted. *"Bastards."*

Jacob watched as he ran into an alley out of sight. "Delightful language for a child so young."

"He probably learned it from his bigger friends." He turned to Jacob, "I think we'd better catch up with the others."

As they walked down a gentle hill, a high-pitched whistle was heard. Bobby stopped suddenly, throwing his head around.

"What on earth is that?" Elijah asked.

Following the sound, Thomas was mesmerised by the massive steam engine pulling three wooden carriages behind it. Puffs of smoke billowed from its funnel at the front as it moved along tracks towards the centre of Plymouth.

Sammy said, "I think that's a train; I remember Mr. Penrose saying his brother saw one in Plymouth when he left Cornwall. I was hoping we might see one while we're here."

Thomas turned around and addressed his family, saying, "Let's keep moving. We need to get to the depot this afternoon."

As the massive steam engine disappeared around the bend, they continued their descent down the hill, anticipation building for their arrival at the depot.

55

After seeking directions, they finally arrived at the emigration depot—a sprawling structure of imposing dark grey stone walls nestled alongside the bustling wharf, its entrance beckoning with a sense of both opportunity and uncertainty.

Thomas and his family walked inside, while Luke and Sammy remained outside with the horse and cart.

Inside, they saw a bare room except for broadsheets advertising work opportunities in Canada and Australia. A second door on their right opened into a big reception room, a large fireplace was lit in the wall on their right, making the room warm and cosy.

There were several benches along the wall to their left and a couple more in front of them. Five young children were sitting quietly on the front bench. Beside them on the floor were several bundles of belongings.

In the corner opposite the door, not far from the fire, was a desk where the man sitting behind was recording information into a large book.

Mary ushered Louisa and the children to sit on a bench as a young man, sitting behind a smaller desk, walked up to them, offering his hand. "Good afternoon. My name is Phillip Hayward, and I'm the assistant depot master here; I presume you're due to sail on a ship leaving soon."

Thomas shook his hand. "I'm Tom Langdon, and these are my sons Ike and Jacob. We were told to be in Plymouth by the eleventh to board a ship sailing to Adelaide."

"Do you have your embarkation orders?"

Thomas pulled the letter out of his pocket, giving it to Phillip. After he had read the orders, he gave them back to Thomas. "And is this all your family?"

"No, Sammy Keslake is outside with my brother-in-law; they stayed with the horse and cart. My brother-in-law will return to Stokebridge tomorrow. Can he stay here tonight?"

"I'm afraid not. These facilities are for emigrants only, but there is an inn about half a mile up the road where he can stay."

"Thank you, I'll let him know. Can we unload our belongings first?"

"Of course, just put them inside the door, and when you are done, take a seat. When Mr. Cowling has finished with this other family, he'll write your family's details into his arrivals book, and then one of the mess men will show you to your dormitories."

"Thank you," Thomas said.

Thomas supervised the cart's unloading, explaining about the inn to Luke. The boxes, trunks, and bedding bundles were removed and taken inside the depot.

Thomas told Phillip, "I'd like to say farewell to my brother-in-law before he leaves."

He nodded. "Of course."

Mary and Louisa walked to the door with Thomas. "We'll be back very soon," he said to his family as they went outside.

Thomas shook hands with Luke. "We can't thank you enough for coming with us to Plymouth. It would have cost us a lot of money to get here otherwise. And please thank Fred Pengelly for letting us borrow the horse and cart."

"I didn't mind coming to Plymouth, but tomorrow before I leave, I'd like to see if I can find something special to take back for Jane." He turned to Louisa. "Would you like to come with me? You may have an idea of what your aunt would like."

"I'd love to Uncle Luke; seeing what else I can buy here in Plymouth would be interesting."

After hugging Luke, Mary asked, "How long do you think it will take you to get home?"

"It should only take me a couple of days. I'll be able to sit on the cart most of the way home, so I won't have to walk, making the journey faster."

"I think Aunty Jane will be glad to have you home again," Louisa said.

"I must admit, I'm looking forward to seeing Jane and the children too."

Thomas shook his hand once more. "We'll say goodbye to you in the morning before you leave."

His big smile brightened his face. "I'll look forward to it."

On their return to the reception room, Phillip Hayward approached Thomas and said, "Mr. Cowling shouldn't be much longer." Before returning to his desk.

Thomas, Mary, and Louisa sat and waited with the rest of the family. A few moments later, Mr. Cowling leaned toward Phillip Hayward and spoke. Phillip walked out a door not far from his desk. Within a moment, Phillip Hayward returned with another young man.

Mr. Cowling turned to the family. "Please follow Mr. Edwards; he'll take you to your dormitory."

Mr. Cowling walked to Thomas, indicating they follow him. "The younger children can remain seated."

Thomas turned around to Elijah, Martha, and Sammy. "Please do as Mr. Cowling says." Thomas pulled his embarkation orders out of his pocket and followed him to the desk.

Mr. Cowling took the papers from Thomas and shook hands with him. "My name is Bill Cowling, and I'm the depot master here. I'll write your names in my ledger and ensure the names and ages correspond with your embarkation orders." Opening the large book as he sat at the desk.

Bill looked at the papers. "You are Thomas Langdon, aged forty-nine and the head of the family, is that correct?" he asked as he looked up to Thomas.

He replied, "Yes, there's also my wife Mary, forty-five, my son Isaac, twenty-one and his wife Louisa, seventeen."

Thomas waited for Bill to check the embarkation orders and finish writing before he continued. "Our son Jacob is also twenty-one."

Bill looked up. "Is he a twin to Isaac?"

"Yes, they're twins." Watching as Bill made a note in his book.

"Go on," Bill said, rechecking the paper.

"My daughter Grace, who's nineteen."

Bill stopped and looked up. "You have been informed the single women stay in their own quarters and have no contact with any other passengers during the time at the depot or on the voyage?"

Thomas glanced at his daughter. "Yes, the agent in Bradford did mention that."

"I'll send Mr. Hayward to fetch the matron soon."

Grace asked, "Will I be able to talk to my parents anytime during the voyage?" Thomas could see she was worried about being cut off from her family.

Bill replied, "You can talk to your mother, but that will be all. And only after the matron has given permission."

Mary gave Grace a reassuring smile before putting her arm around her shoulders.

Bill looked back at his book and the list. "Is the next child Elijah?"

"Yes, he's fourteen, and Martha is ten."

Bill counted the names on the list. "That leaves only Sammy."

Isaac spoke, "Sammy Keslake; he's my wife's brother; he's nearly thirteen."

Bill wrote his name in the book, leaning towards Phillip. "Will you please fetch Mrs. Pearce?"

Phillip walked through the same door as before.

Bill looked up at Grace. "Miss Langdon, will you please get your belongings? The matron will be here shortly."

While Mary and Grace were sorting through the bundles, Phillip returned with a plump, grey-haired woman. She walked to the depot master's desk.

When Mary and Grace returned, Bill said, "This is Mrs. Pearce. She's the matron for the single women while you're in Plymouth."

"Good afternoon," she said, smiling at Grace. "I presume you're the young lady who'll stay in my quarters until it's time to board your ship."

Grace dropped her bundles and turned to Mary, wrapping her arms around her neck before turning to hug Louisa, her father, and her siblings. Picking up her bundles of clothing and bedding, she turned with a tear in her eye. "I'll not see you again until we reach Australia." She followed Mrs. Pearce through the door.

Bill looked at Mary as she watched her daughter leave. "I can assure you Mrs. Langdon, Mrs. Pearce will look after your daughter."

Thomas saw tears in Mary's eyes as she could only nod at the depot manager.

Bill continued, "Now." He consulted his ledger. "Mr. Jacob Langdon, Master Elijah Langdon, and Master Sammy Keslake will stay in the single men's quarters for their time in the depot and on board."

Jacob returned to the bench and began looking for his belongings. "Elijah, Sammy, grab your things; we're going to our quarters."

Thomas asked, "Will we be able to speak to them at any time?"

"The single men will join the families for meals while in the depot, but once you board the ship, they will only be allowed on deck, not in any other quarters."

Mr. Cowling gave Phillip a nod and Phillip walked through the same door as before, returning shortly with a little white-haired man in his forties.

Bill said, "This is Mr. Gregory. He's in charge of the single men." He glanced at Thomas before turning to the young men, "Will you please go with him?"

Thomas saw Louisa watch her brother as he walked away with a smile.

After Jacob and the two young boys left, Thomas asked, "Are we allowed to leave the depot to walk around the city? We'd also like to say goodbye to my wife's brother before he leaves for Cornwall in the morning."

Bill replied, "Yes, you can. There are some shops and market stalls about half a mile from here, but I ask you to advise us of when you are leaving and report back to us when you return." He rubbed his forefinger and thumb on either side of his nose before he continued. "Please don't be too long tomorrow morning. The doctor will be here after breakfast, and you must be examined."

"Of course."

"Phillip, please show Mr. and Mrs. Langdon to the dormitory?" He turned to Thomas. "If your boxes are going into the cargo hold, I can arrange for them to be taken to the storage area if you wish."

"Thank you very much." The five remaining family members picked up their bundles of clothing and bedding.

Thomas glanced at the trunks. Bill said, "You can leave those trunks and bedding here for now, Mr. Langdon. Just take your clothing. Come back for them after you have been shown to your dormitory."

Thomas, Mary, and Martha picked up their bags while Isaac grabbed both bags of clothing. Louisa picked up her basket and followed Phillip out the door.

Walking along a long corridor, they passed a door with a sign 'Halifax, Canada,' and after turning a couple of corners, Phillip opened another with a sign 'Adelaide, Australia.'

"This is the mess hall for all emigrants sailing to Adelaide, as you can see by the sign." He stood aside to let the family walk in.

The first thing that struck Thomas was the size of the room. He had never seen a room as big as this, and the ceiling was at least fifteen feet high. A large staircase was directly opposite them in the middle of the room. On each side of the staircase towards the main door was a row of ten columns from the floor to the ceiling, dividing the room into three sections.

The centre section was left bare for easy access to the staircase, and the sections to the left and right of the columns were furnished with many long tables and benches. Some of these were occupied with people sitting and talking. They could feel the heat of a blazing fire to the right of the door they had just walked in.

Phillip walked towards the stairs, indicating for them to follow. As they reached the top, a passageway ran across to the left and right, but he opened the door just across from the stairs.

"This is the dormitory for married couples and young children."

Thomas looked around the room, noticing the bunks were wooden platforms built into each side; there was a row on the bottom, then another platform above, giving another row of beds. He noted that you had to crawl in from the end, not the side, to get into the bunk. In the middle of the room was a long trestle table with bench seats on each side; a passageway in between gave them access to the bunks.

Phillip turned to Thomas. "Now, Mr. Langdon, let's find your bed." He began looking at names on blackboards at the end of each bunk, walking along the passageway on the left side of the room.

He was over halfway along when he stopped. "Here we are." Pointing at the name written in chalk on the top bunk. "Thomas Langdon." Glancing at the next one along. "Isaac Langdon."

Martha bent to look at the names on the bottom bunks. Pointing to the board on the bunk below her father. "Here's your bed, Ma." Indicating the adjoining bunk. "There's Louisa's and mine." Lifting her bag of clothing onto her bunk.

Phillip smiled, "Well done, Miss Langdon."

Thomas looked at the back of the dormitory, spotting a few trunks lined up against the back wall.

Phillip turned to Thomas. "For the moment, the trunks are kept in the back of these quarters, but once you board the ship, they'll be placed in the cargo hold."

Mary turned to Phillip. "What if we need our summer dresses?"

He gave a gentle laugh. "When the weather warms up, they'll be brought up so you can change into them."

Isaac nodded. "Thank you, Mr. Hayward."

Phillip turned to the door but stopped before walking outside. "Return to the reception room to collect your belongings and trunks. I'll arrange for someone to fetch your other boxes, which are going in the cargo hold."

He was about to close the door behind him but opened it within a few seconds and poked his head back in. "Once you've done that, come down to the mess room, we'll get you something to eat. You're probably all hungry."

Isaac nodded. "Aye, we are." Phillip closed the door, leaving the family alone.

Thomas put his bag of clothing on the bare boards of his bunk, turning to Isaac, "Let's get those trunks and bedding, " he said.

When they returned, Thomas and Isaac found the ladies sitting on the bench. Thomas put the bundles on the floor and turned to Mary. "We'll get the trunks now," he said.

~

While the men were gone, Louisa helped Mary and Martha unroll the bedding and began making their beds. When Isaac and Thomas returned with Mary's trunk, they had just finished the lower bunks.

Isaac turned to Louisa. "We'll get yours now."

"Thank you."

Louisa was about to lift her clothing bag onto her bunk, and Mary spoke firmly. "Don't you dare lift that; I'll do it."

She stood up quickly. "I'm sorry, I was only trying to help."

Mary sighed. "I know you were, but I don't want anything to happen to you or the baby. Ike would never forgive me."

Louisa nodded. The door opened, and the men walked inside with her trunk.

Thomas's stomach growled as he threw his clothing bag on his bunk. He laughed as he looked down at his belly. "We'd better get downstairs for some supper," he said. Mary and Martha followed him to the door.

With her sewing basket in hand, Louisa turned to Isaac, her expression a mix of anticipation and apprehension as they contemplated their uncertain future together. "I might be able to start making some clothes for the baby while we wait for our ship; I packed the material and buttons Mother gave me in my trunk."

"Ma may like to help you with that; I know she made all our clothes when we were little."

"That's a good idea; I'll ask her later."

Isaac put his arm around Louisa's shoulders. "We'd better get downstairs too." He glanced at the sewing basket on her arm. "Aren't you going to leave that here?"

Louisa shook her head and lowered her voice. "All our money's in it. I'd rather not let it out of my sight if I can help it."

Pulling her closer, he said, "Very wise."

Reaching the bottom of the stairs, Louisa found Mary waiting for them, and she whispered, "Louisa, just a quick word before we get examined by the doctor tomorrow." Isaac walked away discreetly. Mary continued in a hushed tone. "If he asks if you're with child, tell him you're not sure; you've only been married a couple of months," she advised, her eyes reflecting concern for her daughter-in-law's well-being.

She scrutinized her mother-in-law for a moment. "Why?" She whispered.

Tilting her head slightly. "It might be safer to deny it, that's all."

Louisa nodded, her mind swirling with Mary's cautionary words as she followed her mother-in-law, determined to navigate the challenges ahead with prudence and resolve.

56

Louisa looked around as they sat at the table, relieved they had finally arrived in Plymouth. Isaac turned to her and said, "I'm sorry Uncle Luke couldn't stay with us tonight; we'll just have to say goodbye to him in the morning."

"That will be so hard." Louisa's voice quivered as she spoke, her heart heavy with the impending farewell to Uncle Luke. She leaned her head on Isaac's shoulder, seeking solace in his comforting presence.

Jacob, Elijah, and Sammy were talking about the journey they had just completed and the upcoming voyage to Australia.

Louisa shook her head when she realized Mary was talking to her.

"How are you feeling after the long walk from Penstowe?"

"I'm feeling fine. Sitting on the cart when it was raining was easier, but it was very bumpy. I found my neck was sore from my head getting thrown about when the cart went into a hole." Mary nodded.

Louisa glanced at Thomas speaking to Isaac and whispered to Mary, "Da looks worried."

Mary looked towards him also, replying softly, "I think he's worried about what to expect when we get on the ship. He told me in St Mellion he's worried we're making a big mistake by emigrating to Australia."

Louisa's voice wavered with uncertainty. "Do you think it's a mistake? Ike keeps asking me if I'm sure about going. I tell him I'll go wherever he goes, and if he's going to Australia, I'm going too. Besides, Sammy can't wait to get there."

"Neither can Elijah or Martha."

"Ma, I told Ike earlier that I might try to make some baby clothes while we're in Plymouth. Would you like to help me?"

"I'd love to. Do you have enough fabric with you, or do you need to buy more?"

"Mother gave me some when she gave me the basket and some buttons. Will you have a look at what baby clothes I have? If you think I need more, I may be able to buy some fabric when I go to the markets with Uncle Luke tomorrow."

"Let's have a look now, shall we?"

Louisa and Mary stood up; as they passed Isaac, Louisa whispered to him, "Ike, Ma and I are going upstairs." He nodded.

Louisa opened her trunk in the dormitory, pulled out the material her mother had given her, and placed it on the table. "I think there's about five yards in this piece of white cotton; I'm hoping I'll only need to make two nightgowns out of it. I have lots of clothes Aunty Jane gave me from when Fran was a baby."

"Let's look at what you have, and then we can decide what you need."

Louisa nodded. Reaching deeper into the trunk, she found the baby clothes and placed them on the table.

Mary touched the little garments tenderly. "It doesn't seem that long ago Martha was wearing something this small."

"I remember Fran wearing them too; now she's six. When Aunty Jane gave these to me, she was saying how quickly children grow up."

Mary agreed. "I'm glad to see you have plenty of baby blankets; you can never have enough of those. Of course, when I had Ike and Jacob, I only had enough blankets for one baby. Our neighbour in Penstowe gave me what she had spare; her youngest no longer needed them."

Louisa asked, "Do you think I'll need to make more clothes?"

Mary smiled, "Your Aunty Jane has given you plenty. I don't think you'll need a lot more, but I'm sure you will enjoy making some just the same. It's always nice to dress the baby in something you've made for him or her."

Louisa hugged her mother-in-law, who understood her desire to make clothes for her baby. "Thank you. I might start making a nightgown tomorrow after I come back from the markets."

Mary helped Louisa fold the baby clothes and said, "Ike told me Lady Trevelen gave you a letter when you finished working for her."

"Yes, she was very sad when I told her I was getting married and gave notice." Louisa reached under her dresses at the bottom of the trunk, finding the letter. "Here it is. Would you like to read it? Oh, I'm sorry. I forgot you can't read."

Mary shrugged. "That's all right, will you read it to me please?"

"Of course."

Louisa opened the letter and read the beautifully sloped words Lady Trevelen had written- not that she needed to, as she knew them by heart.

Trevelen Manor,
Stokebridge,
Cornwall

18th September 1855

To whom it may concern,

Please be advised that the bearer of this letter, Mrs. Isaac Langdon, is a fine seamstress who has served my household for the last four years.

Louisa's skill with needle and thread are hard to surpass, and I am sure she would be a valued servant to any person who requires her services.

Yours sincerely,
Lady Victoria Trevelen

"That was nice of her to write such a lovely letter; she must have thought highly of you."

"She was always happy with the dresses I made for her and the children. I also made some for her friends."

"Did you make many for her friends?"

"Yes, I made several. I'd make them while at the manor, and then her friends would pay Lady Trevelen. They were so pleased that occasionally they would give me a few extra shillings."

"You're a very talented young lady, Louisa."

"I was thinking the other day, that it was while I was at Aunty Jane's having sewing lessons, that Ike and I got to know one another. It's strange how things happen. Maybe it was meant to be."

Mary smiled. "Maybe it was."

Louisa's mind drifted back to the twists of fate that had brought her and Ike together, each step of their journey shaping their shared destiny.

Mary helped her pack the baby clothes in her trunk before they returned to the mess hall to rejoin the others.

~

After supper, with the echoes of conversation still lingering in the air, Louisa withdrew her notebook from her basket and quietly began to write, the words flowing from her pen as she poured her thoughts onto the page.

10th December 1855

> *We finally arrived at Plymouth this afternoon, and it was such a relief to be inside after three days of walking in rain, sleet, and wind. Crossing the Tamar River meant we had left Cornwall for good.*
>
> *Tomorrow, we must say goodbye to Uncle Luke before he returns to Stokebridge; our last link to our old home will be gone. I'm not sure if I can bear the sadness, but if Ike and I want to make a new life for ourselves, we have to make this journey.*

57

The following morning, Louisa, Isaac, and Luke walked around the markets looking for a present for Jane.

Louisa was fascinated by the array of items for sale: stalls with all types of food, fish, meat, and vegetables, stalls with tin pots and pans, and another selling tobacco.

A diverse blend of aromas filled the air, from the tantalizing scent of freshly baked bread to the pungent aroma of tobacco. Each stall beckoned with its own unique fragrance, enticing passersby to explore its offerings. Further along, the smell of a freshly killed pig triggered Louisa's nausea again. Grabbing Isaac's arm, she quickly led him and Luke away.

Soon, they found a shop with ladies' finery near the market stalls.

Luke and Louisa went inside; Isaac waited outside. Looking at the displayed items, Luke asked, "What do you think your Aunty Jane would like?"

Louisa glanced at the beautiful garments and baubles. "I know she wouldn't want you to waste your money on something impractical. You should buy her something she'll appreciate and use often."

Louisa picked up a beautiful black woollen shawl with thin white stripes and tassels. "Maybe something like this; I think she'd love it, and it'll be very useful in cold weather."

"I can just imagine Jane wearing this. It will do nicely." Luke paid the merchant, who wrapped the shawl in brown paper and tied it with string.

"Are you going to buy anything, Louisa?"

"I'm not sure. I have to be careful about how much we can take on the ship, but I will buy more reels of cotton; you can never have too much." Picking up six reels in assorted colours. "I'll also buy a few yards of shirt fabric in case I need to make new ones for Ike or Sammy."

Louisa paid for her purchases and walked outside to join Isaac.

They wandered along the next street, admiring the beautiful buildings and stately homes for a short time.

Luke eventually said, "I think we should be getting back now; I'll come back to the depot to say goodbye, then I must return to Stokebridge."

Tears welled in Louisa's eyes as she gazed at Luke, her voice trembling with emotion. "We're going to miss you so much, having you with us on this part of the journey has been wonderful." Her words choked with unspoken sorrow.

Isaac shook his hand. "I'll let Ma and Da know you're coming."

Louisa held Luke's arm as they walked to the inn. She kissed him on the cheek before saying. "I wish we didn't have to say goodbye."

Luke patted her hand tenderly. "I know."

~

Bobby was happily munching hay when Luke walked into his stall. "Come on, old man. We've got a long way to travel today."

Luke was not surprised to see his sister and her family gathered outside, waiting for him to arrive.

Mary hugged him. "Were you able to find something nice for Jane?"

"Yes, Louisa found a lovely shawl; I'm sure Jane will love it. But I really must leave."

Thomas shook Luke's hand. "We can't thank you enough for your help over the last few days; we're very thankful." Glancing at his family, he added, "I know we're all going to miss you very much."

Mary hugged him again, followed by Martha and Louisa. Isaac, Jacob, and Elijah all shook his hand.

Sammy unashamedly hugged him. "Goodbye, Uncle Luke. I'm going to miss you. You've been more like a father to me, and not many boys can say they were lucky enough to have two Das."

Luke was surprised by Sammy's farewell; he did think of him like a son. "I'm going to miss you too, Sammy," Luke said, ruffling his hair. "But who's going to make sure Billy and Harry behave themselves now that you're leaving?"

Sammy stood back and laughed. "I think Hannah would love to do that."

"I'm sure she will." Luke laughed as he climbed onto the cart. "Don't forget to write."

Isaac said, "Don't worry, Uncle Luke. We'll write so many letters that you may not have time to read them all. I think I speak for all of us."

Louisa said, "I agree; we'll write as often as possible."

Thomas asked, "How far do you think you'll get tonight, Luke?"

"I'm hoping to get as far as St Mellion, and with some luck, I should be able to reach Stokebridge in time for dinner tomorrow."

He flicked the reins, and Bobby moved along the street quicker now that the cart was empty. Luke turned once more to wave as he reached the corner.

~

When they returned inside, Phillip met them. "The doctor is here. You'll need to be examined. Can you return to the mess hall immediately?"

Louisa entered the curtained-off section and sat on the chair. After the doctor had checked her general health, he looked at her and asked, "Are you with child?"

She took a quick breath, this is what Mary had warned her about. She would deal with him exactly as she used to deal with her mother. Her father always said she was headstrong, and she never needed that quality more than now.

"I'm not sure; I've only been married a couple of months. Would it be a problem if I was? My husband's mother is a midwife." Louisa carefully chose her words, hoping to convince the doctor of her willingness to take the risk of sailing while pregnant, driven by her unwavering determination to remain by Isaac's side and start their new life together in Australia.

"It can be." Tilting his head sideways. "If anything happens during the voyage, it could be potentially dangerous to you."

"In what way, doctor?" Louisa swallowed, hoping the butterflies in her stomach would keep still.

"Sometimes seasickness can have devastating effects on women who are with child."

So many thoughts went through her mind. Should she tell him the truth about her condition? If she did, would he prevent her from boarding the ship?

She did not want to stay in England; her place was with Isaac. Her baby was due at the end of June, and she hoped they would have been in Australia for at least a few months by then.

Sitting straight, she clasped her hands and looked directly at the doctor. "My husband is leaving on the ship for Adelaide, and if I must remain in England, I'll have nowhere to go. I don't want to be left behind simply because I *might* be expecting a baby."

The corner of the doctor's mouth curled on one side at her feisty attitude; she suspected he may have guessed the truth of her condition.

"Very well, as long as you're aware of the danger you could be placing yourself in, I'll pass you as fit for the colonies."

"Thank you." Breathing a sigh of relief as she walked out, she immediately found Mary and told her what the doctor had said.

~

Sitting at the table, enjoying the warmth of the fire, Thomas turned to Mary and said, "I'm glad we've all passed fit for Australia."

Mary replied, "I was a bit concerned about Louisa, her being with child, but he seemed happy with her."

Shortly, Bill Cowling placed five canvas bags on the table. "These are for your clothes. Canvas is stronger than fabric, less likely to rip."

Louisa picked up one of the bags and looked at it. "I'll sew our names on them, but what about Grace, Jacob, Elijah, and Sammy?"

"They'll have theirs given to them in their quarters." He turned to address Thomas. "Now you've all been examined; we need to explain how things are run in the depot and on-board ship." He sat opposite Thomas.

Bill continued. "Now, there are some questions I need to ask you and your wife, and I'll assume you'll have some for me. First question, Mr. Langdon, would you like to take the position of a constable on board ship?"

"What would I have to do?"

Bill sighed, "The constable supervises the fumigation and drying of the steerage decks, which must be cleaned with various disinfectants and deodorising liquids. He also coordinates the meals and the daily cleaning, scrubbing, and disinfecting of the mess tables, the berths, the floors, and the water closets in steerage."

"That sounds like a lot of responsibility," Thomas replied cautiously.

Bill grinned. "Do you have somewhere else to be? Besides, you won't be doing it alone; at least three other men will work with you. Between the four of you, you'll also have to assign men from steerage the tasks needed."

"That would make the job a bit easier, is there anything else the constables need to do?"

"Yes, they coordinate the collection of boiling water for tea and the retrieval of cooked meals from the galley for both the married and single quarters. That's why we start here in the depot, to get you used to the routine on board ship."

"Well, I may as well do the job; it's not like I have to work in fields."

Bill grinned. "Good, and you'll be paid a gratuity when you arrive in Adelaide."

"How much is that?" Thomas asked, keenly interested.

"That's up to the captain, but it could be as much as three pounds."

"Well, that would be very useful when we get to Australia."

Bill grinned again. "Most people say that."

He turned to Mary. "Mrs. Langdon, would you like to take on the position of matron for the single women? Especially as you don't have young children."

Mary glanced at her ten-year-old sitting beside her. "What about Martha?"

Louisa put her hand on Mary's. "Don't worry about Martha Ma. She can stay with me, and we'll be able to see you if we need to." Turning to Bill, she asked, "Won't we?"

"Of course, you can," he replied reassuringly, "But there are usually classes for children on board during the day, which she may like to attend."

"Hmm. What does the matron have to do?"

"The matron assists the surgeon with inspections and acts as the moral guardian for the single women, a chaperone. Furthermore, you'll also be paid a gratuity."

Mary thought for a moment. "Yes, in that case, I'll take the position; at least I'll be with Grace, and she won't feel so isolated. Will I have to sleep in the single women's quarters?"

"Yes, but not until you board the ship; Mrs. Pearce is the matron while the emigrants are in the depot."

She nodded.

Standing up, Bill shook hands with Thomas. "Thank you. Bob Gregory, the gentleman who took the single men to their quarters yesterday, will show you your responsibilities at supper time."

Later that evening, Thomas joined Bob Gregory, learning to supervise the cooking and distribution of the meals. Later, as he sat with Mary, Martha, Isaac, and Louisa, he said, "I don't think the constable's job is going to be hard; Bob said it's the same on the ship."

Isaac asked, "Are there still people who are going to Adelaide yet to arrive?"

"According to Bob, only about half of the people are here, but he thinks more will arrive tomorrow. I'm glad I've taken on job of constable; at least I feel useful."

Mary replied, "Well, at least I won't have to move into the single women's quarters until the start of the voyage."

Louisa looked up at her mother-in-law. "You don't have to worry about Martha while on board the ship. Ike and I will look after her."

Mary's smile widened with pride as she looked at Louisa, her confidence in her daughter-in-law's nurturing abilities evident in her gentle touch. "I know you will," she affirmed, her voice filled with unwavering trust.

Louisa stood up and turned to Isaac. "I might go to our dormitory and start making baby clothes."

Martha stood up also. "Can I help you, Louisa?"

Louisa smiled at her sister-in-law. "That would be lovely."

58

The following day, Isaac sat at the table with his wife and mother, a mixture of excitement and apprehension brewing within him as they prepared for their journey to Australia. Louisa's nimble fingers danced across the fabric as she sewed a nightie for the baby, her concentration evident in the furrow of her brow. Isaac couldn't help but admire her skill, each stitch a testament to her dedication.

She knotted the cotton at the end of the seam and reached into her basket for the scissors.

"Louisa," he said, his gaze softening as he watched her work, "I've noticed you never use your teeth to cut the thread like I've seen Ma do when she's sewing."

Mary turned towards Louisa; Isaac could see she was keen to hear the answer.

Louisa giggled, a warmth spreading across her features. "When I started having sewing lessons with Aunty Jane, she saw me biting the thread and said very sternly, '*You don't eat your food with your scissors, so don't cut the thread with your teeth.*' Since then, I have always used my scissors."

Mary laughed. "Sounds like the sort of thing Jane would say."

~

Jacob, Elijah, and Sammy had invited Isaac to walk around town, but he decided he'd prefer to enjoy the sights of Plymouth with Louisa. They still had at least two days before they were due to leave; there was no need to rush.

Isaac sat talking with Louisa and his mother; their voices mingling with the bustling atmosphere of the mess hall. The room echoed with the chatter of fellow travellers, each with their own hopes and dreams for the future. The aroma of food filled the air, mingling with the sound of clinking utensils and murmured conversations. His attention was drawn to some new arrivals, their faces bore the marks of a long journey, yet beneath the exhaustion, there was a glimmer of anticipation for the adventures that lay ahead.

Phillip led them to the family quarters, then returned to the mess hall. He entered the kitchen door to the right of the main staircase and walked out a moment later with Thomas, obviously talking about the new arrivals.

Ten minutes later, the family descended the stairs. The father looked around before leading his wife and children to the curtained-off section.

Isaac observed the people seated at the tables, some couples alone, others in family groups. Waiting for a ship to take them to Adelaide was the one thing they had in common.

Isaac looked up when Thomas talked to the father, as he and his family emerged from their medical examinations, he was carrying a young child. The newcomer smiled as he shook hands with Thomas, indicating that the man and his family would follow him.

Thomas led the new arrivals to their table. The older girl carried a basket containing pewter plates and other eating utensils, a boy carried two cooking pots, and a younger girl walked behind, a rag doll clutched in her hand.

Isaac stood up as Thomas approached. "May I introduce my son, Ike, his wife Louisa, and my wife Mary? Ike, this is Mr. James Newman and his wife Eliza."

Putting the child on the floor, James shook hands with Isaac. "Please call me Jim." Turning to the children, he pointed at each one: "Rachel, Jimmy, Edith, and Harry." Louisa waved at the youngest boy, about four years old, who was hiding in his mother's skirt.

Eliza laughed a little. "Our Harry is a little shy with new people, but once he gets to know you, he won't leave you alone." Picking him up, he buried his face into her neck. Turning back to Mary. "Our eldest daughter, Bella, is with the single women."

Thomas nodded. "Our eldest daughter is there as well, but once we board the ship, Mary will be the matron for the single women, so at least you'll know she'll be looked after."

Eliza looked at Mary. "That's comforting."

Thomas continued. "We have another daughter, Martha, but she's attending classes. Our other two sons are walking around Plymouth with Louisa's brother; you'll meet them later."

He gestured toward the bench. "Please sit down. Dinner will be served soon. You must be hungry after your journey."

James looked at Thomas. "Yes, we are."

Thomas turned to leave. "I've got to help with serving the food. I'll return shortly."

"Of course," James replied.

"Where do you come from, Jim?" Isaac was curious after hearing the Devonian accent.

"We lived on a farm just outside of Exeter."

"Have you always wanted to go to Australia?"

James sighed as he leaned on the table. "I have a cousin who emigrated to Sydney a couple of years ago; in his letters, he said what a wonderful place Australia is."

"Our brother did the same last year, which is why we're going there." Isaac replied.

James said thoughtfully, "Eliza and I realized there weren't much future in Devon for the children if we'd stayed there, so when the chance came to go to Australia, we decided to take it."

Isaac nodded. "It's not an easy decision, but sometimes you have to have faith you're making the right one."

James and Eliza nodded in agreement.

~

A short while later, Jacob, Elijah and Sammy returned from their walk, and Martha returned from her lessons. Isaac introduced them to James and his family.

Sammy talked excitedly about their walk. "We walked along the water's edge. There was a large grey building, and it had lots of windows."

"What was it?" Isaac asked.

Elijah replied, "We asked someone if they knew what it was; they said it was the Stonehouse Barracks."

Sammy continued. "The man we were talking to said a lot of soldiers live there."

Isaac grinned at his brother-in-law. "Well, maybe you can show us tomorrow. Louisa and I plan to walk around Plymouth in the morning."

He replied, "We can also see if there're any ships in the harbour."

Isaac looked at James. "Would you like to walk around Plymouth with us tomorrow, Jim?"

James shook his head. "Not tomorrow, maybe the next day if we can. It took us a while to walk to Exeter from our farm, and then we rode the train to Plymouth."

Eliza said, "It was very exciting for the little children, especially Harry."

Louisa nodded. "I wish we could have taken a train; it took us three days to walk here from Stokebridge."

Isaac said, "I'm sure by the time we get to the sheep farm in South Australia, we'll have done a lot more walking."

James sat up, looking at Isaac. "Are you going to a sheep farm?"

"Yes, we have to meet an agent in Adelaide to be taken there; Da has our letter of introduction."

"I wonder if it's the same one we're going to," Jim replied.

After a brief silence, Eliza said, "Jim, I hope we can walk around the town. I would love to see more of Plymouth before we leave England."

James patted her hand. "Of course, my dear; we still have a day or two before we board the ship."

Thomas returned to the table. "Come with me, Eliza; bring your pots and collect your food."

Eliza stood up after she had put Harry on his father's lap and followed Thomas and Mary through the door to the kitchen.

Returning with pots of food, the two families sat down, eating their meal in silence.

The women left to wash pots, plates, and cutlery; while the men sat talking at the table.

Isaac said, "Da, Jim and his family are also going to a sheep farm in South Australia."

Thomas's eyes opened wide as he pulled the letter from his jacket pocket. Holding it in front of Isaac, he said. "Read what it says, Ike."

Unfolding the paper, Isaac said. "We're working on a sheep farm owned by a Mr. Coates. When we reach Adelaide, we have to see the agent in King William Street; a representative from the farm will take us there."

James reached into his pocket, pulled out his letter, and gave it to Isaac; he scanned it briefly. "It says the same thing; you're working for Mr. Coates also." Handing the letter back to James.

Thomas said, "Well, Jim, it looks like we're going to be working together."

James smiled at Thomas, "Who'd have thought we'd meet people in Plymouth going to the same sheep farm as we are."

Thomas explained, "The agent in Bradford said many men are abandoning their employers to look for gold."

"I hope Jacob and Elijah don't run off to the gold fields," Mary said.

"I hope not," Thomas replied, "That's why farmers are looking for families; they're more likely to stay and work."

Martha said, "I'd rather stay with my family."

Mary hugged her daughter. "I'm glad to hear that."

~

Louisa remained sitting in the mess hall after Isaac had gone to the dormitories. She reached into her basket for her journal and began writing.

12th December 1855

> *We met a family today, Jim and Eliza Newman from Devon, they have five children. They're going to the same sheep farm as us. It's quite funny to watch their youngest boy, Harry, he spends most of his time hiding in Eliza's skirt.*

Louisa capped the ink bottle, replaced it, and the journal in her basket. She stretched her back and shoulders before walking up the stairs.

$$59$$

Sammy sat at the table with Isaac and Louisa, waiting for breakfast. Pulling his penny knife from his pocket, he opened and closed the blade. As he closed it for the third time, Isaac reached into his own pocket, retrieving his knife with a grin. "Use my knife to carve your initials into the handle."

Sammy smiled as he looked at the '*IL*' in the handle. Opening the blade, he slowly carved '*SK*' in his own before handing the knife back.

"Thanks, Ike," he murmured.

Isaac tucked the knife back in his pocket. "Da gave Jacob and me these when we turned fourteen; it's special to me, too."

Sammy traced the initials with his thumb. "I'll always think of Da whenever I use it," he said sadly. "I'm going to miss him, Ike."

Louisa looked up, concern etched on her features. "Do you want to return to Stokebridge?"

Sammy's eyes narrowed. "No, I'm going to Australia with you."

Louisa and Isaac grinned at each other as Sammy put the knife in his pocket.

~

Isaac and Louisa prepared themselves for their walk around Plymouth, with Elijah and Sammy eagerly joining them.

After informing Bill Cowling they were leaving, Sammy asked, "Would you like to see the barracks first?"

Isaac nodded in agreement. "Yes, let's take a look before heading to the main town centre."

Sammy led the way to the Stonehouse Barracks, the chilly wind blowing leaves around their feet.

Two soldiers guarded the three archways at the front of the building. The centre arch was large enough for horses and carriages, but the other two would only allow soldiers to walk through.

Standing across the road, admiring the barracks, Louisa said, "It's a very impressive building."

"I wonder how many soldiers live there?" Isaac said.

Elijah replied, "I think it would be lots because if you look around the corner, you can see how big it is."

As Isaac walked further along the road to the corner, the enormity of the barracks became clear. It was nearly as long behind as it was at the front. "Magnificent!" Isaac was mesmerized by its sheer size.

Elijah asked, "Ike, do you mind if Sammy and I walk a while longer? We might go to the other side of the town centre and see what's there."

"I don't see why not. Try to make sure you're back before dinner, or you'll have to wait until supper before you get something to eat," Isaac replied.

"We will," Elijah said.

Isaac called out after they walked away. "And Sammy, don't get up to any mischief; I don't want to explain to your father that you were sent to Australia as a convict."

"Don't worry, Ike," Sammy assured him, returning the grin. "We'll behave."

As Isaac and Louisa approached the depot, sounds from the waterfront filled the air—the cries of seagulls, and the crashing waves against the wharf walls, mixed with the shouts of men. After listening for a moment, Isaac said, "Probably fisherman." He patted her hand looped through his arm. "Come, let's see if any new ships have arrived."

Standing in the depot shelter, they watched the activity on board a ship tied up at the wharf.

So many adults waited their turn to walk up the gangplank, standing with bundles of bedding and clothing. Several children held the hands of little brothers and sisters.

Louisa put her hand around Isaac's arm. "That'll be us in a couple of days."

"Yes, it will, but let's go back inside; it's cold out here."

Louisa laughed as she walked beside him. "And the smell of fish is overpowering."

Inside the depot, Isaac looked around and noticed more people in the mess hall than when they had left for their walk. Isaac and Louisa sat with Mary, James, and Eliza. Harry sat on his mother's lap.

Isaac looked around. "Where are the children?"

James replied, "At classes."

When Thomas returned to their table, Isaac said. "We saw lots of people boarding a ship at the wharf. Do you know where it's sailing to?"

Thomas nodded. "Canada. Mr. Hayward told me this morning. It was supposed to leave a few days ago but some ships are late because of bad weather."

James turned to Thomas, "I thought we were due to leave tomorrow?"

Thomas shook his head. "Mr. Hayward said we might not be for another few days yet. We'll have to wait until our ship comes in."

James looked at Eliza. "Would you like to go for a walk tomorrow?"

Eliza looked at her young son sitting on her lap. "I don't want to take Harry out in this cold weather, although it would be nice if we could go to the market briefly."

Louisa said, "I'll look after Harry if you want to walk around the town. Ike and I enjoyed our walk this morning."

"Thank you, Louisa, that would be lovely," replied Eliza.

Sammy and Elijah walked in and leaned on the end of the table.

Sammy said excitedly, "Did you see that ship at the wharf?"

Isaac replied, "Da said she's sailing for Canada today."

Elijah tapped Sammy on the shoulder. "Let's ask Mr. Cowling when the ship is leaving. It would be nice to watch her sail out of the harbour."

Thomas laughed as they rushed out the door. "Don't those two ever stop?"

~

Sammy followed Elijah down the corridor to the reception room. Bill Cowling was busy writing in his ledger; Phillip Hayward looked up as they walked in. "What can I do for you boys?"

Elijah asked, "When is that ship due to sail?"

"I presume you mean the one at the wharf."

Sammy nodded. "Yes, people are boarding it now."

"That's the *Duchess of Clarence*; she's sailing to Halifax, Canada, on this afternoon's high tide." He informed them. Grinning at the two boys, he continued, "Not thinking of stowing away on it, are you?"

"No." Sammy smiled at Phillip. "We want to watch her when she sails, that's all."

"Well, you can watch the ship depart, but don't get in the way of the crew or the men working on the quay. Remember to let me know you've left the depot, even if it's only to go to the wharf."

"Thank you, Mr. Hayward," Sammy waved as they returned to the mess hall.

Sitting at the table, Elijah turned to Isaac. "That ship's sailing this afternoon; we thought we'd walk around town after dinner, then watch it sail."

Isaac looked at them. "All right, but once the ship has sailed, please come back inside."

Walking along the road from the depot, Sammy and Elijah admired the beautiful homes along the waterfront.

"The people who live in those houses must be rich," Elijah said.

"It looks like they have many servants," Sammy replied as they ambled.

Sammy and Elijah spent time walking around Plymouth, enjoying the sights. Mid-afternoon, they returned to the wharf, finding a position to observe the *Duchess of Clarence* leaving the harbour for Canada.

Men guided the last passengers up the gangplank while others pushed carts loaded with provisions.

Sammy pointed to other men waiting on the wharf. One stood by a crate of chickens, and another held boards, occasionally turning them to keep four pigs from running away. Behind him, a man held a nanny goat. They were all waiting their turn to go up the gangplank.

Sammy looked at Elijah and said, "I wonder why they need a goat on board?"

"Milk, I guess."

Sammy pointed to another man throwing sacks onto a cart. "What do you think would be in them?"

Elijah replied, "He's not being very careful; I guess they might be taters. The ships are out to sea for a long time; they'd need a lot of food."

Sammy and Elijah watched, fascinated, as the last passengers and provisions were taken on board. Sailors began hauling on ropes, expertly lowering barrels and boxes into the cargo hold.

A man dressed in an immaculate dark-coloured uniform moved behind the ship's wheel and began giving signals. More crewmen pulled on ropes, and the anchors rose from the water on heavy chains and secured above the waterline.

The ship began to move away from the wharf as ropes were untied, and more ropes were secured to the steam-powered tug boats, and they slowly pulled the ship towards the open sea. The *Duchess of Clarence* was ready for departure.

Sammy and Elijah watched as the ship was guided past the rock wall. Sails were raised as the ropes were thrown to the tugs below. The sails billowed, and her bow leisurely dipped up and down as she sailed away, rounding the island outside the harbour's entrance before disappearing.

Sammy looked at Elijah. "That was amazing to watch."

He nodded. "Hope our departure is that smooth. Come on; it must be nearly time for supper."

When Louisa put her hands out to take Harry from Eliza, she was pleased he was happy to go to her.

Eliza said, smiling at Louisa, "It didn't take Harry long to get to know you." Bending down, she kissed him on the top of his head. "You be a good boy for Mrs. Langdon. Da and I will be back later."

Louisa looked at Eliza and said, "I'm sure he'll be good." Then she looked down at Harry and laughed at his cheeky smile.

James turned to Eliza. "Come, my dear, are you ready for our walk?"

Eliza picked up her shawl, putting it around her shoulders. Waving at Louisa and Harry, she put her hand on her husband's arm, and they left the mess hall.

When James and Eliza returned to the emigration depot later, they sat at the table with Isaac, Louisa, Mary, and Jacob. Harry was seated beside Louisa, playing with a piece of wood roughly carved to look like a ship.

"Where did you get that Harry?" Eliza asked.

Jacob looked over and smiled, "I made it from a piece of driftwood I found on the wharf; it gave me something to do."

Harry smiled at his mother. "A ship, Ma." He moved the toy up and down as if it were in the water.

Eliza looked at her son with a gentle smile. "Did you remember to thank Mr. Langdon for the lovely toy he made for you?"

Jacob nodded. "Yes, he did."

"Did you enjoy your walk?" Louisa asked.

James looked up. "Yes, it was very enjoyable. Thank you."

Eliza pulled Harry onto her lap. "Plymouth reminds me very much of Exeter."

~

The following morning, Jacob joined Isaac and Louisa for another walk.

Walking towards the wharf, they stopped to watch seagulls as they flew overhead, occasionally, diving into the water to retrieve a fish thrown overboard by a fisherman.

Isaac said, "There's only fishing boats here. It doesn't look like we're leaving today."

Louisa pointed at the rock wall at the entrance of the harbour. "That must be the rock wall Sammy was talking about when the ship sailed yesterday."

Jacob followed her finger. "Probably. Once we pass that wall and the island in the distance, we won't stop until we reach Australia."

Isaac stamped his feet to ward off the chill, tucking his hands under his armpits for warmth. "That wind's freezing. Shall we go back inside, or would you like to walk around Plymouth again?"

"Let's go back to the warm fire in the mess hall," Louisa suggested, smiling. "Looks like we'll have other days to explore the town."

~

For Louisa, the days blended into one another. The routine remained the same. Breakfast, dinner, and then supper before going to their quarters to sleep. Most of the emigrant children, including Martha, attended classes daily, where they were taught to read and write, and some parents joined their offspring.

Louisa joined the class teaching basket weaving, bag making and straw plaiting.

They looked for Bob Gregory every morning and asked if their ship had arrived, but he only shook his head.

~

Breakfast had been consumed after a week in Plymouth, and Elijah and Sammy left for their daily walk. Isaac turned to Louisa, saying light-heartedly, "Surely they'd have walked every street in Plymouth by now."

Louisa laughed. "Sammy's so excited about being in a town rather than our small village."

"I thought he'd want to wait in the depot; he's so eager to get to Australia." Isaac finished his cup of tea and stood up. "It's a lovely day outside. Why don't we go for a walk, too?"

She smiled at him, "We can look at the beautiful homes."

"Why not?" He replied, offering his arm.

Despite the clear sky, a biting chill lingered in the air, prompting them to bundle up tightly in their warmest clothing.

Stopping to look at a large house on the top of a hill, Louisa asked, "Do you think we'll ever have a home as grand as that?"

"I don't know if I'd want one that big; I only want a home where we can live with our children and be happy."

Louisa leaned on his arm. "Sounds cosy."

Not far from the depot, they saw stray dogs hanging outside a butcher's shop. A medium-sized black dog with a brown face and paws caught Louisa's attention as he struggled to keep up with the others. His hip, shoulder, and rib bones showed as he used the last of his strength to follow the other dogs.

"The poor thing," holding Isaac's arm.

The butcher threw some bones, and the dogs rushed for their share. Although the black dog tried to grab a bone, the others snarled at him and chased him away.

Louisa marched towards the dogs, but Isaac held her back. "Don't, they might attack you."

She turned to him, tears streaming down her face. "I can't stand by and watch as the poor thing is chased away from the food."

Jerking her arm free, she strode purposely to the butcher's shop and opened the door with such force that Isaac thought she would tear it off its hinges.

A moment later, Louisa emerged holding a meat-covered bone. As she approached the pack, he rushed to her side. "Be careful, the others might try to take it from you," he said, reaching for the bone. "Let me try to give it to him; I'd hate for you to get bitten."

She nodded, giving him the bone.

Isaac slowly walked toward the dogs. The black one stood closest to him, looking longingly at the bones the other dogs were chewing.

Isaac approached the dog. "Here boy, you can have this bone." Holding it in front of him. The dog turned with sadness in his eyes as he stepped backwards; fear prevented him from taking it.

Louisa took the bone from his hand. "Ike, you're scaring him; stand back and let me try."

Isaac moved away and watched as she crouched down, offering the bone to the dog. His timidness slowly faded as he stepped closer to Louisa, but still not close enough to reach the bone.

In a soothing voice, Louisa said, "It's all right; I won't hurt you." Stretching her arm further. The dog slowly leaned forward, snatching the bone from her hand, staggering across the street, looking for a safe place to enjoy his prize.

Overwhelmed with compassion, Louisa rushed into Isaac's comforting embrace, tears streaming down her face once more. "That looks like the first food he's had for ages. He'll probably die soon; he's so thin."

He leaned back, smiling as he looked into her tear-streaked face. "Yes, maybe, but his last memory will be of the beautiful, kind lady who gave him a bone."

Giving a painful half smile, she wiped her eyes with the heel of her hand.

"Come on, love, we'd better get back; it's cold out here." Putting his arm around her shoulder, he asked. "By the way, how much did you pay for that bone?"

"A halfpenny," Louisa replied.

Isaac laughed. "That butcher was a rogue. It was only worth a farthing." Pulling her closer, they walked to the depot together.

~

Just before dinner, Sammy and Elijah returned from their walk. They sat with Isaac, Louisa, Jacob, Mary, James, Eliza, and Harry.

"Look what we have," Elijah said with a smirk.

All eyes turned to Elijah and Sammy as they pulled an apple from each coat pocket.

"Where did you get those?" Isaac asked, looking at the fruit and shaking his head. "Never mind. I don't want to know."

Jacob pulled his penny knife from his pocket and whispered, "How about we eat them now in case someone asks where they got them?""

The smiles disappeared from Elijah and Sammy's faces as they realized the seriousness of what they had done.

Jacob cut the apples, giving pieces to everyone at the table.

Isaac addressed the two boys sternly. "I thought I told you not to get up to any mischief. Tomorrow, *if* you go for a walk, I'm coming with you, to make sure you don't do anything like this again."

~

Bob Gregory approached Thomas as he sat eating breakfast with his family and the Newman family.

"The *Emily Catherine* arrived last night. There's still some maintenance to be done, but when that's finished, she'll be sailing for Adelaide."

James's eyes lit up with excitement. "Is that the ship we're sailing on?"

Bob smiled, "Yes, that's your ship."

Thomas enquired, "Do you know when we'll be leaving?"

"Probably the day after tomorrow," he replied with a grin before walking off to inform other families.

Thomas let out a long breath. "Thank goodness, no more waiting. I was nearly ready to forget about going to Australia and return to Penstowe."

Isaac sat up. "After everything we've been through to get here, we're not returning to Cornwall."

Jacob patted him on the shoulder. "Amen to that brother. The next part of our journey is about to begin."

Elijah repeated the ship's name. "The *Emily Catherine*."

Sammy said excitedly, "What it's called is not really important. It's our ship to Australia, and that's all we need to worry about. We'll be leaving England soon!" He gently slapped Elijah on the back.

Louisa said, "The only good thing about the wait is that I've managed to make some clothes for the baby."

Mary turned to Thomas and said, "Tom, the clothes Louisa has made are beautiful. Our grandchild will be the best-dressed baby in South Australia."

Louisa added. "But you helped too, Ma."

Mary laughed. "I only sewed on a few buttons; that was all."

~

Dinner was being eaten when Phillip Hayward walked into the mess hall. Standing on a bench, he called for their attention. When the chatter died down, he spoke loudly: "On tomorrow's evening tide, the *Emily Catherine* will be sailing for Adelaide." A collective cheer echoed around the room.

Phillip waited for the noise to die down before he continued. "In the morning, can you gather your belongings from the quarters and bring them to the mess hall. When it's time to board the ship, you must collect your bundles and walk to the wharf. Also, I must remind you that no one is allowed near the stern cabins. Now, does anyone have any questions?"

Someone called out. "What about our trunks?"

"Bring them down also; they'll go in the cargo hold first. Any other questions."

There were murmurs from people seated, but no one had any questions for the assistant depot master.

"I wish you Godspeed." Phillip jumped down from the bench and left.

~

Later, Louisa moved to an empty table to write in her journal.

20th December 1855

We've just heard that we're leaving on tomorrow's evening tide; our days of waiting in Plymouth are nearly over.
Now, we face over three months of sailing to the other side of the world.
May the Lord protect us.

Closing her book, she returned it to her basket. Finding her writing paper, she wrote to her parents.

20th December 1855

My Dearest Da and Mother,

We're leaving for Australia tomorrow. Ike's Da was told our ship was due to leave on the 13th of December. Uncle Luke would have told you we reached Plymouth in plenty of time, arriving on the 10th, but the 'Emily Catherine' was late getting into port because of bad weather.

We've been here a few more days than we expected. Since we arrived, we've been staying at the emigration depot near the harbour. The married couples and children sleep in one dormitory, the single men in another, and the single women in another.

The depot has been set up like the ship, with a mess area and bunks. We also had to learn the cooking and cleaning routines, keeping our beds clean and aired, and using the water closet. At least we'll know what to expect when we finally board.

We were all given a health check, and anyone thought to have any disease was sent away and not allowed to stay in the depot. Thank goodness we were all passed as being in good health.

Ike and I have walked around town, but sometimes the cold winds make it very uncomfortable, and we quickly return to the warmth of the depot.

Ike's Ma was very strict with me in the nicest way during our journey from Penstowe, not letting me lift or carry anything. Still, I should be doing something to help with the belongings we had to carry. Ike insisted I look after myself rather than worry about our worldly goods. I carry my sewing basket; I'll not let anyone else carry it, that's my responsibility.

We met another family going to the same sheep farm as us. They have five children, and Martha has become good friends with their daughter Rachel, who's the same age as Sammy.

370

Sammy loved every minute of the journey to Plymouth. He never got bored with the scenery, even when it had stayed the same and remained unchanged for miles. He was so excited when we saw some deer.

He and Elijah have become inseparable. They've spent the last few days exploring Plymouth. One day, they came back with four apples. I have no idea where they got them, and I'm not sure I want to know, but they both had sheepish grins on their faces. Ike and I had a good talk with them, warning them not to do that again.

I'll write again as soon as possible, but that will probably be after arriving in Australia.

God bless you.

Your affectionate sons and daughter,

Louisa, Ike, and Sammy

Louisa sealed and addressed her letter before walking to the reception area to inform Phillip Hayward that she was on her way to post it.

"No need for you to do that, my dear, I walk past a letter box on my way home. I'll post it for you this evening."

Louisa handed the letter to the assistant depot master. "Thank you very much."

Thomas spoke solemnly as they ate supper: "Tomorrow will be our final day in England. After we board the ship, we'll bid farewell to Cornwall and this country forever."

"That's frightening, but it's also exciting." Louisa admitted.

"Yes, it is," Thomas replied. "I think we'd better have an early night. We have a big day tomorrow."

Louisa was up early helping Mary and Martha bundle their bedding and clothing, placing them in piles for Isaac and Thomas to take to the mess hall.

Louisa picked up her sewing basket, looked around and turned to Mary. "I don't think anything has been left behind."

Mary nodded. "Let's go downstairs for breakfast."

Thomas and Isaac picked up the last bundles and walked downstairs with them.

Mary smiled as she put her arm around Martha, and they walked out the door for the last time.

Thomas and Isaac added the bundles to the pile near the wall.

Mary addressed Jacob, Elijah and Sammy sitting at the table. "Have you got all your belongings and put them in your bags? We don't want to get on the ship and find something has been left behind."

Jacob replied, "I looked around after we got up but couldn't see anything."

Mary nodded.

Thomas looked up from buttering a piece of bread and said, "Bob said I'm relieved of my duties until we board the ship. All we can do now is wait."

~

Mary was talking to Louisa when Bob Gregory approached her. "Mrs. Langdon, the single women will be boarding first; you must board with them. Please collect your belongings and follow me."

Standing up, she gave Thomas a kiss on the cheek and hugs for Martha and Louisa before picking up her bundles. As she was about to walk out the door, she turned and looked at her family sadly. "We'll be together again in Adelaide," she said.

Mary followed Bob along the corridor until he opened another door. Looking inside, she saw another large room, smaller than the mess hall. Several benches were in the middle of the room and around the walls. There was another door in the opposite wall.

The corner fireplace gave off little warmth; only a few coals remained. She pulled her shawl tighter around her shoulders.

"Please be seated, Mrs. Langdon; Mrs. Pearce will be here shortly." Bob walked to the fire and threw more logs on the coals, using the poker to entice the wood to ignite.

Mary sat on a bench and placed her bundles on the floor as he walked out of the door they had just entered. Her hands shook as she wondered what to expect on the voyage. Would the ladies listen to her? She hoped they wouldn't sneak out to meet with male passengers or crew.

A few minutes later, the door opened, and Mrs. Pearce walked in, followed by the single women.

Mary stood up, smiling as Grace dropped her bundles and rushed to hug her. "Ma! I didn't think I'd see you until we reached Adelaide."

Relief washed over Mary as she leaned back, clutching Grace's arms, her heart swelling at the sight of her daughter's relieved expression. "I'm going to be the matron for the single women during the voyage."

Grace turned to the dark-eyed, dark-haired girl standing beside her. "Ma, this is Bella Newman." Wiping a tear from her eye, she said, "Her family is also going to work on a sheep farm."

Mary looked at her and said, "I'm so pleased to meet you, Bella. You must be Jim and Eliza's daughter."

Bella nodded. "When Grace told me your family were going to a sheep farm, we wondered if it was the same one."

Mary smiled at the young girl, "Yes, it is."

Mary looked around and saw the ladies settling themselves on benches. As Mrs. Pearce approached them, she pulled her shawl tighter. "Mr. Cowling told me you were going to be the matron for the single women." Glancing at the ladies as they settled themselves on benches. "There's only forty-five ladies for this voyage and they're all well behaved."

"What happens now?"

"The ladies will be taken on board first; I'll come with you to see them settled into their quarters and into your care. Then the families, followed by the single men."

Mary nodded and glanced at the young women. They, too, were pulling their cloaks and shawls around themselves to keep warm.

"Very well," said Mary. "When do we leave?"

"I'll find out if the men are ready for us yet," Mrs. Pearce said, walking out the other door in the room. Mary noticed it led to another small room, only six feet before the outside door. Even though the outside door was closed, Mary shivered as cold air seeped from the smaller room.

Mrs. Pearce returned a few moments later. "It's freezing out there," she said, shivering as she pulled her shawl around her again. "The men are ready for the single women to board."

Mary was happy when Mrs. Pearce took charge and turned to the women, saying, "Come along, ladies. It's time to board your ship."

Mary was taken aback by the sudden flurry of activity as the women searched the room, shuffling about, and rummaging under benches for their belongings.

Mrs. Pearce turned to them as they were about to walk outside. "Please be careful; it's very foggy outside."

Following the matron, Mary relied on little yellow dots amidst the grey fog, her gaze fixed on the back of Mrs. Pearce's shawl, her only guide through the mist. The fog obscured everything, muffling sounds and reducing visibility to mere shadows. A distant voice called out from the wharf, barely audible through the thick mist. "Over here, Missus."

Mary hated the fog, ever since she got lost in the woods when she was a child. She jumped when she felt a hand on her arm; relaxing when she realised it was Mrs. Pearce. "This way, Mrs. Langdon."

"Follow us, please," Mary called out, hoping to hear the reassuring footsteps of Grace, Bella, and the other ladies behind her. She hoped they would not fall off the edge as they walked carefully along the wharf. Men's voices became louder. The black shawl suddenly stopped.

Mary accidentally stepped on Grace's foot when a sailor appeared before her. Turning to her daughter, "Sorry, can't see anything out here." Turning back to the sailor, "You scared me."

"Sorry, Missus. didn't mean to frighten you. Follow me, and we'll take you to the ship."

Mary could barely see the sailor as he walked ahead with Mrs. Pearce. She did her best to keep them in sight.

As the ship's bow came into view, men moved on deck, calling out as they lowered boxes on ropes into what Mary assumed was the cargo hold.

Mary observed as the sailor and Mrs. Pearce halted near a small bridge leading to the ship's deck. She called to the ladies following, "Please wait here."

Mrs. Pearce addressed Mary. "Mrs. Langdon, I'll lead the ladies up the gangplank. Can you follow at the end?"

Mary nodded and stepped aside. "Follow Mrs. Pearce, please." She wondered if Grace and Bella could see her smile as they walked past.

Mary stood at the end of the gangplank, gripping the rail tightly, her heart pounding with each step the girls took. When no more girls were waiting to board, Mary followed the last woman, turning towards the ship's bow.

She found Mrs. Pearce talking to a crew member while the ladies stood in little groups on deck. Mary looked at her charges, some reaching into their pockets for handkerchiefs as they sobbed.

Mrs. Pearce turned to Mary. "I'll take you to your quarters." She marched briskly, stopping near an open hatch and turned to Mary. "These are your quarters during the voyage. Please be careful going down the ladder."

Mary looked into the hold, then slowly turned around to walk down the ladder backwards, holding her bundles in one hand and the rail in the other. When she reached the floor of the quarters, she dropped her bundles and called for Grace to pass hers down and climb down the ladder, too.

Mrs. Pearce descended after the last girl. She looked at the bunks on either side and did a mental count. "There are sixty berths, so some ladies will have to sleep on the top bunks."

After placing her bundles on the lower bed near the ladder, Mary looked around the hold. It was illuminated by several oil lanterns, their warm glow casting faint shadows against the wooden walls, creating an atmosphere of subdued comfort. Similar to the quarters in the depot, the hold included a long table in the middle with benches on either side.

Looking at the tables, Mrs. Pearce approached Mary and said, "The young ladies eat in these quarters; they don't mix with any other passengers during the voyage."

Mary nodded. "Where do we do the cooking?"

"The cooking is done on deck and brought down to you."

Mary didn't say anything; so many things were going through her mind. Was she doing the right thing by being the matron? Glancing at Grace, she realised she was. The ladies needed her.

Turning to Mary, Mrs. Pearce offered reassurance. "Don't worry, Mrs. Langdon. If you have any questions, I'm sure the ship's surgeon will be more than willing to assist you." Placing a reassuring hand on Mary's arm, Mary nodded. "Now I must get back so Mr. Gregory can get the families on board."

Mrs. Pearce had only climbed two steps when she turned around. "Godspeed," she said, lifting her skirts as she quickly left the quarters.

As Mary made her bed, a voice called from the hatch opening.

"Mrs. Langdon, my name is Dr. Matthew Parker; I'm the ship's surgeon. May I come down, please?"

Mary walked to the bottom of the steps and looked up. "Of course, Dr. Parker." Mary said, stepping aside as he climbed down the steps with the agility of a monkey. Jumping to the floor, he turned to face her. Mary looked at the slim young man, immaculate in his uniform. His tall figure was commanding but not threatening. His kind face and smile made her feel safe in his presence.

"Pleased to make your acquaintance, Mrs. Langdon. Welcome aboard the *Emily Catherine*." He bowed his head slightly.

"Thank you, Dr. Parker." Looking around at the women getting settled. "Mrs. Pearce said there are forty-five ladies all together."

Dr. Parker nodded. "Were you informed you're to assist me with the inspection of the family quarters?"

"Yes, Mr. Cowling did tell me, but what about inspecting the single men's quarters? I'm not sure if they'd be happy about that."

Dr. Parker chuckled. "I'll get one of the constables to assist me with that."

Mary called out as he turned to walk up the companionway. "Dr. Parker, I've noticed there's a couple of ladies in the family groups who are heavy with child and may give birth on board. I'm a midwife, if I may be of any assistance, please send for me."

"Thank you for letting me know." He climbed the ladder and was gone in a few seconds.

Thomas watched Bob Gregory take family groups to the waiting room. Eventually, it was their turn. Benches scraped the floor as they stood.

Bob turned to Jacob, Elijah, and Sammy. "You single men wait here; you'll be the last group to board. Mr. Newman, your family can come as well."

Leading the two families out of the door, he turned left. "This is the quickest way to the waiting room; we only use this corridor when passengers are boarding the ships. You'll be called from here to the wharf. We don't want people getting on the wrong ship." He said, giving a small chuckle.

Other passengers were seated inside when he opened the door. Thomas turned back to Bob. "Will someone else take us to the ship?"

"No, I'll do that." Closing the door behind him. "I'm going to see if the men are ready for the next group to board. I'll come and fetch you when it's your turn. Please be seated."

Thomas was grateful for the warmth of the room after leaving the cold corridor. Martha settled beside Thomas, who reached out and gently squeezed her hand, offering reassurance. Eliza sat close to the fire with Harry, covering his bare legs with her shawl.

Bob returned, quickly shutting the door behind him. Rubbing his hands together, he called out. "Mr. Elliot, I'll take your family to the ship now, can you follow me please. Mr. Chambers, you and your wife can come too."

Mr. Elliott picked up as many bundles as possible, his wife holding the hands of their two small children. Bob picked up the last two remaining canvas bags.

Thomas glanced at Mrs. Elliott as she walked towards the door. There was no doubt in his mind her baby would be born on board.

When Bob returned, he said. "Tom, your family can come now, Mr. Newman, yours too. Please be careful, although the sun's beginning to rise, it's foggy out there."

Thomas buttoned up his coat, and picked up as many bundles as he could. Isaac did the same, while Louisa carried her sewing basket.

Despite the chill in the air, Thomas's primary concern was ensuring the safety of his family as they followed Bob, his eyes fixed on the silhouette of Bob's dark coat disappearing into the fog.

Bob turned to the little group as they reached the gangplank. "Looks like the fog is beginning to lift."

The sound of hammering came from the ship, Isaac asked, "Are there carpenters still working on the ship?"

Bob replied, "I believe they're doing some last-minute repairs to the passenger accommodation,'" he said, gesturing toward the stern. "Don't worry, they'll be off the ship before she sails this afternoon. You can see there's cargo still being loaded, not to mention the stowing of food and heavy baggage."

Isaac turned to Bob. "Do we wait for someone to tell us when we can board?"

Bob replied, "Someone will come and get you shortly, I must get the next family and bring them out here." He put a hand on Thomas's shoulder. "I hope you have a good life in Australia, Tom."

Shortly a tall thin man walked towards them on the gangplank. His smile emphasised his fine face as he spoke in a well-educated voice. "Welcome aboard the *Emily Catherine*. My name is Dr. Matthew Parker."

With his hands full, Thomas could only nod. "Thank you, I'm Tom Langdon, one of the constables. And this is my son, Ike."

Dr. Parker nodded to Isaac. "Please follow me, I'll take you to your quarters." He turned and walked along the deck.

Thomas looked around as they walked, there were ropes everywhere, stretching from the top of the masts, and attached to pulleys on the deck or on the bulwark. Also, it seemed about every two yards, there was a bucket of sand, obviously in the event of a fire. He hoped they wouldn't have to use one.

Dr. Parker led the two families to a hatch in the middle of the ship. "These are your quarters, please go below and find your bunks. I'll take my leave to welcome the next group." He tipped his hat. "Good day."

Throwing his bundles through the hatch, Thomas turned around, and climbed down the companionway backwards. It brought him to one end of the hold, he stood for a moment and looked around.

Isaac threw his bundles to him, tossing them into a pile to his right. Isaac climbed down, followed by Louisa, still clutching her sewing basket, Eliza, and the children. James was the last to climb down the ladder, with Harry riding piggy-back.

Thomas stood looking at their accommodation. In front of them was the centre bench with two water closets on either side near the hull. He realised they were the only place where anyone could have any privacy. Opening the door to briefly look, he was pleased to see they emptied into the sea, and that sea water was used to clean them.

The quarters stretched along the ship's lower deck, a dimly lit tunnel-like space nestled between the bustling main deck and the cavernous cargo hold. The bunks were built into each side of the hold, like the ones they had slept in at the depot. Several upright support posts were attached to the beam above in the middle of the quarters.

The centre table was three feet wide and built around the posts, with fixed wooden benches bolted to the floor either side.

The space between the benches and the ends of the bunks was barely enough for two people to pass each other. Above the table was another shelf, on a slight angle. A few small trunks were stored underneath the ladder, there was little room to put them anywhere else.

Dead moths stuck to the glass of the oil lamps dimmed the light. Reaching to pick a moth off, Thomas threw his hand back from the glass. "We're going to have to clean these lamps if we don't want any accidents down here, and it needs to be done soon. They'll need to be extinguished first."

Hearing the heavy tread of sailors on deck as they went about their duties, Thomas looked towards the ceiling, wondering if their constant footsteps would prevent them from sleeping during the night.

~

Louisa turned around when she heard someone crying. A woman further down the quarters was wiping her face, her husband stood beside her with his hands in his pockets.

The woman turned to her husband. "This is where we have to stay for the next four months." Wiping her face again. "I'm not sure I can bear it. I told you I *didn't* want to leave Somerset."

Eliza also heard the woman complaining and turned to Louisa while she put bedding on their bunks. "I'm looking forward to going to Australia, but I'm not looking forward to the voyage."

Louisa scanned their cramped quarters, searching for a silver lining but finding none. With a sigh, she finally spoke, "The *Emily Catherine* is going to be our home for a while. We'll just have to make the most of it. I only hope we have a safe journey."

Thomas said, "Louisa, it looks like there's room to stow things underneath the lower bunks if you want to put your sewing basket there."

"I'm not sure, Da, if water comes in, it'll get wet. I'm not very tall, there'll be room to put my basket at the top of my bunk, less chance of it getting wet."

Eliza looked around. "We might put our extra belongings at the head of the little children's bunks as well."

With a grunt, Isaac climbed onto the top bunk from the bench, his weight causing the wood to creak beneath him. "Looks like that's the only way to get up here."

Louisa replied with laughter in her voice, "Please be careful, I don't want you falling on top of me."

Amidst the clamour of voices and shuffling footsteps, parents hurriedly searched for their designated bunks, the air thick with anticipation and anxiety. Louisa saw the heavily pregnant woman making a bed not far from her own, there was also another woman on the other side of the hull, who'd most likely give birth during the voyage. Louisa hoped they'd reach Australia long before her baby arrived.

Louisa and Martha finished making the beds, and wriggled to the end. Isaac helped them stand up. "I wonder how the rest of our family are settling in?"

Martha's voice held a slight quiver. "Will I be able to see Ma sometimes?"

Louisa put her arm around her shoulders. "We'll find out soon if that's possible." Pulling the ten-year-old closer and kissing the top of her head. "I miss her too."

Louisa sat on the end of her bunk, watching as more families walked down the ladder to the quarters. Standing up, she grabbed Isaac's and Martha's hands, leading them up the companionway.

Martha looked around. "What are we doing up here?"

Finding a place behind the sheep pen on the deck, she hoped they wouldn't interfere with the crew while they worked. Sitting on a sack of what she assumed were turnips, she replied, "I'm sorry, I wanted to get away from the noise down there."

Isaac laughed, "It's just as noisy here." Raising his voice to be heard over the bleating sheep.

Martha reached to rub the face of a sheep, then turned to her brother. "Don't you want to watch as we sail out the harbour?"

He sat beside Louisa, putting his arm around her shoulders as he replied to his sister, "Yes I do, we'll never see England again."

~

Eventually, the little steam tugboats towed the *Emily Catherine* towards the open sea. Sammy stood on the quarter deck with Elijah, watching men put up sails.

Noticing some men on the wharf, standing with their high hats and great long coats, they watched the ship as it sailed away. Sammy wondered if they were the owners of the *Emily Catherine.*

As they passed the rock wall, a crewman about the same age as Elijah came up to them. "Enjoying your last sights of Devon? It'll be over three months before you see land again."

Sammy could not contain his excitement. "We thought we'd come and watch as we leave England."

"You're welcome to come up on deck, but please don't get in the way of the crew, especially when we're setting sails."

Sammy shook his head. "We certainly wouldn't do that." Giving him a grin, "I'm Sammy, and this is Elijah. Maybe we can help you during the voyage."

"If you're not too sick, any help is appreciated. My name's Johnny." He shook both their hands before walking to his duties.

Standing side by side, Sammy and Elijah gazed at the receding coastline until it vanished from view, swallowed by the vast expanse of the sea.

When land was no longer in sight, Louisa, Isaac, and Martha returned to the quarters. Finding her journal, Louisa sat at the bench to write.

Isaac settled beside her. "Do you want me to hold the ink bottle?"

Swaying gently with the ship's rhythmic motion, Louisa nodded in acknowledgment, "Thank you." The last thing she wanted was for it to be broken so early in the journey.

Louisa was about to dip the nibbed pen into the ink, when the ship lurched, she narrowly missed stabbing Isaac's hand. "Goodness. I'm so sorry."

Isaac chuckled softly, his eyes sparkling with amusement. "No harm done," he reassured her, offering an encouraging smile. "Let me know if you need anything," he added, gesturing towards the ink bottle.

She laughed also. "All right." Turning her attention to the book.

21st December 1855

Day 1, we boarded the Emily Catherine today. Our quarters aren't big, and I was trying hard not to be disappointed. Then I heard a woman crying, I was very close to joining her. I even thought of telling Ike I wanted to go back to Cornwall, but then I thought about Sammy, how could I leave him? But 3 to 4 months is only a short time in our lives, so we must make the best of the voyage.

Later, Ike, Martha and I were on deck, watching the ship as it sailed past the island we could see from the wharf. When the bow of the ship pointed towards the open sea, I looked back to the harbour. I felt a strange sense of loss for the life we were leaving behind, unsure of what our life would be like in a country on the other side of the world.

Lots of seagulls squawked as they flew overhead, and I wondered if they were laughing at us, knowing we would never see them or Cornwall again.

The dull metallic smell from the ink became overpowering, Louisa took the bottle from Isaac's hand and capped it. "That might do for today." Picking up her belongings, she returned them to her basket.

~

Day 2, I couldn't believe the snoring last night in our quarters, is it going to be like that every night? I thought the movement of the ship might lull me to sleep, instead, it made my stomach churn. Some passengers have been sick, including Martha. So far, Ike and I have been spared that horror, but I've a feeling it won't be long before it happens to us. Eliza is worried about Harry; the poor boy is vomiting all the time.

~

Louisa sat at the bench with Martha beside her, she wanted to write in her journal while Isaac was on deck.

For the first time since they left Plymouth, she had a momentary reprieve from the seasickness. Turning to her sister-in-law. "Martha, can you hold the ink bottle while I write? I don't want it to fall off and break." Louisa saw her face losing colour. "I'll try not to be long."

Martha nodded.

Dipping the pen in the bottle she began.

I'm not sure what day it is, it could be six or eight days since we left Plymouth, I've lost count, and to be truthful, I don't care. Everyone is sick from the movement of the ship. Many times, we hear people yell, 'Leave me alone, I'm dying'.

Ike was telling me he spoke to Sammy when he was on deck. He said he hasn't been sick at all. How I envy him.

The surgeon has times for when we rise, eat, and go to bed. When the weather is fine, we must air our bedding daily.

Right now, I can't be bothered with any of that, because we seem to spend all day in our bunks, wishing the Good Lord to take us, so we can end this misery.

The pungent smell of ink stirred Louisa's nausea again. Hastily taking the ink bottle from Martha, she pressed her free hand over her mouth, fighting back a wave of sickness. Pointing towards the water closet, Louisa urged her younger sister-in-law, "Off you go." Calling out to her as she ran, "Mind you don't get it on your dress." Louisa stowed the ink bottle and notebook in her basket before following Martha.

64

It was Isaac's turn to operate the pumps. Gripping the handle attached to one of the parallel wheels on either side of the pump, he steadily turned it to expel water from the holds.

On the opposite side, Bill White shared the laborious task. It couldn't have been more monotonous. They leaned forward on the handle, pushed down, pulled it back up, and repeated the motion. As Isaac's hands descended on his handle, Bill's rose, and vice versa. Neither man exchanged words, wholly absorbed in their assigned duty. Isaac conceded that, at times, it distracted him from the seasickness and the looming waves threatening to engulf the ship as they traversed the Bay of Biscay.

The handle became harder to push. Glancing over, Isaac saw Bill doubled over the side, vomiting. Isaac persevered with the pumping as best he could, but it was strenuous work for one person. Eventually, Bill returned, wiping his hand over his mouth before taking up his position on the other handle.

They had been manning the pump for about fifteen minutes when another wave of nausea hit Isaac. He kept swallowing, hoping he may be able to stop it, but a minute later he knew he had to vomit. Releasing the handle, he rushed to the ship's side.

Standing up, he gripped the edge, aware his stomach was empty. But that didn't stop him retching every time a wave hit the vessel, leaving him with a bitter taste in his mouth.

It had been nearly two weeks since they left Plymouth and he thought his body would have gotten used to the motion by now. Looking down the ship he saw his father not looking much better. Several other passengers were vomiting over the side as well. Isaac saw Sammy helping

Johnny, wondering why he wasn't sick. His thoughts turned to Louisa in the quarters. Since departing from Plymouth, she had seldom left her bunk or eaten much.

Dr. Parker had been to see Louisa; he was worried she might lose the baby. At this stage of her confinement, it could be fatal; and he could never forgive himself if that happened.

As his stomach settled, Isaac returned to the pump, his gaze fixed on the horizon in an attempt to ward off the returning seasickness. After half an hour, their replacements arrived and Isaac and Bill were happy to let them take over.

Isaac walked towards his father, the grey flecks in his dark hair shimmered in the sunlight as he slumped on the bulwark. "Da, I'm going below to see Louisa."

His father could only nod before he vomited once more.

~

Upon returning to the family quarters, Isaac found Louisa still asleep. Martha lay beside her, while Rachel and Edith Newman slumbered nearby. Isaac sat on the bench and spoke to Eliza as she sat on the end of her bunk, her back against the supports, Harry's head on her lap.

"How's Harry?" he asked.

Eliza's gaze shifted to her son. "He's still very sick, Jimmy and the girls seem to be better."

James sat further up the seat, his eldest son beside him, Isaac turned to him. "How long does it take a person to get used to the movement of a ship? I saw Da on deck, he's not looking well either. What about you?"

James replied, "Just when I think I'm getting over the sickness, my stomach says otherwise."

"Sammy's crewman friend, Johnny, told me not to look down at the deck, but to look at the horizon or straight ahead. I was surprised, but it did make a difference. Sammy said Jacob and Elijah are sick too."

James shook his head. "I hope this doesn't go on until we reach Adelaide."

"Johnny said the sickness usually lasts a couple of weeks, then we should start to feel better. Personally, that can't come quick enough." Louisa began to stir, and Isaac went to her. "How are you feeling?"

She smiled at him, "I think I'm feeling a little better." Inching her way to the end of the bunk. "Could we go up on deck? It's so stuffy in here. The fresh air might help me feel better, maybe even walk around a bit."

"If you want to, but the ship's still moving a lot." Isaac helped her from the bunk, and they cautiously walked towards the companionway.

Louisa stood on the top rung of the ladder, enjoying the salty breeze as it blew in her face. "That feels lovely." Isaac was one rung behind her, holding her arm.

Sammy sat with Johnny on a box near the centre mast. He quickly walked to her, a piece of rope in his hand. "Louisa, I'm so glad to see you're walking around, you had us worried for a while."

"I'm feeling better at the moment, how are you?" she replied.

"I'm all right, I haven't been sick, must be one of the lucky ones." He grinned. "Johnny's been showing me how to splice ropes and tie knots."

"I'm sure that'll be a useful skill when we get to Australia. I hope you haven't been a nuisance."

Johnny took a step forward. "Sammy's been helping me with the sails and other jobs, he certainly hasn't been a bother."

Louisa smiled, "I'm glad to hear that."

As the two boys returned to the centre mast with their ropes, Isaac and Louisa savoured the fresh air, standing side by side on the ladder. The occasional drop of sea water hit their faces. Walking on deck was impossible, so they returned to their bunks.

~

Seated at the bench with her notebook, Louisa was joined by Isaac, who smiled as he sat beside her, holding the ink bottle.

> *It must be about a month since we left Plymouth, most of the passengers are getting used to the movement. The change in everyone is dramatic, food is something to look forward to, and no longer an object of torture.*
>
> *The meals are plentiful. Breakfast is usually tea and coffee, (I did try the coffee, but I didn't like it, but Ike enjoyed it.) And we can have as much bread and butter as we want,*

sometimes there's even jam or molasses. The baker on board is a little Welshman in his fifties, every time I see him, he always seems to be laughing at something.

Dinner is usually salted pork or beef and potatoes. We are encouraged to eat preserved cabbage, or a pudding made from dried peas. Dr. Parker said this is to ward off scurvy, though some passengers refused to eat it. I can't blame them, it's not nice, but Ike and I eat it, we don't want scurvy.

We've been using sea water to wash our clothes. The only problem is that it makes our clothes very stiff. Also, using the sea water to wash ourselves is causing problems too, some people have complained of boils on their skin. Dr. Parker said this sometimes happens.

We have been on deck a few times; it makes a change from being cooped up in our quarters. But every time we look around, it's the same, water and waves. No land. All we can do is trust the captain knows where we're headed.

We saw Sammy and Elijah helping the crew, pulling up buckets of sea water for cleaning. Sammy always seems to have a smile on his face, even when he's cleaning the water closets. I don't know how he does it.

Martha has been attending classes held on the poop deck, along with most of the other children. Even a few fathers from our quarters attend. Sometimes, I join the classes too, not to learn, but to help the teacher, Mr. Walters. He's most grateful for my help with the children's reading.

We all enjoy Sunday services on the poop deck because we get a chance to see Ma, Grace, and Bella, even if it's only to wave to them. The single women aren't allowed to mix with the other passengers, and Ma keeps a close eye on her charges. Ma comes to our quarters once a week with Dr. Parker for inspections. The first time Martha saw her, I thought she would knock her over in the rush to greet her.

Yesterday, our trunks were brought up from the cargo hold, and we were able to change into our summer dresses, the

Flexing her fingers to relieve the cramp, Louisa turned to Isaac. "That'll do for today, I can't stand the smell of this ink any longer."

He grinned as he screwed the cap and handed it to her. Louisa kissed him on the cheek before neatly stowing away the writing materials. Together, they made their way to the companionway.

One afternoon, while Isaac manned the pumps on deck, Louisa busied herself tidying up their bunks. The children were attending classes while the adults made the most of the calm seas, enjoying the sunshine. Louisa cherished the rare moments of peace and quiet in the family quarters, relishing the opportunity to write in her journal undisturbed.

After tidying the beds to her satisfaction, she sat on the bench to write. She was just about to open the ink bottle when a cold shiver ran down her spine. It brought back memories of Robert Engels at Trevelen Manor.

Looking around Louisa could only see Eliza on the bunk with Harry, gently stroking his hair as he slept with his head on her lap. Returning her attention to the notebook, she read what she had previously written, but the feeling of being watched persisted. Closing her book, Louisa stood up and looked around the quarters. In the dim light, she noticed Humphrey Chambers peering over the end of his upper bunk, not far from where she stood. She stepped back when he jumped down and walked closer. Wearing a smug smile, he grabbed her arm and for a split second she was back in the scullery at Trevelen Manor.

She stood firm when he tried to pull her closer. "How about a kiss Darling? I know you'd enjoy it."

"Get your hand off me this instant." Giving her best Mrs. Tremaine imitation. Desperately trying to pull her arm away, she said loudly, "Let me go."

Breathing a sigh of relief when she heard Isaac's loud footsteps. "You heard what she said. Let her go."

Humphrey released his grip and backed away a step. "I was only playing with her; she was the one who wanted a kiss."

"You liar," Came a voice from behind them, breaking the tension.

The look of disbelief on Humphrey's face, should have made her laugh, but that was the last thing she felt like doing.

Isaac gently guided her behind him with his left hand, positioning himself protectively between Louisa and Humphrey. With a swift motion, he swung his right fist, catching Humphrey by surprise as it connected with his cheek. Louisa nearly clapped with satisfaction when she saw Humphrey sprawled on the floor, clutching his face in pain.

Louisa turned to see Thomas behind her. "What's going on here?"

Humphrey scrambled to his feet, feigning innocence. "He punched me, *for no reason.*"

"You lying bastard." Isaac's voice dripped with disdain as he turned to Louisa, Eliza and his father. "Sorry ladies. Da, this…" Scrutinizing Humphrey up and down as he stood before him. "…worm, was trying to kiss my wife."

Thomas took a step closer to Humphrey, his gaze piercing. "Is this true? Because I doubt Ike would punch anyone for no reason."

Humphrey, now backing away nervously, relented. "All right, I was only having a bit of fun, there's not much else to do on this ship."

Thomas grabbed Humphrey by his jacket lapels, drawing him closer until their faces were inches apart. "Now I'll tell you this once, if you do *anything* like this again, I'll tell Captain Williamson to lock you in the brig. Understand? Or better still, I might let Ike deal with you." Thomas released his grip and pushed Humphrey, causing him to stumble backwards. Although he tried, he couldn't avoid falling on the floor again.

Thomas stepped on his hand, preventing him getting up. He squatted, pointing to his cheek. "If anyone asks, you got that black eye when you hit a post as the ship was moving."

He stood up again, keeping his foot on Humphrey's hand, he leaned down to him, pulling his eyebrows together, creating hoods over his eyes. "And if I find out you've told anyone that Ike hit you, then I will get the captain to throw you in the brig, but not before I tell your wife. Is that clear?"

Thomas lifted his foot and turned to Isaac, Louisa, and Eliza. "I'm going to report this incident to Captain Williamson, but we'll keep this between us. All right?"

Louisa breathed a sigh of relief, grateful when Isaac and Eliza nodded in agreement.

Thomas snorted in disgust as he turned to Humphrey when he stood up and straightened his jacket. "My advice to you, would be to take a long walk on deck if you know what's good for you."

Humphrey, visibly chastised, chose to circumvent Isaac and Thomas by walking around the bench to use the other passageway. Thomas followed closely behind, ensuring Humphrey's retreat.

Isaac turned and enveloped Louisa in his arms. "Are you alright?"

She nodded, stepping back to rub her arm. "I might have a bruise there tomorrow."

"You're not the only one." Isaac laughed as he shook his hand and rubbed his knuckles. "I was coming down to ask if you wanted to take a walk on deck, it's lovely in the sunshine. But we'll forget about that."

Louisa sat on the bench. "I think I'll stay here and write in my journal; I don't want to face him right now." Giving a painful half smile as she looked at Eliza. "Besides, I'm not on my own."

"All right, I'd better go to the captain's cabin with Da to explain what happened." After a brief kiss, he swiftly ascended the companionway.

Eliza checked Harry was still asleep and sat beside Louisa. "Are you really alright? You've gone very pale."

Louisa's tears flowed as she looked at her shaking hands. "Oh Eliza, if I tell you something, will you promise not to say anything to anyone else, especially Ike?"

"Of course. I can see something's bothering you, what is it?"

Pulling a handkerchief from her pocket, Louisa wiped her eyes. She told Eliza about the attempted rape by Robert Engels in the scullery of Trevelen Manor, and his subsequent murder.

"I didn't tell Ike what happened, but when Mr. Chambers grabbed me, the memory of what Robert Engels tried to do to me came rushing back."

Eliza put her hand on Louisa's. "No wonder you're shaking." Pulling a strand of hair away from her eyes, she added, "And you say, they never found out who killed him?"

She shook her head. "Ike's Da thinks it may have been the father of a girl he attacked, so there could be several suspects."

"Well, you can relax now, I'm sure Tom will keep a close eye on *Mister, Humphrey, Chambers,* in future."

Louisa laughed at the disrespect in Eliza's voice.

Sammy paused in his sweeping duties, squinting against the sun as he spotted a dark silhouette on the horizon.

"Johnny, there's another ship out there. It looks like it's sailing towards us."

A shout of "Sail Ho" sounded from the crow's nest above.

Looking in the same direction as Sammy, he said, "Don't get too excited, Sammy; that may just be a pirate ship."

Sammy strained his eyes to look closer. "How can you be sure? Looks like it's flying a British flag."

"Don't be fooled by that. I'm going to find the captain," he said, as he walked towards his quarters under the quarter-deck.

Captain Williamson returned with Johnny a moment later and stood beside Sammy; opening his spyglass, he looked out to sea. "You may be right Johnny." He turned to the other crew members leaning against the bulwark. "Keep an eye on that ship for me. I'm going to record this in the log and come right back. If it looks like it's getting closer, come and fetch me immediately."

Sammy and Johnny continued to sweep the deck while the crew looked out to sea.

Johnny looked up again. "I hope the captain comes back soon. That ship is getting closer, and they've pulled down the flag."

Sammy's heart began to race as he moved his broom, hoping Johnny couldn't sense his fear. "What will they do if they get near us?"

Johnny's gaze remained fixed on his broom, his voice barely above a whisper as he confided in Sammy, "I've heard stories about pirates from other crew; I hope we don't suffer the same fate."

Sammy turned at the sound of footsteps. "Here comes Captain Williamson now."

Captain Williamson stood tall by the bulwark, his fingers tapping an impatient rhythm against the weathered wood, his eyes fixed on the approaching ship.

Soon, the captain cupped his hands around his mouth and shouted. "We only have passengers, no cargo." Repeating this several times.

The ship drew uncomfortably close, its ominous silhouette revealing figures scurrying on deck, their intentions unclear; as they changed sails, the ship slowly sailed away, much to Sammy's relief. He walked up to Captain Williamson. "Was that really a pirate ship?"

The captain let out a long breath as he watched it bob in the waves away from them. "I'm afraid so; I never trust a ship without a flag. I'm glad they didn't try to board us; it would have terrified the passengers."

The captain turned towards Sammy, his eyes assessing. "Have you ever considered joining a ship's crew? I've been watching you; it didn't take long to learn how things work, and you didn't get seasick."

"Thank you for asking," Sammy replied with a grin. "But when we get to Adelaide, that's where I'm getting off."

"That's a pity; you would've made a good ship's hand." The captain replied, patting him gently on the shoulder.

"Captain Williamson. I was wondering how the ship got its name." Sammy saw Johnny out of the corner of his eye, smirk and shake his head.

A smile played at the corners of the captain's mouth. "No one's ever asked me that before. It's quite simple, really. There are two owners of this ship, and she was named after their wives."

Eliza was woken by someone shaking her leg; sitting up, she saw Anne Elliott standing by the end of her bunk, one hand on the upright timber, the other holding her bulging belly. She whispered, "Eliza, I think the baby's coming. Can you help me?"

Eliza wriggled to the end of her bunk and quickly put her dress over her nightgown. It was hard to see her face in the dim light. Leading Anne to the bench, she asked. "What woke you up?"

"The pain in my back and the cramps in my stomach," Anne replied.

Anne bit her bottom lip as another contraction started.

"All right, Anne, it looks like the baby might be coming; I'm going to see if I can take you to the infirmary. Stay here."

As the dawn approached, hues of pink, grey, and yellow painted the eastern sky, casting a surreal glow over the ship's deck. Walking to the officers' quarters under the quarter deck, she knocked on the surgeon's door.

Dr. Parker opened the door after a minute. "What can I do for you, Mrs. Newman?"

"Mrs. Elliott is about to have her baby; can I bring her to the infirmary?"

"Yes, I'll get dressed and help you," the Doctor replied, shutting the door.

Eliza waited until the surgeon opened the door a minute later, and they quickly returned to the family quarters. After a brief examination, Dr. Parker confirmed Anne was in labour.

Anne clung to Dr. Parker's arm for support as they ascended the companionway, her face contorted with each contraction. They eventually reached the infirmary, only stopping occasionally when pain gripped her.

Dr. Parker helped her onto the bed. "You don't need to stay, Mrs. Newman, I can manage."

Anne pleaded with the surgeon. "Would you mind if Eliza stayed?" Desperately glancing at Eliza, she added, "Even if it's only to hold my hand."

Dr. Parker chuckled softly as he moved his hands over her stomach. "Of course, she can hold your hand."

Anne's face distorted as she gritted her teeth through another contraction. "I don't think this one will wait much longer."

"You may be right." Dr. Parker turned to Eliza and asked, "Can you return to your quarters and ask Mr. Elliott if he can find the baby clothes and a couple of baby blankets." He turned back to Anne and continued, "You do have some baby clothes with you?"

"Yes, they're in a bag on little Annie's bunk."

Eliza left the infirmary, returning about five minutes later with the bag.

Dr. Parker said, "Thank you, Mrs. Newman, it won't be long before this baby's born."

Eliza quickly knelt on the floor beside Anne and held her hand. "It's all right, you're in good hands."

Within an hour, Anne was holding her little baby boy. She looked up at Dr. Parker. "Thank you."

Dr. Parker smiled as he wiped his hands on a towel. "Don't thank me; you did all the hard work."

Seating herself on the bunk beside Anne, Eliza offered a reassuring smile. "You did that all by yourself. We were just here to lend a hand."

Dr. Parker turned to Eliza. "Mrs. Newman, would you mind staying with Mrs. Elliott for a moment? I must inform the captain of the birth; he needs to record this little boy's arrival in the ship's log."

"Of course." Turning to Anne, Eliza asked, "Have you decided on a name for him?"

"Patrick." She remarked, smiling at the baby in her arms.

When Dr. Parker returned a few minutes later, he said, "You can stay in the infirmary for a while before returning to your quarters."

"Thank you, Dr. Parker."

Eliza stood up, asking Anne, "I'll tell Pat, shall I?"

Anne nodded before returning her attention to the baby.

~

Eliza guided Anne down the companionway two weeks later when she returned to the family quarters with her new baby.

Anne's eyes brimmed with gratitude as she gazed at Eliza. "You've been a godsend, Eliza. I don't know what we would've done without you."

Eliza looked at the other passengers, replying, "We all took turns fetching meals for Pat and the children."

Another woman chimed in, "We didn't mind, and if you're feeding the little one when it's mealtime, we'll happily fetch your family's food."

Anne replied, "How lucky we are to travel with such caring people. Thank you all, from the bottom of my heart."

Isaac and Louisa leaned against the bulwark, their gazes fixed upon the vast expanse of the ocean stretching out before them, the *Emily Catherine* gently swaying with the calm seas since crossing the equator. Occasionally, a spray of seawater would hit their faces. The seasickness had left them temporarily, and they were enjoying more time on deck.

Isaac held an empty bottle while Louisa looked at the words she had embroidered on a piece of fabric. A tender smile played on her lips as she traced her fingers over the words *'Isaac and Louisa Langdon sailing to South Australia, 1856.'*

She looked at him with mischief in her eye. "Shall we do this, Ike?"

Isaac smiled, "It's pure folly, but if you wish, let's."

Isaac removed the cork, Louisa folded the fabric, placing it inside the neck of the bottle. Replacing the cork, he gave it to her.

Holding the bottle by the neck, Louisa raised it above her right shoulder and looked at him again.

Isaac grinned. "Go on. Throw it."

They both laughed as she threw the bottle as far as she could. "I wonder where it'll get washed up."

"I don't know; it could be floating around the ocean for many years before that happens." He watched the bottle as it bobbed about in the water.

She giggled. "When I saw the empty bottle lying on the deck, I thought it would be fun to put a message inside and throw it in the ocean."

"Yes, it was, but whoever finds it will wonder who we are and why we're travelling to South Australia."

"I can tell you why we're going there." Turning to face him, she grabbed his hand and placed it on her growing belly. "To give our son or daughter a better life."

Isaac kissed her, and they walked around the deck a while longer, enjoying the sun's warmth before returning to their quarters.

~

Louisa opened her notebook, and began to write.

> Yesterday, we crossed the equator; everyone from the family quarters was on deck, one of the crew dressed up as King Neptune and buckets of seawater were thrown around; a lot of passengers got wet, but no one cared; it was all part of the fun, the children had a wonderful time.
>
> This morning, Ike and I threw a bottle into the ocean with a message inside. It was fun watching it bob about in the water. I wonder where it will get washed up?
>
> Three days ago, one of the men from our quarters threw himself onto his bunk and landed heavily. Everyone turned around at the sound of creaking timbers and saw his whole bunk and bedding fall onto the bunk below. Thankfully, it was empty. Ike's Da asked the captain if Jacob could be brought in from the single men's quarters to repair the broken bunk. It was nice to see him, even if only for a little while.
>
> The water is beginning to smell. The crew opened a new cask today, and we lined up with our tin cups. One of the constables informed Dr. Parker, he tasted it. He said it was all right to drink, but putting in a few drops of lime juice would make it taste better. I will admit it did cover up the smell.
>
> I saw Sammy on the deck; he told me one of the single men died a few days ago; when I asked him how, he said he had a bottle of rum in his bag, drank most of it, and got quite drunk. They didn't realize he had been sick during the night and choked on his own vomit.

The days are becoming very hot, and the conditions in our quarters have become unbearable. Dr. Parker permitted some passengers to sleep on the deck in the cool breeze, and each passenger was given a turn. Most of the time, everyone cooperates, but occasionally, there are arguments among the passengers, even a couple of fights. This hot weather is making everyone irritable.

The baby has been moving for a few days now. It's a lovely feeling, like the fluttering of butterflies, but unfortunately, Ike hasn't felt it yet.

~

As the day wore on, Sammy observed families basking in the warm sunlight on deck, among them Louisa and Isaac, their faces glowing with contentment amidst the serene surroundings. Leaning on the bulwark, he looked at the rubbish floating around the *Emily Catherine*. Turning to Johnny standing beside him, Sammy asked, "Why has the wind died down?"

"We're in the doldrums, just south of the equator; there's not much wind around here." Johnny responded.

"What'll happen now?" Sammy asked.

Johnny screwed up his face as he looked at the sagging sails. "We hope the wind picks up again. We're drifting towards South America. Hopefully, we'll pick up the roaring forties soon."

"Are they the winds you were telling me about?"

Johhny nodded in reply, "Yes, but if we drift much longer, Captain Williamson may reduce rations."

"Couldn't he go to a port in South America and get more provisions?" Sammy continued.

"He could, but the captain prefers to avoid Rio De Janeiro. The city isn't clean, and we could pick up diseases from the food and water. Cutting rations is less risky."

~

While Louisa rested, Isaac savoured the tranquillity of the calm seas and the gentle warmth of the sun. He leaned on the bulwark, smiling as his father joined him.

Thomas turned to him, "Do you realize we'll be the first Langdons from Cornwall in Australia? With three sons travelling with me, I'm sure it'll be a name that will carry on for many generations."

Isaac replied, "I know. To start another branch of the family in a new country, that's something special."

"It certainly is. And there's already a start, with your baby on the way." Thomas smiled at him before gazing out to sea.

~

With a refreshed spirit, Louisa awoke to find the quarters nearly deserted. Pulling her book from her basket, she sat on the bench and wrote in her journal.

> *The wind has died down, and we've spent over a week drifting with the tide; there's nothing the captain can do.*
>
> *Last night, a young girl died from croup; it was terrible to hear her coughing all the time; she kept us awake the last few nights. Then, last night, the coughing stopped, and we were pleased to finally get some sleep. This morning, we found out that she had died. So sad for her parents.*
>
> *Sammy was telling me there's been a lot of gambling in the single men's quarters. One man was accused of cheating, and a fight broke out. The captain went to their quarters and confiscated the cards; he said they'd all go in the brig if it happened again.*

Putting her book away, she went on deck to find Isaac.

Louisa jolted awake, her senses instantly alert to the piercing scream that shattered the silence of the night. Wriggling to the end of her bunk, she called out. "What's happened?" She had yet to learn where it came from.

The scream was replaced with sobbing; in the dim light, she saw Anne sitting on her bunk holding little Patrick.

"Anne, what happened?" Louisa asked again. Other passengers had been awakened by the scream and were sitting in their bunks watching them.

Anne's body convulsed with heart-wrenching sobs, her words choked by the weight of her grief. "I think he's dead."

Louisa took the baby boy from his mother, looking at him; his little chest wasn't moving. Patrick was dead. Louisa placed him on the bunk. "Anne, please tell me what happened."

Between sobs, she said, "I woke up because my breasts were full and hurting; I looked for Patrick so I could feed him. I found him under me; I must have rolled on him during the night."

Louisa enveloped Anne in a comforting embrace, as her cries echoed in her ear and throughout the dimly lit quarters. "I killed my own baby."

Louisa tried to comfort Anne, sitting with her until she cried herself to sleep.

Sleep eluded Louisa when she returned to her bunk. Pulling her journal from her basket, she began writing in the lantern's dim light.

Dr. Parker examined Patrick in the morning, "I'm sorry, Anne, Pat, but I'm afraid he's dead. I'll take him upstairs, and we'll throw his body overboard later."

The parents stood watching the surgeon as he walked up the ladder with their tiny baby in his arms. As Dr. Parker ascended the ladder, carrying Patrick's lifeless form, the weight of loss bore down upon Anne and Pat, their grief enveloping them in a suffocating embrace as they sought solace on each other's tear-stained shoulders.

70

The *Emily Catherine* surged forward with newfound velocity, propelled by the relentless force of the roaring forties. Sammy was helping Johnny with the sails to match the intensity of the ship's movement.

Johnny looked at the darkening sky and said, "Looks like there's a storm approaching; it's going to be rough sailing when it hits us."

"How rough?" Sammy asked.

"Captain Williamson will probably order the passengers below and close the hatches."

Sammy looked up from securing a rope. "Will I have to go down in my quarters too?"

"You'd better; sailing through a storm isn't for an inexperienced sailor. We don't want you falling overboard."

"All right, Johnny, but I might tell Ike first." Sammy waved, heading to the family quarters.

Sammy called to Isaac through the hatch and waited. Shortly, Isaac climbed the rungs of the ladder, and with only the top of his body visible above the deck, he whispered, "Has something happened?"

"Not yet." Sammy knelt on one knee and replied softly, "But it looks like there's a bad storm brewing, and the captain will close the hatches; Johnny's even told me to go below. It may get a bit rough; I just thought I'd let you know."

Isaac looked at the sky and affectionately grabbed him on the upper arm. "Thanks for telling me; some people have been sick again."

Sammy waved. "I'm going below now. I hope it's not too rough."

~

Isaac walked down the ladder and saw many passengers lying on their bunks or sitting on the bench. He opened his mouth to tell them of the approaching storm, but the ships movement stopped him before he could speak. Reaching for a post to steady himself against the tumultuous sway of the ship, he could only watch as those sitting on the benches were thrown onto the floor whilst people on bunks were rolled around in their beds.

Isaac called out. "In case you don't realize it, a bad storm is coming."

Pat Elliott picked himself up off the floor. "Pity you didn't tell us earlier."

Isaac replied, "I've just heard myself; we need to secure our belongings."

He stepped aside when Sarah Andrews and Susannah Walker rushed past him to the deck.

~

Eliza looked around as she released her grip on the upright post at the end of her bunk. Thankfully, her children were all in the safety of the quarters.

Polly White gave an involuntary groan as she sat on the bench with her husband, Bill.

Eliza leaned forward and put her hand on Polly's arm. "Is your baby coming?"

Polly looked up. "I'm not sure, but I've been having pains all day, but that one took my breath away."

Eliza stood up, encouraging Polly to stand. "I don't want to alarm you, but I think you'd better see Dr. Parker straight away."

Louisa wriggled to the end of her bunk. "Do you need help getting to the infirmary?" She asked them.

Polly shook her head. "No, I can manage; I don't want you falling over if the ship moves too much." Polly stood up, gripping the bench tightly as she strolled towards the ladder. Turning to her husband, she requested, "Bill, maybe I need some help; I don't want to fall as I try to get up to the deck."

The lurching ship forced Eliza to grip the side of the companionway firmly as she climbed to the deck. Her eyes were immediately drawn to the darkening sky to the east. Turning around, Bill put his arm around Polly's back to help her to the deck.

George, a crewman, approached Eliza as she reached for Polly's hand. "You'd best get below, folks; there's a bad storm approaching; you'd be safer down there."

Polly stepped onto the deck and grabbed his arm. "I'd be grateful if you could help us to the infirmary; my baby's coming."

George called another crewman to close the hatch while he grabbed Polly's free arm, guiding them to Dr. Parker's infirmary. Both women struggled to walk on the deck as the ship rocked violently.

George knocked on the door and turned to leave.

Polly called out, "Thank you," as he walked away.

Eliza and Polly stood hanging onto the rail near the door while they waited for the surgeon.

Polly didn't hesitate to say, "Dr. Parker, I think my baby's coming." The surgeon reached to assist Polly and turned to Eliza. "Thank you, Mrs. Newman, for bringing her here, but it would be safer for you to return to your quarters now."

Eliza put her hand on Polly's arm. "Hope it's over quickly for you." Giving a brief wave to Polly, Eliza reached for the stern cabin wall to steady herself.

~

Dr. Parker turned his attention to Polly after Eliza left. "Come in, my dear, and lay on the bed; let me look at you."

Polly eased herself onto the bunk, lying down while being examined.

Dr. Parker stood up again. "Yes, Mrs. White, you are in labour, and I don't think it will be long before your baby arrives."

Polly grabbed the side of the bunk when the ship lurched again and gave a slight giggle. "I hope I don't fall out of bed during the birth."

The doctor chuckled, "Let's hope that doesn't happen."

~

Eliza clung to the mast, her knuckles turning white with tension, as she awaited George's assistance in opening the hatch. Susannah Walker struggled to keep her balance as she hurried her two boys towards her. Eliza accepted George's hand when she turned to descend into the quarters.

Reaching the bottom, she stepped aside as eight-year-old Tommy reached the ladder's bottom rung, his older brother Danny a few steps above. Susannah held George's hand as she turned to climb down.

The ship lurched, and both boys fell. Danny landed on top of Tommy, and the younger boy screamed in pain.

Susannah wrenched her hand from George's grip, descending the ladder quickly. Still, it was Eliza who reached Tommy first. She could see his left leg wasn't straight. Louisa rushed from the other side of the bench, reaching Tommy a moment later. "I think his leg may be broken."Eliza shouted to George as he looked through the hatch. "Go fetch Dr. Parker."

"Can you do it, Missus? I'm supposed to close the hatch and secure the rigging."

"Good heavens!" She lifted her skirts and rushed up the ladder. The rain had begun to fall, making the deck slippery. As she went to the surgeon's cabin, Eliza held onto anything she could.

Knocking on his door, she called out, "Dr. Parker, can you come to the family quarters quickly?"

Within seconds, he opened the door and stared at her as the rain dripped down her face. "What's happened, Mrs. Newman?"

Her eyes darted to the family quarters, "Danny Walker fell down the ladder and landed on his brother; now the poor boy's screaming in pain."

"Did you see if he was injured?"

"His leg's twisted."

Dr. Parker turned around, glancing at Polly lying on the bed. "Can you stay with Mrs. White while I check on the boy?"

"Of course." Eliza obliged.

~

Dr. Parker raced to the family quarters; even with the hatch closed, he could hear the child's screams. George opened the hatch as Dr. Parker turned to him. "Leave the hatch unsecured; we may have to bring the boy out."

Torrential rain cascaded through the hatch, dousing everything in its path as he descended the companionway into the dimly lit confines of the quarters. Dr. Parker carefully avoiding the boy as he lay near the bottom of the ladder.

Susannah stood up as he leaned over her son and looked at his crooked limb. "I'm afraid he's broken his lower leg, Mrs. Walker; we'll have to get him to the infirmary so I can treat him."

Dr. Parker wondered if Susannah heard what he said over Tommy's screams.

Dan, Tommy's father, knelt closer to the doctor and shouted in his ear. "How do we get him there?"

Dr. Parker stood up. "He can't climb, and I don't know if we can carry him; I think we'll have to get some rope and tie it onto a blanket to lift him out." He turned around and quickly climbed the ladder, returning within a minute with some rope, his wet clothes clinging to his body.

The lurching of the ship forced him to stand with his legs apart as he spoke to the child. "Tommy, I know your leg is hurting, but please try to stop crying. We're going to take you to the infirmary."

The boy nodded and tried to control his tears.

Susannah pulled a blanket off her bunk and gave it to the surgeon; he laid it beside Tommy. Dr. Parker gently rolled him onto his left side and moved the blanket under him before rolling him onto his back again. The movement caused Tommy to scream once more.

The doctor found the ends of the rope and tied them around the ends of the blanket; he gathered the middle of the rope into a bundle, climbed halfway up the companionway, and lifted the hatch open. Water splashed down the ladder onto the injured boy and his parents.

Once on deck, he signalled to George, giving him the rope. "We've got to lift the injured boy out." Dr. Parker looked around and saw Johnny coming down the centre mast; he called him over before returning to the quarters again.

The rain and waves splashed through the open hatch with annoying regularity. It sloshed around the floor, about an inch deep. Dr. Parker turned to the little boy again, wiping water from his face. "Now, Tommy, we're going to lift you out of the hatch. Your leg may move, and it will hurt, but we'll be as gentle as possible."

Tommy nodded as the surgeon wiped away the boy's tears.

He looked up to George and Johnny. "Pull him up, but please be careful; we don't want to hurt him anymore."

The slack of the ropes disappeared, and as the ends of the blanket were pulled up, Tommy screamed again.

"Gently!" Dr. Parker shouted and began climbing the ladder, putting his hand under the boy's back to relieve some pressure from the ropes.

Once on deck, Dr. Parker pulled the blanket away from Tommy and picked him up, walking as quickly as possible on the slippery surface. Susannah followed close behind.

Dr. Parker placed Tommy on the spare bunk inside the infirmary and held his hand tenderly. "I'll tend to you shortly, Tommy."

Turning to Susannah, he continued, "I'll have to get someone to look after Mrs. White, but first I must set his leg." Moving to Tommy's feet, he said. "Mrs. Walker, can you hold him around the hips while I pull." Susannah did as she was asked as Dr. Parker pulled Tommy's leg, and then his crying stopped. The only sound in the infirmary was Polly's groans.

"What happened?" Susannah asked.

Dr. Parker put his hand under Tommy's nose, reassured when he felt his breath on his fingers. "He's fainted."

Kneeling beside her son's bed, Susannah gently stroked his forehead.

Eliza remained sitting on Polly's bunk and asked, "Is there anything I can do, Dr. Parker?"

He nodded. "Can you stay here while I fetch Mrs. Langdon from the ladies' quarters? She'll have to help Mrs. White."

Dr. Parker closed the infirmary door and grabbed a rail to steady himself as the ship lurched again. He headed towards the bow and the ladies' quarters. George opened the hatch as he shouted, "Stay here, I'll need you to escort some women to the family quarters."

He swiftly climbed down the ladder as George shut the hatch behind him. Even over the sound of the storm, he could hear women retching in the water closet.

Mary approached him, "Is there something wrong, Dr. Parker?"

"Yes, I need you to help Mrs. White; she's in labour. Tommy Walker has broken his leg, and I need to help him."

"Of course." Mary reached for her shawl and wrapped it around her shoulders, knotting it under her chin. She followed the doctor up the ladder and gratefully accepted George's hand as they returned to the infirmary.

Mary walked inside; Dr. Parker turned to George. "Get another crewman; these ladies will need help returning to the family quarters." George nodded.

When Dr. Parker entered, he turned to Mary. "Mrs. White will have to return to the family quarters and have her baby there. I need to care for Tommy; his treatment is more urgent now."

Mary glanced at the young boy lying on the bunk, then turned her attention to Polly. "Can you get up and walk with me to the quarters?" Polly nodded and slowly stood up.

Dr. Parker opened the door and saw George standing outside with Josiah. "Can you help these ladies to the family quarters?" He turned to the three women, "Please be careful, we don't want more injuries during this storm."

Mary nodded at him before they made their way to the quarters.

71

Without the assistance of George and Josiah, Mary, Eliza, and Polly would have struggled to reach the family quarters safely amidst the violent convulsions of the ship.

Bill White rushed forward to lend his aid as they descended the ladder. "Why are you back here?" He asked.

Seawater and rain cascaded into the hold while the hatch was open, and once the women were inside, George battened it closed. The storm continued to rage outside.

When Polly's feet touched the floor, she doubled over as a contraction gripped her.

Mary turned to Bill. "Help me get Polly to her bunk."

Navigating through the waterlogged quarters, Mary surveyed the scene. She asked, "Can we hang some blankets to give this poor woman some privacy. Also, can someone give me a penny knife?"

In response, several women hurriedly stripped their bunks of blankets, fashioning makeshift curtains for privacy. Polly's dignity was preserved, but the available light was reduced, with no light coming in through the hatch.

Mary asked, "Tom, can you bring a lantern to Polly's bunk?"

Without hesitation, Bill White hung a lantern and handed her his penny knife. Mary put her hand out to steady herself as she turned to take it. "Thank you."

"You're welcome, Missus."

Mary pulled the blanket back and called out. "Eliza, can you help me please? Grab someone else; this is going to be difficult."

Eliza and Anne Elliott knelt on the bunk beside them. Eliza held Polly's right hand and used her other hand to hold onto the upright posts at the head of the bunk. Anne was doing the same with Polly's other hand, and Mary was positioned at the end of the bunk.

Mary laughed. "Polly, I've never had to deliver a baby on a ship before. It'll be a rough time, but I hope you'll have a beautiful baby at the end."

Polly held her breath through another contraction. Once it had passed, she said, "You'd think the little blighter could wait until the storm was over before he arrived."

Mary laughed as she wiped the sweat from her brow. "Babies are not known for their timing, Polly." Mary had no sooner finished speaking when the ship rolled to the port side, and the four women were forced to hang on for dear life.

~

For the next harrowing hour, they clung to one another, their collective strength tested against the relentless onslaught of wind and wave. Isaac was lying in Eliza's bunk, wanting to be near Louisa. She had tied her basket shut, securing it near the head of her bunk with some strips of fabric. She had one arm around the lower part of the post, the other arm protectively around her swollen stomach.

His father had ordered the passengers to their bunks, and they were hanging on to any sturdy piece of timber. Occasionally, Isaac heard people retching, but he swallowed quickly, trying to keep his own seasickness at bay.

The noise of the waves crashing against the side of the ship was deafening, and water poured through the closed hatch frequently, soaking everything in its path. It mixed with the vomit, and before long, there was six inches of foul-smelling muck floating around the floor of their quarters, sloshing about every time the ship lurched and rolled.

Isaac hoped he would wake up and the nightmare would end, but he knew he wasn't asleep. The other passengers were also huddled in their bunks. The screams from the children were quite disturbing, urging his mother to call out, "Nothing to worry about; it's only a storm; the sea is just a bit rougher than usual. Once it passes, we'll be fine, so please try to stay calm for Polly's sake."

Isaac heard some passengers muttering prayers and joined them; he was sure he was about to meet his maker. He reached out to put a hand on Louisa's shoulder, and for a moment, he saw a half smile.

A woman began singing '*bide with me,*' and soon, they all joined in. For the storm's duration, many hymns were sung, the passengers trying to take their minds off the wind's noise and the ship's rolling.

Isaac thought things couldn't get worse, when he heard a loud creaking sound from above. The ship seemed to stand still for a moment, then fell with a sickening drop. Objects not packed away were flung around the quarters. Isaac saw a book land on Pat Elliott's shoulder, and he cried out in pain.

"Mary, Mother of God, where did that come from?" Pat exclaimed.

Isaac looked at the offending book as it was tossed about in the unpleasantness swilling around their quarters.

The sounds of waves crashing over the deck, creaking timbers, the occasional canvas sail tearing, crew members running on deck, and the howling winds were all mixed with Polly's groans as Isaac's mother helped her baby enter the world.

Isaac began to think the ship would sink and his life would end without getting the chance to meet his own son or daughter. He could only pray that some miracle would save them from a watery grave.

~

Mary was thankful the ship's movement had subsided when Polly's baby was born. The cries could be heard over the dying wind and waves.

Mary and Polly struggled to stay in the bunk; if it hadn't been for Eliza and Anne, they probably would have fallen out.

"It's a little girl," Mary whispered as she reached for a blanket. She cut two strips off the edge using Bill's penny knife, tied, and cut the cord.

A voice from the other side of the quarters called out. "What is it?"

Polly laughed as she shouted, "I'm sorry to tell you, Bill, but your son has become a daughter."

Mary wrapped the baby in the blanket and gave it to her mother. "Well, Polly, I won't forget this birth for a long time."

"Neither will I," Polly answered, "When she's old enough, I'll have a story to tell her about the day she was born."

"Have you decided on a name?" Eliza asked.

"Hmm, I'll name her 'Emily Catherine' after the ship."

Mary replied, "What a lovely idea, now get some rest if you can"

She was still kneeling on the bunk and stepped back into the passageway, straight into water past her ankles. She looked down at her wet boots, shaking her head. "Good thing I've got a spare pair of dry stockings." She said to herself.

Mary had her arm around Martha as she sat on the end of her bunk. Martha's head rested on her shoulder while they waited for the storm to pass over them.

After what seemed like an eternity, the crewman opened the hatch. Mary watched the rancid air escape like a cloud of steam, billowing upwards. The odour inside the quarters was overpowering, but leaving the hatch open during the storm would have been impossible.

After giving Martha a hug, Mary searched for the surgeon, holding onto the bulwark as the ship still heaved with the heavy seas, the sudden movements caused her to stumble, occasionally banging into rigging and masts along the way. As Mary reached his quarters, she let go and knocked on the door.

"Mrs. Langdon, is everything all right? Has Mrs. White had her baby?"

"Yes, Polly had a baby girl."

"When?"

"A short while ago." Mrs. Langdon smiled reassuringly.

"Are they both well?"

"Yes, everything's fine with them," Mary said with a laugh. "But it was hard trying to stop ourselves from falling out of the bunk."

"I can imagine. I had a similar problem with the boy. Thank you for letting me know, I'll record the birth later."

"How is the young boy?" Mary thoughtfully asked.

"He's in a lot of pain, I gave him some laudanum, and he's sleeping now. Hopefully, he'll feel better in the morning."

"I'm glad to hear that; I'll return to the ladies' quarters now if you don't need me any longer?"

"No, thank you very much."

Mary turned around and carefully walked to the bow of the ship and the single ladies' quarters. It had been an eventful afternoon.

72

Louisa, lying on her bunk, awaited Susannah Walker's return to the family quarters the following afternoon, eager for news of Tommy.

Susannah rushed to her husband, wrapped her arms around him and cried on his chest. "Oh Dan, Tommy's dead."

He was stunned. "How? He only broke his leg." He pushed her away from him to look into her face.

Dan guided Susannah to the bench, where she wiped her eyes with the back of her hand. "He was in a lot of pain, then this morning he was finding it hard to breathe." She looked up at her husband and continued, "Dr. Parker said it sometimes happens with broken legs." Putting her head in her hands, she burst into tears again.

Danny stood nearby, tears streaming. "It's my fault he died. I fell on him."

Dan stood up, put his arms around his son, and spoke softly into his hair. "You must never blame yourself; it was an accident, nothing more."

Louisa could see he was doing his best to hide his own tears over the loss of his youngest son.

~

Louisa sat at the bench, writing in her journal, Isaac beside her, holding the ink bottle.

*A few days ago, we sailed through a severe storm. Just as
the winds began to blow, Tommy Walker fell down the ladder and*

broke his leg; he was taken to the infirmary. Then, in the middle of the storm, Polly White's baby decided to arrive. Dr. Parker was busy with the young boy, so Ike's Ma had to help Polly. I don't know how she managed it, as the ship was tossed about like leaves going over rocks in a stream. But Polly had a beautiful baby girl that she named after the ship.

Tommy's mother came back to our quarters the day after the storm to say he had died. We were all stunned.

When Tommy's body was thrown overboard, the crew had run out of rocks to put in the canvas wrapping. Susannah stood by the bulwark and cried as she watched his body bob beside the ship all day.

Louisa recapped her ink bottle, stowed her journal in her basket, and smiled at Isaac. She asked him, "Shall we walk around the deck?"

"That would be nice. Let's enjoy some fresh air." He replied, offering his elbow.

Movement of the ship was steady as Louisa and Isaac followed other people on the deck. Leaning against the bulwark, they stopped to look at the ocean.

Louisa saw something shine near the horizon, and as she pointed at it, said to Isaac, "I wonder what that is. It looks like the sun reflecting on a window."

Turning at the sound of footsteps, Sammy approached them. "What are you looking at?"

Isaac pointed. "Something's shining over there; we were just wondering what it might be."

Sammy looked and said, "I can see it too. I might ask Johnny."

When Sammy returned with Johnny, he asked, "Where is it, Mr. Langdon?"

Isaac pointed to his right, explaining, "It was just over there, but it's gone now."

Johnny nodded, "I can't see anything, but from what Sammy said, you may have seen an iceberg."

"Iceberg?" Louisa exclaimed.

"Yes," Johnny replied, "We're getting closer to Antarctica, so we need to keep an extra watch out for them."

Sammy looked out to sea and asked, "Do you think we'll see many more before we reach Australia?"

"I hope not, and we certainly don't want to hit one. Two things the captain is always concerned about during a voyage are fire and icebergs."

~

Isaac stood on the deck with Elijah and Sammy, watching Johnny on the quarter-deck tidying ropes near the bulwark. The men were standing with their feet slightly apart, following the sailor's trick to cope with the rhythmic movements of the ship.

Isaac turned to his brother and brother-in-law. "Are you looking forward to arriving in Adelaide?"

Elijah replied, "Once I got over the sickness, I enjoyed the voyage, but I'll be glad to walk on land again."

"What about you, Sammy?"

"I'll be glad to walk on dry land, and I'll be sad having to say goodbye to Johnny, but this is only the first part of the adventure, and I'm looking forward to seeing the sheep farm too." Sammy replied.

Isaac was about to return to his quarters when they heard a cry from the quarter-deck. Turning around, he saw Johnny desperately grappling for ropes, trying to regain his balance. Isaac froze as he watched the young crewman fall into the ocean.

Out of the corner of his eye, Isaac saw Sammy run to the life buoy ten yards from where they stood. Within seconds, he pulled it off its peg, put his arms and head through the middle of the ring and jumped over the side.

Isaac rushed to the bulwark and called out, "Sammy!" Watching as he fell into the water, holding onto the life buoy.

He turned around and yelled, "Man overboard!" He then turned to Elijah, shouting, "Get a crewman."

Isaac held the thick rope tied to the life buoy, peering over the side, looking for any sign of the two boys. Frantically scanning the water, Isaac saw Sammy swimming towards Johnny, who was in the trough of a wave. Isaac watched as Sammy reached Johnny, struggling to keep his head above water. Sammy grabbed hold of his jacket and linked his hands together around Johnny.

Sammy turned towards the ship and nodded at Isaac, who pulled on the rope. Soon, Elijah and other crewmen joined him, heaving to pull the two boys nearer to the ship. Another life buoy was thrown over the bulwark, and Sammy put it over Johnny.

Isaac stepped back as Captain Williamson raced to them, watching as the two boys were pulled from the water. A step behind him, Dr. Parker had several blankets over his arm. The crew members reached over the edge, quickly dragging the two boys onto the deck.

"What happened, Johnny?" The captain asked as Dr. Parker put the blankets around their shoulders.

Through chattering teeth, he replied, "I was tidying some ropes on the quarter-deck; I turned around; I must've slipped on some water just as the ship lurched. The next moment, I was falling over the side. Fortunately, Sammy saw me and jumped in."

The captain looked at them both. "Well, Sammy, we must thank you for saving Johnny's life, but you could've drowned as well."

Sammy looked at the captain, and also spoke through chattering teeth. "It all happened so fast, I guess I was only thinking about saving Johnny. He'd shown me where the life buoys were, so I grabbed one and jumped in. I knew Ike and Elijah had seen us and would raise the alarm."

Dr. Parker wrapped more blankets around them. "Well, I'm sure Johnny's mother and sister will be very grateful to you for saving his life, but right now, I think you boys need to get out of those wet clothes before you catch a death of cold. Come with me to the infirmary straight away."

Elijah said, "I'll get some dry clothes for Sammy."

Isaac watched as they walked with the surgeon; he turned to the captain. "Sammy's right, it did happen quickly, but I'm glad I don't have to tell my wife her brother was lost at sea."

"And I'm glad that I don't have to write in the log that we lost a sailor overboard. Your brother-in-law did a brave thing, Mr. Langdon; that water would've been freezing." Captain Williamson shook Isaac's hand. "Now, if you'll excuse me, I'll note this incident in the log, but it'll be nice to write that a heroic passenger retrieved the sailor from the water."

Isaac returned to the quarters, telling Louisa and his father what had happened.

"Why didn't you stop him?" She shouted.

"There wasn't time," Isaac replied, "One second, he was standing beside us; the next, he was jumping over the side. Captain Williamson said he was a hero."

"Da wouldn't have seen it that way if he'd have drowned."

"Well, he didn't, and he saved Johnny from drowning, too. Louisa, your brother was brave; you should be proud of him."

Louisa looked at Isaac and slumped her shoulders. "Yes, I am proud of him. I only hope Da doesn't fall over from shock when I tell him."

Isaac pulled his wife towards him, put his arms around her, and kissed her head. "I'm sure he'll be proud too."

~

During supper that evening, Louisa listened to the passengers' conversations. Everyone was talking about how Sammy had saved Johnny from a watery grave.

James turned to her. "You have a very courageous brother, Louisa; I wouldn't know what to do in that situation."

Isaac replied, "It all happened so fast; by the time Johnny was pulled out of the water, it was only a minute or two. My only concern is they don't get sick from being in the freezing water."

Thomas said, "I'm sure Dr. Parker will look after them both."

Isaac replied, "It was only by the grace of God that Sammy saw him fall and jumped in to save him."

Everyone agreed and finished eating their meal.

~

Before retiring, Louisa penned her thoughts in her journal.

Today, Sammy saved Johnny after he fell into the ocean. I was angry with Ike for not stopping him jumping in the water, but I realized if he had, Johnny would have been lost at sea. Sammy was very brave, but I'm glad he wasn't lost at sea as well.

~

The following day, Louisa visited the infirmary, finding both boys in bed. "How are they, Dr. Parker?"

"I think they'll be alright; they were only in the water for a few minutes, so hopefully, they should recover swiftly." Dr. Parker consulted her.

"May I talk to Sammy?" Louisa asked.

"Of course you can, my dear."

Louisa walked over to her brother's bed, sitting on the edge. "I hope you don't do that sort of thing again." She flicked the hair hanging in front of his eyes.

"When I went into the water, it was so cold it took my breath away, but my only thought was that I had to reach Johnny. I couldn't breathe again until we got on deck."

"Captain Williamson said you were a hero for doing what you did."

"I'm not a hero; Johnny had fallen overboard; I just helped him out of the water."

Johnny sat up in bed. "Don't you be fooled by that, Mrs. Langdon; he's a hero to me."

"Well, I'm glad you're both safe," Louisa said as she stood up. "I'll check on you both later."

~

Returning to her quarters, Louisa retrieved her journal from her basket.

I saw Sammy in the infirmary today. Dr. Parker assured me he and Johnny would recover from their time in the ocean.

I don't think I could bear it if anything happened to him.

Sammy has become good friends with Johnny during the voyage, but after pulling him from the ocean, I'm sure their friendship will last much longer.

73

Isaac and Louisa were enjoying a stroll around the deck when Isaac said, "Do you realize we've been on this ship for nearly three and a half months?"

Louisa giggled. "Really! I thought it was an eternity." She said, resting her head on his arm.

Suddenly, a cry of "Land Ho!" echoed from the crow's nest.

Isaac scanned the horizon, finally spotting land. They both joined in the cheer from the crew and passengers on deck.

Louisa turned to him and smiled, "Our journey is nearly ending."

He put an arm around her shoulders. "As well as our torturous conditions."

Isaac saw Sammy helping with the sails as they walked towards him. "Do you know if that's Adelaide over there?"

Sammy replied, "Johnny told me the first land we'll see will be Kangaroo Island; after that, it'll be a few days until we reach Port Adelaide."

Isaac added, "I don't know about you, but I'll be glad to see trees again instead of the ocean."

Sammy smirked, "I will be too, but I've had so much fun on the ship."

"That's only because you didn't get sick," Louisa grinned. She turned to Isaac. "Let's go below and tell Jim and Eliza."

Isaac found them sitting on the bench talking, and James looked up.

"Hello, Ike, you look happy."

"I have great news; we should arrive in Adelaide in a few days." Isaac informed them.

Eliza looked heavenward. "Thank goodness, even though I've gotten over the sickness, I'll be glad to get off this ship."

Louisa sat on the bench, rubbing her hands over her swollen abdomen. "So will I; we didn't want our baby born on the ship if it could be helped. It hasn't enjoyed the motion any more than I have."

Eliza reached over and touched Louisa on the hand. "Looks like your baby will be born in Australia after all."

"I'm glad about that, after seeing Polly when she had her baby." Giving a little laugh. "That was so hard for Ike's Ma."

Eliza laughed also. "I doubt if she'll have to deliver another baby like that again."

"But everything turned out well, Polly has a beautiful baby girl."

"Let's hope everything goes well when your time comes." Eliza said.

"I hope so, too."

~

Three days later, Thomas went to fetch breakfast for his family, and as soon as he stood on the deck, he saw land as they sailed past. He looked towards it. It was close, tantalizingly close; their journey was nearly over.

The cook tapped him on the shoulder and asked, "Are you looking forward to leaving the ship, Tom?"

"Yes, I am. How long before we reach Adelaide?" he replied as he kept his focus on the land.

The cook replied, "It'll be a little while before we arrive in Holdfast Bay."

"Holdfast Bay?" Tom said, turning to the cook.

"That's the harbour where we anchor."

"Do you think we'll arrive today?" Thomas asked as he looked at the land again.

The cook replied, "Maybe, but you won't get off for at least two weeks."

Tom turned back quickly; his eyes wide open. "Why not?"

"The doctor from Adelaide must make sure none of the passengers have any diseases which could spread through the town. Once he's sure you're all healthy, you can disembark."

Thomas took the food below, repeating what the cook had said, "I was hoping after we've eaten, we could pack up all of our belongings and leave the ship."

Eliza glanced around the hold. "I'll be glad to get off this ship also; even if I hate Australia, nothing will persuade me to get on another ship and return to England; we're here for good now."

"So are we, Mrs. Newman," Thomas said, "So are we."

Thomas sat on the bench, gazing at the ceiling, listening to the heavy footsteps and the crew's shouts as they bustled around the deck. He would like to have watched the crew prepare for their arrival in Adelaide, but the passengers had been ordered to their quarters.

He turned to James. "Well, Jim, our life in a new country is about to begin."

"I hope it was worth the journey we've endured." James replied.

"I hope so too; our son Jack's in Brisbane; he said Australia's a wonderful country; I only pray he's right."

~

Isaac and Louisa sat on the bench in the quarters when the chains rattled, signalling the lowering of anchors. He turned to Louisa. "We've arrived."

Thomas stood up. "I'll find out if we're allowed to go up." He climbed up the ladder, standing two steps from the top and called out. "George, can we come on deck now?"

Isaac heard a reply, "All right, but don't get in our way."

"Thank you," Thomas replied as he stepped down the ladder.

Isaac reached for Louisa's hand, asking, "Shall we?"

The low sun hit Isaac squarely in the eyes as he turned to help Louisa to the deck. He put his arm around her shoulders as they stood by the bulwark, looking at the homes and buildings on the shore.

Louisa leaned against his chest. "I didn't think this day would ever come, but we've finally arrived in Australia."

"Yes, we have."

Louisa turned her face to the soft breeze, observing the sunset shimmer on the water. "Ike, I'd like to name a daughter, 'Catherine', after the ship. What do you think?"

He wrapped his arms around her shoulders. "That would be nice." Giving her a little squeeze. "Shall we go below?"

She nodded, and they made their way back to their quarters.

Louisa sat at the table, penning her thoughts in her journal again.

6th April 1856

Today, we finally anchored in Holdfast Bay. There was excitement in everyone as we realized we'd finally arrived. Praise the Lord for bringing us safely to our destination.

74

In the morning, Louisa walked with Isaac and other passengers on the deck; children ran around them as they made their way to the bulwark. They looked at the shore; it was close yet out of reach. They could see other ships anchored in the bay; they watched as Captain Williamson and Doctor Parker were taken ashore in a tender.

Isaac pointed towards the shoreline. "Look, some men are putting a sheep and a pig in a boat. Wonder if they're bringing them to our ship."

"It'll be nice to have fresh meat instead of salted pork." Louisa moved to sit on a box near the centre mast, and Isaac sat beside her. "Sorry, my feet are hurting."

"Well, Dr. Parker did say for you to rest." Isaac reminded her.

"Yes, he did. I might go below and lie down." She picked up her basket, kissed Isaac, and walked to their quarters.

~

Louisa lay in her bunk; for some reason, the men's snoring seemed louder than usual to her. She gave up on the sleep and decided to write more in her journal, straightening her back after wriggling out from her bunk.

7th April 1856

This morning, we had some fresh food brought aboard and some fresh water casks. When the water cask was opened, we all lined up. I scooped my tin cup into the cask and drank deeply.

It tasted so good after the smelly water we've been drinking for the last few weeks. Ike and I were on deck when the cabin passengers were taken ashore. We could only gaze at them jealously.

~

Louisa stood patiently in line on deck, awaiting her turn to be examined by a doctor from Adelaide. Upon being called, she entered the infirmary and saw Dr. Parker standing with a middle-aged man.

"Come in, Mrs. Langdon; this is Dr. Hurren from Adelaide; he's going to check you're healthy." Dr. Parker said.

Dr. Hurren walked over to Louisa and began his examination. Once he had finished, he looked over the top of his half-moon spectacles. "How long do you think it'll be before you give birth, my dear?"

Louisa replied, "Hopefully not for a couple of months, I think. Ike's Ma is a midwife, and she'll be able to help me when the time comes."

Dr. Parker spoke to the visiting doctor; "Mrs. Langdon is a skilled midwife, so I know Mrs. Isaac Langdon will be in very capable hands."

"Well, that's good to hear. I shall pass you as healthy. All the best in South Australia, Mrs. Langdon."

13th April 1856

We've been sitting in the harbour for a week now. This morning, we were all examined by a doctor. Hopefully, we'll be leaving the Emily Catherine soon.

Louisa was enjoying the mutton stew when Thomas said, "Everyone in the family quarters has been passed as healthy. Tomorrow, the single men and women will be examined, and if they're all fit, we'll be allowed to leave the ship soon."

James drained the last of his tea from his tin cup. "I was beginning to wonder if we'd ever get here, especially when we were drifting."

Eliza added. "At least we won't get seasick again. I don't think I've ever felt so helpless, unable to keep my food down. I was really worried about Harry then, but eventually, he got better."

Louisa glanced at Harry, who was eating his food with much

enthusiasm.

Isaac lifted his cup. "To our new life in a new land."

"Hear, hear." A rousing call came from most of the passengers seated on the bench.

Thomas cheered. "Yeghes Da!"

~

Isaac was sitting with Louisa and Eliza when a strange man, holding a large book, walked down the ladder into their quarters. He coughed upon entering and pulled a handkerchief from his pocket, holding it over his nose. He stood on a step not far from the bottom, removed his handkerchief and called out. "May I have your attention, please? My name is George Brooks, and I'm the immigration officer; I need to record your names before you can disembark."

He waited for silence before stepping down the last couple of steps. He moved to the bench, making room on the table as close to the hatch as possible, flicking out his coattails as he sat. He opened the book and announced, "May I have everyone whose family name begins with the letter 'A'."

One family walked towards him. Isaac was only six feet away from George Brooks and could hear what he was saying to the people in front of him. His actions and the tone of his voice gave Isaac a clear indication that he would rather be anywhere else than writing down the names of new immigrants.

George turned to the husband. "How many in your family? Not including single men or women."

"Five."

George looked at his ledger. "Family name, please."

"Andrews."

Without looking up, George asked, "First name, age, occupation and county you came from in England."

"William, thirty-one, a farmer from Dorset."

George wrote the details in his ledger without looking up. "Wife and children's names, age and county."

"Sarah, twenty-five, also from Dorset. John, aged seven, Maryann, aged four, and Benjamin, aged one, all from Dorset."

George wrote down the names. "Thank you, that'll be all."

Still looking at his ledger, he called out again. "Now may I have all the people whose family name begins with the letter '*B*'."

Isaac watched as two more families got up to have their details recorded. The silence was deafening. When it was the Elliott family's turn, Louisa whispered in his ear, "I feel sorry for Anne. Not being able to record little Patrick as an immigrant." He gave her hand a gentle squeeze.

When George called for families with the letter 'L', Isaac stood up with Louisa and Martha. Thomas walked from the other end of the quarters. The clerk removed his glasses and rubbed his eyes; he glanced from his ledger to Thomas and Isaac. Isaac did not need to be told George Brooks was bored as he replaced his glasses, turned back to his ledger and mumbled. "Family name, please."

Thomas replied, "Langdon."

The clerk wrote the information; he continued to look at the ledger and asked, "How many in your family? Not including single men and women."

"Five," Thomas replied.

"Names, please." He held his nibbed pen over the ledger, ready to write, still without looking up.

Thomas replied, "Thomas, my wife Mary, my daughter Martha, and my son Is-."

The clerk looked up, interrupting Thomas. "I also need your age, occupation and what county you came from in England." He was about to turn his attention back to his ledger when he noted only four people were standing before him. The clerk looked at Louisa directly. "Are you Mrs. Thomas Langdon?"

She replied indignantly. "No! I'm Mrs. Isaac Langdon."

He looked back at Thomas again. "So, there are only three people in your family." His impatience was audible as he let out a big sigh. "Now, Mr. Langdon, can you tell me where your wife is?"

Isaac watched as his father turned his head to look at him, rolled his eyes, took a deep breath and turned back to the immigration officer. "She's the matron for the single women and will go ashore with them."

The clerk returned to his ledger. "So, your name is Thomas. May I have your age, occupation and county."

Isaac had to bite his lip to stop laughing as his father took a long breath and replied, "Thomas Langdon, forty-nine, and I'm a farmer from Cornwall."

The clerk wrote the details, without looking up, he added, "Your wife's name, please."

Thomas replied, "Mary Langdon, forty-six, she's a midwife from Cornwall." He waited until he had stopped writing. "Our daughter Martha, aged eleven, also of Cornwall."

The clerk glanced at Isaac and looked back down at his ledger. "Your name."

"Isaac Langdon, twenty-one, a farmer from Cornwall."

When George had recorded this information, he leaned his head on his left hand and sighed deeply. "Your wife."

Isaac had had enough of dealing with this idiot and his 'holier than thou' attitude. Louisa put her hand on his arm. He glanced at her, and she slightly shook her head. How did she know how much he wanted to pick him up by the collar and knock some sense into him. He didn't think it would be a good way to start his new life in this new country, so he followed his father's example, took a deep breath, and remained calm.

"Louisa Langdon, eighteen, also from Cornwall."

James and Eliza had their details recorded, and George Brooks finished before too long. He quickly climbed the ladder out of the hold, obviously glad to be in the fresh air after the smelly confines of the family quarters.

There was a collective sigh from most passengers when Eliza said, "What a ghastly man. I hope the rest of the people we meet aren't like him."

Isaac glanced back at the ladder. "I hope so too, Mrs. Newman."

~

16th April 1856

We are one step closer to leaving this ship, although it has been our home for the last 4 months, we shall be so glad to leave. This morning, an immigration officer came on board to record our details. But his attitude was dreadful, and I thought Ike was going to punch him. I had to put a calming hand on him, or we may have been sailing on the next ship back to Cornwall. Hopefully, we'll be leaving soon, bound for Adelaide.

75

Thomas accompanied the three other constables to the captain's cabin and stood with them just inside the door; Captain Williamson and Dr. Parker were waiting for them.

The captain greeted them cheerfully. "Good morning, gentlemen. I've called you here today to give you the gratuity for your service during our voyage." He handed each man three sovereigns as payment.

Thomas looked at the coins in his hand; he had never seen so much money. He looked at the captain. "Thank you very much, Sir," he said, shaking his hand.

Dr. Parker spoke, "Even when you were seasick, you still managed to do your duties." His face broke into a broad grin. The captain and the doctor shook hands with the men before they left the cabin.

~

Mary walked behind Dr. Parker as he accompanied her to the captain's cabin to receive her gratuity.

"Thank you for your excellent service during the voyage; you chaperoned the single ladies admirably."

"My daughter also helped, especially when I had to deliver Mrs. White's baby." Mary pointed out.

Captain Williamson chuckled as he glanced at the doctor. "Dr. Parker told me about the birth during the storm."

Mary laughed. "I certainly don't want to deliver another baby like that."

"We always sail through at least one storm during the journey to Australia, but that one was quite severe." Captain Williamson agreed.

"Well, thank you for bringing us safely to Adelaide, Captain Williamson."

He bowed slightly to Mary. "Glad to be of service, Madam."

~

Sammy was mystified as to why he had been summoned to the captain's cabin and why Johnny was accompanying him. He looked at his friend but he only smiled as he knocked on the door. Johnny patted him on the shoulder and walked away when invited inside. The captain was writing in his logbook at his desk. He smiled and said, "Ahh, Sammy, thank you for coming." The captain stood up to shake his hand.

"What can I do for you, Sir?"

Captain Williamson grinned. "You have no idea why I sent for you?"

Sammy's eyes widened as he slowly shook his head. "No, Sir, I'm afraid I don't."

Captain Williamson walked to his desk and opened a small box. He reached in and pulled out some coins, smiling as he handed them to Sammy.

Sammy looked at the sovereigns, then back to the captain. "Sir, why have you given me these?" he asked.

The captain laughed. "You still don't know why, do you?"

Sammy shook his head once more.

"That's for your gallantry when you saved Johnny's life."

"I only wanted to help him, that's all."

"That may be so, but if it hadn't been for your bravery, Johnny would have been lost at sea. We want you to know that the crew and I are grateful for your heroism." The captain smiled as he shook his hand.

Sammy returned the smile. "Thank you very much, Captain Williamson, but I wasn't expecting this."

The captain gently patted him on the shoulder. "God bless you, young man. I hope you have a good life in Australia."

Sammy put the coins in his pocket and left the captain's cabin.

~

Louisa lay on her bunk, struggling to sleep, excited knowing they would be disembarking in the morning.

She sat up and reached into her basket, pulling out her journal, pen, and ink bottle. Wriggling to the end of her bunk, she sat on the bench and wrote.

19th April 1856

> *Tomorrow, we finally leave the Emily Catherine. I don't know if I'm scared or overjoyed. It will be wonderful to be out of these quarters, but once we leave this ship, we begin the next part of our journey.*

After recapping the ink bottle, she picked up her journal and returned to her bunk. She looked at Martha asleep beside her, hoping she would fall asleep too.

~

Isaac lay on his bunk, hands behind his head, looking at the cobwebs on the ceiling in the dim light. He wondered what would happen when they disembarked in the morning.

He looked at his father in the next bunk, realising he was awake. "Da," he whispered, "Can't you sleep either?"

"No," he whispered back, "I keep thinking about what it will be like to be off the ship after all this time at sea."

"It'll be strange, but at least we're not moving so much now."

His father sighed. "Try to get some sleep, Ike. We've got a big day tomorrow."

As hard as he tried, Isaac couldn't sleep. Pulling on his trousers, he climbed down from the bunk and up the companionway to the deck. He leaned on the bulwark; it was strangely quiet as hardly any crew were walking about. Looking at other ships in the harbour, he watched the reflections of their lights as they danced about with the ripples of the water.

Turning at the sound of light footsteps, he smiled when he saw Louisa walk towards him, her dress pulled over her nightgown.

He extended his hand to her and asked, "Couldn't you sleep either?"

"I saw you leave your bunk, so I thought I'd come up here too," she said as she looked to the sky. "The stars are so different here from Cornwall, but I guess we'll get used to them soon."

"Hmm." Kissing her on the neck.

Moving in front of him as she looked at the water, he placed his hands on her belly, fingertips touching, protectively holding her. He could feel the baby move under his hands; he loved feeling their baby this way. He would meet this little person they had created in another few weeks.

He gave a huge sigh.

Turning around to face him, she asked. "What are you thinking about Ike?"

He kissed her on the lips and grinned. "Tell me what *you're* thinking about."

She put her hands behind his neck. "*I* was thinking about our child growing up in this new country."

"Well, I was thinking about our future and how our life in this new land is about to begin. We can only hope it'll be a success."

Louisa stood on her tiptoes and kissed him once more. "Only God knows that, and He'll tell us, in His own way."

~ The End ~

KESLAKE FAMILY

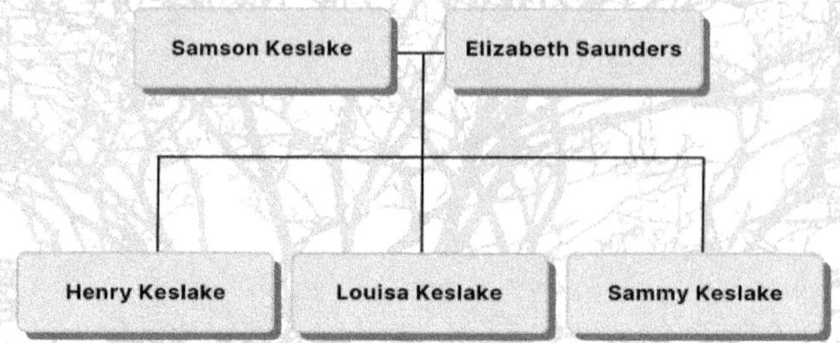

PARSONS FAMILY

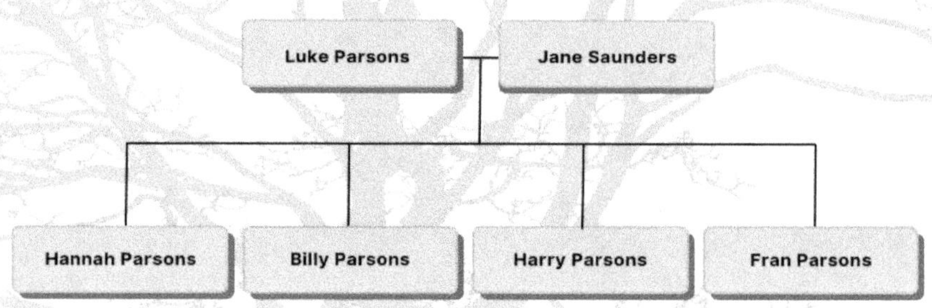

LANGDON FAMILY

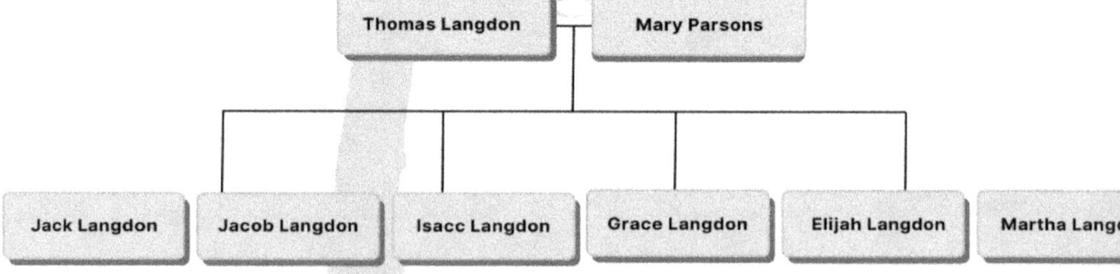

GLOSSARY

'Allo me ansum	Cornish greeting.
Bulwark	An extension of a ship's sides above the level of the deck.
Companionway	Set of steps leading from a ship's deck down to sleeping quarters or lower deck.
Crog loft	Room under the roof of a cottage, usually accessible by a ladder.
Dreckly	Very soon/shortly.
Fishing creel	A wicker basket with a leather strap, used by gentry to hold their catch.
Flounce	Wide strip of fabric gathered and sewn onto a dress or skirt.
Forge	Blacksmith's workshop.
Grand	Wonderful/great.
Hedge creeper	19th century prostitute.
Heller	Naughty child or person.
Little maid/maid	Young girl.
Pixies	Fictional beings, like fairies.
Proper Job	Good job.
Sneck	Old fashioned mechanism for opening or closing a door. Pushing the plate (about the size of a thumb) above the handle, releases the arm from the hook which allows the door to be opened or closed.
Stook	Group of sheaves of grain stood on end in a field.
Taters	Potatoes.
Tup	An entire male sheep.
Yard	91.5 cm
Yeghes da!	Pronounced 'yecki-da' – Translation: Cheers!

Author's Note: In the 19th Century, women wore long, loose-fitting cotton drawers made with either a waistband and button, or a simple drawstring. The crotch was open almost from waistband to waistband. From an early age, women were taught how to pull up their skirts and hold their undergarments to keep them dry and unsoiled. Upon completing her business, a woman simply fluffed her clothing back into place.

ACKNOWLEDGEMENTS

The biggest thanks must go to my cousin, David Copson for giving me the idea to write a book in the first place. For believing in me and giving me encouragement.

Crystal Leonardi, my editor, and publisher. Thank you for the incredible cover, I love it. And for the fantastic, marvellous, outstanding, amazing, wonderful (and any other flattering adjectives you can think of) job of editing. We may have had our differences of opinion over the course of editing, but we got there in the end. I didn't think that I would ever see my story in print, but thanks to you, here it is.

My husband, Daryl. You never said you thought I was crazy for trying to write a book. And even though you don't read books as a rule, you did say you thought it was a good story. I hope you're right.

Melissa, my daughter, for letting me talk through ideas about the story. That was so helpful. Brian, my son-in-law, for helping with the creation of the front cover design. And Erin, my granddaughter. Thank you for drawing the wonderful map of Stokebridge Village. And to the other members of my family, there are many reasons why I'm grateful to you.

Eve Locke, a dear friend, thank you so much for our long talks over the phone, or over a cup of tea at your table, allowing me to bounce around plot lines and ideas. I hope you enjoyed those brainstorming sessions as much as I did.

My oldest friend Sandra Smrecnik, your assistance with horse knowledge, handling and care was invaluable. Also, for the name of Arthur Pendragon.

Sue Stubbs, a dear friend from the Ipswich writers circle. Your feedback was so instrumental in putting me on the right track with the story. A big thank you is way overdue. And to Bronwyn. I'll always be grateful to you both for your encouragement when I was ready to give up.

My Friend, Alison Johnson. Your input with some very difficult scenes made them so much better.

Sofia Aves, author, mentor, and friend. For your support and the useful workshops you held which gave me lots of ideas.

Sandra Smrecnik, Sharyn Petersen and my daughter, Melissa (a grammar perfectionist). For taking the time to read the proof copy, pointing out errors that had been missed. That was so helpful.

Cheryl Sullivan, encouragement from you was so appreciated when we would meet during the 'Writing Friday' sessions at the QLD Writers Centre, held at the State Library.

Tony Pratt, lecturer in Horticulture in Wiltshire. Your information on livestock prices in Cornwall was critical, being able to put an accurate price for animals was so much easier than making an incorrect guess. Thank you.

𝓕ROM THE PUBLISHER

In 'The Narrow House of Clay: Forbidden Love,' author June English weaves a captivating tale of love, duty, and the secrets that bind families together.

Set in 19th century Cornwall, the historical setting is brought to life with such vividness that it feels as though readers are stepping back in time. June's research is evident in every detail, from the picturesque landscapes of Cornwall to the intricacies of daily life in the 1830s.

'The Narrow House of Clay: Forbidden Love' is a compelling historical romance that will appeal to fans of the genre. With its lush prose, compelling characters, and gripping storyline, it is sure to leave a lasting impression.

Congratulations June, on showcasing your talent as a writer. I have no doubt that readers will be eagerly awaiting the next instalment in the Langdon Family Saga and wish you all the best on your journey as a published author.

Crystal Leonardi

Bowerbird Publishing

www.crystalleonardi.com